STANDS A CALDER MAN

Janet Dailey

Thorndike Press • Thorndike, Maine

Library of Congress Cataloging in Publication Data:

Dailey, Janet.
  Stands a Calder man.

  1. Large type books. I. Title.
  [PS3563.A29S7 1983b]   813'.54   83-9131
  ISBN 0-89621-460-5 (lg. print)

Large Print edition available through arrangement with Pocket
Books, a Division of Gulf & Western Corporation.

Cover design by Andy Winther.

I

Stands a Calder man,
Young and proud is he,
Wanting to decide
What he's born to be.

1

An indifferent sun sat in the endless stretch of Montana sky, blazing down on the confused and bawling steers that jammed the cattle pens next to the railroad track. The chugging hiss of the motionless locomotive could barely be heard above the bewildered lowing of the steers and the clatter of cloven hooves on the wooden ramp of the loading chutes. The noise was punctuated by shouts and curses from cowboys as they poked the steers with long prods to force them up the chute and into the rail cars.

"Eighteen!"

With one cattle car filled to capacity, the locomotive rumbled out of its idle snoring to pull its string of cars ahead so the next one could be loaded. Plumes of smoke rose from its stack as the lumbering train's clanks and rattles added to the existing cacophony. Loading cattle destined for the slaughterhouses in the East was a tedious chore, made more unpleasant by the noise and the collective stench of penned animals.

Benteen Calder watched the proceedings from the sidelines. The wide hat brim shaded his sun-creased features and partially concealed his restless, assessing gaze. His dark hair was shot with silver and the middle fifties had put some weight on his big-boned frame, but there was no mistaking that he was of the kind that produced the cattle kings. Piece by piece, he had carved out the Triple C Ranch with his sweat, his blood, and his cunning. He'd fought outlaws, renegade Indians, and greedy neighbors to keep the ranch. There would always be someone wanting it. And the man christened Chase Benteen Calder knew that.

The cattle being driven up the loading chute carried the Triple C brand, marking them as the property of the Calder Cattle Company — his ranch. The dry summer had left the steers in less than top condition for market, but the weather in eastern Montana was seldom ideal.

After nearly six weeks of roundup, Benteen was conscious of the soreness in his aging muscles. Absently, he rubbed at the stiffness in his left arm. He picked up a movement to the right and shifted his head slightly to identify the figure approaching him. The corners of his mouth lifted in a silent greeting as Benteen recognized the railroad man, Bobby John Thomas.

"Oughta be through loadin' here in another hour," the man observed without any preliminary greeting.

"More or less," Benteen agreed with a faint nod.

The local railroad man's sharp eyes spotted a steer with an odd brand among the penned cattle. "I see you picked up some estrays. Diamond T." He read the brand and frowned. "Don't recall seeing that brand around here."

"I think it's a Dakota brand." It was impossible to know the various brands of ranches located outside of the state, and Benteen didn't try. "All told, we've got fourteen estrays in this shipment."

A description of each was listed on the shipping manifest. Given the wandering tendencies of cattle and their lack of respect for boundary lines or fences, it was inevitable that a beef roundup would include cattle owned by other outfits. Reps from neighboring ranches were always on hand for just that reason. If there was no representative for a given brand with the crew, the animal was always included in the market shipment. Left to roam, the estrayed cattle would eventually die of old age, benefiting no one. More important, it would eat grass that could have supported the range owner's cattle.

When the estrayed steer arrived at the terminal market, a brand inspector would spot it and payment for its sale would be forwarded to the animal's rightful owner. Such a practice, by both the rancher finding the estray and the brand inspector, was regarded as a courtesy of the range, observed by all and rarely abused. It was the Golden Rule put into practice – "Do unto others as you would have them do unto you."

Another railroad car had its load of steers and the door was slid shut. The train's engine began a racing chug to bring the next car into position. During the short respite in the loading operation, one of the cowboys stepped down from his perch on the chute and removed his hat, wiping his forearm across his brow, then jammed his hat back onto his nearly black hair all in one motion. A brief glimpse at his angular features, the color and texture of richly grained leather, was enough to hint at a similarity between young cowboy and the owner of the penned cattle.

Bobby John Thomas looked at Benteen. "Is that yore boy Webb?"

There was an imperceptible tightening of Benteen's mouth as he nodded an affirmative answer. A troubled light flickered in his eyes, put there by a gnawing worry that wouldn't go away.

"He sure has growed since the last time I saw him," the railroad agent remarked.

"Yeah." The abruptness of the response seemed to carry a negative connotation. Benteen didn't volunteer the information that, so far, Webb had only grown in size. The promise his son had shown in his early years hadn't yet developed in adulthood.

There was much about the tall, huskily built youth for Benteen to be proud of. At twenty-six, Webb was one of the top hands on the Triple C Ranch. He could ride the rankest bronc, rope with the best of them, and turn his hand to almost anything. Webb never shirked from hard work, so Benteen couldn't fault him for that. It was responsibility that Webb avoided, accepting it only when it was forced on him. On those rare occasions, he handled it well, making few wrong decisions. But it was that lack of interest in assuming an active role in the management of the ranch that troubled Benteen. The more he pushed Webb about it, reminding him that the Triple C would be his someday, the less interest Webb displayed.

Lorna didn't help the situation by insisting that Benteen was expecting too much from their son. It was her opinion that Webb was still too young and needed time to sow his wild oats before taking on any responsibility in running the ranch. Maybe she was right, but he'd been the same age as Webb when he'd driven the herd of Longhorns north from Texas to found the Triple C Ranch. It worried him to think he'd raised a son who was content to take orders instead of giving them. The future of the ranch depended on his son.

Moving his attention from the leanly muscled frame of his big-boned son, the source of his vague anxiety, Benteen half-turned toward the agent. His face showed none of his inner disturbance.

"Ya been keeping busy, Bobby John?" he inquired.

"We've been busy, but we haven't been makin' much money," the agent declared on a rueful note.

Benteen's mouth quirked in a dry line. "That's always the railroad's complaint. And it gets harder to swallow every time I see the freight rates go up."

"It's a fact." Bobby John was a loyal company man. "We may haul a lot of cattle out of Miles City in the fall, but we don't haul enough in or out on a regular basis. We just ain't got the people here, or the goods."

"I suppose," Benteen conceded.

"That might all change, though." The comment was made, then left to lie there like a baited hook allowed to settle near a submerged log where a big fish rested.

Benteen's interest in the conversation was no longer idle, his curiosity aroused by the remark. "Why is that?"

"Some fella plowed him some ground up around the Musselshell River and planted him some wheat. Rumor has it that he harvested forty bushels to an acre." He saw the skepticism in Benteen's dark eyes. "He used that dryland method of farming like they developed in Kansas."

Benteen had a sketchy understanding of the principle involved in such a method. In arid land where there wasn't a local water source to provide irrigation, crops were planted on only half the acreage while the other half was left fallow. This idle land was plowed and harrowed so no plant life would consume any moisture that fell on it. The next year, that half would be planted to crops. It was a way of conserving the moisture from rain and snow for the next year's use.

"It won't work here," Benteen stated flatly, regardless of the evidence just given to the contrary. "This is cow country. That's all it is

13

good for. Besides, I've never heard of a farmer yet who could make a living on just eighty acres." That was half of the one hundred and sixty acres entitled for homestead, and the only part that was productive at any one time under the dryland method of farming.

"That may be true," Bobby John admitted. "But I've heard talk that there's a proposal bein' presented to the Congress to double the amount of acreage allowed under the Homestead Act."

Benteen's chin lifted a fraction of an inch in reaction to this new information. An uneasy feeling ran through him as he looked beyond the cattle pens of the railroad yard to the grassland.

In the autumn afternoon the stark Montana landscape looked like a sea of tanned stalks. It was the best damned grass any cowman could hope to find. The idea of its being ripped up by a plow and replaced by wheat was more than he could stand. A lot of things were different from the way they had been when he had first arrived in the territory, but this was one change Benteen wouldn't accept. He'd fight any attempt to turn this cow country into farmland.

"They'll never be able to push that bill through Congress." There was a steely quality to his voice, but the prospect of a battle, political or otherwise, added its weight to the tiredness in his bones.

"I wouldn't be too sure about that," Bobby John Thomas warned him. "It ain't just a bunch of land-hungry farmers that wants to see it pass." But he added no more than that.

Benteen silently cursed himself for speaking without thinking through the opposition. Farmers were the least of his worries. It was the railroads. They were land-poor in this part of the West, owners of thousands of square-mile tracts of land along their right-of-way, deeded to them by the U.S. government for laying track. The railroads would use an enlarged Homestead Act like a carrot to lure the farmers out here and end up selling them land for farms or townsites. They'd create a land boom that would bring settlers in, tradesmen as well as farmers. People needed products, which meant more freight generated for the railroads.

It didn't take much intelligence to figure it out. The railroads had done the same thing in Kansas, Nebraska, and Colorado, where that prairie sod was now sown with some Russian strain of wheat. But this land wasn't the same. Methods that worked there couldn't work here.

The proposal coming before Congress had to

be stopped, and stopped swiftly. Benteen knew in his gut that he couldn't waste any time, yet the six-week-long roundup had left him in a state of fatigue. Even if he looked the physical equal of his son, he no longer had the resilience of his youth.

"Guess I'd better be gettin' back to my office." Bobby John Thomas shifted his position in a show of reluctance to put his words into action, but Benteen said nothing to invite the railroad agent to stay longer and chat. "Give my regards to your missus."

"I will." An image formed in his mind of Lorna waiting for him at the hotel in town. He suddenly felt an overwhelming need to be with her. Benteen barely noticed the agent move away, his attention already traveling down another channel. His glance swept the cattle pens and loading platform in an effort to locate Barnie Moore, then came to a stop on his son. Dammit, it was going to be his ranch and his land someday, Benteen thought with a frown of irritable concern. "Webb!" There was an edge to his voice as he raised its volume to make himself heard.

With a turn of his head, Webb looked over his shoulder and saw the single motion from his father that indicated he wanted to speak to him. He swung down from the loading chute onto the platform and handed the long prod to another cowboy to take his place. As Webb approached his father, he experienced that strange feeling of pride and resentment — pride for the man that Chase Benteen Calder was and the wide swath he'd cut across this land practically single-handedly, and resentment for the same reasons.

He didn't want to be his father's son; he didn't want to be singled out from the other hands because his name was Calder; he wanted to earn his right to command, even though he was born in the position to inherit it. He would rather have been born Webb Smith than Webb Calder, so his was a quiet rebellion — never overt, always subtle — denying himself the right to claim what was his by birth. Webb made it a practice not to assert himself or his opinions with the other ranch hands. In spite of that, all the cowboys, except the older ones who had come north with his father, turned to Webb whenever there was a decision to be made, deferring to him because he was a Calder. That angered him, although he seldom let it show.

Webb knew his father was disappointed in him. He'd been lectured enough times about accepting responsibility. Only once had Webb tried to explain the way he felt, his determination to be accepted because of his ability, rather than rest on the circumstances of his birth. His father had brushed it aside as a foolish whim, needlessly reminding Webb that he couldn't change the fact that he was born a Calder. Rebuffed by this lack of understanding, Webb had taken the lonely path, not able to be just one of the boys and refusing to assume the role his father wanted for him. More than once, he had considered tying his bedroll on the back of his saddle and riding away from the Triple C; then he'd think about his mother and he'd stay, hoping something would change.

"Yes, sir?" Webb stopped in front of his father, letting the inflection of voice question why he had been summoned. He hadn't addressed him as Pa in more than six years.

There was nothing in his son's attitude or expression that showed more than casual interest. Benteen probed, hoping to find more. He never knew what the boy was thinking — or if he was thinking. A father should know what was going on in his son's head. Benteen knew he didn't.

"I want you to go to the telegraph office and send some wires for me," Benteen stated. "One of them goes to Frank Bulfert, the senator's aide, in Washington. In the wire, I want you to ask him the status of the proposal being brought to Congress to enlarge the Homestead Act and what kind of preliminary support it's getting. Ask for the same information from Asa Morgan in Helena. The last wire I want you to send to Bull Giles at the Black Dove Bar in Washington with the same request for information." The lack of interest Webb showed made him feel weary. "Have you got all that?"

"Yes, sir." Behind the smooth exterior, his mind was running over the possible significance of the information being sought and how it might affect the ranch. "Is there anything else?"

"No." His lips thinned into a tired line. "Don't you want to know why this information is important?" Benteen asked, and had the satisfaction of seeing his son's steady gaze waver briefly.

"I figured you'd tell me when you thought it was right for me to know." There was no hesitation over the reply, and the invitation to ask the question wasn't accepted.

Frustrated by his son's behavior, Benteen half-turned from him, muttering, "Go send the wires, and have the replies directed to the hotel."

As Webb moved away, spurs rattling with each stride, the aching numbness returned in

Benteen's left shoulder and arm. He rubbed at the soreness, kneading the muscles with his fingers.

"What's the matter with your arm?" The voice asking the question belonged to Barnie Moore.

Benteen let his right hand slide down the arm and shrugged aside the nagging ache. "Too many nights sleeping on cold, hard ground, I guess."

"I know what 'cha mean." Barnie arched his back, as if flexing stiff muscles. "Neither one of us is as young as we used to be." His gaze followed Webb. "I remember when that one was just a pup, playin' around with my boy. Now both of them is full-growed men."

Benteen sighed irritably. "I wish I knew where I went wrong with him."

"Webb?" Barnie frowned at him. "There isn't a better cowboy on the ranch than him."

"It isn't a cowboy I want," Benteen replied, but didn't confide the doubts he had about Webb's ability to become the ranch's leader. "How many more carloads of steers do we have left?"

Barnie took the cue to change the subject. "About eight or nine, I'd say." When he noticed the haggard lines etched in Benteen's features, he concealed his concern by casually rolling a smoke. "No need for you to stick around. We can handle the rest."

Benteen hesitated, but the constant din at the railroad pens grated on nerves that were already raw. "I'll be at the hotel if you need me."

Barnie nodded acknowledgment, although he didn't look up as he tapped tobacco from the pouch onto the trough of cigarette paper.

When Benteen stopped at the hotel desk to pick up the key to the suite, there was a message waiting for him. "Your wife said to tell you she'd gone shopping, Mr. Calder," the clerk informed him.

Annoyance flickered across his expression as he closed his fingers around the key and clipped out an automatic "Thank you."

"Be sure to let us know if there's anything you need," the clerk offered, not wanting the hotel to be responsible for the displeasure of a guest as important as Benteen Calder.

"Have someone bring up a bottle of your best whiskey," he ordered.

A quick smile spread across the clerk's face. "Your wife has already seen to that, sir. It's waiting in your room."

As he climbed the stairs to the suite, Benteen made a silent wager to himself that there would be a fresh cigar waiting for him in addition to the bonded whiskey. He won the bet. It was his wife's thoughtfulness that softened the hard curves of his mouth more than the cigar and the sipping whiskey. Shrugging out of his jacket, he dropped it and his hat on a chair in the suite's sitting room and sat down in the second chair, stretching out his legs full length in front of him.

Although the whiskey he'd splashed in the glass was barely touched, the cigar was half-smoked when Benteen heard the soft laughter of female voices in the hotel corridor. A key was turned in the lock and the door was pushed inward. His instinct was to stand, but a lethargy seemed to have control of his muscles as Lorna swept into the room with a rustle of skirt and petticoats.

Her arms were laden with packages. The young, blond-haired girl who followed her into the suite was similarly burdened. Benteen couldn't help noticing that Lorna didn't look that much older than the teenaged girl. She claimed there were gray strands in her dark hair, but they were so few that they didn't show. Her figure retained its slim, youthful curves and her complexion was china-smooth, showing only fine hairline cracks of age — thanks to the lotions she used to combat the effects of Montana's harsh climate. No one looking at her would guess at her inner strength, or the hardships she'd suffered in the early years. Her struggle to come to grips with this land had been as great as his own. With Lorna at his side, Benteen felt there was nothing he couldn't handle.

"I hope Daddy won't think I spent too much," young Ruth Stanton declared with a trace of apprehension.

Neither woman had noticed Benteen yet. He didn't mind. He liked the opportunity to watch Lorna unobserved. After setting her packages on the table just inside the room, she was unpinning the feathered blue silk hat.

"Your father wanted you to buy nice things for yourself," Lorna insisted, still addressing the daughter of her late friend. Since pneumonia had claimed Mary Stanton's life last winter, she had taken Ruth under her wing. Benteen suspected it filled a void in both lives, easing their grief. As a surrogate mother to Ruth, Lorna had acquired the daughter she had always longed for, while Ruth had an older woman to act as adviser and role model.

Ash was building on the end of his cigar. Benteen tapped it off. It was either his movement or the smell of cigar smoke, or both, that suddenly attracted Lorna's attention to the side of the room where he was sitting.

"Benteen." Lorna set the blue hat atop the packages as she crossed the room to greet him, her dark eyes radiant with delight. "No one at the desk mentioned you were here. Why didn't you say something when we came in?" Bending, she brushed her lips against the roughness of his cheek, then straightened, letting her hand rest on his shoulder to maintain contact.

"I knew you'd notice me sitting here sooner or later." A smile touched the corners of his mouth. "It looks like the two of you bought out the town."

"We tried." Lorna winked at Ruth in mock conspiracy.

An attractive girl with curling blond hair and quiet blue eyes, Ruth Stanton was innately shy. Even though Benteen had been the closest thing to an uncle all her life, she wasn't able to directly meet his gaze. Her glance skipped quickly back to Lorna.

"I'd better take these packages to my room." She almost pounced on the excuse to leave.

"We'll meet you in the dining room at six." Lorna didn't attempt to detain the girl. "Webb will be there, too. Why don't you wear your new pink dress?"

"Yes, I will." The suggestion brought a flush of pleasure to Ruth's cheeks. With a circumspect nod to Benteen, she slipped out the door to cross the hallway to her room.

When they were alone, Benteen tipped his head back to eye his wife. "Are you sure Webb's joining us for dinner?" With the roundup over and the cattle on their way to market, most of the Triple C riders would be doing the town. And Webb counted himself among them.

"He'll be there if I have to drag him out of the saloon myself," Lorna stated with a determined gleam in her eyes.

His mouth crooked in a wry line. "Maybe it won't be a saloon he's in," he suggested dryly.

"It won't make any difference." She moved away from his chair, recrossing the room to the table with the packages. "Do you mind if I ask you something?" She sounded too casual.

"What?" Benteen was instantly alert, prepared for almost anything.

"Is it true that Connie the Cowboy Queen had a dress embroidered with the brand of every outfit from here to the Platte?" When Lorna turned to look at him, there was a beguiling innocence about her expression that made Benteen shake his head.

"Where do you hear about these things?" Even after all these years, she still managed to surprise him now and again. Connie the Cowboy Queen had been one of the more notorious prostitutes in Miles City in its heyday.

"Women do talk about things other than sewing, cooking, and children. I promise that I looked properly shocked," she assured him with a mocking glance. "Was the Triple C brand embroidered on her dress, Benteen?"

"How should I know?" Amusement glinted in his eyes.

But she wasn't buying his attempt at ignorance. "A man can frequent such establishments without sampling the wares. Or maybe you just never saw her with a dress on?" Lorna pretended to accuse him of infidelity.

"When I had more woman than I could handle at home?" Benteen countered with a lift of one eyebrow; then it straightened to its natural line. "As for the dress, there was such a thing. And it wouldn't have been complete without the Triple C brand on it." His gaze narrowed on her with wary censure. "I hope this isn't the sort of thing you tell Ruth. The poor girl probably hasn't been kissed yet."

"No, I haven't gotten around to discussing any intimate topics with her." The implication was that the day was coming when Lorna would. Turning sideways to keep Benteen within her vision, she began untying the strings around the packages. "I'm certain Ruth is more than a little in love with Webb."

"Is that why you're going to make sure he comes to dinner tonight — and why Ruth is going to wear her new pink dress?"

Lorna paused to gaze wistfully into space. "Wouldn't it be wonderful if our son and Mary's daughter eventually married?" She barely controlled a sigh as she resumed the opening of her parcels. "It seems only fitting to me."

"I wouldn't hold out much hope." Benteen bolted down the half-jigger of whiskey in his glass in an effort to burn out the sour taste in his mouth. "You'll probably have about as much success trying to marry Webb off to Ruth as I've had trying to turn him into a rancher — which is zero."

"You're too impatient." Lorna gave him a mildly critical look. "You grew up in a different time, under different circumstances, so you can't judge Webb by your life."

The glass was abruptly set on the table next to the chair as Benteen pulled his feet under him and pushed upright. "Maybe that's the problem," he declared grimly. "I haven't been hard enough on him. I've let you spoil him."

"Me?" She stiffened at the challenging statement.

But Benteen was following the thought through aloud while he prowled restlessly around the sitting room. "Everything's been handed to him since the day he was born. He's been fussed over, coddled — the center of attention. Everyone's always smoothing the way for him. He's never had to fight for anything in his life."

"That isn't true." Lorna's maternal instinct rose with a rush as she confronted Benteen and forced him to stop his pacing. "Just look at how hard Webb has worked to earn the respect of the other riders. He's never let them treat him any differently because he's the boss's son."

"Why doesn't he work that hard to earn *my* respect?" Benteen insisted, his dark brows puckering together in a wistful line. "I can buy a dozen cowboys as good as Webb is at working cattle for thirty dollars a month and found. I don't need another workhorse in harness; I need someone who can hold the reins."

"Give him time," Lorna argued.

"There isn't that much left." He sighed and turned away from her. Defeat was tugging at his shoulders, but he kept them squared. "He doesn't give a damn about the ranch." He was beginning to believe that.

"Yes, he does." Her voice was steady, firm in its conviction. "It's his home."

"I'll take your word for it." He wished he

hadn't brought up the subject. Long, stiff strides carried him to the table, where he crushed out the cigar. "I'd better shave and get washed up for dinner."

Before he'd taken two steps toward the adjoining bedroom, there was a knock at the door. He paused, waiting to find out who was outside, while Lorna walked to the door, the exaggerated bustle of her dress wig-wagging huffy signals at him.

"Hello, Mother," Webb greeted her as the door swung inward. A gentleness softened the hard edges of his raw-boned features, giving them a warmth of expression they usually lacked.

"Webb." For an instant, Lorna faltered in surprise and sent a darting glance over her shoulder at Benteen, hoping Webb's arrival on the heels of their discussion wouldn't precipitate a second and, perhaps, angry one. She didn't like being caught in the middle, her loyalties divided between husband and son.

The ease went out of Webb's expression as his gaze traveled past her to his father. The atmosphere seemed thick with tension, strong undercurrents running between his parents.

"Come in, Webb," his father stated in a voice that sounded grimly resigned. "Your mother and I were just talking about you."

29

When his mother's glance faltered under his silent inspection and she moved out of the doorway to admit him, Webb stepped into the room. Obviously he'd been the subject of disagreement between them. He didn't want to be the cause of disharmony for his parents. He just wanted to live life his way, on his terms.

"Yes, we were," his mother agreed with commendable aplomb. "I was just threatening to drag you out of whatever saloon or bawdy house you were in so we could all have dinner together tonight. Now that you're here, your father can be spared that embarrassment."

"I came by" — Webb paused to direct his explanation to his father — "to let you know that all the wires have been sent. The replies will be coming to you here."

"Wires?" Lorna sent a questioning look at Benteen, mildly curious because it seemed a less quarrelsome topic, and because he hadn't mentioned telegraphing anyone. "What's this all about?"

"Nothing that needs to concern you."

"Someday I hope you'll explain to me why you always insist something is none of my business when other people are around, and then tell me about it later when we are alone," she lightly taunted him. "Men seem to think the only place they can talk to their wives is in the bedroom. But it isn't true, Webb," she advised her son.

The corners of his mouth deepened with a hidden smile at his mother's daring. Webb noticed his father was wavering between irritation and amusement.

"I'll try to remember," Webb murmured dryly.

"I thought I married a quiet, tractable woman." Benteen shook his head in affectionate exasperation. "I hope you have better luck, son."

"That reminds me," Lorna inserted. "We'll meet you at six this evening in the dining room." She ran a mother's critical eye over his dusty, smelly clothes and beard-roughened face. "That will give you time to bathe and change clothes. Ruth came to town with me to do some shopping, so she'll be joining us for dinner, too."

That last bit of information left Webb feeling a little unsettled without knowing why. He liked Ruth. She was practically family – a younger sister.

Yet his mother had been quite insistent about him cleaning up and changing clothes. Surely a man didn't have to make a special point about that for a girl who was like a sister. Unless his mother didn't want him to regard

Ruth as a sister. A glint of amusement appeared in his eyes at her subtle maneuvering.

"It was good of you to bring her to town, Mother," he commented. "I know it hasn't been easy for her since Mary passed away. She needed to get out and away from the house."

"That's what I thought," his mother agreed with a pleased smile.

"I'd better get cleaned up." Webb started to turn toward the door to leave.

"Oh, Webb —" She called him back, faltering for a second. "Be sure to notice the dress she's wearing tonight. It's a new one."

"I will." He was smiling as he left the suite. A compliment was expected to be issued about the new gown. It didn't seem to matter how old he got; his mother still felt obligated to remind him about his manners and gentlemanly behavior. Or was it another attempt to arouse a more personal interest in the woman wearing the new dress?

Lorna closed the door and leaned against it, chewing thoughtfully on the inside of her lower lip. When she became aware of Benteen watching her, she straightened. "While you're washing up, I think I'll help Ruth fix her hair."

"Matchmaking is like leading a horse to water. You can't make him drink," Benteen cautioned.

"No, but maybe he'll remember where the water is and find it again himself when he's thirsty," Lorna reasoned. She wasn't sure if it was the fading afternoon light or whether she simply hadn't looked at him so closely before, but Benteen suddenly looked tired to her. "Maybe you should lie down and rest a bit before dinner."

"I'm fine." An impatient frown deepened the lines already carved in his face. He started once again for the bedroom and stopped. "The last address we had on Bull Giles after he left Denver — was it the Black Dove in Washington?"

"Yes." It was her turn to frown.

"That's what I thought." He nodded absently.

"Did you have Webb send a wire to him?" She had already guessed the answer was affirmative. "Why?"

"He may have dropped out of the political scene, but he's bound to have some connections yet. There's a bill coming before Congress that has got to be stopped," Benteen explained vaguely. "It would throw this whole state open to homesteaders and plows. I don't want to go into it just now, not until I find out the particulars."

"That's what's been troubling you, isn't it?"

"Partly." He rubbed a hand along the side of his neck. "And I'm tired. Tired of struggling to keep what we've got. It wouldn't be so bad if my son was fighting with me. It's battling alone—"

"You're not alone," She glided quickly across the space that separated them and curved her hands around his forearm, tipping her head back to look at him.

"No, I'm not alone," Benteen agreed, but there was a sad light in his brown eyes. "I don't really mind the fight. But I'm not getting any younger. What happens when I'm gone, Lorna? I worry about you and how you'll manage on your own. I can't depend on Webb to look out for you anymore."

She caught her breath on a rising note of fear. "You're just tired, Benteen." She made a desperate attempt to dismiss his remarks as exaggerations. "Things will look better after you've rested a couple of days."

"Yeah." But he didn't sound convinced as he patted her hand and moved away toward the bedroom.

2

Most of the time, Webb took Ruth's existence for granted. It seemed she'd always been there in the shadowy background of his life, never seeking any attention and not expecting it. She was so quiet that it was easy to forget she was even around.

At the dinner table that evening, Webb had noticed the determined way his mother had drawn Ruth into the conversation, soliciting comments from her when none were forthcoming. It seemed impossible that a girl with blond hair and blue eyes could appear plain. Her features were comely, and her figure was adequately rounded, yet she wasn't at all striking. Her fair coloring seemed muted, fading into nothingness, like her personality.

Still, there was a subtle difference about Ruth. She seemed more feminine tonight. Webb wasn't sure whether it was the pink gown with its softly ruffled neckline or if it was the pale curls of her hair. With a faint degree of cynicism, he suspected it was more likely six weeks with cows as the only female company.

It was his mother's initial prompting to take notice of Ruth's appearance that centered his attention on her, but it was the air of vulnerability in her blushes and shyly dropped gaze whenever he said something nice to her that finally claimed his interest. There was no coyness in her actions; they were purely natural. Perhaps that's what prompted Webb to want to put her at ease with him.

When they left the dining room after a long, leisurely meal, Webb allowed his parents to lead the way to the hotel stairs while he followed with Ruth. Nate and the boys were waiting for him to join them at a saloon down the street. With dinner over, he had a perfect excuse to take his leave of Ruth and let her retire to her room for the evening as his parents were doing, but he didn't use it. He curved her hand along the inside of his arm and let his gaze slide down to study her profile.

"Would you like to step outside and get some fresh air?" Webb was surprised by the invitation he voiced.

Her startled glance revealed a similar reaction, but her eyes were brighter. He felt the slight tremor in her hand where her fingers touched his arm.

"Yes, I'd like that," Ruth accepted and kept her eyes directed straight ahead.

"It will be chilly outside. You'll need a wrap," Webb advised.

"I have one in my room. It will only take me a minute to fetch it." She sounded anxious, as if afraid he might change his mind and withdraw the invitation.

"I'll wait here for you." Webb paused beside the newel post at the base of the staircase to the rooms as she picked up the front of her skirts and rushed up the steps, trying not to appear unduly hurried. For Webb, it was a novelty to be with someone who demanded so little from him. She seemed to have no expectations for him to live up to. That was rare indeed. If it wasn't his father, then it was some local cowboy wanting to test his skill with a rope. Even whores expected more from him because he was a Calder, whether it was money or sexual prowess.

As he glanced up the staircase, wondering how long it would take her, Ruth appeared at the top of the steps. A drab-looking coat of brown wool covered the pink gown, nearly destroying the feminine illusion he'd formed, but the anxiety he briefly glimpsed in her face was wiped away by relief when Ruth saw him waiting for her. She came quickly down the stairs to his side, a little breathless.

"That didn't take long." His glance strayed to the incongruous brown coat, an unflattering choice for an evening wrap.

"This is the only warm thing I brought with me." She offered the explanation almost apologetically, aware it wasn't appropriate.

A smile broke the hard line of his mouth. "At this time of year, you'll need the warmth of that coat. I was just thinking it was a shame that anything has to cover that pretty pink dress." He attempted to make her feel less self-conscious about her appearance and tucked her hand along the inside of his arm to escort her outside.

Night shadows crowded close to the edges of the gaslit streets, lurking near the corners of buildings and spilling onto portions of the sidewalks. It was relatively quiet, most of the muted noise coming from saloons down the street. There was a sharp bite to the cold air that turned their breath into vaporous clouds.

"Will you be returning to the ranch tomorrow?" Ruth inquired.

"I expect so," Webb responded absently.

"You'll probably be glad to get back after being on the roundup for so long," she murmured.

"That's for sure." His glance ran over her, noticing the way she had burrowed her chin so deeply into the collar of her coat to keep out the cold. "Are you warm enough?"

"I'm fine." But her teeth chattered a little.

Their strolling pace had carried them a block from the hotel. Webb suspected Ruth wouldn't complain even if she were freezing.

"I think we'd better turn back anyway. It's colder out here than I realized." He guided her into a wide turn without increasing their pace.

"Yes, it is," Ruth admitted.

"What are you going to do now that you've finished school?" He didn't mention the recent passing of her mother.

"I thought about teaching some of the younger children at the ranch. Mrs. Calder — your mother — mentioned that maybe we could turn one of the smaller cabins into a day school."

"That sounds like a good idea."

"There aren't many jobs for a girl around here . . . proper jobs," she added on the heels of a raucous female laugh that came from a saloon across the street. "My father needs me right now, anyway, so I want to stay close by him for a while."

"Some cowboy will come along and sweep you off your feet," Webb declared with a faint grin. "You'll probably be married before you can decide about teaching school or working someplace else."

"No. That's not going to happen." She sounded so positive that Webb's curiosity was aroused.

"Why not?"

"Because —" She almost looked at him, then lowered her glance and shrugged. "Just because it won't."

"You don't want to marry a cowboy?" There was an edge in his voice as he wondered whether she was like other girls — setting her sights higher.

"No, it isn't that," she rushed to correct that impression. Once she met his gaze squarely, she seemed unable to look away.

"Then what is it?" Webb tried to fathom the cause for the helpless way Ruth seemed to be staring at him.

She broke away from his locking eyes, withdrawing and becoming more subdued. "I guess I just don't think I'll ever get married."

"Why not?" He had never heard a woman forecast her own spinsterhood. "You're a pretty girl, Ruth. The right fella is going to come along some day and see that blond hair and blue eyes and fall in love with you on the spot."

"Maybe." She conceded the point rather than

continue the subject.

Lights streamed from the glass windows of the hotel. "Here we are, right back where we started." Webb opened the door and followed her into the heated lobby. "I'll see you safely to your room."

"Are you staying here, too?"

"No." If his father'd had his way, he would have, but Webb preferred to bunk with the rest of the Triple C riders. That's why he slept in the bunkhouse at the ranch rather than in The Homestead, as the main house was called.

They climbed the stairs in silence, with Webb staying slightly behind her. He sensed awkwardness in her; she seemed uncertain how to behave. It became stronger when they reached the door to her room. She jumped visibly when Webb took the key from her and unlocked the door.

"Do you want me to check inside?" he asked as he handed her back the key.

She shook her head, tension showing on her face. "I enjoyed the walk." It was apparent in the murmuring tone of her voice, too. "Thank you."

"It was my pleasure, Ruth," Webb insisted politely and waited for her to enter the room.

But she continued to stand on the edge of the threshold, looking at him and appearing anxious, unsure of herself. Her blue eyes were rounded in a silent plea. It was a full second before Webb recognized the expression of puppylike adoration. She wanted him to kiss her good night.

His indecision didn't last long. In the dim hall light, her blond hair shimmered like creamy silk and her blue eyes were pools of blue sapphires. Without conscious direction of his movements, Webb let his hands close on the coarse wool of the brown coat and find the round points of her shoulders while his head bent closer to hers.

Her lips clung to his the instant they touched, yielding and soft, eager and inexperienced. It should have ended there, but Webb let the kiss draw out to an improper length. There was sweetness here and the taste was fresh and new.

Reluctantly he drew away, although his attention stayed on the moistened curves of her lips. A gentleman didn't indulge his baser needs on young ladies such as Ruth.

"Good night, Webb," she whispered on a note of lilting happiness.

His gaze flicked upward to the shining light in her eyes. "Good night, Ruth," he murmured huskily. "I guess we'll probably be seeing you more often around The Homestead if you start teaching school there."

"Yes." She swayed slightly toward him.

"You'd better go inside," he advised.

Ruth continued to smile at him, not letting him out of her sight as she entered the room and closed the door. Webb stared at the closed door a second longer, then moved toward the staircase. Almost immediately her image faded into a blur, hazy around the edges, nondistinct. At the top of the steps, he passed a messenger boy from the telegraph office on the way up, probably with a reply from one of the wires that had been sent. Webb paused to light a long, narrow cigar, his side glance following the messenger down the hallway until he stopped at the door to his parents' suite.

Shaking out the match, Webb held it between his fingers and puffed thoughtfully on the cigar as he started down the steps. The Homestead Act had been in existence for years. His father had used it, twisting it a little, to build the Triple C Ranch to its present size. Yet he seemed to regard the proposed amendment to it as some kind of threat to the ranchland.

Stepping out of the hotel into the crisp October night, Webb stopped and tossed the dead match into the street. He lingered there for a few minutes, wondering if the new bill might not be a benefit to the ranch by increasing the amount of land they held actual title to, then turned and walked down the street to the saloon where the rowdy group of Triple C riders had gathered.

The door swung open just as Webb was about to reach for it. The cowboy lurching out the door nearly bumped into him, then rocked back on his heels to squint at him. The noise of loud, boisterous voices and the heavy-handed piano playing rushed out into the night.

"Where are you goin', Johnny?" Webb let a faint grin lighten the hard angles of his face. "The party's just startin'."

The cowboy finally recognized him in the bad light and grabbed him by the arm to pull him inside. The air in the saloon was warm and stale, pungent with the smell of whiskey and beer. The smoke from cigars and cigarettes hung in layers over the long room.

There were a few locals in the saloon crowd, but mostly it was made up of the crew from the Triple C outfit. A couple of the cowboys were swinging two of the floozies around the room – dancing, by their standards. Riders without a female partner were dancing with each other. Some were leaning against the long bar, offering their encouragement and criticism of the dancers. In the back of the saloon, a poker game was in progress.

"Hey, boys!" Johnny shouted, his voice slurring slightly. "Look who finally showed up!"

Webb was greeted with a motley collection of shouts and demands to know where he'd been. Someone yelled his name from the right. His glance went in that direction just as a whiskey bottle was lobbed through the air for him. In quick reflex, he made a one-handed catch of it.

"You better get started!" Nate advised, waving a filled shot glass in a salute. "You got a lot of drinkin' to do to catch up with the rest of us!"

Webb pulled out the cork and raised the bottle to his mouth, tipping it up and guzzling down a couple of swallows of the fiery liquid. His action was met with cheers from the rowdy cowboys as he was swept toward the bar.

The next morning he remembered little of what had transpired after that point. He heaved the saddle onto the back of his rangy black gelding, then had to rest a minute until the violent throbbing in his head subsided to a dull pound. He stank of cheap perfume and his loins ached. Every movement was jarring, sending shafts of pain from his head down. Gritting his teeth, Webb strung the strap through the cinch ring and tightened it. There was some consolation in knowing that the other riders saddling up felt as rotten and miserable as he did.

Gingerly he pushed his hat a little farther down on his forehead. It felt like it was sitting on a balloon about to burst. The black gelding snorted and shifted sideways, rolling an eye at Webb. He changed his mind about climbing into the saddle and grabbed the trailing reins to lead the horse out of the livery corral and walk some of the humps out of its back before climbing aboard for the usual morning buck.

A team of sorrels was hitched to the ranch carriage parked in front of the livery stable. The slanting rays of the sun hurt Webb's eyes, and he dipped his chin down so more of his hat brim would shade out the sunlight. As Webb led his horse past the back of the carriage, he noticed his father standing by the front wheel. He felt the close inspection of those keen, dark eyes and bridled under it.

Stopping, he checked the tightness of the saddle cinch again and caught the movement out of the corner of his eye as his father approached. Webb gave no sign that he was aware of him, feeling the waves of irritability sweep through his system.

"I'll be spending the next few days in town,"

his father stated. "Your mother is riding back to the ranch with Ruth. If it wouldn't be too much trouble, I'd appreciate it if you'd keep an eye on her while I'm away."

His teeth came together as a muscle jumped along his jawline, but Webb merely nodded. "I'll check on Mother."

"Fine." Benteen kept his lips thinly together, bothered that he felt he had to make such a request of his own son. "Barnie's going to let Ely know, since he'll be in charge till I get back."

It would have been an opportune time to give Webb a taste of running the ranch in his absence if his son had shown any leadership potential in the past. But he couldn't risk it, and that was another worrisome point to Benteen.

When Webb made no comment, Benteen felt goaded into continuing the one-sided conversation until he got some kind of response from his son. "If I can arrange a meeting within the next week and get this new Homestead Bill nipped in the bud —" He paused, noticing the unexpected flicker of disagreement in Webb's expression. "Do you have something on your mind?"

Webb hadn't intended to venture an opinion, but everything seemed to rub him the wrong way this morning. Instead of keeping his customary silence, he met his father's narrowed look and decided to openly voice his differing view of the situation.

"I don't see why it's important to keep that bill from going through," he said flatly. "This land out here still isn't any good for farming. If anything, the proposal would probably be more beneficial to the cattleman than the farmer by extending his title to range he's already using."

At first his father's reaction was one of impatience for his apparent ignorance of the bill's ramifications, but it changed quickly, a speculative gleam appearing in his eye.

"That's what you think, huh?" he challenged, something close to approval touching his mouth. "Well, you're wrong." His father appeared to mentally shake away any lingering tiredness, energy suddenly returning to him. "Unsaddle your horse, Webb. You're going to attend that meeting with me. Nothing is ever secure — least of all, the Triple C."

Webb started to reject the idea that it was important for him to be at the meeting. Before he could say anything, his father read it in his expression.

"That's an order, Webb," he stated. "I'm not asking you."

There was a testing of wills before Webb

turned and hooked the stirrup over the saddle-horn to loosen the cinch. The black gelding twisted its nose around to snort at him to make up his mind.

The telegraph in Miles City was kept busy that week transmitting messages back and forth from the nation's capital to arrange a date for the meeting that all parties could keep. When a train from the East pulled into the depot ten days later, Webb and his father were on hand to meet it. Asa Morgan, having arrived from Helena the day before, was with them.

As soon as the private railroad car was separated from the others and pushed onto a siding, they converged on it, crossing the cinder-bed tracks to swing onto the rear platform. A uniformed black man admitted them into the private car, bowing with servile respect.

The interior walls were paneled with oak, and a thick gold and green rug covered the floor. It was ten years, maybe more, since Webb had seen the large, muscled hulk of a man seated in the overstuffed leather chair, but he recognized Bull Giles immediately. One leg was stretched out in front of him and a cane rested against the side of the chair. A second, heavyset man was standing by the window, no doubt having observed their approach to the train. Turning, he stepped forward to greet them as they filed into the car. His ruddy face was wreathed in a welcoming smile.

"Benteen, good to see you again." He vigorously shook his father's hand, then turned his shrewd glance on Webb. He doubted if the man was in his thirties yet, but there was an age-old look of political cunning behind the good-natured facade. The old-young man with the portly build was a back-scratcher with an itch of his own. "You must be a Calder, too," he guessed as he firmly clasped Webb's hand.

"This is my son, Webb." His father completed the introduction. "Frank Bulfert, the senator's aide." Then he included the third member of the Montana party. "And I'm sure you remember Asa Morgan, with the cattlemen's lobby."

"Of course I do. How are you, Asa?" Frank Bulfert greeted him with a kind of back-slapping gusto.

Benteen turned his glance on the brutish-faced man in the chair, who hadn't appeared to age since the last time he'd seen him. Theirs was a longtime acquaintance, dating back to his Texas days and those early years in Montana. Benteen didn't regard Bull Giles as a rival anymore, but neither did he call him friend, yet he trusted Bull Giles as he trusted few men. The man had saved his life once, crippling his knee as a result. It was something Benteen had never forgotten.

Despite an appearance that suggested all brawn, Bull Giles was shrewdly intelligent. During the long years he'd spent in Washington as companion and associate to Lady Elaine Dunshill, he had enlarged upon her connections in political circles and exercised considerable influence behind the scenes.

"Hello, Bull." There was a glint of respect as Benteen greeted him. "Don't bother to get up." He motioned him to stay in the chair. "How's the leg?"

"Stiff, but I've still got it," Bull Giles replied with a twisting smile. "How's Lorna?"

"Fine." He nodded briefly.

Then Bull turned his head to look at Webb. "It's been a long time, Webb. I'd forgotten how long it had been until you walked through that door to remind me. You're not a fresh-faced boy anymore."

"No, sir." Webb leaned down to shake the man's hand, stirring vague memories of his childhood, of the way he used to trail after this bear of a man.

Frank Bulfert's voice broke into their exchange. "Everybody, make yourselves com-

51

fortable. Percy" — he addressed the black servant — "pour these gentlemen a drink."

There was a lull in the conversation as they settled into the chairs grouped around the brass-appointed heating stove. After the servant, Percy, had passed around the drinks, Frank Bulfert opened a box of cigars and offered them around. Smoke from the aromatic tobacco collected in the air above the select group.

An unwilling participant, Webb was impatient for the talk to get around to the purpose of the meeting, but he seemed to be the only one. He took a sip of imported whiskey and wished he'd kept silent ten days ago. He'd be back at the ranch instead of here in this private car, involved in a meeting that he didn't think was necessary.

"The senator asked me to be sure to extend his regards to you, Benteen." Frank Bulfert leaned back in the cowhide chair and hitched the waistband of his suit pants higher around his middle. "My instructions are to lend you any assistance I can. The senator knows the value of your support." After this formal assurance was made, his serious expression took on a wry amusement. "I've heard stories about the way you ranchers get out the votes in this part of the country. It's been reported that sometimes your cowboys vote twice to make sure the right candidate is elected."

"They've been known to get too enthusiastic in their support," Benteen admitted with a faint smile.

"Seems to me you have men who follow orders," Frank Bulfert concluded.

"They're loyal to the brand" was the only reply to that. "What about this new Homestead Bill?"

"I'm afraid you're not going to like what I have to say," the aide warned and closely watched Benteen's reaction. "It's getting strong support from several quarters."

"The railroads being the most vigorous?" Benteen sought confirmation of his own opinion.

"Certainly they are looking at the substantial benefits to be derived from increased freight and passenger usage to bring new settlers out west. And I'm sure they are hoping to sell off their extensive landholdings. Yes." Frank nodded. "They have a vested interest in the passage of this bill."

"But it isn't only the railroads that want it," Bull Giles inserted. "You have to understand the situation in the East. The cities are filling with immigrants. The West has always been a safety valve to siphon these so-called dregs of

53

other nations out of populated areas and prevent any social or political unrest. The slums are overcrowded; there's complaints about cheap wages in factories and talk of unions and strikes for better working conditions. So all the big businesses are behind this bill to keep order by sending as many as they can to the frontier."

Benteen grimly expelled a heavy breath, recognizing he was opposing a formidable group. "But this isn't Kansas. They'll starve out here the same way they're starving in the cities."

"Do you think any of the big companies care?" Bull scoffed. "If they die, it makes room for more." He paused briefly. "The big-money men in the East aren't interested in settling the West. They just want to get rid of a lot of poor, unwanted immigrants. They don't give a damn where they go. The Indians were forced onto reservations on the poorest lands. If the immigrants wind up on the same, no one in the East is going to give a damn."

"So far," Asa Morgan spoke up, adding more gloom to the subject, "that new dryland method of farming has shown some impressive results. It's difficult to argue against the kind of success they've been having with it."

"Successful now, yes," Benteen agreed.

"With their method, they can raise a crop with only fifteen inches of rainfall a year. What happens if there's successive dry years with less than that, like what happened twenty years ago?"

"Twenty years ago isn't today." Frank Bulfert dismissed that argument.

"It sounds like sour grapes coming from a cattleman." Bull eased his stiff leg into a less cramped position. "You big ranchers are highly unpopular. Public opinion is against you. Most of the Europeans coming into the country look on ranchers as feudal lords. They came here to escape that system of large, single landholders. There you sit on a million-plus acres. They want to bust it up so everybody can have a chunk of it. They come to America filled with dreams about owning their own land."

"In other words, you are saying that we don't have a chance of defeating this bill," Benteen challenged.

"We can keep it in committee for a while," Frank Bulfert said. "But it's bound to pass once it gets out of there. It's what the majority wants."

There was a brief lull as everyone waited for Benteen to respond. He stared into his whiskey glass, idly swirling the liquor around the sides.

"They want it because they see it as a way of taking land out of the hands of the rancher and putting it with a bunch of immigrants," he stated finally. "But what if they become convinced that the bill won't accomplish that objective?"

"How?" Frank Bulfert drew his head back to study Benteen with a curious but skeptical eye.

There was another short pause as Benteen glanced at his son. "Webb thinks the new bill would let cattlemen get free title to more land. What do you think would happen, Bull, if certain factions heard that stockmen were in favor of this proposal to enlarge the Homestead Act?"

The burly man chuckled under his breath. "I think they'd come to the same conclusion Webb did. They'd be afraid they weren't breaking up the big beef trusts and worried that it would make them more secure instead." He turned to the senator's aide. "Benteen's found their weakness."

Frank nodded. "That just might be the tactic that will work." He glanced at Asa, who also nodded his agreement. "It will take some fancy footwork."

Later, after the meeting broke up in the early-evening hours, Webb and Benteen headed back to the hotel to clean up for dinner. They walked most of the distance in silence.

"Did you learn anything?"

The challenging question drew Webb's glance to his father. "What was I supposed to learn?"

"That you came up with the right answer for the wrong reason. You didn't think the proposal all the way through. You have to see how a thing can work against you as well as for you."

"After listening to Giles and Mr. Bulfert, I think it will be defeated," Webb concluded.

"It isn't as simple as that," Benteen stated. "This is just the first skirmish. The railroads still want more people out here, and the eastern cities have thousands they'd like to ship out. All we're going to accomplish right now is postponing what appears to be the inevitable." He lifted his gaze to scan the reddening sunset. "Those damn farmers will come — like a horde of grasshoppers; only, instead of grass, their plows will be chewing up sod."

There was a prophetic sound to his words that licked coldly down his spine. It didn't sound possible.

Two and a half years later, on February 19, 1909, Congress responded to the public cry for more free land and passed the Enlarged Homestead Act. Claims could be filed on 320 acres of land, providing it was nonirrigable, unreserved, and unappropriated, and contained no marketable timber. That description fit almost twenty-six million acres of Montana land.

II

Stands a Calder man,
Flesh and blood is he,
Longing for a love
That can never be.

3

Wild flowers covered the long stretches of the broken plains, wide sweeps of yellow, red, and white dancing over the low, irregular hills. The black gelding cantered through a thick mass of them growing out of the tangle of tightly matted grass. A plume of dark smoke lay against the blue sky far in the distance. Webb saw it and traced it to the locomotive bearing down on the tiny collection of buildings that made up the settlement of Blue Moon.

It was officially a town now, with a general store to supply the local ranchers, a saloon to wet the throats of the cowboys, a blacksmith shop to repair their wagons, and a church to forgive them their sins. Since the railroad had laid tracks through it, they had a freight depot and regular mail delivery.

Off to the left, a horse-drawn buckboard rattled over the rutted track across the plains that served as a road. There were supplies to be picked up and some freight due at the depot that necessitated the trip into town. Neither would be done with any amount of haste, so there would be plenty of time to catch up on local happenings and trade information.

The shrill, lonely whistle of the train punctured the quiet of the starkly masculine landscape as it let off steam and signaled its imminent arrival at the small town. The black gelding shied beneath Webb, spooking at the sound, then settling back into its rocking gait.

The buildings were growing larger, becoming more discernible now in the vast plain as the contingent from the Triple C Ranch drew closer. Webb judged that they would arrive about the same time that the train pulled in.

When they reached the outskirts of Blue Moon, Webb reined the gelding alongside the buckboard and slowed it to a trot. There were more people in the streets than he was accustomed to seeing in the little cow community.

"Busy place," Nate observed from his seat on the buckboard.

"Probably just more people out because of the train." It was an event that brought folks out of their houses.

But there seemed to be a lot of unfamiliar faces on the street. Webb saw only a few people he knew. A frown began to gather on his face as he tried to figure out what had brought all these strangers to town, and where they'd come from.

"Shall we go to the depot?" Nate asked as they neared the general store.

"Might as well." Nearly everyone was heading in that direction, so they let themselves be swept along with them. Two new buildings had sprung up on the street. Nate noticed them, too, and exchanged a questioning look with Webb.

The skittish gelding danced sideways under Webb, trying to see everything at once. Ahead, the depot was crowded with empty wagons hitched to teams of horses shifting nervously at the closeness of the "iron monster." It chugged idly, hissing puffs of steam. Nate had to swing the buckboard to the far end of the depot platform where there was room to park it. Webb reined the fractious gelding around to the far side of it as Nate set the brake and wrapped the reins around the handle.

Passengers were streaming out of the cars onto the depot, mostly men, but a few women with children, too. None of the men were dressed like cowboys or traveling salesmen. On hand apparently to greet the arrivals was a short, fox-faced man in a spanking white suit and a white straw hat. Taking it off, he waved it over his head to get the attention of the passengers.

"This is it, folks! Your journey's end!" He sounded like a preacher announcing to his flock that they had reached the Promised Land. "These wagons are going to give you a close-up look at America's new Eden! Now, I know you all are tired from your long ride and want to stretch your legs a bit. While you take a few minutes to get the stiffness out of your bones, I want you to look around. Take a gander out there at that grass." He gestured to the expanse of plains beyond the railroad tracks leading into town. "It's purty nigh belly-deep to a tall horse. You look at that grass — and picture wheat in your mind!"

Nate slid a sharp glance at Webb from the wagon seat. "What the hell is he talking about?" he muttered under his breath, but clearly didn't expect an answer as he swung off the seat to the trampled and packed ground.

Webb took another look at the empty wagons lined up in front of the small train station. On both sides of the wagon beds, planks were laid, forming two benches to accommodate human freight. The new wood contrasted with the weathered-gray boards of the rest of the wagon and revealed how recently they had been converted to accommodate a passenger load.

As he dismounted and tied the gelding's reins to the back of the buckboard, he sized up the milling group of people. There were a scant few who looked like farmers, the ones with permanently sun-reddened faces. The vast majority of the group had the paleness of the city about them, but their tired faces were alive with hope. Webb realized their expression was more positive than hope. The belief was shining in their eyes that they had now been led to the Promised Land.

My God, he thought with a mixture of amusement and anger. The poor fools don't know what they're gettin' into.

Nate was already heading for the small building that housed the office of the station agent to check on the freight for the Triple C. A handful of the newly arrived passengers had wandered to the end of the train where the buckboard was parked, providing Webb with a closer study of them.

His dark gaze moved over the young girl at the vanguard of the little group, then came back to her. She stood poised on the edge of the limitless plains, facing the benchland of tall grass with its hidden coulees and flat buttes. Her chin was lifted to the wind blowing in from the land as if she were drinking in the air's freshness, free from the city stench of smoke and congestion.

Wisps of dark auburn hair were whipped loose from a coiled knot at the back of her head while the sun's direct rays highlighted the fiery sheen in her dark tresses. A limp blue hat dangled by a ribboned string held in her hand and the black shawl had fallen off her shoulders. The wind flattened the faded gingham material of her dress against her slim body, showing Webb the swelling curve of high, youthful breasts and the outline of slender hips and legs.

Vitality and excitement seemed to flow through every line of her. It was more than just her young female form that drew and held his eye. There was something else that pulled his interest and wouldn't let it go. Without conscious direction, Webb let his course to the depot widen so he would pass closer to the girl.

Her motionless stance was broken as she turned to look over her shoulder and search the milling group of passengers for someone, her parents more than likely, since Webb doubted that a young girl would come out here alone. Evidently she spied them, because she started to glance back at the rolling grassland, sweeping aside strands of hair that the wind blew across her face. But when she did, she noticed his approach.

With bold curiosity, she stared at him. Her eyes seemed to take in every detail from the dusty crown of his cowboy hat to the heavy denim material of his Levi pants and the spurs riding low on his boots. Then her gaze swung upward to linger on the rough cut of his features. Montana born and raised, he unknowingly carried the print of the land on him, big and strong, with a certain harshness in the uncompromising lines of his face. His flatly sinewed chest was broad and strong, throwing an impressive shadow on the ground.

Webb was indifferent to the impression he created. He was caught up in the blue of her eyes — as blue as the Montana sky overhead. Just like looking into the sky, he seemed able to see forever. The sensation gripped him, unnerving him a little.

His attention had been so obvious that his sense of propriety demanded a greeting. He touched a finger to his hat brim as he came within two feet of her, his easy stride slowing. "Good morning, miss."

"Morning." Her head dipped slightly in response, her eyes never leaving his. "Are you a cowboy?" The question rushed from her, followed by a smile that seemed to laugh at her own impetuousness.

"Yes." His mouth quirked in a humorous line. It didn't seem necessary to explain that he was a rancher's son. By profession, he was a cowboy.

"I thought so." Her smile widened at his affirmation. "You're dressed like the cowboys that were in Mr. Cody's parade."

There was a second when he didn't understand the reference to the man; then the confusion cleared. "You mean Buffalo Bill Cody and his Wild West Show," he realized, amused by the falsely exaggerated impression it had created for thousands about the West. "Have you seen it?"

"No." She shook her head, laughing softly as if such a possibility were out of her reach. It prompted Webb to notice again the dress she was wearing, guessing it was probably her best, yet it was faded except where the seams had been let out to compensate for her maturing figure. It was wrinkled from traveling, but clean. It was obvious that her family didn't have the money to spend on such frivolities as a Wild West Show, and her next statement confirmed it. "We couldn't afford the admission price, but they had a parade with Indians and everything."

"Where was this?" Webb asked, curious to know where she was from — this innocent woman-child who couldn't be more than seventeen.

"In New York. That's where we live — used to live," she corrected herself, excitement beaming in her face, thoroughly enchanting Webb with her eagerness for life.

"What are you doing here?" He struggled to break the crazy spell of her, forcing his gaze to the scattered clusters of the train's former passengers.

"This is where we're going to start a new life." There was an absolute certainty in her voice that it would also be a better life. His glance slid back to study her profile as she looked expectantly at the surrounding plains, as if Utopia were just over the next rise. "We're going to have our own land and grow acres and acres of wheat."

"If that's what you want to grow, you belong in Kansas. This land is only good for grass and cattle," Webb stated grimly.

Her attention was fully on him once again, a determination he hadn't seen before suddenly surfacing in her clean features. There was even a shade of defiance glittering in her eyes. "That isn't what Mr. Wessel says."

He tipped his head to one side. "And who is Mr. Wessel?"

"That's him over there." She indicated the

man in the white suit. "He's a locater. He's going to show us the best sections of unclaimed land so we can choose which one we want to file on."

It wasn't difficult to imagine the promises of riches the man had made to these ignorant and inexperienced settlers.

"He's going to find land for all these people on the train with you?" Webb guessed.

"Yes," she stated with a challenging tilt of her chin. "All of us signed up with him because he's the only one who knows where this land is located. No one else has seen it but him. We're going to be the first."

"Besides the ranchers and the cowboys who have traveled every inch of this country." He lightly mocked the boasting claim that originated with the white-suited Mr. Wessel. "I suppose he's told you that all you have to do is plow up the sod, sow some wheat, and you'll be rich overnight. It isn't that easy."

"Nothing worth having is ever easy." She seemed to be speaking from experience rather than simply mouthing a wise phrase. "We've read all the brochures the railroad printed, telling about richness of this soil and the dryland method of growing wheat. The railroad has checked into it and they have evidence that proves it can be successfully grown."

Webb didn't argue that point, because it couldn't be disputed. Considering his father's steadfast insistence to the contrary, it was a fact that troubled him. Wheat had been harvested in profitable quantities. Most of Webb's opposition to turning this ranchland into wheat farms came from an ingrained resistance to any change of the present lifestyle that focused on cattle and cowponies.

"Lillian!" A male voice called out the name and the auburn-haired girl turned in response. Webb wasn't quick enough to pick out the man who had called to her from the group of settlers gathering around the wagons.

Feeling her glance return to him, he looked back. There was a troubled quality about her expression, a kind of resigned regret, but it wasn't quite that, either. Then it was gone, replaced by a polite but friendly smile.

"I have to go now. They're loading up the wagons to take us out to the new land," she explained unnecessarily.

"I hope you and your family find what you're looking for," Webb offered. "Either here or someplace else." There was a barely formed thought that he didn't want this to be the last time he saw her as his fingertips gripped the front brim of his hat.

"Yes." It was a preoccupied reply.

Drawing her shawl up around her shoulder, the young woman named Lillian turned to rejoin the others. At first, she moved sedately away from him, but her steps quickened when she drew closer to the group.

Webb took the tobacco sack out of his vest pocket and used the business of building a cigarette to screen his interest in the girl with the dark chestnut hair. She approached an older man in an ill-fitting suit and spoke to him. He was tall, a slight stoop to his shoulders as if they carried the weight of many hard, lean years. His gaunt features were mostly covered by a hoary white beard, silver tufts of hair poking out from the flat-brimmed black hat on his head. Yet he looked rock-solid, a laborer rather than a farmer, using the muscles in his back and the sweat of his brow to eke out a living for himself and his family.

Raking a match head across the rough denim material covering the back of his thigh, he cupped the flame to his cigarette and dragged the smoke into his mouth. He was shaking out the match as Nate Moore approached him, coming from the direction of the depot.

"Our stuff's in." Nate confirmed the arrival of the ranch's shipment. His glance strayed to the motley assortment of travelers climbing into the converted wagons. "As soon as they

72

get gone, we can drive the buckboard over and get it loaded up."

"Good." Webb pinched the match head between his fingers to be sure it was cool before tossing it into the grass near the cinder track.

What few belongings the new settlers had brought with them were stacked on the depot platform along with the other freight. After they'd selected a homesite, they'd be back to collect it. The baggage was a clear indication of their intention to stay, and a desperate statement that they had no home to go back to, their roots pulled up to be replanted in Montana soil.

"Did ya ever see such a ragtag bunch?" Nate remarked, following the direction of Webb's interest. "The station agent says they're just the beginning. The railroad's cut the fares coming from the East down to next to nothin'. But they're only sellin' one-way tickets. It wouldn't surprise me if some of those folks didn't sell nearly everything they owned just to raise the price of the fare. They'll be lucky if they got a dollar in their pockets."

"What do they need money for?" Webb countered with wry cynicism. "The land is free." He mocked the ignorance of the settlers who had arrived here with a pocketful of dreams and little else.

As the wagons loaded with eager settlers pulled away from the train station, their modern-day Moses was at the head, leading the oppressed poor to their so-called Promised Land.

"Let's get that buckboard over by the depot." Nate pushed his lanky frame into motion, but Webb dawdled a second. His gaze traveled after the rumbling wagons, trying unsuccessfully to pick out the one the young woman had climbed in.

When the freight was secured in the back of the wagon, they headed back to the main part of town. The general store had the distinction of being the original building in the small settlement. It bore little resemblance to its log-cabin beginnings, especially with the false front dressing up the entrance side. Although it still bore the name of Fat Frank Fitz-simmons, his widow had sold it several years ago when Frank died and she decided to go back east where she had family. The new owner was a man named Ollie Ellis, middle-aged and aggressive in seeking trade with the ranchers in the area. He believed in serving his customers, anxious to discover their needs and fill them so they wouldn't take their business elsewhere. Few ranchers did.

The Triple C Ranch represented a big account to the merchant. When Webb walked into the store, Ollie Ellis came out from behind the counter to greet him. He was a stocky man with a shock of sandy hair, businesslike in his attitude. "It's good to see you again, Mr. Calder." Even though Webb was the son of the owner, Ollie always addressed with the respect he felt was the due of the heir apparent to the Calder Cattle Company. "We've been having a fine spring, haven't we?"

"The weather has held nicely so far," Webb agreed, resenting that he was acknowledged and Nate was relegated to second place in importance.

"Hello, Nate." Ollie was freer with the cowboy, a back-slapping quality to his greeting. "How's the tobacco holding out?"

"I'll be needing another can," Nate replied, not seeing the slight Webb saw.

Taking the list of needed supplies from his pocket, Webb handed it to the store's proprietor. The man looked it over without comment as he walked behind the counter.

"Did you happen to notice those wagons filled with new settlers that went through town just before you came into the store?" the merchant asked as he began filling the order.

"We were down at the station when they

came in." Nate nodded in reply. "They are figurin' to file homestead claims hereabouts."

"That's what I heard. Rumor is they are going to start streaming to this area." Ollie Ellis looked skeptical. "It's for sure the railroad is out there beating the drums to bring them in." Aware of where his loyalties belonged, he quickly made certain Webb was informed of them, too. " 'Course, I don't put much stock in all that talk about turning this land into one giant wheatfield. This has always been grazing land for cattle or sheep – and before that, for buffalo and antelope."

"That's what they said before the farmers started fencing in Kansas and stopping all the trail herds." Some of that Webb remembered from his childhood. "Dodge City is about as tame as towns come now, filled with farmers on market day instead of cowboys blowing off steam after months on the trail."

"That's true," the merchant conceded. "But I don't see farmers taking over Blue Moon and turning it into a farm town. Not that I wouldn't appreciate their business, you understand. New customers are always welcome in my store, but a man just doesn't forget his regular customers. That's like biting the hand that feeds you."

"This bunch doesn't look like it came with

much money in its pockets," Nate remarked. "So I don't think they'll be doin' too much buyin' for a while."

"I noticed there are a couple of new buildings in town," Webb said.

"A guy named Wessel owns one of them. He's a land speculator, from what I've heard," Ollie replied. "He dresses real flashy — wears a white suit. He tells me that a bank is going into the second building."

"A bank? In Blue Moon?" Nate looked more than skeptical.

"That's what he said," the merchant confirmed, and smiled crookedly. "If those new settlers are as broke as you think, they'll need a bank to loan them money for seed."

"The land's free." Nate looked at Webb as he spoke, recalling the phrase he'd used at the station. "But they'll have to sell their souls to grow anything on it."

A humorless smile of agreement flashed across Webb's mouth. "While you fill our order, Ollie, Nate and I are going over to the saloon."

"I'll have it ready for you in less than an hour," Ellis promised.

"There's no rush." He knew they wouldn't be in any hurry to leave the saloon to make the long ride back to the ranch.

Up until ten years ago, the saloon had been a small room off the general store. Then the railroad had put a spur into Blue Moon and Sonny Drake had arrived in town and built a roadhouse, complete with a bar to lure trade into his establishment. Competition and an expanding merchandise business had combined to finally close the saloon side of the general store.

Like Ollie Ellis, Sonny Drake catered to the local ranchers and their hands, happy to serve them whiskey, then rent them a room to sleep it off when they had too much. The separate building with a bar on the first floor and a half-dozen small sleeping rooms upstairs also had the added enticement of being only a dozen yards from a log shack located in back of the building where Miss Fannie Owens quietly plied her ancient profession.

In the early noon hour, there was only one customer leaning against the long bar made out of hand-carved wood, imported all the way from Chicago. When Webb and Nate walked into the local roadhouse, the interior seemed dark after the bright sunlight. Sonny was sweeping the floor, most of the chairs still turned upside down on the tables, with the exception of one. A curly-haired man had set the chairs upright and sat reclining in one with his boots propped atop the table. A whiskey bottle was on the table within reach to fill the shot glass he was nursing.

His gaze lifted from its study of the contents when he heard the combined jingle of spurs. The hard, brooding look that had been on his face vanished when he recognized Webb. A smile broke across his face, giving it the good-natured expression Webb usually associated with Doyle Pettit. Doyle was a couple of years younger than Webb, the son of a rancher. Only Doyle wasn't just the son of a rancher anymore. His father, Tom Pettit, the owner of the TeePee Ranch, had died three years ago, and it now belonged to Doyle.

"Hey, Webb, Nate. Come on over here and join me!" He waved them to his table. "It's been a helluva long time since I've seen you fellas! Sonny," he called to the husky owner/bartender. "Bring these boys some glasses."

"What are you doing in town?" Nate pulled out a chair and slumped into it, resting his arms on the table.

"I'm drinking to the end of the cattle business." Doyle lifted his glass in a mock toast, then downed the drink.

It was fairly common knowledge among the ranch community that the TeePee had been going steadily downhill since Doyle had taken charge. It was a combination of poor management and a declining cattle market.

"You aren't thinking of selling out?" Webb raised an eyebrow, surprised that Doyle might be quitting. It was good land, the best next to the Triple C.

"Hell, if the cattle prices get any lower, I won't have a choice." Momentarily disgruntled by the implied failure, Doyle Pettit refilled his glass, then poured whiskey into the two that Sonny set on the table.

"They'll go up. They always do." It was just a matter of riding out a poor market and paring down expenses.

"I laid off most of my hands yesterday." Doyle sighed. "I just barely met the spring roundup payroll. I'll let them all go if I have to, but I'm going to hang on to that land. It's going to be a gold mine."

"No cowboys mean no cattle, so I don't know where you're going to find that gold," Nate said dryly.

"Gold as in wheat." A bright gleam leaped into his hazel eyes. "Wheat means land. And, Lord knows, I own enough of it."

"You don't really believe a fella can grow wheat out here?" Nate scoffed, eyeing the rancher as if he'd lost all his wits.

"Hell, no, I don't believe it, but those dry-landers do." Doyle laughed. "When all that free land gets snapped up, they're gonna start buying it."

There was sense in what Doyle was saying, but Webb couldn't approve of the plan. The idea of breaking the Tee-Pee up into wheat farms seemed a traitorous act for a cattleman. He kept his silence only because Doyle had been a good friend for so many years.

A lull followed that was silently critical. Swinging his feet off the table, Doyle sat up and leaned forward, anxious to convince his friends of the wisdom of his plan.

"It's the smart move," he insisted. "Those suckers coming out here are hungry for land. Nothing is going to stop them. Now that they have started, it's going to be like a flood. You just watch; the land values around here are going to shoot sky-high. It isn't going to matter anymore how many head of cattle you own. It will be how much land. Anyone who tries to stick with ranching is a fool. A man can get rich with land."

"You overlooked something." Nate shifted in his chair. "Every boom has a bust. When those farmers can't grow a crop to meet their notes, they're going to lose their land."

"That's the beauty of it." A grin spread his

mouth wide. "Think of how many times a man can sell the same chunk of land!"

"It don't sound right to me." Nate shook his head.

"It's no different than horse-trading," Doyle declared. "If the buyer can't see for himself that the horse is spavined, then he deserves what he gets."

It was apparent that Doyle considered the comparison an adequate justification. Webb also realized that Doyle had covered every angle. This wasn't just idle talk to be bandied around the table and forgotten. It was going to be followed through.

"What do you say about all this, Webb?" Nate turned to him, seeking vocal support for his opposition.

"I say it's a damned good thing old Tom Pettit is dead and in his grave." There was a certain stiffness in his movements as he took a quick swallow of whiskey.

Doyle reddened slightly, his hazel eyes narrowing. "My pa was just like yours is, Webb. All he knew was cattle and that ranch. As far as he was concerned, there wasn't any world outside the boundaries of his range. That's old-time thinking. He put nearly thirty years of his life into that ranch. When he died, he left me a bunch of cattle, but no money —

not a dime after thirty years. That's what you're going to get, Webb — cattle and all the headaches that go with them. I'm not going to waste my life the way my pa did."

"A man's gotta do what he thinks is right," Webb murmured, but Doyle's words had made him uneasy. This time it had nothing to do with being the son of Chase Benteen Calder and the future owner of the Triple C. It was something else that gnawed at him. Some new thought that hadn't occurred to him before.

"Your pa left you a good piece of ranchland," Nate reminded him.

"And I'm going to take that land and turn it into money," Doyle stated, less defensive. "I've been talking to Harve Wessel about maybe setting up a partnership. Have you met him yet?" He shot a glance at Webb.

"I've only seen him."

"That guy could sell beaded moccasins to reservation Indians," he declared with a grin. "We've been considering buying up some land for speculation. Since his heart attack last winter, Evan Banks is talking about selling the old Ten Bar spread. Harve is sure we can convince the bank to loan us the money to buy it."

"Instead of being cattle-poor, you're going to be land-poor," Webb warned.

"I'll be land-rich," he corrected and let his

glance swing back to Webb. "If your pa was smart, he'd sell off at least some of his land. The days of the big cattle ranches are over. He'd better be thinking about trimming down the size of the Triple C, or he'll find himself losing it all."

More than an hour went by before Webb and Nate took their leave of Doyle and left the saloon to get a bite to eat. They paused outside the door, studying the one-street town. Nate hitched his pants higher on his hips and darted a squinting glance at his friend.

"What do you think?" he asked.

Webb didn't have to ask what he meant. "I think Doyle is going to do it. He's going to sell off the TeePee."

The knowledge didn't set well with either of them. Times change, and both men had seen a lot of change. More was coming, it seemed, and they didn't like the looks of it.

Surrounded by the rolling plains of eastern Montana, the immigrants listened wide-eyed to the man in the white suit. Tall stalks of grass rubbed their heads against his knees. Harve Wessel had carefully chosen the place for his lecture on the dryland method of wheat farming. As far as the eye could see in any direction, there was virgin grassland, government land free for the taking. Time and the elements had carved a cutbank into the side of a small rise in the land, giving him a naturally elevated platform from which to speak.

With the confidence of a salesman convinced his product was sold, he invited questions. "Is there anything you don't understand about the dryland method?"

Everyone looked around to see if anyone else was going to speak. Stefan Reisner made a negative shake of his head when the locater Harve Wessel looked squarely at him. He was in the front row of the immigrants, with Lillian standing by his side, her head tipped slightly back to view the locater.

"Now, for those of you who are short of funds" – which was virtually all of them, as Wessel knew – "I can help you obtain a loan from our new bank – your new bank – so you can buy seed and the equipment you need. The interest is ten percent, but the land is free," he emphasized. "Any questions?"

"What will we do about a place to live?" someone asked.

"Wagons or tents will get you through the summer until you sell your first crop. There's going to be a lumberyard in Blue Moon where you can buy wood to throw you up a place. Borrow money from the bank for that, if you don't want to wait. Or" — he paused, "you can build you a sod house out of all this 'prairie marble.' "

A woman spoke up. "What will we use for fuel to cook with and to heat our homes in the winter? There aren't any trees around here."

"I'm glad you asked that," he stated and looked down at Lillian Reisner. "Young lady, hand me a chunk of that black rock by your feet."

There were any number of shiny black rocks at her feet, broken from the wide seam showing in the exposed earth of the cutbank. Bending, Lillian picked up a large, rough-edged chunk and handed it to him. A curious frown narrowed her eyes because the rock had looked just like coal.

"Now, I've been telling you people what treasures you can find in this land. This is one of them." Harve Wessel held up the piece of black rock for all to see. "It's coal. It's a few feet underground just about anywhere you want to look. And in places, like here" — he pointed to the coal seam in the cutbank — "it's at the surface. There's your fuel!"

Slowly Lillian swung her attention to Stefan. She had no more doubt about the wisdom of coming to Montana. It was only a matter of finding their piece of land.

4

The wind rustled through the green-growing grass, bowing its tall spring stalks and creating shimmering hues of emerald, jade, and turquoise under a sapphire sky. It seemed a jewel-studded land with wild flowers of ruby red and topaz yellow strewn all around and a horizon that was limitless. At last, the promises of riches that had lured her parents to America's shores were about to be fulfilled.

With her head lifted high to the shining sun, Lillian Reisner filled her lungs with the freshly scented air. Blind hope had been her traveling companion for such a long distance. To be standing here in the middle of this vastness made her feel as if something wonderful were bursting inside. It was a sensation of freedom beyond expression.

No more buildings crowding in to block out the sun. No more smoke-clouded skies and air that choked the lungs with the stench of sewage and animal waste. No more living on top of neighbors, hearing all their quarrels and crying.

"Listen to the wind, Stefan." She turned her shining face on the tall, square-jawed man. "I can't ever remember hearing the wind before."

"And the birds, too." His speech was laden with the guttural accent of his native Deutschland. "My ears have so long heard only pigeons that the songs of birds in the meadow I forget. I vas a young man vhen ve left Germany – your papa and me. You vere only a gleam in your papa's eye."

It was a story Lillian had been told many times: the long ocean voyage in steerage, her parents' ardent wish that their first child be born in America where the streets were paved with gold. She was a native citizen, raised in the German ghetto of New York City. Both of her parents had believed in the dream of America all the way up to their deaths within a few months of each other. It hadn't mattered that the streets weren't paved with gold. The markets held more food than they had ever seen. To them, it had remained a land of plenty, untarnished with disillusionment.

Listening to Stefan's thick accent, Lillian remembered how once she had been so ashamed of the way her parents talked, how intolerant she had been, unable to appreciate the strength and courage it had taken to leave their homeland for a strange, new country with a different culture. To her deep regret, it was a discovery she had made after they were gone.

Now she had made a journey so very much similar to theirs — traveling across this huge continent of America, eager, yet unsure of what she would find waiting for her. This big, open stretch of land was awesome — a long, lonely distance from anywhere. But she wasn't intimidated by the empty landscape.

Her father and Stefan had shared a dream of owning their own farm in America. She was here with Stefan, taking her father's place, to make that long-ago dream a reality. Respect and deep affection were in the look she gave the forty-three-year-old man who was her husband. Despite the grayness in his hair, he was iron-strong, yet kind and good.

In her own way she loved him. If the emotion lacked passion, Lillian wasn't troubled by it. Romantic love was a luxury of the rich who could afford such things. A common woman had to be more practical and pick a man who could provide her food, shelter, and companionship. Lillian was satisfied with her choice.

"You have waited a long time to have land you could call your own." Lillian watched the pride of possession steal into his eyes, then turned to make a sweeping gesture with her arm. "Here it is, three hundred and twenty acres."

"That Mr. Vessel, he said he vould show us the best." He nodded in satisfaction, his stoic features altering their expression not at all, but the look in his eyes was very expressive.

Yesterday they had filed the homestead claim, made arrangements at the bank for a loan with Mr. Wessel's help, and purchased seed, equipment, and the supplies they needed to start a new life. With the team of draft horses and a used wagon, they had picked up the belongings they'd left at the train station and driven here to their property where they would build their home. It was twenty miles from town and six miles from their closest neighbor, but after traveling so far, they were undaunted by these distances.

"Look at this, Lillian." Stefan indicated the ground at his feet and nudged the grass aside with the toe of his high-topped leather shoe. When he crouched down for a closer study, Lillian did the same, smoothing her skirt close to her legs so it wouldn't be in the way. His callused and blunt-fingered hand exposed the tangle of grass stalks that held the soil together. "Ve vill make to grow the vheat dis thick."

"Yes, we will." She knew he was seeing it happen in his mind's eye, the transformation of this sea of grass into an ocean of waving wheat.

His hand closed around a clump of grass and gave a steady pull, muscles straining to break the tenacious grip of the grass's roots in the soil. That Stefan Reisner succeeded in ripping it out of its earth bed was a clear measure of his physical prowess. He tossed the clump aside and clawed out a handful of dirt. With smiling eyes, he looked at Lillian and offered her the soil. She cupped her hands while he crumbled the chunks into them.

"Our land," he said simply.

The brown dirt was cool against her palms. She closed her fingers around the dry earth, feeling its roughness and reminding herself that this soil was a source of food for plant life. This was fertility in her hands, the first chain in nature's cycle.

"On this spot, ve vill build our home," he said as he pushed to his feet. "First, ve must plow the ground and plant our vheat."

"We'll need to plow a space for a garden, too, so we can grow our own vegetables," Lillian added.

Behind them, one of the horses stamped the

ground, rattling the harness chains. Lillian straightened and brushed the dirt from her hands without getting it all. While Stefan walked to the wagon to begin unloading it, she lingered to make another slow study of the rolling grassland sprinkled with wild flowers.

For so long, this land had been unproductive, solely the domain of cattle and the men who tended them, the cowboys. The corners of her mouth were edged with a faint smile by the latter thought. The first one she'd met in the flesh hadn't turned out to be anything like what she had expected a cowboy to be. She had thought they were wild and rowdy, always ready for a fight, but the one she'd met had been polite and friendly.

She could still remember his dark eyes and the way they looked at her, frankly admiring and alive with interest. He'd always had elbow-room, never confined or crowded. It showed in his manner, the way he carried himself, so loose and at ease with his surroundings, accustomed to the bigness of the sky.

There was a difference in him that came from living his life in the outdoors. His features were browned by the sun, making Stefan appear pale in comparison. He looked proud and vigorous, his shoulders squared, not stooped like Stefan's. He was strong, and rugged, like this land, possessing an earthiness that Stefan didn't have.

With a mute shake of her head, Lillian realized that it wasn't fair to compare Stefan with the cowboy. Stefan was easily fifteen years older. Perhaps when he had been in his prime, the differences wouldn't have been so marked. Besides, it wasn't wise to begin building up images of that cowboy in her mind.

And it was equally foolish to stand around daydreaming when there was so much work to be done.

Riding fence was a lonely job, but Webb had never minded the loneliness of it, the long days with only his horse, the land, and a big chunk of sky for company.

While the mouse-colored dun horse walked along the fenceline, Webb reached out to check the tautness of the wire wherever it appeared to be slack, and test the posts to make certain they were solidly in the ground. His actions were automatic, leaving his mind free to wander along its own trails.

The horse's stride made long swishes through tall grass already making its early-summer change from green to yellow. The sound and the color prompted Webb to try to conjure up a picture of this land covered with golden stalks of wheat. It was a tame sight that didn't seem to belong in this wild, open range.

For the last two months, the grumblings in the bunkhouse had centered on the drylanders, the term being given to the homesteading farmers. They were being called a lot of other things by the cowboys, too — bohunks, nesters, and honyockers. Since spring, these immigrants had been arriving by the trainload. Homesteads were springing up on the plains like weeds, threatening to take over the rich grasslands that had been the ranchers' domain.

Webb didn't like the idea any more than the next cowboy, but he'd become more philosophical about it. In his father's time, this country had been the last area of free range for the cattleman. Now it was the last area of free land for the farmer. It had always been so in the settling of the western lands. First came the trapper, then the rancher, and finally the farmer. No amount of resistance by the established order had ever changed the outcome. The invasion of the plow had begun.

With that historical perspective, he regarded his father's continuing efforts through his political connections to halt or check the flow of homesteaders pouring into the area as both futile and unrealistic. Five years ago, his father had forecasted the coming of the farmers, and Webb couldn't understand why he was fighting a war that was already lost.

As the mouse-colored horse topped the gentle slope of a hill, its head came up, its ears pricking with sudden interest at some object on the other side of the fence, outside the Triple C boundaries. Webb felt the horse's sides expand to whicker a greeting to the team of draft horses in the wide hollow of the adjoining section of land. They were leaving a brown wake behind them, a straight swath through the grass.

It was strictly reflex that caused Webb to rein his horse to a stop. The rattle of harness chains came clearly across the silence of the rolling plains. Coming into view behind the muscled haunches of the draft team Webb saw, first, the man driving them, then the plow, a descendant of the famed sod-buster that had tamed the prairie of the Midwest. The old iron plow of early settlers couldn't cut through the densely matted sod that was baked rock-hard by summer heat and frozen solid by winter's cold until a man named John Deere invented a plow with a revolving blade and a steel mold-board that was able to cut the sod and turn it over.

There were refinements, but the principle

was the same in the modern version of the implement Webb saw. He relaxed the checking pressure on the bit and let the gray dun start down the slope to the hollow where the homesteader was plowing up the virgin sod. The working team were too busy to respond to the cow pony's whinnied greeting except to swing bobbing heads in its direction.

The man at the reins wore suspenders to hold up his loose-fitting trousers. Sweat was leaving wet stains on the front of his shirt, nearly reaching the patches under his arms. The small-billed cap on his head shaded little of his sun-reddened and whiskerless face.

When Webb noticed the homesteader's cheeks were smooth-shaven, he realized he had thought the man might be the father of the girl he'd met at the train station. But the man was not only beardless, he was also younger, about Webb's age. Still, his gaze swept past the dryland farmer and his horse-drawn plow to follow the trail of newly turned earth until he found its starting point.

About a quarter of a mile from the fenceline, the weathered boards of a wagon nearly blended into the tan background of the plains. His eye was caught first by the dull-white slash of a tent roof; then the wagon took shape. Two small children were playing in front of the tent, supervised by an older girl-child. All of them were fair-haired, making it unlikely that they were related to the girl he'd met with dark copper hair. Webb's gaze came back to the man.

Like his horses, the homesteader was too intent on his work to notice the horse and rider approaching him on the opposite side of the fence. It wasn't until Webb was nearly level with the horse team that the man saw him. His reaction was to instantly halt the team, his gaze darting warily over the tall rider.

From what Webb had heard in the bunkhouse, the homesteader's attitude was understandable. The railroads and the small-town businesses had welcomed the immigrants to the area, but the reception from their neighbors — the ranchers and cowboys — had been on the frigid side, varying from icy disdain to blatant hostility.

The mouse-colored horse wanted to stop and become acquainted with the equine new-comers, so Webb let it. The saddle leather groaned as Webb shifted position and pushed his hat to the back of his head. The gelding stretched its neck over the barbed wire to nose at the near horse, as indifferent as its owner to the overture of interest.

"It looks like it's going to get hotter as the

day wears on." Webb remarked on the weather, since it dictated conditions that affected both rancher and farmer.

An affirmative response was made by the downward movement of the drylander's chin, but not once did his eyes leave Webb to inspect the skies for himself. Webb turned his glance to the churned-up earth behind the plow.

"Are you planning on sowing this in wheat?" He asked the obvious.

The chin came up again with a defiant thrust. "Yes."

"Isn't it a little late in the year?"

Something flickered across the man's face. Webb wasn't sure whether it was doubt or simple concern. It was too quickly replaced by a desperate determination that he would later recognize as a quality common to virtually all the drylanders. For a fleeting second, he let his thoughts run back to the auburn-haired Lillian, glad that her family had been among the early arrivals, because their crop would have time to mature, provided there was rain. This man was gambling there wouldn't be an early killing frost.

"Mr. Wessel said we had time to plant and harvest." The drylander's voice had an accent Webb couldn't place, but the conviction of belief was unmistakable.

Impatience with the man's blind faith in this land promoter Wessel thinned the hint of friendliness from Webb's features, turning them hard. His stony gaze veered to the distant wagon and tent, and the children playing so carefree under the warm sun.

"That your family?" Webb slashed the same narrowed glance at the farmer.

There was worry behind the man's bristling posture, as if Webb's reference to his family were somehow threatening, but Webb was wondering how those youngsters would make it if the crop failed, as it probably would with such a late planting, and there was no money to buy food for the winter.

"That's my Helga and my children," the man stated.

"Do you have any idea how rough it's going to be out here for them?" Webb seriously doubted it.

"I have gun." The drylander returned Webb's steady look. "If trouble comes to my family, I will use it."

Although there was no outward change in his expression, Webb was startled by this response. He had been referring to the hardships inherent in this land and its climate. He hadn't meant to imply any other source of physical harm to the man or his family. Had there been instances of violence or harassment by ranchers or cowboys that he hadn't heard about?

At this point, it didn't matter. But what was clear to Webb was how easily it could occur. Lord knew, the bunkhouses had plenty of hot-headed cowboys eager to fight over anything. If they bumped into an equally belligerent dry-lander, violence of some sort was bound to result.

Webb shifted his hat, bringing the front down on his forehead, while he subjected the man to his narrowed study. "What's your name?" he demanded.

"Kreuger. Franz Kreuger." It was issued with a combative pride that silently challenged Webb to make some disparaging remark about his nationality.

"Let me tell you something, Franz Kreuger." Webb walked the dun horse along the fence until he drew even with the man. "Most of the ranchers around here are old-timers. They've shot it out with renegade Indians and rustlers — and sometimes with each other. They know which end the bullet comes out of. When they see a gun, they don't regard it as a warning. They figure it's going to get used. My advice to you, Mr. Kreuger, is to give that gun to your wife. You'll all be safer if you do."

With his piece said, Webb reined his horse away. This section of fenceline could wait to be checked another time, after he had cooled down. It was fool-talk like that said to the wrong man that started incidents.

As Webb pointed his horse toward the crest of the hollow's ridge, he heard the homesteader slapping the reins and clicking to his team. He kicked the gelding into a lope, letting the pounding of its hooves block out the sounds of the draft horses straining against their collars.

Before he reached the top of the gentle incline, a trio of riders was skylined on the ridge to his right. Webb shifted his angle of ascent to join up with them. Since he wasn't due to be relieved for two more days, his curiosity was aroused. Most of it dissipated when he recognized his father as one of the riders. They pulled in at the ridge crest and waited for him to ride up.

A space was made for Webb next to his father's horse. Was he required to take the position beside him because he was the son or because the boss wanted to talk to one of his riders? Webb swung his horse behind the trio of riders and walked into the opening between his father's mount and Ely Stanton's. Judd Turner, a drifter who'd come to work for the outfit a year ago, was on the outside.

His father gave him a brief side glance that was never satisfied with what it saw. "Everything all right?"

It wasn't a query about the condition of the fence in this sector. Benteen Calder wanted to know about the homesteader on the other side of the Triple C boundary. Webb looked down on the scene from the vantage point of the ridge. The homesteader was sending anxious glances at the men on horseback, but he kept the team of horses moving.

"Everything's fine." Webb didn't mention the father's challenging assertion that he had a gun. Talk like that would fly through the bunkhouse, and somebody was bound to harass the man out of sheer orneriness.

The sunlight angled off the plow just right, reflecting on a blade as it furrowed into the grass-matted sod and turned over dark earth. Webb sensed, rather than saw, the quiet rage that filled his father. It seemed to crackle through the air.

"Turner is here to relieve you," his father stated, although Webb had guessed as much. The glance Benteen darted at the cowboy was a silent order to assume Webb's duties.

The drifter urged his horse forward, flashing the three of them a smile. "Don't forget you left me out here," he joked.

102

When the cowboy was out of earshot, his father said, "Bull Giles is arriving by train the day after tomorrow. You're coming with me to meet him."

A part of Webb wanted to ask the reason behind Bull's visit, but his father didn't appear to be in an explaining mood. So he said what he thought instead. "The homesteaders are here. The army couldn't get them out now. More are coming, and there's nothing you or Bull Giles will be able to do to stop them."

"So I shouldn't try, is that it?" The full, cold fury of his father's gaze was leveled at him. "Look down there, Webb — just ahead of that team of horses. Do you see the grass?"

"Yes." It was a clipped answer as Webb looked where he was told, not seeing the point.

"Take a good, long look, because it's the last time that earth will ever grow that grass again." His voice was harsh. "It's like the rape of a virgin. You can never put back what she's lost. Maybe you can watch it happen and not try to stop it, but I can't."

It crossed Webb's mind to point out the many historical precedents to this moment when the farmer invaded what had previously been the rancher's domain, but it was wasted breath on his father. The implication that he was a quitter rankled.

"Time changes places and people," was his only reply.

"I've lived through a lot of them, son," Benteen Calder reminded him. "But this is one I don't want to live to see." A grim despair cut through his voice as his gaze swung back to the homesteader. The short silence was followed by a slow shake of his head. "I don't know whether I admire the fool guts it took that drylander to come out here — or to hate the stupid bastard for what he's doing to this land." His voice vibrated on the last with the deep intensity of his emotions.

The violence that Webb heard below the surface reminded him of the fighting stand the homesteader had been so ready to take. It seemed to reinforce how volatile the situation could become.

"If this dirt can grow grass, how can you be sure it won't grow wheat just as thick?" It was a subtle challenge, a little open rebellion against his father's black-and-white world that left no room for gray.

"For the same reason a rocky field won't grow corn and there's no rice growing in the desert." The answer was swift and stabbing. "There's certain things land can support. No matter what man does or tries, he can't change it — not permanently. That man down there is

104

a stranger to this country." He motioned toward the homesteader. "His ignorance is at least a partial excuse for what's he's doing. But you should know better. I'll never understand why people have to learn the hard way." He gathered up the reins to his mount and turned its head away from Webb.

Yet no explanation had been given, no proof offered, that convinced Webb the rancher was right and the farmer was wrong. The last thing he wanted to see was the Triple C turned into a giant wheat farm, but that didn't mean farmers weren't potentially turning the land to its most profitable use. It was for sure there wasn't any money in cattle – not this year or the last couple of years. Webb didn't know what kind of shape the ranch was in financially, since he hadn't inquired, but it couldn't be good.

5

The single street of Blue Moon was a quagmire of sticky mud that clung to the wheels of the Reisner wagon, but Lillian was all smiles. Yesterday had provided the first good rain they'd seen since they arrived in eastern Montana, except for a couple of brief showers that did little more than settle the dust. She had laughed and danced in it, and tried to coax Stefan out of their tar-paper cabin to join her, but he had stayed in the shelter of the doorway, content to watch her and the ground-soaking rain falling on their burgeoning wheatfields.

Since it was too muddy to work outside, they had hitched the team to the wagon and taken the opportunity to come to town for more supplies. As crowded as the street was, it seemed all the other homesteaders were doing the same thing. Lillian couldn't help noticing the happiness in the people's faces. She knew what they were thinking because it had to be the same as she was: This was supposed to be dryland – and it had rained!

What did it matter if the wet soil was like thick gumbo that clumped on your shoes and sucked at your feet? All that rain would make the wheat grow. Come autumn, they would harvest their first crop. The smell of success was in the air. Stefan had cautioned her about counting chickens before the eggs hatched, but she had seen the relief in his eyes and knew she was only expressing what he was inwardly feeling.

"Ve vill first fill the vater barrel," Stefan declared as he pulled the team to a halt in front of the blacksmith's shop.

Since the arrival of the drylanders in the Montana plains, the blacksmith's well had become the source of water for the home-steaders who weren't close to a river or hadn't sunk a well on their own property, which was most of them. For a small fee, they filled the water barrels from the smithy's well and hauled them home. Now that it had rained, it seemed a minor inconvenience – and only temporary.

Other wagons were clustered around the blacksmith's with the same intent. Lillian searched the faces of the women on the wagon seats, but didn't see anyone she remembered from the train. She smiled and nodded to the ones who looked her way and they did the same back, while their menfolk waited for their turn at the well, as Stefan was doing.

As her attention swung to the street, Lillian saw the half-dozen riders that were escorting a buggy into town. Two women were riding in it.

Suddenly she found herself staring at a familiar face. A little rush of pleasure tingled through her at the sight of that cowboy she had spoken to the day they'd arrived here. He seemed taller than she remembered, but maybe it was the added height of the horse that created that impression.

When his slowly roving gaze wandered her way, Lillian unconsciously held her breath. She was sure that he looked right at her, but he gave no sign that he recognized her. She felt crazily deflated when his eyes failed to linger on her.

Then his head suddenly jerked around to look in her direction. She could almost feel the probing search of his gaze. Hard, male features that appeared cast in bronze took on a warm, gentle quality of recognition. Her pulse seemed to pick up its tempo, beating a little faster.

There was a hint of a smile about his mouth as he raised his hand and touched the rolled point of his hat brim. It was the same gesture he'd made when they'd first met. With a small nod of her head, Lillian acknowledged the greeting. Then he was past her and the eye contact was broken as he continued with the group of riders escorting the buggy, apparently to the train depot.

She darted a quick glance toward the well, picking out Stefan from the other homesteaders, then looked back to the entourage of cowboys. They were all riding horses, marked with three *C*'s on their left hips. Lillian remembered the marks were called brands. She wondered what the three *C*'s meant, but it was simply another way of wondering about the cowboy.

"Did you see that?" A homesteader in a billed cap had also noticed the passing of the riders. He offered the question to anyone who would listen, and immediately captured Lillian's attention. He turned his head and spat at the ground. "They ride into town like they own it."

The man talked as if he knew who they were, what ranch they were from. Lillian leaned forward in her seat, a question forming even while she bit at the inside of her lip to hold it back.

But it came out anyway. "Who was that?"

"Calder." Dislike shimmered in the man's

blue eyes as he said the name. "He owns the biggest ranch in this area. There are lords in America just like in Russia."

Others were listening, some of them craning their necks to see the band of riders that had passed. Lillian's gaze traveled after them and lingered on the wide-shouldered cowboy.

When her attention returned to the well, she looked around at the other homesteading families. These were proud, working people with backgrounds of poverty and struggle very similar to hers. She didn't think the cowboy had suffered as they had.

"How do you know them, Kreuger?" another homesteader questioned the Russian.

"My place touches his land. One of his men comes by when I was plowing my field and warns that harm might come to my family." He paused to inspect the hushed reaction around him and stood a little straighter, adopting a swaggering pose. "I told him I have rifle and I would shoot it."

A voice rose above the hum of whispers that followed. "What happened then?"

"He made more threats, then rode off." He addressed his words to the men. "We must stick together, all of us. These ranchers think because they were here first that they own everything. We must show them we can't be frightened."

The phrases seemed echoes from the past. Lillian's gaze drifted downward to the blue gumbo of wet earth around the well. It was caked on Stefan's high-topped shoes. In the New York tenement where they had lived, she'd heard that kind of men-talk before — the angry grumblings to organize so they could stand united against the robber barons. Despair always seemed to give birth to violence.

This was a new land. It should be the place for a new beginning, where a person could build something with the pure sweat of labor — without hostility or fear. But this empty-looking land wasn't as serene as it appeared.

At the train depot, Webb dismounted with the other riders and tied the horse's reins to an upright post. Stepping up to the wooden floor of the roofed platform, he stamped the sticky mud off his boots. Restless surgings were creating a tension inside him, putting him on edge. The other riders shifted around him, making way for Benteen Calder as he joined them.

"Curley, check with the agent and find out when the train's due," Benteen ordered.

"Right, boss." The rider angled toward the depot office with the typical rolling gait of a cowboy.

Then Benteen's cool glance fell on Webb.

111

"Give your mother and Ruth a hand over that mud."

With a nod, Webb turned to the horse and buggy parked within a couple feet of the platform. There was a split-second hesitation when he caught the warmth of Ruth's gaze directed at him. A ripple of unease flowed through his muscles as he approached the buggy, but it didn't show in his face.

"Need some help to keep your skirts out of the mud?" He smiled at the quiet, blond-haired woman standing in the buggy with one foot resting on the outside step.

"Please." Ruth returned his smile, but in her own reserved way.

His gloved hands gripped her slim waist and lifted her in a gentle, swinging motion that spanned the two feet of muddy ground and deposited her on the wooden floor of the platform. He felt the lightness of her hands on his shoulders for balance and the slow way they were withdrawn. Then he was turning away to help his mother out of the buggy.

"I can't recall when I've seen so many people in town," his mother declared as she straightened the fall of her caramel skirt.

"They're mostly drylanders," Webb stated. "The rain's driven them out of the fields into town, I imagine."

"This sun is going to dry the ground in a hurry," she said with a frown. "They'll need a chisel instead of a plow to get back into their fields tomorrow."

Webb smiled in response to her observation. Montana mud did become rock-solid when it dried. The rains came so seldom that he tended to forget that.

"I pity those poor people," Ruth murmured, drawing Webb's eyes to her with the comment.

"They seem determined to make it," he said. But he was noticing the rose-colored dress Ruth was wearing and the smoothness of her skin, like a white pearl. A picture flashed in his mind of the homesteader girl, Lillian, in her cheap gingham dress and skin that was already browning from the sun. He'd passed right over her when he'd first seen the group of wagons around the well. This raw land was already having its effect on her.

It was strange how he hadn't recognized her. He hadn't caught the flash of red in her hair until the second time he looked. Something else had triggered his recognition. Maybe it had been the coiled eagerness of her — that vitality of body and spirit.

"It will take more than determination, I'm afraid," his mother said. Her lips widened into a smile. "But I like seeing all these people in town, even if a certain Mr. Calder thinks that is a traitorous remark." She boldly lifted her gaze to the man just joining them, teasing him in a loving fashion.

If anyone else had said that, they would have received a steely glare, but Benteen merely gave his wife an indulgent smile. "The train's a half-hour late," he advised them. "The agent told Curly there's two cars full of drylanders on it. I hope that makes you happy, Lorna."

She took a breath and said nothing in reply. "Since we have to wait for the train, we might as well find a comfortable place to sit." She looked to Ruth. "Would you like to come inside the depot with me, or stay here on the platform with Webb?"

"I think —" Ruth paused and looked at Webb, reluctant to voice her approval of Lorna Calder's maneuvering to put the two of them together.

This nonassertiveness was nothing new to Webb. She never presumed anything in their relationship, always letting it be his initiative and never showing dissatisfaction over his snail's pace. Webb himself wasn't sure why he held back and avoided courting her outright.

"Ruth needs some fresh air after being shut up in the schoolhouse so much." He made the decision for her and noticed the pleased look in his mother's eye.

"Are you coming with me, Benteen?" She tucked her hand under the inside curve of his arm, not waiting for his answer.

Webb reached into his shirt pocket for a tailor-made cigarette and watched his parents walk arm in arm to the depot office. Since Ruth had never objected to his smoking, he didn't bother to ask her permission before lighting up. An Indian woman had her wares on display and approached Webb, offering a pair of moccasins for his inspection. He shook his head and she moved back to her blanket to wait for the train.

"I hope those primers I ordered for the children have arrived," Ruth said, uncomfortable with the silence.

He squinted his eyes against the curling smoke. Maybe he was like Nate claimed to be, not the marrying kind. There were others on the ranch, his age or younger, with children in Ruth's school. His life was too aimless. A wife and family meant settling down and becoming his father's man, which Webb flatly rejected. Instead of just drifting along, it was time to decide whether he wanted to stay at the Triple C or strike out on his own.

"You should get married, Ruth," he said abruptly. "You should be teaching your own children instead of someone else's."

"You sound just like your mother," she replied. "Except she said I should be teaching her grandchildren."

"That's not likely." The answer came out before Webb had considered it, but it was a true feeling. He realized it said something about his intentions toward Ruth — or the lack of them. "Have you ever been to Texas?" He changed the subject, aware that she was directing her attention elsewhere to avoid looking at him.

"No, I haven't." Her voice sounded small. She had been waiting for Webb to notice her for so long. It seemed he had. He'd come to see her once in a while, have dinner at her house, and he had kissed her at least a dozen times. Each year, she thought it would be the one when he'd ask her to marry him. He wasn't seeing anyone else. Lorna Calder had assured her of that.

"I've only been there a couple of times myself. My grandparents are still living in Fort Worth. Mother keeps talking about visiting them, but . . ." He frowned and didn't complete the sentence.

The lonely wail of a train whistle sounded in the distance. Those waiting on the platform stirred and began drifting to the trackside. It was the same in the street. The arrival of the train was an event that drew onlookers to the station. It was a link with civilization for the residents of this isolated community in the middle of nowhere.

When the train whistle blasted its approach signal again, three wagons came rattling down the street. The white-suited figure in the first wagon Webb recognized as that land promoter Wessel, but his eyes narrowed at the sight of the second man sitting on the wagon seat with him. It was Doyle Pettit from the TeePee Ranch. That day in the saloon, Doyle had talked about throwing in with the land promoter. As Webb had suspected, it hadn't been just talk; but seeing the two of them together was another thing. When he glimpsed the drivers of the other two wagons, it was even more difficult to accept. They were longtime hands with the TeePee outfit, nearly as much parts of the ranch as Barnie Moore and Shorty Niles were at the Triple C. It didn't set well when Webb considered these men — these cattlemen — would be driving wagonloads of nesters out to help them find land to homestead.

"Isn't that Doyle Pettit?" His father spoke from Webb's right as the train chugged and hissed to a stop at the station. "And Charlie — and Jingles?"

117

"Yeah." Webb faced the train rather than watch the defection of his contemporary to the other side.

The first two passenger cars behind the freight cars were painted with signs proclaiming them to be the Northern Pacific Special. It didn't matter where a person looked anymore. There was always a visible reminder of the drylanders. Families of them filled the special cars. Webb silently watched them pouring out to be greeted by Wessel striding into view in his eye-catching white suit. His father wore a tight-lipped expression and there was a hard gleam in his eyes.

"Look at that bunch of bohunks." The muttered words of contempt came from one of the Triple C riders. It didn't matter which one, since he voiced the sentiment of all.

"There's Bull." Lorna Calder was the first to spot the broad hulk of the man as he swung down from the train steps, relying heavily on his cane for support. A black porter followed with his satchel.

They lost sight of him behind the swelling tide of emigrants clustering around the land locater. Wessel hopped onto a wooden crate so all could see him.

"Welcome to the future wheat capital of Montana!" His voice carried like a preacher's.

"I hope you didn't come here looking for dry-land. All we've got is mud!"

Subdued laughter and wide smiles spread through the large group of new settlers. The only ones shaking their heads grimly were the members of the Triple C outfit. As Bull Giles limped into view, Webb pushed the voice of the locater extolling the virtues of this region into the background of his hearing.

Built like a circus strong man and just about as ugly, Bull Giles wore a tailor-made black suit. The jacket was unbuttoned, revealing a silver brocade vest and a diamond stickpin. Despite his hulking physique, he appeared every inch the gentleman. The impression was stronger as Bull Giles singled out Lorna Calder for his initial greeting. There was a softness in his features that belied his powerfully built body and craggy face.

"You haven't changed a bit, Lorna. If anything, you are more beautiful." He took her hand and bowed gallantly over it, kissing the top of her white glove.

"And you haven't changed a bit, either, Bull," she declared. "You are still the flatterer."

"If your husband wasn't standing here, giving me the baleful eye, I would attempt to convince you that my admiration isn't insincere." There was a lightness in his reply that didn't match the intensity of his gaze. Then he was turning to Benteen before anything more could be read into his manner toward Lorna. "I guess I don't need to ask how things are," Bull said as he shook Benteen's hand. His glance swerved to the emigrants flocked around the promoter.

"They're blacking this land like a plague of grasshoppers." Benteen put them in the same category of disaster, which seemed an unwarranted exaggeration to Webb. "I hope you've come up with something."

"The dam broke, Benteen," Bull stated. "It would take an act of God to stop this flood of people now."

The pronouncement was no different than Benteen had expected, yet it didn't lessen his displeasure at actually hearing it voiced. There was a brief lull in the conversation as Bull paid the porter for carrying his satchel. Benteen motioned to one of the men to stow the satchel in the buggy.

"The town has really grown." Bull looked up the street, noting the many new buildings that flanked the muddy thoroughfare. "Is that a lumberyard?" He nodded toward the stacks of green wood piled against an unfinished building.

"The lumberyard's the most recent," Benteen admitted. "Blue Moon even has a bank. And there's optimistic talk going around about building a granary."

"Nothing stays the same, I guess." Bull thoughtfully studied the wide spot in the road that had grown into a full-fledged boom town in less than a few months. "Things change."

"The changes aren't always good."

Bull's mouth twitched in a dry smile. "You'll have a hard time convincing the merchants of that."

"The problem with greed is that it feeds on itself." Benteen seemed to shake off his dark mood with an effort and made the opening gambit to depart from the station. "Let's go have a drink while Lorna does her shopping."

"Good idea," Bull agreed. "It's a long, dry ride to the ranch, as I remember."

For the short ride up the street, Benteen climbed in the buggy with his wife, Ruth, and Bull Giles. The muddy ground was getting thicker as it slowly dried in the hot sun. It was like walking in glue as Webb untied his horse's reins and moved to the near side to mount.

As he stepped into the stirrup, Nate backed his horse away from the post to give Webb room. The driver of the bench-seated wagon closest to them was a black cowboy dubbed

Jingles because of the belled spurs he wore. He pretended not to see the Triple C riders filing past to accompany the buggy.

But Nate forced an acknowledgment, stopping his horse beside the wagon seat. "Jingles, what are you doing in that box?" He frowned. "A top hand like you oughta be in the saddle."

"The ranches around here are layin' off top hands. They ain't hirin' 'em." His voice was hollow with resentment for the menial job he was doing, but he had a wife and family to support. "At least I'm gettin' paid to ferry these pilgrims across this ocean of grass."

"You keep ferryin' em," Nate replied, "and it won't be grass no more. Without grass, there won't be cattle. You're gonna wind up puttin' us all on the grubline."

Jingles pushed his hat lower on his forehead to cover the guilt in his eyes as his chin came down. Nate urged his horse after the rolling buggy. Webb said nothing to add to the black cowboy's miseries as he rode by. The plummeting cattle market had made hard times for all ranchers. To cut expenses, most of them were operating with skeleton crews. The Triple C hadn't hired its usual contingent of seasonal riders, running strictly with its corps of permanent hands.

His father had said change wasn't always

good. Jingles would agree with him. As Webb scanned the homesteaders' wagons scattered up and down the street of Blue Moon, he recognized they welcomed the change, and so did the merchants. Whether change was good or bad seemed to depend on a person's perspective.

A team of pale sorrels stood placidly in the trace chains of the wagon parked in front of the new bank. Their feathered fetlocks were encased in mud, disguising their white-socked legs. But the Belgian bloodlines of the two draft mares were unmistakable. For a cowboy, it was second nature to study animals and note their owners; almost as automatic as breathing.

When Webb spied the Belgian draft mares, he knew without taking a second look this was the team hitched to the wagon the girl Lillian had been sitting in earlier. But the wagon seat was empty now. And he didn't see her among the pedestrians walking on the boards laid across the mud.

A long breath sighed from him as he looked around. A rawness worked on his nerves and coiled his muscles. That edgy feeling was back, a sense of dissatisfaction without knowing for what. Webb wasn't sure if it had ever left him. He didn't understand this restlessness, or its source. Was it the drylanders and the change they were bringing that was working on him? Or was it something inside himself?

His horse broke into a trot, reacting to the restlessness of its rider. Webb checked its pace with an irritable tug on the bit and clamped his jaw down on the urge to sink his spurs into the horse and ride away while he could.

6

The mug of beer in front of Webb was warm and flat. He had taken only one swallow from it. His father and Bull Giles were discussing politics, but he wasn't listening.

The other Triple C riders had gathered along the bar, supervising a billiard competition in progress. Their loud, rowdy voices and guffawing laughter emphasized the distinction between themselves and Webb's brooding silence. He felt tied and bound by the Calder name, not one of them. He reached for the beer mug, then pushed it away and stood up. He turned to avoid the sharply questioning look his father sent him. "Where are you going, Webb?"

"My mother and Ruth will probably be needing a hand with their packages." It was merely an excuse to leave the table and the saloon in obedience to the agitation that charged him with a raw energy.

Bull eyed the younger Calder as he crossed to the door. "What's eating at Webb? He's like a range bull on the prod."

Benteen glanced after his son and lifted a shoulder in a vague shrug. "Maybe he and Ruth had a falling out." But he didn't believe that for a minute.

"Ruth certainly doesn't take after her mother." As if sensing Benteen's reluctance to discuss his son's behavior, Bull turned the conversation down a different path.

"That's true," Benteen admitted. "She's definitely her father's daughter, quiet and gentle just like Ely."

"Is Webb engaged to her?"

"Half the time, I'm not even sure he's courting her. If he's got marriage on his mind, he's taking his own sweet time about showing it," Benteen concluded with a disgruntled sigh, irritated by his son's avoidance of all responsibility even in the shape of an amenable wife.

Outside the roadhouse-saloon, Webb paused to survey the street. The buggy was parked in front of the general store next door. Beyond it was a wagon and the team of Belgian mares. Wide planks covered with muddy footprints were lying on the bare ground, providing solid footing to connect the board sidewalks of the two establishments. Webb waited on the saloon side while a family of drylanders with four children crossed on the planks. The youngest, a boy of four, tipped his head way back to stare wide-eyed at Webb.

"Where's the Indians, Mommy?" he questioned as he was forcibly urged past his first close-up look at a real cowboy.

A wry curve made a fleeting play across his mouth as Webb stepped onto the mud-slick boards and started across. The street seemed more crowded than ever, with more wagons arriving than leaving. It wasn't often that a family in this raw and lonely country — farmer or rancher — made a trip to town. When they did, it usually turned into an all-day affair.

The general store had been expanded to accommodate more business, but it had more than it could hold. There was an overflow onto the board sidewalk outside. Webb didn't see one pair of heeled boots or a Stetson hat among the trousered and bib-overalled men in front of the store. Once this town had known only cowboys — just a few short months ago. This had been his town. It was strange to feel out of place.

As he made his way to the door, the farmers moved aside to give him a clear path. Webb was conscious of their measuring stares. He nodded to one of them, but the man was slow to nod back.

The door was blocked open. Webb entered and stepped to one side, the hum of voices sounding louder in the confined space. He searched the crowd of customers and spotted the man named Franz Kreuger who was homesteading the section of land adjoining the Triple C's eastern boundary.

During his second scan of the enlarged store, he caught a glimpse of blond hair in the dry-goods side. Webb shouldered his way to that department, where his mother and Ruth were busy fingering bolts of material. He glanced at the gingham-gowned women also gathered there, but didn't see any with dark copper hair.

When he touched his mother's shoulder, she turned with a slight start. Her expression cleared into a smile when she saw who it was. "I hope your father isn't ready to leave," she declared, guessing Webb might have come to hurry them along. "Ruth and I haven't had a chance to do our shopping. We stopped by the church first before coming here. We only arrived a few minutes ago."

"No, he didn't send me. I thought you might need somebody to carry your packages," Webb explained, glad they didn't since the crowded store was giving him a bad case of cabin fever.

"Not yet, but don't go too far," his mother admonished. "A woman can always use a pair of strong arms, can't she, Ruth?"

Ruth feigned an agreeing smile, but didn't look at Webb. A harried-looking Ollie Ellis, the proprietor of the general store, came bustling forward.

"I didn't mean to keep you waiting, Mrs. Calder," he apologized for his lack of prompt attention. "What can I help you with today?"

"I was here first." A bird-faced woman pushed Ruth aside to demand the owner's attention. "They just came in."

"Go ahead and help this lady, Mr. Ellis." His mother showed cool indifference to the woman's rudeness, courteously giving way to the woman's obviously rightful claim. "Ruth and I haven't decided which material we want."

"Thank you, Mrs. Calder," the merchant murmured, plainly relieved that she had acquiesced so graciously.

Someone accidentally jostled Webb from behind and offered a hasty apology. The air in the crowded store was stifling. "I'll wait for you outside," he told his mother.

Her nod acknowledged his decision before he moved away, taking the most direct route to the front door. Webb didn't pause once he was outside the building. The sidewalk was too congested with gossiping farmers, so he recrossed the planked ground to the porch sidewalk of the saloon and roadhouse. Except for passerbys, Webb had the porch all to himself. This lot of homesteaders were evidently a bunch of teetotalers, since none had been in the bar, either.

Leaning a shoulder against an upright post supporting the porch roof, Webb lit up a factory-made cigarette and let his gaze roam around the busy street. His eye caught a few details he'd missed earlier. At the new lumberyard where carpenters were hammering on siding for the unfinished building, a black-lettered sign was propped against the front wall. It read Pettit Lumber Company. The swinging shingle above the land company's office identified the business as the W P Land Locaters, confirming that Doyle Pettit had become Wessel's partner. The former rancher's name showed up again in small lettering under the sign for the Blue Moon Hardware & Supply store across the street.

It didn't take much guesswork to suspect that Doyle was also the one behind the proposed granary. It was a clever circle the former rancher had drawn, helping the homesteader to find land, selling him the tools to work it, and the lumber for his house. In time, Doyle would probably buy the man's crop. The farmer might never get rich, but Doyle sure as hell would. It was probably good business practice, but Webb didn't like the smell of it.

A set of light footsteps mounted the saloon porch to his left. With a partial turn of his head, he recognized the slim girl in the wide straw hat. With a snap of his thumb and finger, he flipped the cigarette butt into the muddy street and straightened from the wooden post.

As he moved to intercept her, he saw the flash of recognition in the blue of her eyes. He felt a run of pleasure at the smile that came so naturally to her mouth. In her arms was a bulky woven basket, the kind the Indians on the reservation had been taught to make.

"Hello." She greeted him first, her voice coming to him with the soothing freshness of a breeze on a hot day.

"Hello." His fingers gripped the rolled point of his hat brim and were slow to let it go. Webb was fascinated by the frankness of her look. She seemed so at ease. Most of the young ladies he'd met, excluding saloon women, weren't very sure of themselves when men were around. Realizing he was staring too rudely, he lowered his hand. "May I carry that for you?" He motioned to the basket.

"I can manage it." Her hold on it tightened

131

ever so slightly, almost in unconscious defense of her property. "It isn't heavy."

"I insist." Webb reached for the woven basket, which she reluctantly surrendered into his care. "Did you buy this off the Crow squaw at the depot?"

"Yes." He could see she was satisfied with her purchase. "She wasn't that anxious to sell it, but it will be so useful to store things in, and decorative, too."

Few of the settlers had brought any furniture with them except family pieces. When they owned nothing, even a woven Indian basket would seem like a lot, he supposed.

"I hope you didn't pay what she asked," Webb stated, aware the price was always inflated.

Her laugh was low and brief, yet with a rich vitality that was such an inherent part of the young woman. "No. I'm very good at bargaining. I always get a better price for something than Stefan does."

It sounded like the innocent talk of sibling rivalry. Webb let the name slide by, figuring Stefan was her brother, therefore of no interest to him.

"Our wagon is in front of the store." She politely hinted that instead of standing in the middle of the porch talking, they should be walking to the wagon.

He shifted around to walk on the outside of her. "Yes. I noticed it there earlier," Webb admitted and wondered if he had been purposely waiting to see her. "I guess you must have settled around here."

"Yes, we have a place about fifteen miles west of town."

West of town would put it near the Triple C boundary. He shot her a curious glance. "Is it anywhere near the Kreuger homestead?"

She looked at him in surprise, pausing a second before crossing the planks to the general store. "He's our neighbor. But how did you know that? He filed on the land not more than a week ago. As a matter of fact, we only met him today."

"It was just a guess." Webb shrugged.

A faint crease made a mark on her forehead as she faced the front again. "I'd forgotten you work at the ranch next to Mr. Kreuger's place."

"How did you know about that, Lillian?" A bemused curve lifted one side of his mouth. He'd used her name unconsciously and wasn't aware he'd done something wrong until she slid him a wary side glance. "It is Lillian, isn't it?"

"Yes." Her attitude toward him altered in

some indefinable way. It was as if she were trying to pull away from him, create distance between them.

But he refused to be put off by it. He leisurely studied her profile, taking note of the sun-golden color of her skin and the faint sprinkling of freckles along her cheekbone. The worn straw hat covered most of her auburn hair, swept up and hidden inside the crown, but a few wisps curled along her neck.

"I was in Texas a few years back to bring a trainload of steers north to fatten on this grass. I saw these flowers growing wild in a ditch. They were dark orange, with black specks coming from the center of the bloom. Someone said they were called tiger lilies. That's what you remind me of, Lilli."

It wasn't a deliberate attempt to flatter her, although Webb wasn't unused to complimenting women. He usually did so out of a sense of duty, either to a saloon's sporting lady who had given him a night's pleasure or to the daughter of a rancher or foreman. There weren't many respectable girls of marriageable age in the area. Most of them he'd known all his life, like Ruth. So everything about Lilli seemed new to him. She aroused his interest as few ever had.

She tried to appear unaffected by his flattering comment, remaining silent to ignore it. His pleasure in her deepened when he noticed she was stealing glances at him out of the corner of her eye.

"Does anyone call you Lilli?" It struck him as being more appropriate, more of a match to her outgoing personality than the formal Lillian.

"No." No one had ever shortened her name, not her parents nor Stefan. She wished she had seen one of those tiger lilies he'd mentioned. It was hard to picture it from his brief description. For once, she didn't mind the trace of red in her brown hair.

When she started to climb the short set of steps leading onto the board sidewalk outside the general store, she felt the light support of his hand at her elbow. It stirred up a warm and pleasant feeling inside her. Turning her head, she gave him a full look, and she liked the raw strength in his sun-browned features.

Lillian had a vague awareness of people dawdling about in front of the store, but she was indifferent to them. It was like being in the city again, where little attention was paid to those on the sidewalks. So she missed the frowning looks given her because of the cowboy walking with her.

"What's your name?" she asked.

"Webb." He offered no more than that.

She wondered if he was spinning one around her, then smiled at such a fanciful thought. "How long have you worked for Mr. Calder?"

Turning his back to the bar, Nate Moore leaned the flat of his elbows on it and hooked a heel on the brass footrail. His beer was gone and he didn't want to spend the money for another when he wasn't thirsty anyhow. The billiard table offered about the only action available. His glance strayed to the far table where Benteen Calder was sitting with the big man, Bull Giles. Webb's chair was still unoccupied. He'd left about twenty minutes ago and hadn't returned yet. Nate supposed he'd been sent on an errand of some sort.

It was getting too quiet in the saloon to suit him. Maybe he'd go find Webb so they could liven things up a bit. He pushed away from the bar and swiveled the upper half of his wiry body to lift a farewell hand to his fellow riders.

"See ya later," he said, not feeling obligated to tell them of his intentions.

His long, skinny legs were bowed a little from a lot of long days forking a saddle. They made little effort to pick up his feet as he ambled across the room. Pausing near Benteen Calder's chair, he adopted a genuinely respectful look for his boss.

"Where'd Webb take off for?" he asked when Benteen acknowledged his presence with a glance.

"He went over to the store to give Ruth and his mother a hand with their packages."

Nate bobbed his head at the information and touched his hat in a casual salute. Webb's errand sounded as boring as this place had become, but Nate decided to go in search of him anyway.

Inside the general store, Stefan Reisner scooped up a handful of nails and sifted them through his fingers until only one was left in his palm. He tested its strength by taking it between his fingers and exerting a little pressure to see how easily it might bend.

"They are cheaper across the street," he was advised by a voice on his right.

When Stefan turned, he recognized his new neighbor, Franz Kreuger. The man's dark and brooding eyes were difficult to meet for long, yet they seemed to have missed nothing. Franz Kreuger had been here for such a short time, yet he had acquired more knowledge about local people and places than Stefan had. Stefan tried to justify his own lack of awareness by reminding himself that he had devoted all his hours to improving his homestead. But he also knew inside that he was a follower by nature. It had been Lillian's father Reinald's idea to come to America, not his. Most of his dreams were shadows of someone else's.

On the other hand, Franz Kreuger was a leader, naturally asserting his opinions as he had at the well when he had denounced that big ranch owner's threats. He had made himself known to all the homesteaders, while Stefan had quietly listened and ventured no opinion.

But Stefan had never wanted to be the center of attention. By being quiet and going on about his business, he didn't attract confrontations such as Franz Kreuger had experienced with the rancher and his men. He was a passive man who never went looking for trouble, so he seldom found it.

"You have bought at the hardware store nails?" Stefan raised the nail he was holding, satisfied with its quality. "Good ones?"

Franz Kreuger nodded affirmatively. "I buy mine there." He looked at the goods around them with displeasure. "The prices in this town are high for everything. So many things I could have bought cheaper in the city."

"Ya," Stefan agreed. "But the cities are far from here. The shop owner must pay freight for his goods to the railroads." He had reasoned out the cause for the higher prices, although it had initially alarmed him when he had realized how much more had to be earned in this country in order to live and pay his debts.

"Are you buying nails to build your house?" the new homesteader probed.

"My house is finished, but furniture ve must have," Stefan replied. "When the ground dries, a vell for vater I must also finish digging."

"When the ground dries, I must get back into the fields with my plow." Kreuger's mouth tightened into a thin line. "The rain did not come at a good time for me. My land is not ready to put the wheat in the ground. Two days I have lost. That is not good. I have not much time left to plant and grow a crop to harvest in autumn."

Stefan could readily understand the man's concern. It seemed to explain the brooding anger that lurked in his eyes. "You said at the vell ve must together stick. My vheat is growing. Vhen the ground dries, I vill bring my plow and horses to your place. Ve vork together to plant your vheat."

A smile formed on the man's face, an expression that seemed alien to its ingrained lines. "And I, Franz Kreuger, will come to dig your well for water." He extended his hand to seal the bargain with a vigorous handshake. "Come. We will go to the hardware store and buy your nails for furniture."

Stefan raised no objection at the way Franz Kreuger was taking charge. It reminded him of that bygone time when Reinald was alive, sharing the workload and doing nearly all things together. He had not been that close to another man since then. Perhaps his new neighbor would change that.

Side by side, they made their way to the door. Stefan had taken one step beyond the threshold when Franz laid a staying hand on his arm. Stefan halted to turn a questioning look at the Latvian to learn why they had stopped.

A frown had narrowed his eyes and darkened his expression, but his attention wasn't directed at Stefan. It went beyond him, focusing on something or someone else. Stefan turned to look.

"That cowboy," Franz said in a low voice, and there was only one individual wearing the clothes of that job. Stefan stiffened when he saw the cowboy was speaking to Lillian. His hand was gripping her elbow in a most familiar fashion. "He's the one the rancher Calder sent to threaten my family. Do you see how he has accosted one of our defenseless young women?

Someone should do something to stop this tyranny."

The words prodded Stefan to act. It was evident that since Lillian's back was partially turned to them, Franz hadn't recognized her. With quick, long strides, Stefan moved to confront this tough-looking cowboy bothering his Lillian.

"How long have you worked for Mr. Calder?" she asked.

"All my life, it seems." Webb couldn't force the smile that might have lightened the flatness of his voice. Nor did he take advantage of the second opportunity to explain he was the son, not just another working cowboy. Sooner or later she'd find out, so he didn't understand his reluctance to make it known to her now.

"I —" She started to make a comment, but a guttural voice, thick with anger, slashed across her words. "You vill leave her alone!"

Before the harsh command was finished, a hand was reaching out to grab Lillian's arm and yank her away from Webb. For a split second, Webb was stunned by the suddenness of it. Anger flared in a purely instinctive reaction to the apparent attack as he faced the bristling drylander planted squarely in front of Lillian.

"What the hell are you doing?" Webb demanded an explanation from the tall, whiskered man.

"You stay avay from her!" The man was past middleage, muscled but gaunt.

"Stefan —" Lillian pulled at the long arm that was keeping her shielded. She appeared confused and shocked by his aggressive hostility toward Webb.

"You don't understand —" She tried to protest, but he wasn't in any mood to listen.

"You vill go to the vagon." Without taking his eyes off Webb, he pushed Lillian to the side. "Franz," he called to a man in a small-billed cap. "Take her to the vagon."

Webb made a quick identification of the man taking Lillian by the arms as the hostile homesteader, Franz Kreuger. He swore under his breath, certain that man's twisted thinking had something to do with the animosity being shown by Lillian's father.

"I don't know what you thought you saw," Webb began curtly, the Indian basket still in his arms. "But I was carrying this basket to your wagon. Your daughter bought it and —"

"She is not my daughter." The man bristled more fiercely. "She is my vife!"

The announcement was a cold shock. His wife! Webb stared at the man more than old enough to be Lillian's father. It seemed a sin against nature that a man past his prime should be mated with a woman who had not reached hers.

The cold shock swelled into an icy rage. The man had no right to possess someone as young and fresh as Lilli. It was dirty and sordid, incestuous. Why? Why had she married him? How could she bear to have those old and callused hands touch her?

His hard, accusing gaze searched her out, finding her being helped onto the wagon seat. Her eyes clung to him, her expression mute in its appeal. Webb trembled with the effort it cost him to contain the fury that was looking for any excuse to bury his fist in the old man's face.

He wanted to crush the basket in his arms, but instead he shoved it at the man rooted in his path. "Your wife's basket." His voice was sarcastic.

There was a moment of hesitancy before the basket was accepted, but the fight didn't leave the man's eyes. He seemed to expect it from Webb, almost invited it. It was difficult for Webb not to pick up the challenge and fight it out — the winner taking Lilli as the prize.

Tantalized by the thought, Webb quickly sized up his possible opponent. Despite the gauntness of the man's frame, he had arms like slender oaks. He'd pack some force, but he was too old to last long. It wouldn't be a contest, and Webb knew it.

"You'd better get out of my way before I forget you are an old man," Webb warned in a low, thick voice.

He didn't wait for the man to step aside. Instead Webb moved forward to shoulder his way past him. But as his body shoved at the man, the man shoved back. The force of it pushed him into the wall. Webb hit it hard, shaking loose the dust between the rafters. He started to come away from the wall, his muscles bunched to lunge at the man.

A wiry-framed body pressed him back and pinned his shoulders to the wall. Blinded by a primitive rage, Webb didn't recognize Nate until the cowboy spoke in a low, urgent tone.

"For crissake, Webb, have you gone crazy?" he demanded. "That's an old man."

"Get out of my way." Webb glared at the whiskered man standing with his fists half-raised only two yards from him, and tried to push Nate aside.

Although Webb was superior in size and weight, Nate was made of tempered steel. "Dammit, Webb," he grunted impatiently. "I'm as game for a fight as the next man, but look around you. If you take that old man, this whole crowd is gonna jump on you."

Some part of the warning penetrated his anger-crazed consciousness, enough to pull his attention to the closing circle of homesteaders. An attack on one of their kind would bring the whole pack into the fray. Only a fool would ignore them, and Webb had never counted himself as a fool. He was breathing hard as he relaxed his muscles.

"Okay," he muttered to Nate.

Nate was slow to let him go. Webb swept the circle with a hard glare, then reached down to scoop up his hat from the board floor. With stiff, jerky movements, he made a show of brushing it off while he centered his cold gaze on the old man, Lilli's husband.

"Ve vill no more be pushed around. And you leave our vomenfolk alone from now on," the man ordered tersely.

It grated Webb to be dressed down without cause. "I was raised to have better manners, mister. Around these parts, a man always carries the packages for a lady. You're a newcomer. But the next time push comes to shove, you won't be standing up when it's over."

He jammed his hat onto his head and angled off the walk. He heard the clumping of a pair of boots behind him, indicating Nate was right on his heels. Webb ignored the planked walk over the muddy ground and headed straight into the street, going to the hitching rail where his horse was tied. He yanked the reins loose and swung into the saddle, turning the horse's nose toward the general store. He glimpsed his mother and Ruth in the dark opening of the building. Both of them appeared bewildered and alarmed.

Then he looked over at the wagon where Lilli sat watching him with an expressionless face. There was not a hint of guilt or regret. He felt the anger rising again and dug the spurs into the horse. He rode out of town at a gallop, with Nate only a length behind him.

7

Hues of scarlet and orange swirled across the western sky as the sun lingered for a last few minutes on the edge of the horizon. Its light cast colored shadows on the rolling plains and darkened the wide stretch of ground, stripped of its native grasses. A rutted track divided the bared ground from the field where a new stand of wheat waved its young stalks in the evening breeze.

The team of Belgian mares, Dolly and Babe, picked up their pace as home came into sight. There wasn't any comfortable barn to welcome them, only a small corral and shed made of green wood. The square house was made out of green lumber, too, its dimensions twenty-four feet by twenty-four feet. The outside walls were covered with tar paper. One window was located in the front next to the door and a stovepipe had thrust its top out of the barely slanted roof, minus any eaves or overhang. A pair of guy wires was stretched across the top of the roof and anchored to the ground on each side so the strong Montana winds couldn't blow the flimsy house down.

But it was home to the man and woman riding in the wagon pulled by the draft team, a home they had built on land they owned — or would own when the allotted time had passed and the other necessary requirements had been met to receive the government deed to their homestead. Yet the couple didn't appear eager to reach the end of the rutted track the wagon traveled. The silence between them was heavy with disapproval emanating from both sides. Not a single mention had been made of the incident that had caused this rift between them.

When the wagon drew even with the tar-papered house, Stefan Reisner leaned back in the seat, pulling on the reins to halt the team. As soon as the forward motion had stopped, Lilli swung down from the wagon, unaided, and walked to the rear to begin unloading the day's purchases from the wagon box. Stefan was slower to climb down, casting a side look at his young wife, as he had done several times before. There was irritation and impatience in his sternly questioning eyes, but he had voiced none of these to her.

"I vill take care of the horses." Withdrawing his glance from her, he bent to unhitch the team and drive them to the corral.

"Supper will be ready in a few minutes," Lilli responded.

Lilli deliberately left the woven basket along with heavier packages for Stefan to carry in after he had the team unharnessed. She juggled the two lighter packages in her arms to pull the latchstring hanging on the outside of the door.

The house was stuffy after being closed up all day long, so she left the door open and set the packages on the bed. Isinglass hung in the window opening. When they harvested their wheat crop, they hoped to replace it with real glass. Lilli rolled up the semitransparent covering to let in air and take advantage of all that was left of the waning light so she could conserve their precious supply of kerosene for the lantern.

Newspapers covered the inside walls to provide insulation, glued there with a paste made from flour and water. Two crude shelves attached to the wall stored cooking utensils and tableware as well as their meager supplies. The cookstove was the only source of heat, the range top also serving as a work counter. There wasn't any table or chairs. The only other piece of furniture in the house was the bed, which

Stefan had built. The mattress was stuffed with grasses and rested directly on the wooden slats that bridged the rough frame.

The few clothes they had were still stored in the cloth satchels, although there were wall pegs to hang hats and coats on. There was one trunk, which held the wash basin and water pail. And the warped floor was bare of any covering.

All the refinements and furnishings would come later. For now, it was an attempt to make do with what they had, and get through the first winter. Next year, they'd build a real frame house. Lilli considered herself fortunate to have this little shanty. A lot of the homesteaders, she'd learned, were living in sod homes. One family was even living in a cave they'd dug in a cutbank.

By the time Stefan had taken care of the horses and unloaded the rest of the wagon, Lilli had a cold supper dished onto a plate and waiting for him. Since they didn't have a table and chairs yet, they had to sit on the edge of the bed and balance the plates on their laps.

It had long been Stefan's custom to eat without talking. The purpose of a meal was to consume food, in his thinking, not to engage in conversation. That came before or after, but not during. With this single-minded attitude, he cleaned his plate before Lilli was half through with her meal, even though the helpings on her plate were smaller than his.

When Stefan stood up to carry his dirty plate to the metal basin, the buzzing fly that had pestered him throughout the meal switched its attack to Lilli's plate. She absently waved a hand to keep it from landing on the few bites of food she had left. Leaving his plate and cutlery in the basin, Stefan stopped to light the lantern suspended by a wire from the middle of the ceiling to chase away the purpling shadows of twilight invading their humble abode.

He glanced at Lilli as he took his pipe from his pocket, but her head was bent toward the plate in her lap. After a meal, he always went outside to smoke his pipe. It was part of the daily routine of his life, so it wasn't necessary to inform Lilli of it.

"Outside I am going to smoke," he said.

A brief nod was her only response. His teeth bit down hard on the stem of the empty pipe as Stefan tramped stiffly out of the house. He paused beside the wagon and made a slow business of filling the pipe bowl with tobacco and tamping it down. Before lighting it, he studied the match flame to make certain the light breeze would blow the smoke away from the shanty. Lillian didn't like the smell of smoke.

151

Stefan knew the reason she didn't, although she had blocked the cause from her mind.

It wasn't surprising that she didn't remember, since she had only been seven years old when the tenement building next to theirs had caught fire and burned to the ground, trapping many people inside. It had been a terrifying experience for a child. And long after the rubble of the burned building had been cleared away, the smell of smoke had stayed in the tiny apartment where they had all lived as one family.

The first stars were flickering in the night sky to join the sickle moon watching over the earth. To Stefan, the stars were like old friends that he hadn't seen since he was a young man in Germany. Most nights he enjoyed watching them grow steadily brighter while he smoked his pipe. This night he was too troubled by his young wife to give them any notice.

Never had there been any serious friction between them. He couldn't remember feeling anger toward her, nor any time when she had seemed angry with him. There had always been a smooth, gentle flow of affection between them, starting from the day she was born and Reinald had placed his daughter in the arms of his best friend. Her little fingers had tried to curl around his big thumb. The first link had been forged from that moment.

Through the years, Lillian had come to represent all the things a female might be to a man. First, she had been like a niece. When the consecutive deaths of her mother and father had left her orphaned, Stefan took on the role of family and raised her as his own daughter. But the scandal-minded gossips in the building had looked askance at a bachelor living with a fourteen-year-old girl. Their talk had emphasized the conflict of emotions he felt watching her mature into womanhood. It had been to ease these desires as much as a wish to keep her reputation unsullied that Stefan had suggested marriage on her fifteenth birthday. Lillian had agreed calmly and without any hesitation. The transition from niece/daughter to wife and mate had occurred with ease, so that neither of them was uncomfortable with the change.

Yet something had altered that today. As he puffed on his pipe, Stefan was gnawed by a fear he couldn't define. Lillian was wise to the dangers of the city, yet she seemed to have abandoned all sense of caution since coming out here. She had heard Franz Kreuger telling how that rancher had sent one of his men to threaten Kreuger's family, so she should have avoided any association with that cowboy or anyone directly connected to the ranch community unless they had established friendly ties with the homesteaders the way Wessel's partner had done.

Perhaps he needed to explain that to her. The fire in his pipe bowl had gone out. He knocked the bottom against the heel of his hand to empty the dead ashes on the ground. With the pipe once again tucked in his pocket, Stefan entered the tar-papered house.

The dishes were all washed and dried and stacked on their portion of the shelf. Lillian was untying her apron when he came in. She looked away from him as she turned, folding her apron to lay it on the trunk by the basin. Stefan hesitated, then walked to the bed and sat down.

"Come sit, *liebchen*," he requested, softening some of the firmness in his tone by his use of the affectionate reference to her. "Ve talk."

With her shoulders naturally squared and her chin jutting slightly forward, Lillian approached the bed and sat sideways on the edge to face him. Her deep blue eyes showed a surface calm and not what simmered behind it.

"You are angered vith me because of vhat happened today." Stefan bluntly broached the issue. "But there is much that you don't understand."

"Yes, I am angry," she admitted. "Because

you wouldn't listen to me. What he said to you was true. He had politely insisted on carrying the basket to the wagon for me. It was a gentlemanly act and that was all."

He listened patiently to her defense of the man and tried not to give rise to the anger that stirred within. When she had finished, he challenged quietly, "Vhat do you know of this cowboy?"

"I don't know very much about him," she grudgingly acknowledged, but qualified it. "Except he treated me with respect. He certainly didn't do anything to deserve the way you attacked him. He had made no unseemly advances."

Stefan sat up straighter, stiffening at her criticism. "I vished only to keep harm from coming to you."

"Why on earth would he want to harm me?" Lillian argued. "Do you remember when we arrived by train and I spoke to a cowboy waiting at the station? That was the same cowboy."

"And that vas also the same cowboy that tried to threaten Franz Kreuger and his family," Stefan declared.

"The same one?" Her expression clouded with a bewildered frown. "Are you sure?"

"Franz pointed him out to me. Yes, I am

sure," he stated, and went a step further. "He is also the son of that rancher Calder."

"How do you know that?" Her frown deepened. "Did Mr. Kreuger tell you?"

"No. The shopkeeper did. He vas most upset that the incident had occurred in front of his store. I heard him apologizing to a lady he addressed as Mrs. Calder. He vanted her to know he vasn't responsible for vhat had happened vith her son."

"I see." The evidence seemed irrefutable, yet Lillian didn't understand why she was so reluctant to accept that he was the son of the powerful rancher.

"Now you see vhy I didn't vant him near you." He was certain she would understand that he had been right to behave as he did.

Lillian didn't answer immediately as she tried to sort through all the conflicting thoughts running through her head. "I'm sure you believe you were justified." She gave him that. "But he had said and done nothing mean to me. He was being friendly and courteous."

"Vhat did he say to you?" Stefan asked patiently. Women tended to be gullible. Perhaps Lillian was acquiring that female trait.

"Definitely nothing threatening," she insisted. "He remembered speaking to me at the train station and asked if we had found a place nearby."

"And you told him?" he prompted.

"Yes." She didn't regard it as a secret. Then she recalled something else and a flash of uncertainty crossed her expression. "He did ask whether our land was near Mr. Kreuger's," she added hesitantly.

"It is obvious that it vas information from you he vas seeking." Now he was fully convinced he had been right in thinking the cowboy was up to no good.

The idea troubled her. Even though she had only met him twice, she had liked that dark-haired cowboy named Webb. Webb Calder. She knew the rest of his name now.

"It is late." He laid a comforting hand on her shoulder. "The sun is sleeping. That is vhat ve should be doing, too."

An unsatisfied sigh came from Lillian as she stood up to fetch their nightclothes from the satchels. There were questions in her mind without answers, and Webb Calder was the only person who could supply them.

Stefan closed the door, securing the latch-string on the inside, and rolled the isinglass down to cover the window opening. Lillian handed him his nightshirt and began unbuttoning her dress as he turned out the lantern. In the near darkness, she took off her clothes and slipped on the long nightgown.

By the time she had combed out her hair and plaited it into a single braid, Stefan was already in bed beneath the quilted cover. She laid beside him in the narrow bed, the bony length of his body next to hers, offering companionable warmth.

"Will you finish digging the well tomorrow?" Lillian tried to force her mind away from the cowboy and onto more essential subjects.

"No. Tomorrow I vill go to Franz Kreuger's farm and help him plow his field so he can plant his vheat," Stefan informed her. "I vill be home before dark."

"What about the well? And the table you were going to build?" She turned her head, trying to see his whiskered profile in the darkness.

"Franz will come to help dig the vell. Then I vill build your table and chairs," he stated. "Ve must all of us help each other. It is good to have neighbors."

"Yes." She rolled onto her side, facing away from Stefan as she unwillingly thought of another neighbor of theirs. "Good night, Stefan."

"Good night." His voice already had a drowsy sound to it.

Lillian didn't find it that easy to fall asleep.

Before first light broke, Webb had roped his horse out of the corral and was throwing on the saddle. There was a light over in the cookshack, which meant breakfast would soon be on the griddle, but Webb didn't intend to wait around for it.

The anger hadn't left him in the nearly two days since his run-in with the aging homesteader. The memory of it continued to gall him like an irritated saddle sore. And the last day and a half spent at the headquarters with his father and Bull Giles had only added salt to the wound. He was riding out before his father could order him to spend another day confined in futile discussions.

With the cinch tightened, he dropped the stirrup and swung into the saddle. The frisky gelding made a few crow-hops, then settled into a brisk walk that carried Webb away from the ranch buildings. Away was the only direction he had in mind; the farther the better. Out of earshot of the ranch, he let the horse set its own pace.

Midmorning found him miles from the headquarters of the Triple C with the fenceline of the east boundary in front of him. The gelding sidled along the barrier, waiting for a command from its rider as to the next direction. Webb applied pressure on the bit to check it to a halt and uncoiled the rope tied below the saddlehorn. He dropped the loop over the fence post and turned the horse away from it, taking a wrap around the horn with the free end of the rope.

A touch of the spurs had the horse straining against the partially anchored weight. The wooden post groaned; then the earthen bed gave way at its base. Dismounting, Webb freed the loop from the post and walked his horse across the downed fenceline, then righted the post again, stamping at the loose earth around its base until it was solidly in place.

When he was in the saddle again, he angled the horse toward the southeast. He knew where he was going now, the destination that had been in the back of his mind all along. He pushed the horse into a ground-covering lope and watched the landscape for a long strip of barren earth.

Perspiration trickled down her neck. Lillian paused in the hoeing of her garden to wipe at it with the hem of her apron. A movement in the distance caught her eye. Thinking it might be Stefan coming back from Franz Kreuger's place, she stopped to take a closer look. He had said he doubted if he would be home until the afternoon, but it was possible they had finished the plowing sooner than he had expected.

But there was just one horse, not a team. And it was being ridden, not driven, so it couldn't be Stefan. More than that, he was riding diagonally through the young wheatfield. Stefan would never risk damaging the young stalks. Lilli gripped the hoe with both hands as she tried to identify the rider.

The shantylike building belonged to the bleak landscape, churned and stripped of its protective grass. A wagon stood in front of it, but Webb noted that the corral was empty of the horse team. His eyes searched the land without finding any sign of horse and plow. He was about to conclude there was no one about when he saw a figure on the south side of the shack. From a distance, the dark color of her dress had blended in with the landscape. Hatless, her dark haired glinted with the sun's fire. Something tightened inside him.

She watched his approach, but didn't come forward to greet him even after he stopped his horse. There was a wariness in her look, a hint of distrust that he hadn't seen in her eyes before. Still, she didn't speak. The custom of the range was to invite a man to step down from his horse, but she made no offer.

"Could you spare some water for my horse?"

Webb broke the silence with his terse request.

"There's some in the barrel." She motioned to the wagon box.

He curtly nodded his thanks and swung out of the saddle to lead his horse to the wagon. Out of the corner of his eye, he was conscious that she followed him, as if she thought he intended to steal something. She gripped the hoe like a weapon.

Since she didn't offer him the use of a bucket, Webb took off his hat and ladled a couple of dipperfuls into the upturned crown. When he turned to offer the water to his horse, he was facing her. His glance slid over her and back to the horse as it buried its nose in the hat to suck up the water.

"Did you get your basket home safely?" He baited her with the memory of the incident, feeling someone owed him an apology.

"Yes." She watched him as if she expected him to sprout horns any minute and was ready to chop them off with her hoe if he did. She tipped her head slightly to one side. "You're Mr. Calder's son, aren't you?"

"Yes." The horse had drunk its fill, and Webb used the moment to empty the rest of the water from his hat. "I'm afraid I didn't catch your last name, *Mrs.* —" He put biting emphasis on her marital status and moved leisurely to the left side of his horse as if to mount it, but the action brought him within two feet of her.

"Reisner. Mrs. Stefan Reisner," she said without a trace of guilt or regret.

"Is your husband about?" His gaze made another arc around the homestead.

"Why do you want to know?"

"Just wondered." Webb brought his attention back to her. Then he looked down to her left hand. "You aren't wearing a wedding ring," he observed.

"No, I'm not." Her gaze faltered under the level study of his. "Stefan and I decided we would rather use the money to come out here than buy a ring."

This time he looked away, struggling against the anger he felt. "You knew that I thought you were single, Lilli," he muttered in a thick, rough voice. "You should let a man know such things before he goes making a fool of himself."

"Our acquaintance has been brief, Mr. Calder —" She was a little pale suddenly.

Webb cut across her defense. "The other day you were ready enough to call me Webb. Have you forgotten that?" he challenged. "And you didn't raise any objection when I called you Lilli."

"The other day I also didn't know you were the man who threatened Mr. Kreuger and his family," she retorted just as swiftly.

"I never threatened that belligerent little farmer," he denied angrily. "I spoke to him, yes, but he was the one who began ranting about having a gun and being willing to use it to protect his family."

Despite his disclaimer, there was still doubt in her eyes. "That isn't the way he told it."

"And you'd believe him before you'd believe me," he snapped. "All I did was warn him that it was going to be rough on his family living in these conditions." He gestured toward the shack to make his point.

Her chin came up. "It's just until next year; then we're going to build a real house."

When he'd ridden up, he'd noticed the partially dug hole on the other side of the house. "And I suppose you're going to sink a well so you can have water."

"Yes. Mr. Kreuger is going to come over and help after Stefan finishes helping him plow his ground."

With an effort, he controlled his exasperation and attempted a patient explanation. "Ranches in Montana have been called chunks of dry ground with a water right to go with it. You don't even have that. You aren't going to find any water. Or if you do, it's going to be so thick with alkali you won't be able to drink it."

"You don't know that." She resisted his prophecy.

"I was born and raised not thirty miles from here," Webb reminded her. "If it's one thing I know, it's the land. I'm not trying to scare anyone into leaving, and neither is my father. But you drylanders won't listen."

"You don't want us here. You want all this land to yourself." She said the words, but there wasn't a lot of strength in them. "That's what Kreuger told Stefan."

"Kreuger again," he muttered.

"Everyone knows your father is trying to keep more people from coming here."

"Yes, he is, because he doesn't want to see the land destroyed by people who think it will grow wheat." Webb defended his father's position.

"But it can grow wheat. You rode through it," she reminded him with a triumphant lilt to her voice. "Your father is wrong."

It was hard to argue when he was faced with the evidence. He released a long breath. "I didn't come here to debate anything with you, Lilli."

She looked at him, meeting his gaze as fully

as she had other times. "Why did you come?"

"Because —" His teeth came together and a muscle flexed in his jaw. He took a step toward her, the reins slipping out of his hands to trail the ground. "Why did you marry him, Lilli?"

Her eyes rounded in vague alarm at his bluntness. "Stefan . . . is a good man . . . and a good husband." She struggled with the answer. "He's warm and kind and —"

"And he's old enough to be your father, if not your grandfather." His hands closed on her shoulders as he ground out the words to finish her incomplete sentence.

Her right hand released its hold on the hoe to push at a forearm in mute protest to his touch. "He is older than I am," she admitted.

"Old enough to be your father," Webb persisted, determined to get that admission from her.

"Yes." It was said with defiance. "More than that, he was my father's best friend. They came over to this country together. I was fourteen when my parents died. If it wasn't for Stefan, I don't know what might have happened to me."

"That's why you married him?" He searched her face, trying desperately to understand — wanting desperately to understand. "Because you were alone?"

"Because I was alone. Because I cared about him. Because he was good to me. Because there wasn't anything else I could do. No one else cared about me." She flung out the reasons that had always been so sound.

"You didn't have to marry him." His fingers tightened their grip on her shoulders. Things were all twisted up inside of him. The only certainty he knew was that she didn't belong with the man she'd married. "You could have gotten a job."

"Doing what? The only job a girl can get is in a factory or —" She clamped her lips shut on the other alternative that didn't need to be drawn for him. "I don't regret marrying Stefan. I would have done it if he was a hundred years older, because I care about him. I am his wife, and I'm proud of it."

The air rang with her declaration. Webb was left with the feeling that he'd lost a battle he hadn't known he was fighting. His hands fell away, releasing her from his hold.

"I guess there's nothing more to be said, is there?" He waited, but she didn't answer.

Turning, he swept up the loose rein and sank a boot in the stirrup. The saddle groaned as it took his weight. A nudge of his spur swung the horse's rump in a quarter-circle so Webb was looking at her. The restless, galling anger was gone, leaving a hollow feeling of loss. He touched a hand to his hat.

"I'm obliged for the water, Mrs. Reisner," he murmured formally and clicked to his horse.

8

As Nate hauled the heavy stock saddle off his horse, he saw Webb ride up. Even as close as they'd been growing up, Webb had always struck him as being a kind of loner. This last month, he'd made himself about as scarce as hair on a gnat's ass. The way Nate figured it, it didn't take no genius to know that Webb hadn't been the same since he'd had that run-in over some farmer's wife. He'd never quite got the full scoop on that.

They nodded to each other as Nate swung his saddle onto the top rail of the corral. Walking back to the horse, Nate used his saddle blanket to begin wiping it down while he watched Webb dismount and flip the stirrup over the seat to loosen the cinch. Webb's back was to him, nothing about him inviting conversation, but that didn't faze Nate.

"Them honyockers are havin' a big whoopde-do celebration in town for the Fourth of July. Are you figurin' on goin'?" Nate inquired.

There was a momentary break in the rhythm of Webb's movements at the question; then he was lifting the saddle off the horse's back. His expression was closed to any probe of Nate's eyes.

"Nope." It was a flat and definite response.

"You're likely to be the only one who ain't. The rest of the boys are plannin' to take in the doin's," Nate informed him, but Webb didn't appear to be swayed.

"Hey, Webb!" Young Shorty Niles hailed him and made a detour from his planned route to the bunkhouse. "The Old Man left word that you are to *dine* at The Homestead tonight." He put bantering emphasis on the fancy word for eating.

Webb acknowledged the message with a curt nod of his head, but otherwise gave no sign that the news wasn't to his liking. Like Nate, he hefted his saddle onto the top railing of the corral and used the blanket to wipe the moisture from his horse's back. Young Shorty leaned on the fence to watch.

"Ike picked up a poster in town today. There's gonna be a big doin's the day after tomorrow to celebrate Independence Day." Shorty's eyes were alight with the news.

"Heard about it," Webb commented with definite lack of interest.

Shorty ignored it. "There's gonna be races an' fireworks — even a dance." He offered a brief list of the activities. "The only good thing them drylanders have done for this country is bring their daughters. I ain't got no more love for those honyockers than the next man, but I don't intend to hold nothin' against their daughters. I'm gonna whirl them little gals right off their feet."

Moving to his horse's head, Webb unbuckled the cheek strap and slipped the bridle off. With a wave of the blanket, he spooked the horse away from the fence, sending it galloping to join its equine companions milling on the far side of the corral.

Nate kept one eye on Webb as he responded to Young Shorty's last remark. "You're gonna have to stand in line to get one of them farmer gals. I think every cowboy for miles has got the same idea."

They could have been talking in Chinese for all the notice Webb paid to their conversation. He hefted the saddle onto the back of his shoulder and spared the two of them one brief glance.

"See you later," he said and headed for the barn to stow his gear.

Lately it seemed Webb had trouble working up emotion for anything. Even the summons to dine with his father had produced only a pale shadow of his former resentment. There had been a scant second when he had nearly been jolted out of his indifference when Nate had imparted the news about the Fourth of July celebration in Blue Moon, but he'd shut that out, too.

He guessed the dinner that night was a farewell to-do for Bull Giles. His planned month's stay should be about over, so he'd probably be pulling out any day now. As far as Webb knew, nothing had been accomplished by the visit.

After a wash, shave, and change of clothes, Webb left the bunkhouse and headed for the big, two-story house with the pillared front that sat on the knoll overlooking the headquarters. It seemed to represent all the bigness the Calder name implied.

The low murmur of voices came from the den when Webb entered the house. Sweeping off his hat, he swung left and walked toward the sound, running his fingers through his dark hair to rid it of its flatness. As he crossed the opened doorway, he saw his mother sitting on the leather sofa in front of the huge stone fireplace. His father was at the liquor cabinet, lifting the stopper on a whiskey decanter.

172

"You're just in time for a drink, Webb. What'll it be?" his father inquired smoothly.

"Whiskey's fine," he replied and wandered into the room. His idle glance flickered over the massive desk and the framed map on the wall behind it. The hand-drawn map delineated the extensive boundaries of the ranch, and the desk represented the heart from which the control flowed to the farthest extremities. Webb swung his attention to his mother, smiling faintly. "Is that a new dress?"

"I'm surprised you noticed. I see you so seldom anymore." The criticism was softened by the warmth of her smile. "Why is it we always have to issue an invitation for our son to have dinner with us?"

He shrugged at the question. "I guess you shouldn't have raised me to be so independent." It wasn't an answer, merely an avoidance of the issue that had strained the relationship with his parents.

Circling around the furniture, Webb stopped in front of the fireplace. A sweeping set of horns from a Longhorn steer was mounted above the mantel. They had belonged to Captain, the old brindle steer that had led the first herd of Triple C cattle to Montana and a dozen more drives in subsequent years. There had been so much crossbreeding on the ranch that the Longhorns had virtually died out. Captain had been the last of his kind.

"I spied a yearling steer the other day carrying a long set of horns," Webb remarked in passing as his father gave a glass of port to Lorna before bringing Webb his whiskey.

"A throwback crops up every now and then," his father replied and returned to the cabinet for his own drink.

"I wonder what's keeping Bull." His mother cast a curious glance toward the open doorway.

"He'll be down shortly." Benteen Calder wasn't concerned. "With that bad leg, it takes him longer to get around."

"I suppose." She sipped at her drink, then turned a bright look on Webb. "Speaking of invitations, have you asked Ruth to the Fourth of July festivities they're planning in town?"

He studied his drink before downing a swallow. "No."

"Are you going to?" his mother persisted.

"I hadn't planned on it," Webb replied.

"She is expecting you to ask her."

"I haven't given her any reason to expect that," he countered. "As a matter of fact, I don't have any plans to go myself. Somebody should stay behind and hold down the fort. The rest of the boys are so eager to go that I thought I'd volunteer to stay at the ranch."

Webb wasn't sure why he was going to such lengths to justify his decision.

"Coming from you, that's a surprise," his father remarked dryly. It was a subtle dig at Webb's expression of concern over the ranch being left unattended.

"Forget the ranch for a minute," his mother impatiently interrupted to continue with her subject. "I want to know about Ruth." The situation had drifted on an aimless course for too long. Webb was thirty. It was time for him to be thinking about marriage and a family, and making a decision about Ruth's role in his future.

"What about her?" Webb lifted his head to coolly meet her challenging gaze.

"Since her mother isn't here to look out for her, I feel it's my place to do it for her." She established that her concern was to protect the daughter of her best friend, rather than her own son. "You have been seeing Ruth on a somewhat regular basis for more years than I care to count. Just what does that mean?"

"It means I like her, but she isn't the only woman I've been seeing." He was irritated by this questioning.

"Is there someone else?" his mother asked sharply, betraying a surprise at the possibility.

"No." He snapped the denial, then realized it

175

required a qualification. "I mean there's no special woman I'm seeing."

"Are you saying that you don't regard Ruth as special?" Her look was far from pleased.

"No, I don't, and I've never said anything that would give her reason to think she is." A dark frown gathered on his hard features as he swirled the whiskey in his glass.

"Maybe you haven't said anything, but your actions have certainly indicated otherwise," his mother insisted. "When a man continues to see a woman over a long period of time, it's natural for her to believe that their relationship will evolve into something more permanent. It's hardly fair to expect Ruth to wait for you to make up your mind when she could be meeting other men."

"I have never asked her not to see anyone else," Webb declared.

"Have you been trifling with her all this time?" she demanded.

"I've known Ruth all my life. Now that we're grown, am I supposed to ignore her?" he challenged in return. "I guess it's what I should have done, since now you're accusing me of trifling with her affections. I may have kissed her a few times, but I've never stepped out of line. And I've never made her any promises."

"Then you have absolutely no intention of

ever marrying her," his mother concluded.

The anger went out of him as the pain returned once more to empty him of feeling. "She's a nice girl, and she'd make a good wife. But she won't be marrying me."

Lorna sighed with regret. The sadness in her heart wasn't just from a sense of loss for a long-held dream that someday her son and the daughter of her best friend might marry. It came more from the knowledge that Ruth was hopelessly in love with Webb and it was all in vain.

"I share your mother's desire to see you married and settled down," his father spoke up, the frosted tips of his dark hair showing up strong in the light. "It's time you stopped avoiding responsibility and made some hard decisions about what you're going to do with the rest of your life."

Something prompted Webb to voice the thought he'd been mulling around in his mind the last few weeks. "I thought after the fall roundup I might head down to Texas and take a look around."

Dark brows drew together in a frown as Benteen Calder eyed his son. "To look around for what? There's nothing in Texas that can match what you've got right here."

"Maybe I just want to see for myself." Webb

shrugged, mentally bracing himself for the argument that was bound to erupt.

"Benteen —" Lorna attempted to play the part of peacemaker. "Maybe it isn't such a bad idea. I've been wanting to visit my parents for quite a while now. With things the way they are, I know it's hard for you to get away for any amount of time." The real truth was that Benteen had no desire to go back to Texas, having cut all ties when he'd left it. In the past, he'd mentioned returning only because he knew it was what Lorna wanted. "If I go with Webb, you wouldn't have to worry about me traveling alone." It was also a way of ensuring that Webb returned with her.

"I'll think about it," Benteen agreed, but under obvious protest.

Uneven footsteps approached the den, accompanied by the thud of a cane on the hardwood floors. "You'll think about what?" Bull Giles paused in the opening.

"Webb's got some wild-goose idea about making a trip to Texas this winter," Benteen muttered into his glass. "As if we aren't going to be short-handed enough as it is."

Bull threw Webb a look and limped into the room. "Are you thinking about trying to get in on that oil boom?"

"I might." Actually, he hadn't thought about

it. In this area, he would always be Benteen Calder's son. Somewhere else, he would be only himself. Texas was just a possible starting point if he finally decided to make the move.

Later that evening after dinner was finished, Benteen suggested that they retire to the den for a glass of brandy. "I think I'll pass that invitation," Bull Giles refused as he rested his weight on the cane. "I'm going to take a turn on the porch instead." He looked at Webb. "Care to join me?"

Concealing his surprise at the unexpected invitation, Webb quickly saw it as a way to avoid another lecture from his father. "Sure," he accepted.

"Go ahead and enjoy your brandy, Benteen," Bull instructed and deliberately didn't suggest that his old friend accompany them.

Outside, the air was warmed by a summer wind. A half-moon was perched drunkenly in the sky, throwing its light across the roofs of the many ranch buildings that spilled out from the base of the knoll. Bull Giles reached inside the jacket of his suit and withdrew two cigars from the inner pocket, offering one to Webb.

"Are you serious about this Texas thing?" he asked as Webb bent his head to the match flame Bull had struck.

Webb lifted his head slowly, trying to read the man's expression, but the flickering matchlight didn't reach the pugnacious features. "I'm considering it. Why?" He tried to sound casual.

"Just wondered." Bull lit his own cigar and sent up puffs of smoke while Webb doubted that Bull Giles "just wondered" about anything. Bull shook out the match and looked at the buildings beyond them. "The first time I saw this place, there was only a log cabin. Benteen has sure built himself quite a spread."

"Yup." It was a noncommittal agreement. "Every bit of land you can see is sitting under a Calder sky."

"It's a big sky," Bull commented with seeming idleness.

"And a big chunk of ground," Webb added.

"It takes a big man to run all this, but I guess I don't have to tell you that." Bull removed the cigar from his mouth and studied the glowing tip.

"No, I don't guess you do." Webb shifted restlessly, feeling he had escaped a lecture from his father only to get it from a longtime friend of the family.

"He's getting tired. He needs to start turning over some of the control to others. It's getting to be too much for him." Bull changed positions to bring Webb into his direct line of sight.

"I suppose the next thing you're going to suggest is for me to start filling my father's shoes."

Something close to a smile broke across the man's face. "Is that what's bothering you? You don't like the idea of walking in your father's footsteps?"

"No, I don't," Webb stated flatly. "He made his mark, and I'm proud of him."

"But you want to carve out your own," Bull concluded, surprising Webb at his ability to understand the situation so clearly. "You're a fool, Webb Calder."

"Sir?" He stiffened at the insult, questioning that he'd heard right.

"I said you are a fool," Bull repeated calmly. "The day your father's gone, you aren't going to be walking in his footsteps. You're going to be picking up where he left off. And if you don't walk strong and tall, you're going to get stepped on."

"What do you mean?"

"I mean I've been watching you. Between the little I've seen of you and a few comments your father has made, I've gained the impression that you're trying to straddle a fence. You try to act like all the other hands and just put in

181

your day's work, but there's a gnawing in you to make some kind of mark so others can see where you've been."

"And?" Webb neither confirmed nor denied it.

"And" — he puffed on the cigar — "you're going to have to get off the fence. You could have this ranch someday. Whether you believe you've done anything to earn it or not, you're going to have to fight to keep it. Because there will be somebody out there who will want to take it away from you. Getting something is easy, but keeping it is the real test of a man. You keep that in mind while you're thinking about Texas."

"I'll give it some thought." He rolled the cigar between his lips, tasting the richness of the blend. "This is a good cigar."

"The best." Bull leaned on his cane and used its support to pivot toward the door. "I guess I'll call it a night."

"Me, too." Webb moved slowly to the steps, his gaze shifting to night-darkened land.

On the Fourth of July, the Triple C head-quarters seemed like a ghost town. Everyone had gone into town to take part in the celebrations, leaving Webb, the antisocial cook Grizzly Turner, and another cowhand named

Budd Pappas behind.

All the odd jobs Webb planned to do were finished by early afternoon. He'd never been comfortable sitting around just idling time away. After a dozen games of solitaire and an equal number of cups of coffee, he prowled restlessly around the cookshack.

"Why don't you light somewheres?" Grizzly Turner grumbled irritably. "You're as edgy as a range bull with mating season just around the corner."

Webb ignored the complaint and carried his cup to the cookstove to refill it. Black coffee dribbled out and barely covered the bottom of his cup before the pot went dry. He shook it and glanced at the cook.

"We're out of coffee."

"Yeah, well, ain't that just tough," the cook snarled. "Why didn't you go into town with everybody else? There ain't nothing for you to do here but make my life miserable."

Webb started to snap an answer about the cook's miserable nature, then shut his mouth on it and set the cup on the stove. The restlessness in him was growing until he wished he had gone into town to blow off steam with the others. The more he thought about it, the more appealing the idea became.

"You've got a good idea there, Grizzly." He

snatched his hat off the wall hook and pushed it onto his head. "I'm heading into town. The ranch is all yours."

"And good riddance to you, too," Grizzly Turner called after him as Webb walked out the door to head for the corral.

9

When he rode into town, the street was jammed with people, horses, and wagons. As expected, there were a dozen horses carrying the Triple C brand tied in front of the road-house and saloon. Webb dismounted and looped his reins around the far end of the hitching rail.

A couple of cowboys were coming out the door as Webb went in. They were laughing and talking loud, but the noise they were creating seemed a whisper compared to the din that Webb found inside. Nearly every outfit within miles seemed to be represented in the throng of cowboys filling the roadhouse. It took him a minute to spot the Triple C bunch and work his way across the room to join them.

"Webb!" Young Shorty Niles slapped him on the back and pushed him up to the bar. "Hell! I thought you were holdin' down the fort!"

"I got bored and thought I'd better check to

see what trouble you guys were getting into,"
he replied and ordered himself a beer.

"Why, we haven't been in any trouble, have
we, boys?" Shorty asked and received a chorus
of vigorous negatives. "We just been picking
out the gals we're gonna dance with tonight.
There's a whole passel of 'em in town."

"If I was you boys, I wouldn't be sashayin'
too close to them honyockers' daughters." The
warning came from a man outside their group,
his voice thick with contempt for the homesteaders. "You just might catch somethin'."

Webb glanced down the long bar, finding the
lantern-jawed man who had made the sneering
remark. Hobie Evans rode for a neighboring
ranch. He was good at his trade by all
accounts, but some said he was a hundred and
seventy pounds of solid mean. He was certainly no stranger to trouble, whether of his
making or someone else's.

Feeling the eyes of the Triple C outfit on
him, Hobie Evans turned his head slightly in
their direction, but remained leaning on the
bar, hunched over his drink. Around his eye
there were the fading colors of a bruise.

"Catch what?" Young Shorty wanted to
know, a devilish light dancing in his gaze.
"Some farmer's fist in the eye?" Chuckling
laughter circled through the Triple C riders.

"Ain't that where you got your shiner, Hobie?"

As he pushed away from the bar to face his questioner, Hobie appeared ready to take umbrage at the question. But his glance swept the ranks of the Triple C outfit and he thought better of it.

"Yeah, I got this from a nester," Hobie admitted, pointing to his blackened eye. "But the last time I saw him, he was stretched out on the ground, and he wasn't lookin' so good, neither."

"What happened?" someone behind Webb asked.

"He claimed I broke the law — said I couldn't spit in the street." Hobie pushed out his chest, his mouth curving down in a jeering smile. "So I proceeded to tell him that we made the law around these parts long before he came here; then I spit on his shirt and asked him if he liked that better. When he threw a punch at me, I just naturally had to defend myself."

The laughs were louder the second time around, showing support for the tough cowboy's actions. Webb's mouth widened into a smile as he leaned sideways against the bar and sipped at the foaming mug of beer.

"This is our town," Hobie declared, raising his voice to make himself heard throughout the room. "Them funny-talkin' nesters think they can just come here and start tellin' us what we can do in it. We was here first. I say, if they don't like it, they can get out!"

There was a rumble of agreement and nodding heads throughout the room. Satisfaction glinted in Hobie Evans's eyes when he heard the response. He stood a little taller, sure of his support.

"They're a plague, that's what they are. Worse than a bunch of damn 'hoppers. Look at the way they're eatin' up the land till there ain't a blade of grass left." He paused, listening to the murmurs in the room. "Has anybody even lifted a hand to stop them?"

This kind of ugly talk didn't set well with Webb. "You're forgetting something, Hobie." He didn't raise his voice, but it carried clearly through the suddenly quieting room. Webb didn't change his position or even raise his glance from the beer mug. "Those drylanders have every right to claim government land — same as you."

"I wouldn't have figured a Calder would be stickin' up for them against his own kind." Hobie eyed him with derision. "Maybe your pa's spread is still sittin' pretty, but you better take a look at the rest of the ranches around here. They're handin' out walking papers right and left. And it's all on account of those farmers."

"Every ranch is feeling the pinch of the low cattle prices," Webb replied, turning his head to study the man. "If some cowboys are let go, you can blame the cattle market."

"Some cowboys." Hobie scoffed at the phrase and turned to the room of men. "How many of you here have drawn your last pay for a brand? I wanta see a show of hands."

It began slowly, first one man lifting his hand, then another and another. When Webb finished looking around the room, about half the cowboys present indicated they were out of work. He hadn't known it was that bad.

"Ain't all of us got a pa that owns the place," the cowboy reminded Webb with deliberate sarcasm. "And if the cattle prices are bad, who's to blame for that?" Hobie wanted to know, then supplied the answer himself. "It's the farmer. The price of grain's so high that the farmers are sellin' it over there in Europe instead of fattenin' cattle with it. They can get more money for their grain than they can for cattle, so they ain't buyin' any steers at the market. They're gettin' rich an' takin' over our grassland, and we aren't doing nothin' about it."

"There ain't nothin' we can do," a disgruntled cowboy grumbled. "The government's given 'em the land."

"Somebody should take it away from them," Hobie suggested and watched the reaction. "Since when has anybody in this territory paid attention to what a bunch of politicians in Washington do?" There was a stirring of discomfort and little, if any, sound of agreement. "Hell, this ain't wheat-growin' land," Hobie argued. "They passed the law without ever comin' out here to look at it. They made a mistake, and we'd just be puttin' it right."

"What you're suggesting is against the law," Nate pointed out dryly.

"What law?" the cowboy countered. "Washington law or range law?"

"Ain't you heard, Hobie?" someone piped up from the back of the room. "They've hired a lawman. Blue Moon's got its own town sheriff now."

Webb lifted his head, his features sharpening. There was a similar reaction around him at the announcement, indicating the knowledge wasn't widespread.

"You can just bet that sheriff was hired to protect those nesters. None of us have ever needed to hire anyone to protect us," Hobbie declared. "We were able to look after ourselves."

"What about the stock detectives and the wolvers?" Webb offered. "They were profes-

190

sionals hired by ranchers to track down rustlers and wolves. It seems to me you're talking out of both sides of your mouth."

"We sure didn't wait around for a sheriff to do it for us," Hobie reminded him. "If we had depended on the law, all the cattle would have been rustled. When the law fails us, we always step in and do what needs to be done. We don't go around bellyachin' about it."

"Ya know, it strikes me that —" Nate took out his tobacco and paper and began building himself a smoke — "that our problem is no different than the Indians' was. No matter how many times we fight, we just keep gettin' pushed back farther. There's more of them than there is of us, and they just keep comin'. We get rid of one, an' three more take his place."

The ground swell of agreement that had begun with Hobie's remark leveled off at Nate's sobering comparison. Like everyone else, Webb had the feeling that Nate's observation was a little too close to the mark.

Before the silence began to grow heavy, Young Shorty slapped Nate on the shoulder just as he was about to lick his cigarette together. It slipped from his hand, tobacco scattering to the floor, leaving Nate only with the paper between his fingers.

"You know what they say, Nate," Shorty

declared. "If you can't beat 'em, join 'em. And that's just what I'm aimin' to do. I'm going to latch myself on to a purty farmer's gal and dance till the sun goes down." His jubilance was contagious, livening up the leaden atmosphere in the bar. Shorty waved a hand at Hobie. "Belly up to the bar, Crazy Horse," he said, likening the cowboy to the famed war chief of the Ogalala Sioux. "And I'll buy a drink."

The invitation broke the spell Hobie had cast over the room, and the noise level rose once more. When Sonny Drake, the bartender and owner of the establishment, brought the whiskey bottle over to refill their glasses, Shorty slapped his money on the counter.

"Dancin' is thirsty business. You better give me two bottles to take along," he stated, then looked at the nearly full mug of beer Webb was nursing. "You'd better drink up, or you'll still be here when they call out to choose your partners."

In the open area behind the lumberyard, a bunch of boards had been nailed together to make a crude dance floor. A flat-racked hay wagon sat at one end, all strung up with banners, to form a stage for the band. A crowd had already begun to gather, an assortment of wagons and buggies rimming the perimeter.

Benteen headed back toward the buggy where he'd left Lorna and Ruth, but there was no sign of them when he reached it. The near horse of the matched bay team nuzzled his shirt sleeve. Benteen stroked its nose as he took a frowning look around, finally spotting them three wagons away talking to Gil Brickman's wife from the Bar M.

"Ah-oo-gah!"

The sudden and loud sound startled the horses. Benteen grabbed hold of the reins under the chin strap and quieted them, but they continued to move restlessly, rolling an eye toward the noisy contraption rumbling past them. Benteen glanced at the new-fangled automobile with disgust, and its aproned and goggled driver with more.

"Tom Pettit would rise out of his grave if he knew what his boy was spending his money on." It was Ed Mace who spoke, his approach covered by the noise of the auto's combustion engine.

"That's a fact," Benteen agreed. "I don't know what he's going to do with that thing way out here."

"Drive it up and down the street, I guess." Ed Mace shook his head at the wasteful use of money. "There aren't any roads around here for those horseless carriages. And there won't be for twenty, thirty years or more, I'd wager."

"It's just a toy." Benteen relaxed his hold on the reins now that the horses had settled down. "You've heard the Pettit boy is selling off parcels of his ranch to the homesteaders, haven't you?"

"I heard it, but I didn't want to believe it." Ed Mace nodded as anger flashed in his eyes. "There's a lot more ranchers that are thinking about selling off some of their land to try to stay afloat until the cattle market turns around. Some of the prices those drylanders are paying for worthless land make it mighty tempting."

"It looks like easy money, I guess." Benteen sighed heavily.

"Damned easy when the banks are charging ten percent interest!" the rancher declared. "I swear they're being run by a bunch of damned shysters." The line of his jaw hardened as he surveyed the cluster of farm wagons in the area. "Did you ever think you'd feel out of place here, Benteen? And more keep coming every day."

"It's just the beginning, I'm afraid." He hadn't found any way to stop it.

"You don't know the half of it," Ed declared. "This country is growing too fast. Little one-building towns keep poppin' up all over the place . . . with names like Popular and Love-joy. It's like somebody plunks down a shack in the middle of nowhere and calls it a town."

"They're worse than a plague of grasshoppers," Benteen admitted. "They're covering more ground than any grasshopper cloud."

"Yeah, well, maybe we ought to dose them with kerosene and set them afire. Burn 'em up like we do 'hoppers." He eyed the families of homesteaders as they gathered in bunches around the dance floor. "Listen to them jabbering. Half of them don't even speak English. And the other half — I wouldn't trade you an old bull for the other half."

A short, wide-hipped man dressed in western clothes ambled toward the two ranchers. He didn't appear in any hurry to reach them, using the time to size the pair up. Benteen caught the flash of a star on the man's shirt, and his eyes narrowed.

"I don't think we've met yet," the man declared when he stopped in front of the two ranchers. "The name's Potter. The town hired me on as sheriff to keep the peace."

"I reckoned that's who you were." Ed Mace nodded and openly showed his indifference to the authority the man supposedly represented. "I'm Ed Mace. I own the Snake M Ranch, east of here."

"Benteen Calder, with the Triple C." He courteously offered his hand in greeting and felt the fairly young man press his hand into his palm, without exerting the effort to shake it.

"I've been meaning to ride out to both your places," the sheriff said, giving the impression he didn't rush into anything. "I'd like you to speak to your boys and ask them not to make any trouble. I know when they come to town it's natural for them to feel kind of frisky. I don't expect that you control that, but I'd like you to see to it that they don't bother any law-abiding folk."

"I don't suppose they will as long as you see to it that your law-abiding folk don't bother them," Ed Mace challenged.

"That Hobie Evans rides for you, don't he?" It was a statement of recollection rather than a quest for information.

"He does." The rancher's look almost dared the sheriff to say more.

"It was nice meeting both of you gents," the sheriff drawled and nodded to each of them in turn. "This is a day for celebration. I hope your boys behave themselves and don't step out of line. I wouldn't like to have to arrest anybody on the day of our nation's independence."

The corners of his mouth were turned up in the closest effort he made to a smile as he bid the ranchers good day and ambled off at the same leisurely pace that had brought him there.

"I heard a rumor the town was thinking about hiring a sheriff, but I wasn't aware they actually had." Benteen sent a questioning glance at the man beside him. "This must have just happened."

"The first of the month."

"Has there been trouble?"

"A few minor incidents, nothing serious." The rancher shrugged. "There isn't an outfit around that hasn't had to let some cowboys go. Most of them have been hanging around town until their money's gone. You know what the boys are like, Benteen. They get bored with nothing to do and start hazing the drylanders. Basically, it's just harmless fun, but they get a little rough sometimes."

The homesteaders were green, so they were the most likely ones to bear the brunt of a cowboy's frustration. And if a homesteader's sense of humor didn't match a cowboy's, the cowboy would be more than willing to back up his opinion on the matter. Benteen was certain a few scuffles had resulted.

"There's been complaints, too, about Sonny's

197

saloon — and the 'criminal element' that hangs out there." Ed Mace stressed the derogatory reference to the men who rode for them. "It happens every time you get a bunch of those high-minded farmers. It won't be long before they'll be wanting to close his place down. God help Fannie when the pious horsefaces find out about her."

"The next thing you know they'll be drawing a deadline the way they did in the trail towns," Benteen suggested in dry amusement.

"With the respectable folk on one side and the cattlemen on the other," Ed Mace elaborated with gathering resentment. "And us forbidden to cross the line. It was us, and men like us, that built this town. Nobody is going to tell me or my men where we can walk in it. Not ever."

"I hope neither one of us sees that day." There were too many changes coming too fast to be able to predict what tomorrow might bring. But the water was simmering in the cauldron. If much more wood was put in the fire, it was liable to boil over. And there didn't seem to be any lack of available fuel. A couple of musicians had climbed onto the makeshift bandstand to begin tuning their instruments. "It looks like the dance is about to start," Benteen observed. "I guess I'd better find my wife."

It wasn't much more than a block from the roadhouse saloon to the flat area being used for the dance, but a cowboy never walks when he can ride. Somebody brought the word that the dance was about ready to start, and the cowboys began spilling out of the saloon onto their horses, some of them taking the time to stuff a bottle into their saddlebags.

None of them were drunk but they were all feeling good, shouting and laughing as they urged their horses into a canter over the short distance. Webb rode right in the midst of them, more sober than most with only one beer under his belt. The wagons were a barricade that kept them from riding right up to the dance floor. Forced to dismount, they tied their horses to the nearest available wheel of any buckboard and worked their way forward to the short wooden platform where the dancing had already started.

At the edge of the platform, they began spreading out, halting in clusters of three and four to review the potential dance partners that were present. All the homesteaders were strung along the opposite side. Webb noticed his parents among the dancers on the floor, and Ruth dancing with the foreman of the Brickman Ranch.

With the exception of a few ranchers'

daughters, the pickings of eligible girls were slim on the cowboys' side of the floor. It was a different story on the homesteaders' side, where there seemed to be an equal number of males and females.

"Look at the bosom on that gal with the yellow braids." Young Shorty nudged Webb with his elbow. "Hot damn! She's the one for me."

Just as Webb spotted the young girl in the white pinafore, he saw Lilli standing beside her and he went still. She was wearing a bright blue dress that he knew had to match her eyes. As she watched the dancers, she swayed in time with the music.

"I spotted her first," Abe Garvey insisted. "You take the one in blue next to her."

"She's married," Webb stated flatly, dropping his gaze and forcing it in another direction.

"The hell you say." Abe frowned.

"I got dibs on Yellow Braids," Shorty insisted. "It ain't my fault, Abe, that you didn't say something before me."

As Young Shorty Niles started across the floor, Abe hurried to follow a step behind him. "When she turns you down, Shorty, just move over, 'cause I'm right behind you."

"Are you gonna try your luck?" Nate

inquired, sending a sidelong look at Webb.

"No." But he sensed the closeness of Nate's scrutiny and let a wry smile lift one corner of his mouth. "I'm going to let them blaze the trail. That way I can travel faster following their sign."

"Don't look like they're doin' too good," Nate surmised.

Reluctantly, Webb let his gaze swing back to the girl with the yellow braids without continuing to Lilli. A tall, stern-looking man of Scandinavian descent was standing next to the golden-haired girl. Young Shorty evidently had already been turned down and stood watching while Abe tried his luck. The girl shook her head in refusal and edged closer to the tall man next to her.

"Maybe she's married, too," Webb suggested, not intending for his voice to sound so bitter.

"Nope. That big Swede next to her is a fella named Anderson. He's got a whole brood of kids and his wife is about the same size he is. Big woman," Nate stated. "They staked a claim on some land buttin' up to the Triple C on the southeast corner. I saw 'em out working in their fields a few weeks back. The gal's his daughter, all right."

As that song ended and another started,

Webb noticed that Abe and Shorty weren't the only ones getting turned down. So were the cowboys from all the other outfits. The drylanders had no intention of letting their innocent daughters associate with the likes of a bunch of no-account cowboys. At least, Webb suspected that was their thinking.

Even the dance floor appeared divided, the homesteaders keeping to one side and the ranchers on the other. Webb realized that the electricity in the atmosphere wasn't all generated by the holiday mood.

At first the cowboys were good-natured about the refused invitations to dance. They were ready for a party and weren't about to be denied it. So they turned their attention on the female members of their own side, dancing with married and single women alike.

As Webb approached his mother, he gallantly swept off his hat and turned to offer her his arm. "May I have the next dance?"

She laughed and tucked her hand under his arm. "I've been saving it just for you." When they were on the dance floor and had completed the first set of waltz steps, she tilted her head to him. "I thought you weren't coming."

"Grizzly chased me off the ranch with a butcher knife." With his mother, he could get away with a light reply, so he did. It was easier than delving into the reasons that had brought him here when he had insisted he wasn't coming.

"Are you going to dance with Ruth?" she couldn't resist asking, hoping he might have reconsidered. She supposed it was the flaw of all women to live on hope.

"I haven't noticed that she's had any shortage of partners," he replied.

"She hasn't. In fact, she's danced every dance."

As they made another circle, Webb noticed Lilli on the other side of the dance floor. She was in the arms of the whiskered and stoop-shouldered man she had married. It grated him to see her smiling face turned upward to the man. It was wrong for them to be together.

"Webb? What's the matter?"

"Nothing." His expression closed up, letting her see none of his feelings, as he faced his mother once more. She looked unconvinced, but didn't press him for a more revealing answer.

When the song ended, he escorted her back to his father's side and returned to stand with his outfit. Disappointment and anger were knotting his insides, twisting him up with reckless urges, stirring up wants that were better left dormant.

The dark grumblings around him seemed to echo his mood. The looks being sent across the dance floor at the unattached females were turning into glares of resentment. The homesteader gals were like candy being dangled in front of a boy with a craving for sweets. And every time he reached for it, he got his hand slapped. And like little boys, the cowboys were growing sullen and restive.

"They think they're too good for us, that's what."

"Some of them gals are downright ugly. We was doin' 'em a favor just askin' 'em to dance."

"Look at 'em, thinking their daughters are so innocent an' pure. I bet they ain't that way out behind the barn."

"They ain't nothing but a bunch of scissorbills. I'd like to know where they got the idea they're better than us."

Echoing comments traveled up and down the clustering line of cowboys, resentment building among the ranks led by Hobie Evans. It wouldn't take much to turn it violent. Webb sensed it, and a part of him didn't care.

When the band began playing another one of those fast folkdance songs foreign to most of the cowboys' ears, they took exception to the accordion music. This time, they didn't confine their complaints to themselves. They said them loud so the dancers could hear.

"Don't you know any good music?"

"Somebody kick that guy with the squeeze-box off the bandstand!"

"Yeah! We want to hear some fiddlin'!"

Nate sidled closer to Webb. "Looks like this might be an excitin' party after all."

"It's either going to be a dance or a fight," Webb agreed. "I don't see the point in waiting to find out which. Get Shorty and Abe. We're going to settle it one way or the other."

When all three were gathered with him, Webb angled for the corner of the bandstand on the ranchers' side. His objective was Doyle Pettit, minus his hat, goggles, and coat, standing by the hood of his shiny black automobile and proudly demonstrating to the curious the function of the crank.

"Hey, Webb! I didn't know you were here!" Doyle strode forward, glad-handing him. "I'll take you for a ride and show you how Ford's invention works. It's the first one of its kind in these parts. I got it —"

"Later." The invitation was curtly rejected as Webb took the man by the arm and propelled him toward the dance floor. "Those drylanders think you're their friend, so they trust you. All five of us are going over there, but it's up to you to convince them to let us dance with their women."

"I don't know if they'll listen to me." Doyle pulled back.

"You'd better hope you picked up some of Wessel's smooth talk" was Webb's reply. "Kreuger's the ringleader, so don't waste your time speaking to anyone else."

Halfway across the dance floor, they were intercepted by a slim, quiet man about their age. The badge pinned on his jacket identified him as the new sheriff of Blue Moon. His attention was centered on Doyle Pettit, although he had taken in the rest of them and marked them in his memory.

"Mr. Pettit, I'm hoping you aren't thinking about starting any trouble," he said calmly.

"I merely intend to speak to them as a friend. I don't want trouble any more than you do, Sheriff," Doyle insisted with an expansive smile.

But the sheriff looked at his companions to ascertain their intentions. Webb's level gaze didn't avoid the silent probe. "We're going over there looking for peace. If it turns out the other way, it won't be our doing."

"You stated yourself plain." The sheriff nodded and moved away, satisfied that his duty was done for the time being.

When they started forward again, Webb

searched the silent-growing band of homesteaders until he found Franz Kreuger. The
man's chin was already aggressively thrust in
their direction. Webb's attention was distracted
by the couple standing next to Kreuger. The
couple was Lilli Reisner and her husband. The
hardening knot in the pit of his stomach told
him he had known all along the two neighbors
would be together. He realized that subcon-
sciously he had been counting on it.

10

When Lilli recognized Webb Calder approaching them with Mr. Pettit, a hint of excitement threaded her nerves while a shaft of apprehension caused her to dart a quick look at Stefan. Seeing the wariness and suspicion in his expression, she was glad she hadn't told him of the visit Webb had paid to their farm. Stefan had spent so much time in the company of their neighbor, Franz Kreuger, that his attitude toward cowmen had hardened. She didn't think she could have convinced him that Webb had been only trying to forewarn them of the problems they would face, not threaten them. Besides, it had been an unsettling meeting in other ways, so it had seemed best not to mention it.

The beat of her heart picked up its tempo as Mr. Pettit stopped in front of their neighbor. Before the dance started, it had been the general consensus among the homesteaders not to associate with the brash and noisy cowhands and thus avoid the unpleasantness that had marred many other occasions in town. At first the cowboys had been so polite and respectful with their invitations to dance that Lilli thought Stefan and the other men had misjudged them. But their increasingly loud and taunting remarks were confirmation that the menfolk had been right.

Still, Lilli didn't want to include Webb Calder in the same category with the other half-wild cowboys. If there was no warmth in the way he regarded Franz Kreuger, then perhaps it was because he was shown none. Her female vanity was pricked by Webb's failure to give her even a passing glance. She hadn't expected him to ignore her. It stung a little. Lilli shifted her attention to Doyle Pettit, eloquently appealing to Franz Kreuger to persuade the homesteaders to change their minds about the cowboys.

He was summing up his argument. "After all, Mr. Kreuger, we have all gathered here to celebrate our country's independence," Doyle Pettit reasoned. "On this special day, I think we should put aside petty differences and join together in the festivity here. I will personally vouch for the conduct of all the members of the ranching community present and assure you their behavior will be above reproach. If any of your womenfolk would care to dance with the cowboys, I promise they will be treated with the utmost respect."

"And if they aren't?" Franz Kreuger challenged with open skepticism.

"You have my word on it." Webb issued the cool reply before Doyle Pettit could speak. "The word of a Calder means something around here, Mr. Kreuger. If any of the boys step out of line, they will personally answer to me." He paused a split second. "Do we have your permission to ask your ladies to dance?"

"I am not a big, important man like you, Mr. Calder. I am just a wheat farmer." The modest disclaimer from Franz Kreuger was issued with a trace of contempt. "I can say you have permission, but that does not mean there is a woman willing to accept such an invitation."

His response was a subtle way of indicating his attitude hadn't changed. The granting of permission was mere lip service that Lilli considered rude and unwarranted. One look at Webb's tightening mouth revealed that he viewed the response in the same light. His request had been reasonable and proper. She was irritated that it had met with such discourtesy from her own kind. After all, Webb had been willing to meet them more than halfway.

The gesture should have been reciprocated, not rejected.

She took an impetuous step forward, leaving Stefan's side. "I will," Lilli asserted, seeing Webb's head come up as his gaze jumped to her. "I'm sure Mr. Calder can be trusted to keep his word."

Webb's cool expression didn't alter, but his dark eyes were warm and approving, glinting with some disturbing force. Lilli felt the restraining hand Stefan laid on her shoulder and turned her head slightly in his direction.

"It will be all right, Stefan," she insisted in a low murmur, but he didn't remove his hand.

She was angry with him for being so unreasonably protective of her. If Stefan objected, she couldn't openly defy him. It would shame him in front of all of his friends. Lilli felt torn by a sense of duty to her husband and the knowledge that her offer to dance was the proper response to ease the rising animosity between the two factions.

As she waited for a sign from Stefan, she looked back at Webb. He seemed to sense her conflict. His attention swung to Stefan as he removed his hat in a gesture of respect and held it against his chest.

"With your permission, Mr. Reisner, I'd like to dance with your wife," he stated calmly.

Her respect for him was raised another notch by this action. Webb Calder had taken the decision out of her hands and placed it in her husband's, indicating he would abide by it and not assume on Lilli's impulsive action. Therefore, there would be no occasion for her to defy her husband's wishes. She silently prayed that Stefan would be as magnanimous as Webb Calder was.

Stefan's large fingers tightened briefly on her shoulder, then relaxed to slide away. Lilli was proud of him at that moment. She beamed a quick smile in his direction, then placed her hand on Webb's arm and let him lead her onto the dance floor.

His hand fit naturally to the curve of her slender waist, his fingers spreading on her back. Her hand was warm and small inside the grip of his as Webb held her less than an arm's length away. She was lithe and graceful, following his steps with ease, as if they'd danced together many times before. Her arms and throat had a sun-golden beauty, while the mass of auburn hair crowning her head gave the impression of stature. For a moment, the vitality of her utterly destroyed his self-possession.

Around them, other homesteaders had relented and given their daughters permission to accept a cowboy's invitation to dance. Not many of them, but enough to show the majority was weakening. Webb had no interest in the possible trouble he'd averted. All his attention was on the girl in his arms.

"You were right, Mr. Calder," she said.

"I was? That's nice to know." The smile came easily to his mouth. "About what?"

"The well. We found water all right, but it was poisoned with alkali, just like you said it would be," she admitted. "We're going to have to depend on a cistern for our water."

"That's one time I'd rather have been wrong — for your sake." He added the last on a husky note.

"We'll manage." She sounded confident, then looked around them. "I didn't know cowboys enjoyed such things as dancing."

"We don't spend all our time busting wild broncs and roping cattle like the Wild West Show would make you believe." Webb recalled that her concept of cowboys had been colored wrongly by that show. "Our tastes are not totally unrefined. Dancing is right up there at the top of the list of a cowboy's favorite pastimes."

"Right next to his horse?" she asked with a laughing look.

"Definitely." He liked her sense of humor. "Our biggest problem around here has been the scarcity of female partners. You could count the number of available women on your fingers. That's why it was so frustrating for the boys to see all those gals on your side not dancing with anyone. I expected any minute for a couple of the boys to volunteer to be heifer-branded."

"What's that?" She tipped her head toward him in the most engaging fashion.

"That's when a cowboy ties a handkerchief to his sleeve to show he's willing to dance the female part," explained Webb. "It's a desperate measure. But around the bunkhouse, a fella can get pretty desperate for entertainment. They've even been known to tie on an apron."

"Have you ever been heifer-branded?" The gleam in her eye stopped short of actually flirting with him, but the interest was there. Webb could see it, whether she was aware of it or not.

"No. I guess I wasn't broke to follow someone else's lead."

"I can believe that," Lilli replied.

When the song ended, Webb was slow to let her go. "I was right about something else," he told her, looking deep into her eyes. "When I noticed you earlier, I was sure the dress matched the color of your eyes. And it does."

It was the intensity of his gaze, that light that smoldered in it, rather than his compliment that disturbed Lilli. She lowered her head, trying to avoid his look and the sensation it caused in her stomach.

"Thank you." Withdrawing her hand from his warm grasp, she turned out of his hold to walk back to Stefan.

Webb fell in step to escort her back, but he didn't want to take her there. He didn't want to give her back into her husband's keeping. He was a man; vital instincts surged in him. For the first time in his life, he begrudged the obligation of his word.

When he stopped in front of Stefan Reisner, he knew he was the better man, but there was little solace in it. He handed Lilli into the man's possession, his features set in grim lines.

"Thank you for the privilege of dancing with your wife, sir." He inclined his head, his dark eyes flashing.

He didn't dare look at Lilli again as he walked away.

Across the dance floor, Ruth watched him return to the sidelines as she had watched him since he had arrived, keeping track of where he was and whom he was with. It was something she couldn't stop doing, even though Webb had not spoken to her once, nor even ventured in her direction.

Her glance ran back to the settler's woman.

Jealousy was a painful feeling. It imprinted all competition clearly in her mind so that she never forgot any female who might be her rival. She remembered the young, auburn-haired girl as the wife of that elderly settler Webb had nearly gotten into a fight with. Despite that, Webb had just danced with her. It worried Ruth, as much as if the girl were single.

As Nate watched Webb striding over to rejoin them, he was reminded of a bull with its tail twisted. A wise rider gave a critter like that a wide berth. He sucked in his breath and said nothing when Webb reached them, letting the others do the talking. If they missed the warning signals, that was their lookout. His glance skipped to the girl in blue, and Nate shook his head in sad dismay for his friend. He guessed he knew what had been eating at him.

"I thought for a while there you weren't going to pull it off, Webb," Shorty declared, but he was always the kind to wonder how deep the quicksand was. "Yellow Braids wouldn't dance with me, but I think I'll wear her pa down the next time."

"Is there any whiskey left in that bottle you tucked away in your saddlebag?" Webb gave no sign he'd heard the congratulatory remark.

"Hell, yes!" Shorty confirmed with a wide grin. "And you've got the right idea. Let's go have a drink now that we've got ourselves a real party goin'."

Webb pushed off, plunging through the maze of wagons to the rear where they'd left their horses. The slanting rays of a lowering sun cast long shadows on the ground as a summer wind carried the band's music away from them. The warm air was pungent with the smell of horses.

Shorty took the whiskey bottle from his saddlebag and tossed it to Webb. "You first."

It was a case of fighting fire with fire as Webb tried to burn out the anger with a long swallow of the fiery alcohol. It shuddered through him, numbing his senses. Lowering the bottle, he pressed a hand to his mouth, the muscles in his throat paralyzed.

"Jeez, Webb." Shorty gave him a reproving look as he took the bottle and wiped at the lip with his sleeve. "For a minute there, I thought you were going to slug it all down."

There was a stirring of activity down the way, the creaking of saddle leather and the jangle of metal bits and bridle chains that indicated riders were mounting up. As Webb turned automatically to look, he recognized Hobie Evans and two more Snake M riders reining their horses away from the wagons.

"Looks like Hobie's a sore loser," Abe Garvey remarked. "He sure was hopin' your play would work the other way. He had a bunch of guys worked up to teach them homesteaders to be more friendly. But your move left him high and dry."

"He never was too successful with the ladies," Shorty concluded. "They aren't rough enough for him. 'Course, with an ugly mug like that, what woman would want him?" He laughed the question and passed the bottle to Abe.

"You got a point." Abe watched the trio of riders heading the horses up the main street of town at a shuffling trot. "Looks like they're goin' to Sonny's."

"One thing you gotta say about Hobie, that fella can hold his liquor," Shorty admired and glanced at Abe as he released a loud, satisfied sigh of approval for the throat-clearing swallow of whiskey. "What d'ya say? Shall we go back and try our luck with Yellow Braids and her pa?"

Webb stuck a hand in the side pocket of his denim Levi pants and pulled out a coin. "I'll buy the rest of the bottle from you, Shorty." He flipped the coin toward the cowboy, who caught it with a quick, one-handed stab.

"Aren't you coming?" Shorty hesitated,

giving him a puzzled look.

"No, I think I'll just stay here and drink for a while." Webb took the bottle by the neck and eased his long frame onto the ground, propping his back against a wagon wheel.

Shorty studied him a second longer, then shrugged. "Suit yourself."

As Shorty and Abe ambled off, Nate lingered to roll a smoke, but Webb gave no indication that he wanted company. Nate lit the cigarette and squinted at Webb through the smoke.

"I guess you know the only thing you'll find in that bottle is a helluva hangover, so I'll just see you later," Nate said in parting and went wandering back through the wagons after his other two friends. "Women," he said to himself. "Ain't nothin' can tie a man into a tighter knot."

Alone with only the sounds of tail-swishing horses stamping at flies, Webb stared at the uncorked bottle. The dance in progress was just a distant hum. He took another long swig from the bottle and leaned his head back against the cradle of the wheel spokes. A high, blue sky was above him, but there were shadows all around him. There were shadows in his heart and mind as well, black ones, directing his desires down a bad path.

Hobie Evans rode in the middle, his mount a step or two ahead of the flanking horses. Passing the roadhouse saloon, they trotted out of town to the west. Hobie was slouched loosely in the saddle, his sullen gaze contemplating the land ahead of them.

"Never thought I'd see the day when a Calder would toady to a bunch of egg-sucking farmers." Ace Rafferty broke the silence.

"Never should have let thè first one of 'em throw up a shanty," Hobie countered roughly, then swung a gleaming, malevolent look at his compatriots. "You ever been inside one of their huts?"

"No." But both showed a sudden interest at the question, guessing he had something in mind.

"There's a honyocker that's got himself a place just a couple three miles from here. Wanta go check the place out?" Hobie grinned.

All three men lifted their horses out of a trot into ground-covering lopes, heading for the settler's shanty up the way.

"It is growing late, Lillian." Stefan took her by the arm as he cast a glance at the sun hanging above the horizon. "The sun vill be down in another hour. Ve should be leaving."

"So soon?" she murmured in protest, but

smiled a reluctant agreement. "I suppose we must," she conceded. There was a lull in the music as the band took a well-earned break.

"Alvays you vomen enjoy dancing, but tomorrow it is vork again," he reminded her. Then he remarked, "You never said if you enjoyed your dance vith that Calder man." They started toward their wagon.

"I enjoyed it, the same as I enjoyed the polka with Mr. Anderson," she replied, although the experiences had been vastly different. "I was proud of you today, Stefan. You were just as much a fine gentleman as Webb Calder."

"Ya?" He seemed to question her observation, but she noticed that he held his head a little higher.

Strangely, she didn't find any satisfaction in the knowledge that she had reassured him. Her blue eyes were clouded by the troubled thoughts in her mind, brought on by the slow discovery that Stefan had asked the question out of jealousy. It was obvious that Webb Calder was younger and stronger, more handsome in the hard way this land had of growing men. She hoped it was merely the jealousy an older man had toward one younger. Stefan was very dear to her. Lilli didn't want him to know a part of her was drawn to Webb Calder. She was certain it was natural to like someone who was more attractive and closer to her own age, but it didn't mean she thought any less of Stefan, although she doubted that he would understand the innocence of the attraction.

Someone called to them before they had passed the first row of wagons around the dance floor. Both stopped to turn and look behind them.

"It is Franz Krueger." Stefan identified the man threading his way through the milling group of homesteaders toward them.

"I'm sure he wishes to speak to you." Lilli had the feeling that their neighbor didn't like her very much, although he had certainly never indicated it in any overt way. "I'll go on to the wagon and wait for you there."

Stefan nodded agreement and started back to meet his friend. Lillie lingered a moment to watch them. In truth, she didn't like Franz Kreuger very much, either. Maybe he had guessed that. He struck her as being arrogant and intolerant toward anyone who didn't share his views. He knew it all and pressed his biased opinions on everyone around him. Lilli suspected Franz Kreuger's distrust of those who had more than he did, like the ranchers especially, was really a mask for jealousy. Of course, Stefan would disagree, but he had been influenced by his neighbor's stronger personality.

Sighing, Lilli turned and began strolling toward their wagon. In places, the wagons were three deep. They had arrived at the dance area late, so theirs was parked in one of the outer rows. It was already evening, but the summer sun was still up and the air was warm. The band was starting to play again, but the music drifted away from her on a dying breeze.

She began humming the melody the band had played when she danced with Webb Calder. She could almost feel the guiding pressure of his hands, leading her through the steps. He was an important person, probably the most sought-after bachelor in the area, and he had danced with her. As a matter of fact, she had only noticed him on the dance floor a couple of times. It was curious the way he had disappeared right after he had finished the dance with her. It made her feel just a little special that she had been one of the few he had partnered. She had liked the way he had made her smile with his amusing tale about cowboys dancing with each other. For a little second, she had been tempted to flirt with him until discretion surfaced.

It was a new experience to have a man pay attention to her, especially one of Webb Calder's caliber. Most of her life she'd been too young; then her parents had died and many harsh realities about living alone had had to be faced. She had missed out on being courted, so the dance with Webb Calder had given her a little sample of what it might have been like. Stefan was so staid and stolid, he shouldn't object if she stole a few minutes of excitement, but Lilli knew he would.

As Lilli reached their wagon, the Belgian mare, Dolly, issued a low, inquiring whicker. "We'll go home as soon as Stefan comes," she assured the animal, the corners of her mouth lifting slightly. Instead of climbing onto the wagon seat, she leaned against the side of the box.

"Lilli." A low voice called her name.

She turned, startled. The vague surprise disappeared the instant she recognized Webb Calder. It didn't occur to her to question what he was doing here or why he had sought her out. For the moment, she felt only the pleasure of seeing him again.

He was framed against the backdrop of the plains. It seemed fitting, because they had shaped him so. It was something she could see clearly, being city-bred herself. With so much room, he'd grown big and tall, but the sun and wind had carved him into flat sinews and bronzed his skin. His smile was slow to come, but it always held meaning. Even when he was looking at her, as now, his dark eyes still showed the habit of looking across far distances.

"Hello," she greeted him easily.

As he walked to her, Webb studied the outline of her body, slim and lovely against the velvet curtain of shadows. There wasn't much left in the whiskey bottle propped against the wheel a few wagons away. He followed a stiff, straight line to her, one foot determinedly planted in front of the other.

Webb stopped when he reached her. Her wide lips were curved in a smile, and he thought he saw extra warmth in the blue eyes for him. The caution that should have been in his head if the alcohol hadn't dulled his thinking was nowhere to be found. After drifting so long, not knowing what he wanted, he seemed to have found it.

"Are you leaving?" His voice stayed low-pitched.

"Yes." She added an affirmative nod. "Stefan stopped to speak to a neighbor, so I came on ahead."

Her words ripped at the fine feeling he'd known so briefly. She belonged to another man; all that bold spirit and beauty were for Stefan Reisner. Webb swayed, like a heartsick wild animal at the end of its tether watching others of its kind run free. Too much pressure was applied against the rope, and it snapped. His hands closed on her shoulders and he felt her stiffen in startled resistance as he gathered her to his body.

Too stunned to struggle, Lilli barely had time to bring her hands up against his chest in an instinctive effort to ward him off. The muscled arm circling her waist pressed her to his hard, strong body; then his hand was gripping the back of her head, holding it still so she couldn't avoid him. She caught the smell of liquor on his breath and realized he was drunk.

A tiny animal cry of struggle came from her paralyzed throat, but it was silenced by the driving pressure of his mouth on her lips. He claimed them with a hunger and need that were jolting. It was not the gently warm and quiet kind of kiss she'd come to know. The sensation was a crazy, downward spiral that seemed to reach all the way to her stomach. She was frightened by the intensity of the feeling.

She shuddered with relief when he dragged his mouth from hers and trailed it down the curve of her neck. She was shaken and raw; the condition didn't improve under his nuzzling exploration and the virile impact of his hard length.

"Lilli, you don't belong with him," he muttered thickly.

The sound of his voice seemed to release her from the numbed silence. Lilli clung to the belief that he wouldn't have forced his attentions on her if he hadn't been drinking. Since he had lost his head, it was up to her to remain calm.

"Mr. Calder, if you don't let me go this minute, I shall have to scream," she informed him. Her voice sounded steady, but she hoped he didn't notice how agitated her breathing was.

She was willing to excuse his behavior and not mention it to Stefan if Webb released her now. Drink caused men to behave in ways they wouldn't consider while they were sober, she kept telling herself, trying to rationalize why she wanted this incident kept secret.

Her threat did not loosen the closed circle of his arms, but he did lift his head, as if to see if she meant it. With an effort, Lilli boldly returned his look to convince him she would scream if he didn't do as she had asked. He shook his head in a silent request for her not to make any sound and cupped a hand over her mouth, his callused palm lightly brushing against her lips. Yet the very gentleness of his action indicated it was not a genuine attempt to smother any outcry.

A second later, he was drawing away from her. The broken look in his expression nearly tore her apart. Lilli discovered something that stirred and depressed her. It was taking hold of her heart, catching her up in a struggle as old as the ages, yet new to her. A raw and wild frustration ran in her.

"Hey! Isn't that smoke?" a man shouted, out of sight beyond some other wagons. "Look there! To the west!"

The cry of alarm claimed Webb's attention, which had been trained too long to alertness not to respond. It sobered him in an instant as his suddenly sharp gaze swept the western horizon, halting on the billowing black plume of smoke rising into the air.

Fire. A man didn't have to live long in this open country to know the kind of devastation a grass fire could do once it took hold. The smoke appeared confined to a narrow area, but it could spread to a whole hillside in minutes with all this summer-dry grass for fuel.

Webb didn't waste time confirming the sighting. He broke into a run for his horse. The area around the dance floor was emptying of ranchers and cowboys, all alive to the dangers of a prairie fire. The green settlers were slower to react, but the alarm of the

Montana natives was contagious.

When Stefan reached Lillian, he didn't waste any more time with explanations than Webb had. He hustled her into the wagon seat and picked up the reins, slapping them on the rumps of the Belgian team. She grabbed hold of the seat with both hands and hung on.

11

Pounding hooves vibrated over the ground as riders and wagons raced toward the growing tower of smoke. Webb was among the first group to arrive on the scene. The fire had started in the tar-paper shack of some homesteader, raged through it, and set the grass around it ablaze. From there, it had begun spreading quickly. The heat from the fire generated its own draft to fan the flames onward.

Cowboys peeled off their horses and paused long enough to strip off saddle blankets and use them to beat the flames. Loose horses scattered and milled, interfering with arriving wagon teams. A wide, plowed strip of fallow land formed a firebreak to confine the spread of flames on one side.

The fire was inching fastest to the west, and the cowboys threw all their energies in that direction to check the spread. "There's no damned water!" someone complained. Without water to wet blankets, they weren't as effective.

Next to the smoldering remains of the shack, there was a charred and blackened barrel that held the drylander's water. The wet contents had kept the barrel from burning, but it was too far away with too much smoldering ground between it and the firefighters to do them any good.

The cowboys had organized themselves into a combat unit, experienced at fighting prairie fires, but the drylanders, for all their eagerness to help, were milling about in confusion, not knowing what to do. As Webb was driven back by the heat of the flames, he noticed the directionless homesteaders advancing uncertainly toward the fire, without blankets or any weapons except their own will to stamp out the flames.

"Where is the fire wagon?" one of them demanded. "Why hasn't it come?"

Webb stifled the run of impatience at the question and pulled down the kerchief he'd tied around his face to keep from inhaling too much smoke. Most of these drylanders came from the cities, where they relied on someone else to fight their fires. But they weren't living in the city now.

"If any of you have water barrels on your

wagons, bring them up here!" Webb shouted the order. "Wet down blankets and jackets, anything you have, and use them to beat down the flames!" No one objected to his directives, relieved to know what they were to do, and Webb suddenly found himself taking charge. "Spread out and form a line! Don't all of you bunch together! If the wind shifts, you'll find yourself trapped in a circle of fire!"

A homesteader came running up to him, stricken and pale. "You got to keep the fire from burning my wheatfield!"

"To hell with your wheatfield!" Webb glared. "If we don't stop this fire, it'll blacken hundreds of square miles!" He pushed the man toward a gap in the newly formed line. "Get in there!"

Two wagons came rolling up, the horse teams plunging and shying at the swirling curtain of smoke that heralded the advancing flames. Both had water barrels in back. Webb vaulted onto the back of one of the wagons and lifted off the barrel cover.

"You ladies!" He waved to women hovering anxiously in the rear. "Start wetting down the blankets for the men so they don't have to leave the line! And if any of you have shovels or tools in your wagons, bring them up here!"

With all hands put to constructive use, Webb

went up and down the line, pitching in himself wherever there were flash points. The fiery heat sweated the alcohol out of his system as adrenaline surged through his blood.

The fire crackled nearly underfoot and the choking smoke filled Benteen's lungs, paralyzing him with a coughing spasm. Webb saw it and grabbed his father by the shoulders, guiding him away from the fire to an unthreatened area near the wagons, where the air was relatively clear of smoke and blowing cinders.

"Are you okay?" Webb paused long enough to ask and see the affirming nod from his father. Then he straightened and called an order to the first woman he recognized. "Ruth, take care of him and keep him here."

Ruth hurried over, bringing a dipper of water for the senior Calder. He accepted it, flicking a grateful look at the girl before his gaze traveled after his son. There were tears in his eyes. Some of them were caused by the burning smoke, but most of them came from pride. His son was finally taking responsibility for something and giving orders.

"Dammit, I knew you had it in you all along, son." Benteen whispered under his breath.

"What did you say, Mr. Calder?" Ruth asked.

"Nothing." He shook his head and raised the

dipper to his mouth, letting the water soothe his smoke-raw throat. God, he was tired, he thought and sank back against a wagon. Maybe he wouldn't have to work so hard now; he'd let Webb take over some of the more arduous chores so he could spend more time with Lorna. The Lord knew she deserved more of his time than he'd given her.

They had nearly beaten the fire to a standstill when Webb sensed something was wrong. He lifted his head, trying to identify the cause, as he scanned the fireline. It was a full second before he noticed the almost imperceptible shift in the wind's direction. There was a sudden crackle and curl of yellow flames, angling toward the wagons.

"The wind's changing!" He shouted the warning to the others far down the line and headed to the fire's new point of attack.

Those closest had already seen the threat and were converging on it. As Webb hurried to join them, he saw Lilli whipping at the shooting flames in a kind of terrified frenzy. She was too close to be effective, and her frantic efforts were fanning the fire, not smothering it.

Before he could call to her, smoke rolled from the hem of her long skirt, and he heard her scream. "Lilli, roll!" Webb started running. "Get down on the ground and roll!" But her fear put her beyond hearing as she first tried beating at her skirt, then turned to run to the wagons.

Webb dived at her, sending both of them crashing to the ground. It seemed he'd never known fear in his life until that moment. Her hands clawed at him, trying to get away, but he kept her down and grabbed the water-soaked blanket she'd been using, throwing it over her kicking legs and the smoldering skirt. He pinned her struggling, heaving body to the ground with the weight of his and pressed the blanket tightly around her thighs and hips. It was long, agonizing seconds before the skirt stopped smoking. But she was still fighting him, sobbing hysterically, her eyes closed.

"The fire's out, Lilli," he assured her and ran a stroking hand down the side of her face. "It's all over."

"I can still smell the smoke," she protested in a choked voice.

"The fire's out," Webb repeated and eased some of his weight off of her as she began to relax. "I promise you it's out."

She brought a hand up to her mouth as if to smother her crying. "I can smell it," she insisted, not opening her eyes.

Webb moved, slipping an arm under her and lifting her up. She weakly buried her face in his shirt, crying softly now. He turned his head to her, his lips tightly brushing the singed ends of her hair. "You brave little fool," he murmured, half in anger for the extreme danger she'd put herself in. He scooped up her legs to carry her when he stood.

Then Stefan Reisner was kneeling in front of him, his smoke-blackened features making him look even older. Anxiety was in his eyes as he reached out a hand for his wife.

"Is she all right?" he asked. "Vhat happened?"

"She caught her skirt on fire, but I think I got it out before she was badly burned." His arms tightened around her possessively. "I'm going to carry her over to the wagons where the women can see to her."

"I vill take her." Stefan insisted it was his right.

"I've got her." Webb stood up, refusing to relinquish her and leaving Stefan with little choice except to agree. Lilli seemed oblivious to both of them, not caring whose arms were around her.

Webb strode to the wagons, with Stefan staying right beside him every step of the way. His mother and several other women hurried forward as soon as they saw him carrying someone in his arms. Ruth was one of the few who hung back.

"Is she hurt?" his mother asked. Immediately she suggested, "You can put her in the back of the wagon."

Someone lowered the endgate so Webb could set her down inside. "I think she's more frightened than anything else," he explained as he surrendered her to his mother's care. "Her skirt caught on fire. There might be some minor burns on her legs."

"The poor dear, she's fainted," his mother murmured, cradling Lilli's head on her lap. "Someone bring me a wet cloth." Webb stepped back and Stefan immediately took his place. "Are you related to her?" his mother asked as Stefan's trembling hand touched the unconscious woman's shoulder.

"Lillian is my vife," he acknowledged. "She vill be all right?"

"I'm sure she will," Lorna assured him and shot a confused glance at Webb, as if questioning why he had carried the girl here instead of letting her husband bring her.

He pivoted away, a nerve leaping along his cheek. He looked right past Ruth, not even seeing her, as he started back to the fireline. They had contained the flames and kept them from breaking through to the wagons. But it wouldn't be over until the last ember was out.

Lilli stirred, a panic surfacing, but there was still a glazed quality to her eyes when she opened them. "The fire . . . smoke . . ."

"It's all right, *liebchen,*" Stefan murmured, patting her hand.

"Stefan?" She turned her head toward the sound of his voice.

"I am here," he assured her, and she drifted back into that unconscious world. His sad eyes lifted to the woman holding the wet cloth to Lillian's forehead. "It is the fire she fears. Vhen she vas small, it burned the building next to vhere she lived. There vere people trapped inside. Her mind cannot forget it."

"I understand," Lorna murmured and guessed it was one of the many bonds that held the older man and this young girl together despite their vast age differences. She wondered if Webb understood how strong such bonds could be. She had seen the look in his eyes when he'd carried the girl in, and her heart went out to him.

There was no leaving until the fire was completely out. All prairie people knew how an apparently dead fire could smolder and break out anew. So they walked along the dead ashes, looking for hot spots in the sun's gloaming. The fire had taken part of the wheatfield, but more than half was undamaged.

A small group of homesteaders had ventured across the burnt ground to inspect the few charred timbers of wood still standing as skeletal evidence that a crude house once stood there. One of the group was the owner. He'd had so little to lose, but it was gone. All he and his family had left were the clothes on their backs, their wagon and horse team, and half of a wheatfield.

"Nothing. There is nothing," he murmured brokenly. Even the plow had been damaged by the fire. In the center of the burned-out shell, there was the charred metal of a broken lantern.

"It vas the vill of God," another offered.

"No God did this," Franz Kreuger declared. "Do you think this fire just happened? Someone started it."

"Vhy do you say this?" Stefan frowned.

"Because it is true." But Franz didn't offer any proof. "They threatened us. Now they burn our homes."

"You think the ranchers did this?" the owner questioned in disbelief. "But they came. They helped put the fire out."

"So it would not burn their land, only your house and your wheat," Franz pointed out. "They are probably sorry only that your entire field did not burn."

239

"We must tell the sheriff," Stefan proposed as the next logical step. The others nodded agreement.

"All of us, we will go tell him together," Franz stated, but the dark cynicism in his gleaming eyes showed his skepticism that it would do any good. In his experience, the little man only got help from others of like circumstance. "Tomorrow we will all come to help build a new house for you."

"I cannot come." Stefan spoke in silent apology. "I must look after my vife."

The homesteader Sokoloff nodded his understanding and offered, "I regret she was hurt."

"We are lucky no one else was." Franz Kreuger gave them all a look that seemed to warn that one of them might be next. He had believed in the plottings of the powerful too long not to see it here.

Assured that the danger was over, there was a general milling toward the wagons and buggies as smoky, soot-blackened families made tired motions to depart. Three drylanders had volunteered to stay on the place and keep watch through the night to be sure no fire flared to life. A half-dozen cowboys had ridden out to catch up the loose horses. Nate came back, leading Webb's black gelding and two others.

"We never did get to see them fireworks they were gonna have in town." There was a dry, dancing gleam in his eye as he passed the reins to Webb.

"I think most of us have had all the excitement we want for this Fourth of July," Webb responded with a twisted smile and swung onto his horse. The purpling sky made indistinct silhouettes of tired figures straggling to wagons a short distance away. Only those close by were distinguishable. And Webb recognized Stefan Reisner carrying a blanket-wrapped figure to his wagon.

"Here come Shorty and Abe," Nate announced, pulling on the reins to back his horse and join the pair. "You comin'?"

"In a minute." Webb threw an absent glance at his friend and kneed his horse forward. When he reached the Reisner wagon, the whiskered man was in the seat, with Lilli huddled against his side. Webb strained to get a closer look at her in the fading light. She was conscious, but there was an unseeing quality about her eyes. "Is she all right?"

"She vill be fine." The man steadily returned his look with a kind of challenge. "I vill take care of her."

Webb's mouth thinned out as he set the gelding on its haunches and pivoted it away from the wagon. As he rode over to rejoin Nate and the others, he looked back once. There was a hard knot in the pit of his stomach at the sight of a slim silhouette resting its head on the stooped shoulders of a second.

In a dull lethargy, Lilli watched Stefan as he approached the bed, carrying a small bowl of gruel and a spoon. At the last minute, she roused herself sufficiently to push into a sitting position. Stefan paused and pulled one of the new chairs he'd built closer to the bed, then sat down. Her blank eyes watched him dip the spoon into the bowl, but it was halfway to her mouth before she summoned a protest.

"I can feed myself, Stefan," she said in a lifeless voice and lifted a limp hand to take the spoon from him.

"But this vay I know you vill eat everything." He ignored her attempt and carried the spoonful of gruel to her lips.

It was bland and tasteless going down. Stefan was not the best of cooks, but he had fixed all the meals for the last two days. Lilli experienced a twinge of guilt at the way he had waited on her, not letting her lift a hand to do anything for herself. Physically there wasn't anything wrong with her. The one or two little burns on her legs certainly didn't incapacitate her. Yet she had been languishing in this bed ever since Stefan had brought her home that night, rarely talking, just lying there as if she were in some kind of trance. Through it all, Stefan had been kindness itself.

"Most husbands would be complaining because they were doing all the cooking and the housework." She looked at Stefan. "You haven't said a word."

"Vhat is two days?" he reasoned with a gentle smile. "You do these things for me all the time. Now, for you, I do it." He dipped the spoon again into the gruel. "Until you are better," he added.

He hadn't even asked what was wrong, Lilli realized and studied him again with marveling confusion. "It was the fire." She felt he deserved an explanation.

"I know," he said and pushed the tip of the spoon to her mouth. "Eat."

A frown knitted little lines in her forehead as she obediently swallowed the smooth mixture. "I don't mean the grass fire. It was just a part of it. It was the tenement next door burning when I was little."

"You don't need to speak of it," Stefan assured her.

"I . . . think I want to." It was a gradual realization, unsure what purpose it would serve. "The other night, I was wetting blankets and taking them to the men fighting the fire. I started to give someone the blanket I had in my hand when I saw those yellow flames suddenly leap up." She looked sightlessly beyond Stefan, reliving the experience that had trapped her in a childhood nightmare. "The fire started coming closer, but I couldn't move. I had to stay there like those people in the burning building. Then my skirt caught on fire and I was one of them." Her chest tightened, the muscles contracting and not letting in any air. "And the smoke. I can still smell the smoke."

"It's over. You are here — and unharmed," he said firmly.

Her lungs relaxed, expelling a sigh of mixed relief. "Yes." A wan smile curved her mouth. "And behaving like a female ninny over it."

"It vas a frightening thing for you." Stefan indicated that he didn't regard her reaction to the incident as abnormal.

"I feel sorry for the Sokoloffs, losing everything they had." She found she could think about someone other than herself. Maybe this dullness that had insulated her against feeling anything was finally wearing off. "It was a terrible thing to happen."

"Terrible, yes." Stefan nodded with grim insistence. "Ve are convinced the fire vas deliberately started. Ve have told the sheriff our suspicions."

"Someone burned their home on purpose?" Lilli frowned at this statement. "But who would do that?"

"Kreuger says one of the ranchers sent his men to do it after he made sure all of us vere in town. It vas da perfect opportunity."

"But why Mr. Sokoloff's house? What had he done?" She found it unbelievable that he would be singled out without reason.

"It vas a varning for all of us. Sokoloff's place vas close to town, so all of us vould see it."

"Did Kreuger say who he thought was behind it?" The minute she asked the question, Lilli realized how insidious the man was. Like Stefan, she was beginning to accept anything Kreuger said, whether or not he could support it with fact.

"He says Calder vould think he is big enough to get avay vith such a thing. And his son left after he danced vith you." Stefan seemed to watch her closely, and Lilli was careful not to appear to be avoiding his gaze. "Maybe he vas not the first one there. Maybe he vas there already."

She knew better, but she kept the knowledge to herself. "What does the sheriff say?"

"It happened outside of town. He says there

245

is nothing he can do." There was a harshness in his voice, reminiscent of Franz Kreuger, that implied the response was what they should have expected. "The sheriff can protect us only vhen ve are in town. Ve must protect ourselves and our property. The next time ve go to town, Franz is going to come, too, and help me buy a gun."

Stefan. Kind, gentle Stefan with a gun. It was so absurd Lilli wanted to laugh, but she couldn't because she knew he meant to do it. What really frightened her was the thought he might use it. She wished she could wear blinders like a horse and not see or know any of this.

"Come. You must eat some more." He offered her another spoonful.

She wondered if her suddenly nauseated stomach would tolerate another swallow of the bland gruel. "Stefan, please, you don't have to treat me like an invalid anymore. I'm capable of feeding myself." With new forcefulness, she reached for the bowl and the spoon. "You have spent so much time looking after me that you must have gotten behind in your work." When he hesitated, Lilli added, "I promise I'll eat every last bite."

"All right." He finally smiled and relinquished his possession of the bowl and spoon.

"I vill let you chase me back to vork."

After he'd left the one-room shack, she let the bowl rest on her lap and stared at the wide patch of sunlight on the floor. Gleaming dust particles danced in the light spilling through the window.

It was July and she felt cold. There were changes going on inside herself that she didn't want to happen. Even Stefan was becoming different. She pressed her fingers to her lips, feeling them. A man had kissed her, and she hadn't told her husband. She hadn't told Stefan she was alone with Webb Calder, even though he was being falsely accused of starting the fire. Why? Because his kiss had made her feel things that were wrong.

During those terrifying moments at the fire, it was his voice, his arms, the feel of his body pressing on hers, that kept her link with sanity. By not mentioning it, she had let Stefan believe it had been his strength and comfort she had relied on. She had vowed to be a good wife to him. She had to keep that vow.

Webb's spurs made a dull clanking sound with each striding step as he crossed the hardwood floor of the entryway to the den. His father was seated behind the big desk, going over the ledgers. Webb removed his hat and combed his fingers through his hair as he approached the desk.

"Barnie said you wanted to see me." He kept his hat at his side, tapping it slightly against his leg in a small show of impatience at the summons.

"Yes, I did." The big chair groaned as his father leaned his weight against the back and ran a calm eye over Webb. "I've decided that I'm not going out on the roundup this fall. I want you to take my place and supervise the operation for me."

"Barnie is more qualified than I am. Why don't you ask him or Ely?" Webb stiffened at this sudden thrusting of authority onto his shoulders.

There was a moment of absolute silence. Benteen glared at Webb with open irritation, but appeared to make an attempt to control his anger. "If I wanted Barnie or Ely, I would have asked them to take charge of it. Dammit, I want my son heading the roundup," he declared roughly.

"Is that an order?" Webb asked.

The corners of Benteen's mouth turned down, forming a hard, grim line. "No." His father dropped his gaze from Webb. "It isn't an order." There was a stubborn streak in him that wanted Webb to accept the responsibility without being ordered to do it. "That's all I wanted. You can leave."

As Webb started to put on his hat, he noticed his father press a hand to his chest and hold it there. He paused, his eyes sharpening in concern. "Are you all right?"

"I'm fine." It was an irritable retort, but the hand was slow to come away. "My chest has been bothering me since the fire," his father offered in grudging explanation. "I guess I got too much smoke in my lungs. It just hurts now and then, but it goes away."

Webb gripped and ungripped at his hat. He was of half a mind to tell his father he'd changed his mind about taking over the round-up. The Old Man did look tired. He'd probably rest easier if he thought Webb was in charge. Webb also knew that Barnie and Ely both would be shadowing him to make certain he didn't make any mistakes. That was the irritating factor about accepting, knowing the two men would be supervising him. They were just "letting" him be in charge.

"The word is going around that the fire was started deliberately," his father mentioned in passing.

"Where'd you hear that?" Webb frowned.

"Somebody picked it up in town." He shrugged to indicate an indefinite source. "I wouldn't be surprised if it was true."

"What makes you say that?" His eyes narrowed.

"There's a lot of cowboys out of work, and a lot of hard feelings between them and the drylanders. It sounds like the kind of cruel prank a cowboy might pull after he's had a couple drinks."

The remark prompted Webb to recall something that hadn't seemed significant before. "Hobie Evans and two Snake M boys left the dance early. It was less than an hour after that the smoke was seen."

"Hobie's got a streak of mean in him." He paused to look at Webb. "Every man does. It's just a question of how wide it is. You might want to keep that in mind."

"Why?" He found that curious advice.

"So you don't underestimate someday what the opposition's capable of doing," his father replied and turned his attention to the opened ledger on his desk.

It seemed a cryptic warning. Webb pushed it to the back of his mind where it lingered as he left the big house to resume his day's work.

12

Stones clattered under the iron-clad hooves of the black gelding inching its way along the coulee where it fell at a fairly steep angle. When the ground leveled out and the footing became more solid, it picked up its pace without any urging from its rider, Webb Calder. It stopped automatically when it reached the young cottonwood tree and the concealing shade of its branches. Black ears swiveled back to the rider, waiting for further instructions.

The Reisner farm was about a mile away at this point, its shanty-house clearly visible. Webb had come upon this hidden approach to the farm about three weeks ago and used it about four times since then. Twice he'd seen Lilli working in the garden beside the house, but neither time had he left the concealment of the cottonwood. Reisner had been in the fields nearby. At least, Webb had been assured that Lilli was all right, although he didn't kid himself that it was the only reason he came.

As he scanned the fields and the area around the tar-paper house, he saw no sign of Reisner. The horses and wagon were gone, too. Smoke was coming out of the stovepipe chimney, which indicated someone was home. He looked over the fields again; then he walked the gelding out from under the tree and crossed the intervening land at an easy lope.

Coming up to the one-room shanty, he slowed the horse to a walk and made a close-up note of the changes since the last time he'd been there. A couple of chickens were scratching up dust under the feed trough in the corral. There was a handpump sitting atop a cistern cover, and a scraggly but determined patch of flowers growing alongside of the house. The air was laden with the yeasty aroma of baking bread, which assured him the lady of the house was at home.

Unhurried, he stepped down from his horse and let the reins trail to ground-tether his mount. The door was propped open, a kind of silent invitation which he readily accepted. Webb paused at the threshold and let his gaze travel over the slim figure of a woman standing at the table with her back to the door. She was vigorously kneading a batch of dough, apparently unaware of his presence. Wisps of hair had escaped from the bun and lay against her neck. The trace of burnt copper was absent from the dark shade of her hair without the bright sunlight to expose it.

Taking off his hat, he ran a hand through his hair, then rapped his knuckles lightly against the door frame. "Anybody home?" His voice was warm and certain of the answer to his question. It was the same in his eyes as he watched the quick turn of her head and the darted glance over her shoulder. There was only the briefest pause in her bread-kneading before she resumed her former rhythm.

"If it's water you're wanting for your horse, you're welcome to draw from the pump," she said.

It pleased him that she remembered the reason he'd given for stopping the last time. "That isn't why I came by." The dull clank of his spurs signaled he was crossing the threshold.

"What is it you wanted, Mr. Calder?" she asked without turning.

He crossed to the table, his glance skimming the interior with its newspaper walls and homemade furnishings. Her dark head was bent to her task, and she didn't raise it when he stopped at the narrow end of the table. The front of her apron was spattered with flour dust and there was a little white smear by her cheekbone.

"We'll be busy with fall roundup at the ranch for the next few weeks and I wanted to check and be sure you had recovered from your burns," Webb offered as his reason.

"That's kind of you, Mr. Calder, but they were really very minor. They healed within days and never left a scar," she assured him and continued pounding and pummeling the dough.

The room's lights and shadows and warm smells took on a strange familiarity. Webb ranged about the table, a sense of comfort and home sweeping over him.

"When I was a little boy, we lived in a log cabin about this size," he mused. "Standing here, it doesn't seem so long ago. I guess this place reminds me of it a little."

"Stefan will be interested to know that you found something nice to say about our home." She shaped the dough into a loaf and slapped it into a pan, pushing it out to touch both ends.

There was a slight narrowing of his gaze at the determined reference to her husband. When she finally lifted her head so he could see her face plainly, it was as if she were wearing a mask. Webb chose to ignore her reply.

"I had forgotten that making bread was such

rough work." He smiled. "I'd be black and blue if I was pounded like that."

"You've got to get the air out, otherwise the bread will be full of holes," she stated and picked up the pan. To avoid passing him, she went the long way around the table to reach the stove and opened the oven door. He watched her crouch down to slip in the pan and test the other bread baking inside.

"It smells good," he remarked.

Closing the oven door, she straightened and nervously smoothed her hands down her apron. He noticed that she was deliberately avoiding looking at him.

"I never did thank you, Mr. Calder, for putting out the fire before I was more seriously burned," she began, saying the words as if she had been mentally practicing them for some time. "I am very grateful. I wish for you to know that."

"You don't have to thank me." Webb tipped his head at an angle, trying to figure out why she was so aloof with him when she'd always been so open before. "I'm just glad I was there."

She dropped her chin again and looked about her as if searching for something. "It was very good of you to drop by and ask after me." She moistened her lips and made an effort to look directly at him. For a few seconds, she was very poised. "I hope you'll understand that I'm very busy with the baking and all, so I can't ask you to stay."

It was a roundabout way of asking him to leave, but Webb didn't believe she meant it. He crossed the short space between them to stand in front of her. There was a hint of agitation in the rise and fall of her breasts.

"You've got some flour on your cheek, Lilli." He reached to wipe it off, but she turned her head away from his hand and brushed at it herself.

"It's true that in the past I might have given you cause to believe you have my permission to speak to me in such a familiar way, Mr. Calder," she said stiffly. "But from now on, I would prefer that you address me properly as Mrs. Reisner if we should meet in the future."

His brows were pulled together in a puzzled and doubting frown. "Lilli —"

"You knew my husband wasn't here when you rode in, didn't you?" she accused suddenly, a wounded and angry look flaring in her eyes.

"I . . . noticed the horses and wagon were gone," he admitted.

"The truth is Mr. Calder, you stopped because he wasn't here." She controlled her voice, taking all the sting out of it and making it hard with reason. Its very smoothness made the words penetrate and twist deeper inside him. "You deliberately came while I was alone. I am a married woman, Mr. Calder, and I do not entertain men visitors when my husband isn't home. It is improper of you to expect that I should. Therefore, I must request that you leave, here and now." But she wasn't through. "And the next time you ride by and my husband isn't about, don't stop. Because if you do, I shall bar the door and refuse you any hospitality."

In good conscience, Webb couldn't argue with her. His position was indefensible, which made it all the harder to take. He was sore with an anger that was unjustified. She was within her rights to order him to leave.

"Why don't you want me here, Lilli?" He deliberately used his nickname for her, challenging her reason for not wanting to see him. "Do I remind you too much that your husband is an old man?"

A raw anger blazed unchecked in her eyes. A split second later, she was swinging a hand at his face, and Webb made no attempt to avoid it, knowing he deserved it for the remark he had made. But it was no weak slap in the face. All her force was behind it and her hand packed power when it struck. It jarred him, sending black shafts of pain through his head, and unleashed what little control he had left.

In instinctive retaliation, Webb grabbed the wrist of the hand that had struck him. The first slap he had deserved, but he wouldn't stand still for a second. After one attempt to twist out of his grip, she simply glared at him, her wrist straining against his hold. Webb could feel the angry tremors vibrating up through her arm. She knew she had no chance to best him in a physical struggle.

"Let me go or I will scream," she threatened in a low, taut voice.

The line of his mouth slanted in a hard smile. "That's what you said at the dance, but you didn't do it then, either."

He reached for her waist, determined to prove he was right in thinking she wanted him here as much as he wanted to be here. He needed the confirmation in order to justify his own conduct. Her wild resistance was easily contained as his arms banded around her to trap her against his body.

With the roundness of her breasts hard against his chest and slim curves of her hips fitted to his loins, it ceased to matter that she carried another man's name. It was a bitter thing to learn that, even sober, he had no conscience — no remorse at taking what belonged to another man.

Her lips tried to rebuff the possession of his mouth, but he persisted in his claim. He could feel the stiffness ebbing from her body and felt the swell of victory course through his blood. He eased the pressure of his hold and she stayed molded to him. This was his proof, undeniable evidence that he wasn't wrong in believing she had wanted this.

When she slowly dragged her lips from his, Webb didn't try to prevent it. Through eyes three-quarters lidded, he saw the yearning ache in her expression before she turned her head away from him and lowered her chin.

"Are you satisfied now, Mr. Calder?" The tortured sound in her voice cut him to the quick. All sense of elation was washed away as a tear was squeezed from her lashes. "Or have I not been sufficiently humiliated?"

"Lilli —" He wanted to tell her this wasn't wrong, but it was and they both knew it. A raw, twisting frustration strangled any false assurance he might have given.

When she turned out of his arms, Webb was powerless to stop her. She walked to the open door, her head bowed as if unable to look at him, but there was something proud about her, too. And it was this he saw.

"Please go now," she murmured in a voice

that was almost emotionless. "And don't come back."

His mouth was grimly closed, a muscle flexing convulsively along his jaw. Webb was riddled with self-loathing as he picked up the hat he'd dropped and crossed to the door. His gaze slid off her face with its pale, composed lines. He'd never felt so low and contemptible in all his life as he did when he walked out that door to his horse.

He didn't need to look to know Lilli was standing in the doorway. Some sixth sense had already relayed the knowledge. Grabbing the trailing reins to the bridle, Webb looped them over the black's neck and hopped a foot into the stirrup, swinging into the saddle all in one motion. For a split second, Webb faced her. It seemed the die had been cast and his course set since the day he'd met her at the train station, only he hadn't known it then. It was inevitable — just as it was inevitable that he had to ride away. There wasn't anything lower than a wife-stealing man, and he'd sunk just about to the depths. He didn't have much respect for himself, so she couldn't have a very high opinion of him, either.

With a slight turn of his hand, Webb neck-reined the gelding away from the opened door and Lilli. As he was about to touch a spur to his horse, he heard the drum of cantering hooves and looked up to see three riders crossing the fallow ground to approach the homestead. All his senses came to a wary alert when he recognized Hobie Evans riding at the head. He lowered both hands to rest on the saddlehorn, not leaving until he found out what kind of business had brought Hobie Evans and two Snake M riders here.

As the three riders neared the shack, they slowed their horses to a snorting, head-tossing walk. There was a wide and wondering smile on Hobie's expression, an interested and calculating gleam in his eye, as he advanced toward Webb.

"I sure never expected to run into you here, Webb," he declared and ran an inspecting look over him. "What brings you this far off Triple C range?"

"I was about to ask you a similar question," Webb returned smoothly, his gaze narrowing. He didn't particularly like that knowing light in the man's eyes or that laughing grin that was just an inch away from mockery.

"Were you, now?" Hobie glanced at his two accompanying riders. "Ain't that interesting, boys?" Then he appeared to notice Lilli standing in the open doorway of the shack and removed his hat, holding it against his shoulder in a gesture of respect that didn't ring true. "Well, howdy, ma'am." He made an exaggerated show of sniffing the air. "That bread you're baking sure does smell good." She inclined her head in a brief and cautious acknowledgment, but remained silent. "Is your man home?" Hobie asked, yet seemed to know the answer.

Lilli flashed a short glance at Webb, her blue eyes clouded with apprehension, but her answer was simple and truthful. "No."

Hobie urged his horse forward until he was alongside Webb, facing him almost knee to knee. The hat went back on his head, but it didn't shade the glitter shining in his eyes. "What's that white stuff all over your shirt, Webb?" he challenged mockingly. Webb's muscles went all tense. "Damned if it doesn't look like flour." Hobie declared and eyed him with a knowing gleam. "I guess you been helping her make bread, huh?"

Webb's hand curled around the saddlehorn. He didn't look to confirm the observation that his shirt had flour smears from Lilli's apron. He wanted to jam his fist down Hobie's throat and blacken those damning eyes that saw too much.

"State your business, Hobie." He ground out the order through his gritted teeth.

"You speak like you're standing on your pa's land, but you got no rights here, Calder." Hobie reminded him, and took pleasure from it.

"I'm telling you to say what you came for," Webb warned, ready to back it up if he had to.

"Now, Webb, there ain't no call for you to get your back up." Hobie laughed in unconcern and pushed his hat to the back of his head. His horse did a little reversing sidestep that put distance between his rider and Webb Calder and brought the auburn-haired girl into Hobie's view. "An unfortunate thing happened over at the Snake M Ranch last night, ma'am. It seems something spooked some of our cattle and they stampeded, tearing down a section of fence. After that, they just scattered to the winds. A bunch of us boys are out looking for them right now. If you see any strays wandering around your place with a Snake M brand, we'd be obliged if you'd point them toward home. Sure would hate to see any of 'em get in your wheatfield."

"I'll tell my husband to keep an eye out for your cattle," Lilli said.

"You do that, ma'am." He nodded, still smiling; then his glance cut to Webb. "See ya 'round, Calder."

"I was just leaving myself, Hobie. I'll ride

with you a ways," Webb stated and eased his hands off the saddlehorn to put his horse in motion.

As they left the house yard, Webb rode on the outside next to Hobie Evans. They followed the tracks made by wagon wheels, dividing the fallow land from the field of ripening wheat. There was nothing Webb could say, no denial he dared make in defense of Lilli's reputation. He had not intended to do her harm, but he had — irreparably.

"Webb, why do I get the feeling you're escorting us off this land?" Hobie asked with an amused sidelong look.

"Couldn't say," he replied stiffly, then turned a slow, leveling glance at the lantern-jawed cowboy. "Maybe you've got a guilty conscience."

"I don't know what I'd be guilty of." Hobie laughed shortly. For several long minutes, the silence was broken only by the shuffle of trotting hooves and the creaking groan of saddle leather. "She wasn't a bad-lookin' woman, for a squatter."

Webb pulled in his horse, a white-hot anger threatening to erupt, as Hobie stopped, feigning surprise. "I wouldn't say any more, Hobie," he warned thickly.

"Hey, Webb, come on." Hobie gestured with

an upraised palm to indicate there was nothing to be upset about, and all the while, his eyes mocked. "A young thing like that probably gets lonely. It ain't nothin' to me if you wanta cheer her up now and then. I might be tempted myself."

"I'm going to tell you this — and I'm only going to tell you this once." His teeth were bared and the blackness in his eyes wasn't to be ignored. "If anything happens here — if any cow strays into that wheatfield, or any fire accidentally starts — if there is so much as a hand raised against . . . these folks, even in so-called fun, I'll take it personally. Do I make myself clear?"

"Clear as rainwater." The amusement had left Hobie's eyes, leaving them cold and brooding.

"Good. Because if anything happens, I'll come looking for you." Webb kept the restraining pressure on the bit. "I'll leave you here."

Hobie swept him with a sizing look, then reined in his horse in a slow semicircle to join the two riders waiting for him. Webb stayed where he was, watching them ride on until they began to grow small with the widening distance; then he turned his horse to cut across to the Triple C fenceline.

After they'd traveled another mile, Hobie Evans allowed his horse to drop out of the trot into a long-striding walk. The mounts of the two other riders matched the slower pace. Ace Rafferty sent an anxious look at Hobie.

"How do you s'pose Calder figured out we started that fire?" he asked.

"He didn't," Hobie stated. "It was just a shot in the dark. Nobody saw us."

"Maybe they found the broken lantern," Ace suggested.

"So?" Hobie challenged. "It was the farmer's lantern. Who's to say it didn't fall and break during the fire?" His gaze made continuous sweeps of the deceptively flat-looking land, a restless and driven quality about his eyes.

The third rider, Bob Sheephead, a half-breed, drifted his horse closer to the other two. "Ain't that gal the one that's married to that old fella with the gray whiskers? The one that's always hanging around with that Roosky?"

"Yeah, I guess that's where I saw her," Hobie agreed without interest in the identity of either of them. They were honyockers, and in his prejudiced mind, that put them in a considerably lower order of life.

"No wonder Calder was prancin' around her like some range stud." The breed smiled. "I'll bet she's more than just lonely. Maybe we should pay a friendly call on her sometime."

"You're crazy." Ace eyed him with a dubious look. "Sometimes I think you're more than half Indian. You heard what Calder told Hobie."

"I'm shakin' in my boots." Bob Sheephead grinned. "Ain't you, Hobie?"

"Yeah," he agreed with a dry, smiling look. "I'm quivering."

"You boys do what you like," Ace declared firmly. "But I ain't aimin' to cross a Calder."

Hobie stood up in his stirrups, looking off to the left. "Would ya look at there?" he murmured. "That's a bunch of Snake cattle, isn't it? They're grazin' awful close to that drylander's wheatfield. It'd be a shame if they got into it."

"It sure would," Bob Sheephead agreed with a widening grin. "We'd better hurry on down there and stop them."

"Yeah, we'd better." Hobie nodded.

The breed let out a whoop and all three riders dug into their spurs to send their horses charging to the left. The cattle spooked and took off running, straight into the tall stand of heavy-headed wheat. The cowboys gave chase with deliberate ineptitude and stampeded the cattle all over the field. The churning, pounding hooves, both cloven and shod, trampled down the wheat stalks, ruining wide swaths of the grain. Every time a cow veered off to escape to the range country, a rider raced alongside to turn it back into the field, damaging more wheat.

The frantic homesteader came running through the field, waving his arms to stop the destruction of his crop. Neither the cattle nor the riders paid any attention to him. In desperation, he grabbed at the bridle on the shaggy buckskin Hobie Evans was riding, violating range etiquette that forbids any interference in a rider's control of his mount. The buckskin reared, lifting the man off his feet and nearly unseating his rider. But the homesteader hung on.

"You must stop!" he insisted. "You're trampling my wheat."

"Let go of my horse, you damned honyocker!" Hobie whipped at him with his rope loop and laid a track across the man's eyes. With a pained cry, the homesteader let go and the plunging buckskin shouldered him to the ground. Hobie indifferently watched the squirming man blindly trying to avoid the horse's sharp hooves, and didn't try to rein his horse away from the man. "Can't you see we're trying to round up these strays?" Hobie declared in derisive scorn. "We tried to head 'em off before they got into your wheat. You just stay out of the way, nester. We know what we're doin'."

With a silent laugh at the drylander's stupidity, Hobie took off again after a turning cow. This time, he shook out his loop and sailed it around the animal's neck. He threw out plenty of slack as he set the buckskin to throw its weight in opposition to the rope. The cow was flipped on its back and dragged a half-dozen yards over more wheat before its flailing legs found footing so it could begin fighting and bucking the strangling loop around its neck.

When the three riders finally tired of their fun and herded the small but destructive bunch of cattle out of the wheatfield, there wasn't much left standing. The homesteader looked about him, his crop virtually left ruined. So little of it was salvageable. There was a stark, broken look in his expression as he stumbled toward his family waiting by their sod home. Blood trickled from the ropecut that had nearly blinded him.

Word of the disaster spread through the homesteaders like wildfire. The following day, more than a dozen converged on the stricken homestead to see the extent of the damage for themselves and offer what aid they could.

From the group present, Stefan Reisner was among the contingent of four selected to go to the Snake M Ranch owned by Ed Mace and demand reparation. Franz Kreuger was unanimously chosen spokesman for the group. They all piled into one wagon and headed for the ranch.

Since Snake M planned to send its outfit out on roundup the following day, nearly all its riders except those at line camps were at the ranch's headquarters checking gear and equipment and selecting the remuda string when the wagonload of drylanders rolled in. It headed straight for the five-room log house. Ed Mace was on the porch to meet them before they got out of the wagon.

All the hands had noted the arrival and were dawdling at their various chores while keeping an eye on the group of drylanders talking to their boss at the main house. The half-breed Bob Sheephead sauntered over to where Hobie Evans was repairing a weak cinch strap. He squatted down beside him and turned a piece of rotting leather from a bridle over in his hand, as if it were the object of interest.

"What do ya s'pose they want here?" the crow-haired cowboy asked Hobie. "Reckon they come cryin' about their wheat?"

"I reckon." Hobie pulled on the cinch to test

its strength and shot a glance through the tops of his lashes at the ranch house. "Looks like we're gonna find out."

Ed Mace was striding toward the barn area where most of the riders were idling. The four homesteaders in their odd-looking farmers' garb followed in his wake. Hobie noticed the dislike in his boss's expression when he glanced impatiently over his shoulder at the trailing drylanders, and smiled to himself.

"Listen up, all of you." Ed Mace called for the attention of his men while the drylanders made a short arc behind him. "These . . . gentlemen" — he deliberately hesitated over the polite term — "have come to inform me that some of the cattle that strayed off our range the other day got into one of their wheat-fields. They also claim that three of you chased the cattle around that field, doing even more damage."

Dropping the cinch strap, Hobie Evans rolled to his feet and pushed his way to the front of the riders. "I think, boss, that they're talkin' about me an' Ace an' the breed. We rounded up a bunch of cattle that got into somebody's wheatfield."

"He's the one." The owner of the wheatfield confirmed it and pressed a hand to the gash along his cheekbone in bitter memory.

"And you're the one that came runnin' out there, flapping your arms like some damned crow." Hobie flung a pointing arm back at the man, then looked at his boss. "We could have gotten those cattle out of there with hardly any damage to the wheat at all if he hadn't interfered. You know what those range cows are like. They're wilder than a jackrabbit. He comes out there and waves his arms, and they took off in all directions."

"He struck me with a rope and tried to run me down with his horse," the owner charged.

"You jumped in front of my horse," Hobie countered. "If I hadn't slapped you out of the way with my rope, he'd have trampled you."

"That is a lie." Franz Kreuger stepped up. "But we did not come here because Otto was struck. We are here because your cattle damaged a wheatfield. Your own men have confirmed it. We demand that you pay for the wheat your animals destroyed."

"It seems to me that my cattle wouldn't have laid waste to so much wheat if it hadn't been for the actions of this . . . gentleman." He indicated the owner with a derisive flick of his hand. "He claims he lost his entire crop. I'm willing to settle damages with him, but I won't pay for the whole field." He named a figure well below what the group had petitioned to receive.

"But I spent more than that for the seed," the homesteader protested and turned to the other three for support.

"It is not enough!" Franz Kreuger asserted angrily. "It is not fair."

"That's my offer." Ed Mace challenged them without wavering. "If you don't like it, take your case to the judge and *wait* for him to set a trial date — and *wait* for the verdict." He stressed the verb to indicate the time that would pass. "That's your choice. Either *wait* and see if the judge agrees, or take my settlement — in cash, right now."

The homesteader looked to Franz Kreuger for guidance, as did the other two, including Stefan. Franz eyed his opponent with a cold, measuring look.

"This judge, do you know him?" he demanded.

A smile broke across Ed Mace's expression. "Judge Paulson? Why, we grew up together."

Franz Kreuger breathed in hard and turned to the homesteader. "Take his offer. If he doesn't give it to you, he will use it to buy the judge."

13

The morning side of the roundup was spent combing the coulees and hollows for cattle. The cowboys fanned to the far corners of a given section of range and drifted any cattle they found toward the center in an ever-tightening circle for the afternoon sorting and occasional branding of any beasts they'd missed in the spring gather.

The air was crisp and clear, with a little bite to it, as if warning of winter's advent and attempting to hurry riders about their chores. Webb hazed his last bunch of cows toward the bellowing herd, composed mostly of Hereford cattle and crossbreds, milling under a dust pall. A quarter-mile from the noon holding ground, an antisocial cow decided to quit the bunch.

As it bolted for open country, the weary but game bay horse under him made a lightning pivot to give chase and turn it back. But it stumbled on the second stride, nearly unseating Webb, and pulled up lame, favoring its right front leg. With no chance of turning the animal now, Webb figured the tail-high cow was waving good-bye to him.

Out of the corner of his eye, he caught a flash of gray and focused on it. A big, iron-gray horse was flattened out in a run to intercept the cow before it reached freedom. Its rider was none other than his father. As Webb dismounted his lame horse, he watched the rider first check the animal's flight, then block any attempt to proceed until the cow finally gave up and turned to join the herd. There was a lot of cow-savvy evident in the work of both horse and rider, but Webb didn't remark on it when his father rode over. A man did his job, and if he was good, people noticed. If he wasn't, they noticed that, too.

When his father stepped down, Webb was running an inspecting hand down the bay's right foreleg. "How is it?" the senior Calder asked.

"Looks like a strained tendon." Webb straightened to pat the horse's neck, already covered in a shaggy winter coat. His father didn't attempt to verify the diagnosis with his own examination. A rider didn't question another man's judgment about his horse. Webb glanced toward the herd and the two riders that had come out to haze his bunch in with the others. "I don't remember when I saw the cattle in better shape."

"And they wouldn't bring half of what they're worth at market," his father replied grimly. "I told Barnie to keep back all but the culls and the old stock. We've got more hay this year for winter feed, so we should be able to carry them through till spring. Maybe the prices will be up by then."

"Sooner or later, the market's bound to turn." Webb understood the gamble his father was taking, holding that many cattle through the winter.

"Don't count on it coming soon," his father warned on a heavy note. "Bull Giles wrote that next year doesn't look any better than this one. He said there'd probably be a short rise in cattle prices next spring, but not to expect it to hold."

There was something else troubling his father. Webb sensed there was a reason behind this information. It was leading to something, but he couldn't put his finger on just what.

"What do you figure — about another week before the roundup's finished?" his father asked with a sideways look.

"Give or take a day." Webb nodded his agreement with that timetable. They'd been more than five weeks out now, and the long hours were beginning to show on the men and horses.

"There's a bunch of the hands I'm going to have to let go — just through the winter, I hope," his father stated. "I can keep the married ones with families on the payroll, but the others —" He shook his head.

Webb frowned. He'd known the situation wasn't good, but he hadn't realized the ranch was in such severe straits that they'd be letting go some of their permanent hands. "Nate? Abe?"

"All of them are welcome to stay on the ranch, sleep in the bunkhouse, and eat in the cookshack, but I can't pay them wages." Benteen Calder didn't single Webb's two bunkmates out, but he included them by implication.

"We're going to be carrying all these extra steers through the winter — with fewer men?" Webb couldn't believe his father intended to take that gamble.

"I don't have a choice" was the short reply.

There was a moment when Webb couldn't respond. He looked across this land that stretched a man's eyes with its limitless reaches. It was raw and wild, a witness to many changes. Webb saw more on the horizon.

"Maybe it's time to take another look at operations of the ranch," Webb suggested with a certain grim reluctance.

"What do you mean?" Benteen eyed him with narrowed interest.

"I mean the ranch is solely dependent on cattle. Maybe it's time to diversify into other things." He moved to the near side of the bay horse and flipped the stirrup over the saddle seat to loosen the cinch.

"Into what? Sheep? The wool market is as depressed as the cattle market is," his father pronounced. "Between Australia and Europe, they've glutted the market."

"I wasn't thinking about sheep," Webb replied, knowing his suggestion would be regarded as akin to blasphemy by his father. "The big money is in grain."

"Wheat?" The word came out in a low shock of anger.

"They're growing wheat all around us," Webb reasoned firmly. "We're already part granger now with all the hay we cut and stack. There's no reason we can't expand the farming side into wheat. It isn't the lack of land that would prevent it."

The angry pain of disillusionment was in his father's eyes when Webb finally looked at him. "I thought you had some intelligence, but you are as stupid as those drylanders."

"You mean the ones that are harvesting wheat?" Webb bristled.

"You think I'm gambling because I'm holding over so many cattle. But those drylanders are gambling with *land*. What happens when they lose?"

"Maybe they won't lose." Webb had seen some of the great shocks of wheat standing in the fields adjoining Triple C range while making the roundup.

"They'll lose, all right," his father stated in a voice that held no doubt. "This plains country has alternating cycles of wet and dry. Lately we've been enjoying the wet years when there's been adequate rain. But the dry ones will come. They always have and they always will."

Webb had a cold sensation that wasn't caused by the nipping breeze. He studied his father with narrowed concentration, listening to the words that came from experience.

"You're probably too young to remember what it was like in the early days." Benteen gave him that much. "Do you see this grass?" He indicated the thick tangle growing tall at their feet. "I've seen it burned brown in the spring of the year, parched roots setting in ground that was dry and hard as a rock. Without the grass for covering to hold the soil, it

279

would have blown away. That's why it's so important not to overgraze it. And those drylanders are plowing up this grass. We'll have a drought again, and when we do, those homesteads of the drylanders will be a desert." He gave Webb a long, hard look. "Every time you try to make the land be what it isn't, it will turn on you and destroy you. If you don't remember that, this land won't be here for your son — if you ever have one."

The grim words seemed to echo in the air as his father turned and swung his lofty frame onto the big gray horse. He reined it away from Webb and pushed it into a canter back to the herd.

After more than a month and a half out on the range rounding up cattle, the band of Triple C riders heading for town were flush with two months' pay and ready to kick up their heels. They'd washed off the grime and sweat, shaved off the scraggly whiskers, and put on their best clothes. All but Webb and one or two others had drawn their last wages, but none of them intended to keep a tight fist on the money. The winter might be lean, but they were going to have one last fling to trade tales about while they were huddled around a heating stove on a cold Montana night.

They were riding along the dirt track that passed for the main road leading into Blue Moon. There were parallel ruts from the wheels of wagons and buggies, while hoof-prints pockmarked the ground in between. A dark object was blocking the trail ahead of them.

"What's that?" Nate eyed the black-colored obstacle in their way.

"It looks like Doyle Pettit's automobile," one of the other riders guessed. "I guess he broke down."

The possibility presented an opportunity to rag the ex-rancher turned entrepreneur that these mischief-loving cowboys just couldn't pass up. With a whoop and a shout, they spurred their horses into a gallop and descended upon the immobile automobile.

"Hey, boys!" Shorty Niles pointed to the rear tire that had been pried from the wheel with a sprung leaf and was propped against the back fender. "It looks like it threw a shoe."

Their laughter didn't faze Doyle Pettit as he examined the tube he'd extracted from the tire, trying to find the puncture. The large tool box on the running board sat open, displaying a wide array of tools.

"Go ahead and laugh, boys." Doyle grinned. "I'll have this tire patched and get to town before you will." He located the hole. "Ah, here it is." He picked up a piece of sandpaper and began rubbing it across the area.

"What are you doing way out here in that thing?" Webb leaned over his saddlehorn to watch the curious procedure.

"I went out to Big Jim Tandy's place. He's thinking about selling off some of his land, and I had a proposition to give him that will make both of us a lot of money. You won't believe the prices of land, Webb." He shook his head in bright-eyed amazement and reached for a bottle sitting in the tool box. "It's tripled since spring, I swear. Harve Wessel got itchy feet. I bought out his share of our partnership. He thinks he's moved on to greener pastures, but nothing can be greener than right here."

"What's that?" Webb nodded at the bottle.

"Benzine." Doyle identified the product. "You wash it over the area around the puncture, then coat the spot with rubber cement and apply the patch." He glanced at Webb and laughed. "I can do this in my sleep. I figure I average three flat tires on a trip between my ranch and town, so I got a lot of practice."

"I thought you had to burn gunpowder to patch one of those things," Webb said.

"That's a hot patch, and it's more complex. Takes more time than a cold patch like this."

Doyle explained in terms that showed off his knowledge. "I oughta stop out and see your pa sometime. There's a fortune to be made in land right now."

"You can talk to him." Webb straightened in the saddle and gathered up the reins to leave. "But I don't think he'll listen." He backed his horse away from the dusty black automobile. "See ya in town, Doyle, and take care or that horseless carriage of yours might buck you off."

"If you don't show up by noon, we'll send somebody back with a horse to get you," Shorty taunted as they pointed their mounts down the road.

Two miles from town, the band of riders heard the belching horn of the automobile behind them. They split into two groups, riding off the road to make way for the faster conveyance. The noisy vehicle rattled and chugged past them. Doyle risked taking one hand off the wheel, usually gripped with both at all times, and gave them a mocking wave. With his passing, the riders were engulfed in a cloud of choking dust and exhaust fumes.

When they rode into Blue Moon, the street was bulging with carriages and buckboards and the high-boxed, heavy-wheeled grain wagons. The granary had ceased to be an item of talk and was now standing at the end of the street near the railroad tracks. Just about everywhere a man looked, there were farmers and their families. The congestion forced the cowboys to hold their horses in a walk. They were strangely silent, feeling out of place in this scene, with few realizing they were an anachronism in this changed society.

From her seat on the wagon so recently converted with the installation of higher sides to haul their grain, Lilli saw Stefan come out of the granary office. There was an exuberance in his stride as he approached the wagon.

"Fifty bushels an acre," he proclaimed the success of their harvest. She summoned a smile to show her pleasure in the news, and wondered why she wasn't as excited as she should have been. It was the culmination of their dream; yet she felt curiously flat as Stefan climbed onto the wagon to sit beside her. "There is talk that Europe might go to var, and they think the price of vheat vill go even higher next year."

"That's good news." Although it didn't seem right to Lilli that they would profit from someone's else's adversity.

"Now ve go to the bank." Stefan took the reins and released the wheel brake.

"Are we going to pay off the loan?" She knew Stefan had not liked being in debt.

"No, ve are going to borrow more money and buy more land vhile it is still cheap," he declared. "And ve vill need money for more seed. Maybe even ve buy a tractor. Franz says a tractor can plow in one day vhat it vould take a team of horses to plow in two veeks. Ve could plant a lot of vheat."

Stefan had not discussed any of this with her, but it was obvious that he had talked to Franz Kreuger about it at considerable length. It was just another example of the subtle way she and Stefan had drifted apart. They weren't nearly as close as they once had been.

"I thought we were going to take the money we made on this harvest and build a real house." Lilli made a tentative attempt to remind him of their initial plans. "Will there be enough to do that, too?"

"The house can vait," he stated. "Next year, ve vill have much more money and ve can build a big house."

But there were a lot of things in between that he left unsaid. Instead of paying off their loan, they were borrowing more money, which meant that would have to be closely budgeted. There would be nothing to spare for luxuries this winter — or even some of the minor necessities.

"Vhen ve go to the store, ve must get plenty of supplies," Stefan advised. "Vinter vill come soon and it may be a long time before ve come to town again."

"Yes." But Lilli was noticing the horses wearing heavy stock saddles tied in front of the saloon. She wondered if Webb were inside. Almost guiltily, her glance darted to Stefan, and the silence between them grew longer. She couldn't decide whether she was changing or if it was Stefan, but things weren't the same between them anymore.

Shorty Niles stared incredulously at the aproned man behind the bar. "What do you mean we can't get anything to drink?" he demanded.

"We don't serve any liquor here until after three in the afternoon," the man repeated. "Now, if you want somethin' to eat, just park yourselves at one of those tables."

"I don't want anything to eat. I want a beer. Where's Sonny?" Shorty looked around for the owner.

"He's back in the kitchen cooking." The man jerked a hand over his shoulder.

"Since when did this become a restaurant?" Another Triple C hand pushed his way to the bar to add his demand for an explanation to Shorty's.

"Since the town passed an ordinance that outlaws liquor being served until after three in the afternoon," the man explained none too patiently. "Sonny didn't see any reason for the place to stand empty all day, so he started servin' food since the town don't have a restaurant."

A half-dozen tables were occupied by diners taking advantage of the roadhouse's additional service. The cowboys had been the center of their attention since they had charged into the establishment. Webb could tell they weren't exactly welcome.

"I don't care what any town ordinance says," another disgruntled cowboy declared. "Let them eat, and give me a drink."

"We got a sheriff that does care about that ordinance," the man retorted. "Now, I told you we aren't servin' drinks until after three. And if you don't like it, I just call the sheriff and let him settle this."

"Why'd they pass a damn-fool law like that?" Nate frowned.

"I guess they didn't want a bunch of likkered-up cowboys on the street molestin' decent women anymore," the man suggested in challenge.

"Tell you what," Webb inserted. "Why don't

you sell us a bottle and we'll go somewhere else."

"Yeah." There was quick agreement within the group. "We'll go see Fannie."

"Fannie ain't here no more. The doc's got his office back there now," the man informed them.

"The doc? This town got a doctor?"

"A certified belly and bones doctor, name of Bardolph."

"What happened to Fannie?" That seemed the greater concern among the men, since they preferred her cure for their ailments to any doctor's remedy.

"The sheriff presented her with a train ticket out of town," the man replied.

"I'm not findin' much to like about this sheriff," Shorty declared.

"What about the bottle?" Abe Garvey raised Webb's question again. "Is it against the law to sell that to us, too?"

"Don't remember there was any mention of that," the man acknowledged. "So I reckon I can. But you don't drink it in here," he reminded them. There was a mocking display of raised hands and solemn oaths being taken.

"Better make that two bottles," someone suggested when the man reached under the bar. "It's a long, thirsty time till three o'clock."

288

"Where are we gonna go?"

They all looked around at one another, trying to think of a good place to do a little serious drinking, until someone finally suggested, "Let's go down to the train station."

Two of the cowboys took a bottle apiece and tucked them inside their jackets. All together, they trooped out of the roadhouse turned daytime restaurant and sauntered down the sidewalk toward the depot. They tipped their hats to all the ladies they passed and paid lavish compliments to the pretty, eligible ones. The responses were always the same. The quiet ones blushed and the others giggled. And the mothers always gave the cowboys stern, disapproving looks and hurried their virginal daughters along.

At the train station, they lounged around on the platform, making use of the benches and freight crates. After lonely months of having no one to talk to but horses and cows, they made up for the silence and lack of companionship with a lot of noise and laughter. They'd barely got a good start on the second bottle when the sheriff strolled into their midst.

"Sorry, boys, but we don't allow any loitering in public places, and this is a public place. You'll have to move on," he stated.

There was a lot of grumbling and a few

choice words muttered underbreath, but they didn't argue. "Hell, I was outa tobacco anyways," Nate mumbled.

"Yeah, let's go to the store." Shorty picked up on the thought. "I been meanin' to buy me a new jacket for winter."

They set out en masse, retracing their steps and passing the saloon to go the general store. An intrepid motorist came chugging into town in another one of those horseless carriages. A homesteader fought to hold his rearing team of horses and keep them from bolting. Distracted by the commotion in the street, Webb walked right into the woman coming out of the store, jostling the packages out of her arms and scattering them on the board sidewalk. He grabbed her to keep from knocking her down as well.

"Sorry, miss, I —" He stopped abruptly as he stared into a familiar pair of blue eyes. "Lilli." Her name came out with the soft breath he released. His hands immediately became gentle on her, the pressure changing to an involuntary caress.

For a fleeting second, he saw a leaping warmth in her eyes; then her lashes came down, concealing it. "It was my fault, Mr. Calder," she murmured, and her shoulders moved slightly in silent request that his hands be removed from them. "I wasn't looking where I was going."

He let her go rather briskly, a raw frustration filling his insides. When she knelt down to pick up her scattered packages, he was driven to help her.

"Let me get these for you," he insisted.

"I can manage," she returned curtly.

"It's the least I can do after nearly knocking you over." Webb gathered up most of the packages and presented them to her. When they were once again standing, he said, "I'd offer to carry them to your wagon, but —"

The door opened and Stefan Reisner stepped outside, carrying a shiny new rifle. Dark suspicion was in his expression when he saw Webb with Lilli. He stepped immediately to her side.

"Is he bothering you Lillian?" he inquired, at least this time asking before he challenged Webb.

"No," she asserted quickly and glanced at Webb through the top of her lashes. "I dropped some of my packages and Mr. Calder was kind enough to retrieve them for me."

Webb noticed the inaccurate description of the incident, but didn't correct her. Whatever her reason for the white lie, he wasn't about to expose it.

"That's a fine-looking rifle, Mr. Reisner." He observed that the muzzle was absently pointed in his general direction. "It will come in handy this winter for hunting, although there isn't much game around here anymore. The rabbits might be pretty thick, though." Webb paused, then asked. "Have you used a rifle much, Mr. Reisner?"

"I know how to shoot it." He was packing a box of shells under his arm.

"I don't know what it's like where you come from, but around here" — he casually reached out and laid a forefinger alongside the muzzle to point it in another direction — "we don't point a rifle at something unless we aim to shoot it. It's considered bad manners."

"I vill remember that."

They continued to face each other while Lilli stood to one side, uneasily watching them both. The air seemed heavy with the veiled antagonism that drifted between them, carefully undefined.

The sheriff interposed. "What's the trouble here?"

"No trouble, Sheriff," Webb replied with an easy look. "I was just admiring Mr. Reisner's new rifle and wishing him good hunting." He tipped his hat to Lillian. "Good day to you, ma'am."

He stepped past both of them to enter the store, and heard the trailing sounds of several pairs of heeled boots belonging to the Triple C riders behind him. A raw and reckless energy was pulsing through his blood. Webb wanted to hit something – anything.

Business was brisk inside the store, wall to wall with customers as entire homesteading families dawdled over purchases of merchandise and supplies. Youngsters in their knickers with a penny to spend were wavering between the candy jar selections, the decision of which to buy nearly as sweet as the stick of candy.

Webb walked to the back of the store far away from the front windows so he couldn't see Lilli getting into the wagon with her husband. All of the Triple C riders stayed together in a loose, noisy bunch, browsing through the goods for sale. Nate was the only one with any intention of making a purchase, so he walked up to the counter to buy his tobacco. Webb prowled restlessly along with him.

A new clerk started to inquire how he could help Nate when Ollie Ellis, the proprietor, came over and sent the clerk to another customer. At first, Webb thought nothing of it despite the owner's stern and businesslike expression. Ollie Ellis had always personally waited on representatives from the Triple C, so it appeared to be no different this time.

"What can I do for you?" The crisp inquiry was not even accompanied by a familiar address.

"I need some tobacco. Better make it a whole can of Prince Albert," Nate added, figuring it had to last him all winter.

"Is that all?" There was something in the owner's tone that seemed to resent such a small purchase.

Behind them, Shorty was trying on a lady's hat, to the hoots and guffaws of the other cowboys. Shorty had always been part clown and part banty rooster, so his hot temper and wild antics were equally well known to the local tradesman.

"Yeah, that's all," Nate replied to Ollie's question and dug into his pocket to pay for the tobacco.

"Then I will thank you to take your tobacco and your friends, and leave the store." The proprietor's request was coached in polite phrases, spoken quietly but firmly. "You have been drinking, and I don't want you creating a disturbance here or offending my other customers."

Webb turned, not quite believing he'd heard right, but there was little respect or softness in the man's expression. "The boys are a bit rowdy, Mr. Ellis, but they're doing no harm." The irritation that he'd been containing was straining to escape. "We've been six weeks in the saddle and come to town to do a little hurrahing. We're not here to cause any trouble."

"All I am asking is that you do your 'hurrahing' someplace else." As Ollie Ellis observed the hardness taking over Webb's features, he added nervously, "I hope you will leave peaceably, I should not like to have to ask the sheriff to remove you from these premises."

"We'll go, all right." There was a deadly quiet in Webb's voice. "But you've got a short memory, Ellis. You and all these townspeople that were here before the drylanders came. It was our trade — the cattlemen trade — that kept your business alive."

"Times have changed," the owner replied a little defensively.

"But greed hasn't. You've caught the whiff of money in another man's pocket and that's all you can think about. Like the dog looking at his reflection in the water and seeing a bigger bone, you've just dropped yours, Ellis," Webb murmured coolly. "Because my memory is longer than yours, I won't forget this."

"Now, see here, you've got no call to talk to me like that," Ollie Ellis protested with affronted dignity. "My request was perfectly reasonable and —"

But Webb had already pivoted away from the counter, not listening to a single word. "Let's go, boys," he snapped to the others. Their initial, loudly voiced reluctance was silenced by the look on Webb's hard features. They quickly trailed after him. It was Nate who supplied the explanation for their abrupt departure from the store.

"Doesn't look like we're welcome anyplace in this town," one of them grumbled.

"I ain't never stayed where I wasn't welcomed."

A few minutes later, the band of riders were trotting their horses out of town. They had no good times to remember, only the bad taste in their mouth.

In bed that night, Stefan made his demand on her and Lilli went to him. After he was through, she lay on her side, staring at the silver path the moonlight made into the room. The physical side of her marriage to Stefan had been a very minor part of their relationship. The act of mating was an occasional, perfunctory thing, occurring only at the initiative of Stefan. Lilli had never regarded it as an unpleasant duty as his wife, an activity to be endured. But she certainly didn't derive the kind of satisfaction that Stefan did from it. As a matter of fact, she never had the impression that she was expected to. It didn't occur to her that she might find some gratification from physical closeness with a man until she had felt curiously stimulated by Webb's kiss. All her life, kisses had been mere gestures of affection. Certainly her mother had never indicated they were anything else. But her mother had died when Lilli was only thirteen. Other than her parents', Stefan's love was the only kind she'd ever known. She was gradually becoming aware there was another. And it was a man other than her husband who was opening her eyes to it.

So she lay in bed, conscious that her own urge to love was unquenched. It was too deeply repressed, because it was an urge for another man. She could feel her heart beat and the blood flow through her veins; yet the center of her felt dry and empty. There was so much she could give, but all those feelings and desires were going to waste. They were withering. She was suddenly frightened by the thought that they might never be used — that they'd die without ever being given. She felt an over-whelming sense of loneliness.

III

Stands a Calder man,
Lonely now is he,
Turning to the land —
To the Triple C.

14

Large snowflakes drifted out of a pale gray sky that shaded into the bleak, white landscape. The air was bitter cold, nipping at the exposed areas of Webb's face. A long wool scarf was tied over his hat and wrapped around his neck, partially raised to cover his nose and mouth. Without tipping his head, he peered upward at the December sky, looking for weather signs, while the hoary-coated black gelding buck-plunged through the snowdrift until it reached an area of wind-swept ground with only two or three inches of snow cover.

The sky had been threatening all morning and the air was brittle with the chill of an Arctic air mass. So far, the wind had remained calm, as if frozen by the icy temperature. But Webb was alert to any shift of the wind into the northeast, the lair of what the Sioux Indians called the White Wolf — a howling Arctic storm that preyed on the land. He could almost smell it in the air when he'd ridden out of the line camp that morning.

His route had taken him nearly full circle around the section of range he patrolled. All the cattle along the outlying areas Webb had drifted closer to camp and the hay stacks that would feed them when the snow became too deep for foraging. The gelding snorted, its warm breath rolling out in thick, vaporous clouds. Without turning his head, Webb glanced in the direction indicated by the pricked ears.

A cow was floundering in the snow, but her ungainly actions weren't warranted by the depth of the snow cover in that area. The animal was obviously injured, a broken leg by the looks of it. Webb reined the black gelding toward the cow. There was an awkward attempt by the animal to elude his approach, but the white-faced cow finally halted in the snow and turned a wild and pain-filled eye on the horse and rider.

Webb stopped the gelding a few yards from the animal, not wanting to increase its panic. The left foreleg was twisted at a crazy angle, unquestionably broken. It was an older stock cow, which was some consolation. In another couple of years, she'd probably be culled from the herd anyway. The injury must have happened in the last few hours; otherwise the wolves would have gotten her by now.

"If the wolves don't get you, the storm will." The thick wool scarf muffled his murmured words and spilled the warmth of his breath over his face. "So I might as well end your suffering, Bossie."

Cold-stiffened leather creaked loudly under his shifting weight as Webb swung a numbed leg out of the saddle and stepped to the snow-packed ground. His gloved fingers had trouble with the leather flap of the rifle scabbard, but he finally managed to grab the butt and pull out the rifle. He stepped in front of the gelding to face the wide-eyed cow and levered a bullet into the chamber.

Snowflakes whirled aimlessly through the silence. He hooked an arm through the tied reins before lifting the rifle butt to his shoulder. He didn't want the gelding to spook at the explosion of a rifle shot and leave him afoot this far from camp. The gelding chanked on the metal bit as Webb sighted on the cow and squeezed the trigger.

The deafening report of the rifle shattered the stillness of the gray morning, drowning out the crunching thud of the cow crumpling to the snow. He ejected the empty shell from the chamber and walked back to the saddle to shove the rifle into the scabbard. With the flap secured over the butt, he put a boot in the stirrup and started to heft his cold-numbed body into the saddle, but the sight of the dead cow and the crimson-spattered snow stopped him.

It was a shame to leave that carcass for the wolves and coyotes to quarrel over. The age of the cow would make the meat tough and stringy, but it still seemed a waste of beef. He could cut himself off a quarter, except he had an ample supply of meat back at the line camp.

Webb knew where his mind was turning, but try as he might, he couldn't stop from thinking of Lilli. Unless a homesteader had a calf of his own to butcher, beef wasn't exactly a mainstay of his diet. Fresh meat came mostly from wild game. And here was a whole carcass of meat.

He turned his head, looking to the east. With the cattle all drifted toward the camp, there was nothing left for him to do but sit in the line shack and wait out the storm. His work was done and it didn't look like the storm was going to break any time soon. There'd be a few hours to ride over to the Reisner homestead and take them the beef, maybe even time to get back before the weather got too bad.

After that, his decision was a foregone conclusion. He slipped the toe of his boot out of the stirrup and reached into the saddlebag for his hunting knife. It was a simple matter to slit the jugular vein to let the cow bleed. It took considerably more time to rig up a travois out of two saplings and lash the carcass onto it with his rope. The snow had stopped when Webb swung into the saddle and pointed the black gelding east.

During all her years in the city, cramped in a small, two-room tenement apartment with three other people, Lilli had never felt so cooped up as she did in the one-room shack. She was restless and irritable, rebelling against all the little tasks that would pass the time. The gray world outside seemed to press in and make the shack even smaller.

The breakfast dishes were still staring at her, a glaring reminder that she was neglecting her chores. Lilli glared back and continued flipping through the well-worn pages of a catalogue, but she wasn't looking at the pages either. Finally she plopped the book on the table and stalked over to the cookstove to heat water for the dishes.

There were an endless variety of things that needed to be done. There was mending to do, bread to be baked, scraps of cloth to be sewn into a quilt, more coal to be brought in for the stove, not to mention the breakfast dishes to be washed and lunch not far off. But Lilli wasn't in the mood to do any of them. She just didn't understand how Stefan could idle away the time without showing any sign of boredom. She would never have believed his quietness could be so irritating, and sent a glaring look in his direction.

He was putting on his wraps, layering clothes to combat the cold outside. She supposed he was going out to check on the horses, but it seemed like desertion to her. It was bad enough trying to talk to her taciturn husband and keep a conversation going, but it was worse having no one to talk to at all.

"Where are you going?" she demanded, ready to take the kettle off the stove and accompany him to the horse shed, rather than stay in this four-walled prison alone.

"Hunting." The one word was the only answer that he felt was required as he reached up to take the rifle from its rack above the door.

She should have guessed, Lilly realized. He'd mentioned they needed fresh meat this morning when he'd gone out to water the horses.

"I'll come with you," she said.

"It is too cold." That was the end of it as far

as Stefan was concerned. Once he made up his mind about something, he rarely budged. Lilli half-suspected that since Franz Kreuger didn't allow his wife to go hunting with him, Stefan wouldn't permit it, either. Stefan seemed to be acquiring more and more of their neighbor's characteristics.

When he came over to kiss her good-bye, she coolly offered him her cheek. She felt the whiskery brush of his beard and the brief warmth of his mouth against her skin, then he was straightening. The affectionate caress meant nothing, its very blandness taking meaning from the gesture.

"I vill be back for supper." He turned and walked to the door.

She didn't offer to send any food along with him or even wish him success in his hunting. As she heard the pull of the latchstring, Lilli suddenly examined her heartless attitude.

The cause went deeper than mere resentment at being deprived of company and left in this small place alone. This inner dissatisfaction had been growing for some time. She could trace it all the way back to that first meeting with Webb Calder.

Plagued by this guilt that always came with any thought of Webb Calder, Lilli hurried to the door that had swung shut. A flurry of snowflakes swirled in when she opened it, letting in another bitter blast of frigid air. Stefan was tramping through the snow several yards from the house, the rifle on his shoulder.

"Stefan!" She hunched her shoulders together, shivering in the opening. When he turned, she felt the old affection and friendship for him flowing through her again. She realized she was being ungrateful and unappreciative of his kindness and goodness toward her. "It looks like it could storm. Don't go too far!" she called after him in concern.

He lifted a hand, acknowledging he'd heard, then turned and began traipsing across the snow, a dark, hunched figure in a gray-white world. Lilli closed the door and hurried over to the stove to warm herself. She looked about their house. When he returned, she vowed to have everything done and a hot supper waiting for him. The kettle was simmering to heat the snow-water in the basin. She poured it in. Working was always the quickest way to get warm, she remembered her mother saying that.

The clouds were flattening themselves close to the barren snowscape, making land indiscernible from sky. The dark plot in the gray picture grew steadily larger as Webb approached it. The smoke rising from the chimney pipe blended into sky. He could smell it in the air, but he couldn't distinguish its wispy trail from the gray-spun clouds.

The snow-covered wagon sat next to the bleached poles of the corral. The wind shelter for the draft team had been closed to create a shed where they could seek protection from inclement weather. At the moment, Webb could see the two mares nosing at the straw scattered in clumps next to the shed, offering them browse. There was a glimmer of light showing from inside the shanty, mostly blocked by the covering over the window.

The black gelding stopped of its own accord near the door, as if sensing this was their destination. Webb's legs were numb and stiff with the cold. They felt like two dead sticks when he tried to dismount, and didn't seem inclined to support him when he did step down. He stamped them to bring back the feeling, with jarring results as pain shot through his body.

"Hello in the house!" he hailed the shack's occupants, notifying them of his presence.

Despite the scarf around his mouth and nose, his face felt numb and his lips were unwilling to form the words. The air was so cold that it hurt to breathe. Much longer out in this cold and he'd turn into an icicle. He moved stiffly to the rear of his horse to unlash the carcass. His call had met with no response from inside the cabin. Webb paused to call again.

"Hey! Anybody home?" He cupped his hands to his mouth and shouted.

The door was opened a narrow crack. He recognized Lilli despite the heavy blanketlike shawl wrapped around her. He stood there for a long second, breathing hard from the cold and the effort of breathing at all. She said nothing in greeting.

"Tell your husband to come outside and give me a hand with this." Webb finally spoke to break the silence, and bent down to continue his awkward attempt to untie the nearly rigid corpse of the cow. Snow crunched under the footsteps of someone approaching him. He glanced up to see Lilli coming toward him.

"What's that?" The shawl was up around her face, muffling her voice.

"One of our cows. She broke a leg and I had to shoot her." He grunted as he tugged at a knot with numb fingers. "Thought you could use the meat. It was either that or stick some poison in her for the wolves to eat." He straightened and looked expectantly toward the house. The door was shut. "Isn't your husband coming?"

There was a long pause before she answered

him. "He isn't here." The blue of her eyes seemed to dare him to say something. Her eyes were all he could see of her face, the rest of it hidden by the dark shawl that covered her hair.

"The horses are here. So's the wagon." He didn't want to be accused of coming here with the foreknowledge that her husband was absent from home. "Where is he?"

"He went hunting this morning and hasn't come back yet," she said.

"He went hunting in this weather?" Webb frowned. The cold was a frigid band of steel across his forehead.

"Yes." She became apprehensive at his reaction.

"All the wild game will have taken shelter with this storm coming. I didn't even see a jackrabbit on the way here," he stated, impatient at the ignorance of a homesteader who had no practical knowledge of living on the land. "Babes in the woods" was a mild description. "Where do you want me to put this carcass?" Then he realized Lilli wasn't any more knowledgable than her husband about such things. "It needs to be in a building of sorts where the wolves can't get to it. Is the horse shed all right?"

"Yes." She nodded. "Can I help?"

"I doubt it." It was easier for him to show

anger toward her; it kept his other feelings at bay. "You can open the door to the shed."

Without another man's muscle to help him, Webb knew, it wasn't going to be an easy trick to get this carcass inside. The simplest way would be to cut it up out here, but it was too damned cold. He checked the lashings to make sure they were still secure and walked to his horse's head, taking the reins to lead it as close to the shed as possible.

He rolled the carcass off the travois directly in front of the door and glanced at Lilli, all huddled inside her shawl. "Go back inside where it's warm," he ordered.

"You'll need help." She showed no signs of leaving.

"Do you know anything about gutting, skinning, and butchering an animal?" he challenged and watched her gaze drop under his piercing look. "That's what I thought. Go inside."

"I can learn," she argued.

"Have it your way." Webb shrugged.

Between the two of them and a rope slung around a rafter beam, they dragged the carcass inside the shed and strung it up. When Webb disemboweled the dead cow, Lilli felt queasy. It was so much larger than the few chickens she'd cleaned. For a few minutes, she thought she was going to throw up. When Webb challenged her to haul the gunnysack of entrails out of the shed and some distance away, she managed to swallow the nauseous lump in her throat and drag them out. The trek into the sharply cold air had a reviving effect. When she returned, he was half-finished skinning the cow, and she was not exactly sorry she had missed the beginnings of it.

"That's good enough for now." Webb stepped back, looking weary and cold. "I hope you've got some coffee hot." He attempted to flex his gloveless fingers, but they resisted closing into a fist. There had been enough body heat left in the animal to keep his hands warm while he worked, but they were chilled and stiff now. He pulled on his gloves before going out in the cold to the shanty. "After I warm up some, I'll go look for your husband."

"You don't think anything has happened to him, do you?" Lilli raised the heavy shawl over her head. Stefan had said he'd be back by suppertime, which was still a couple of hours away, so she wasn't alarmed that he hadn't returned yet. Stefan had gone hunting on other winter days and come back safely. Even if a storm was coming, it wasn't here yet, so she didn't understand why Webb appeared concerned.

"He's probably all right," Webb conceded as he opened the shed door and waited for Lilli to go first. "The Lord has a way of looking after babes and pilgrims." The last was muttered to himself as he stepped outside into a thickening snowfall, stirred now by a fluctuating wind.

Inside the shack, Webb began peeling off his outer garments while Lilli stoked the cooking and heating stove with more coal. He rubbed his arms briskly, trying to stir up the circulation, as he moved to the source of heat. Lilli poured them both a cup of coffee, and Webb warmed his hands with his, aware of the strained silence and quietly studying her.

"You'd better take off that shawl," he advised. "Or you never will get warm." She seemed reluctant to forsake the protection of the shawl, but it could hardly have been for the warmth. When she did remove it, she was wearing a long and heavy, high-necked sweater. "That, too," Webb stated.

She darted him a wary glance that resisted his suggestion. "I always wear this inside. The cold seeps through the walls and I —"

"You can put it back on later, but take it off for now," Webb insisted. "It's blocking out the stove's heat, so it'll take you a lot longer to get warm."

Following his sensible advice, Lilli tugged

the sweater over her head and folded it to lay it aside. Then she was taking up her cup of coffee and crowding close to the stove. There was a high color to her cheeks, nipped by the cold, and her dark auburn hair was attractively disheveled. Webb wanted to run his fingers through it and remove the loosened pins that swept the mass of it atop her head. He stared at his cup. His limbs were starting to tingle with needle-sharp jabs radiating from his nerve ends as the cold-induced numbness began to wear off.

"Thank you for the meat." Her voice came to him, soft and clear, unaffected by any coyness. Webb shut his eyes, tortured by the things he wanted to say and had no right to voice. He breathed in and caught the disturbing scent of her, so near to him.

"Like I said, it was either bring it here or turn it into wolf bait." He sounded gruff. He had to, or he'd find himself regretting the alternative. He downed a quick swallow of coffee, letting its heat thaw his insides. "Do you know which direction your husband took when he left?" Webb deliberately mentioned Stefan Reisner to remind himself of the man's existence.

"He headed west — toward Franz Kreuger's place." She wouldn't be surprised if Stefan had stopped there for the noon meal and gone out hunting with Franz in the afternoon.

Webb tipped back his head and drained the coffee from his cup, then handed the empty tin mug to Lilli, his glance sliding away from her. "I'd better ride out a ways and see if I can find any sign of him before the storm breaks."

"Will you come back?" She held the cup, looking at it instead of him, but he sensed the tension and let his gaze wander over her profile for a long second.

"I guess it will depend." But he didn't say on what. "Hand me the coal bucket and I'll fill it before I go, just in case I don't get back." He picked up his heavy wool-lined jacket and shrugged into it.

He couldn't help thinking that if he hadn't come here, he'd be sitting snug and cozy in the line shack instead of venturing out into this subzero weather with a blizzard on the way. He'd be better off there, and Webb wasn't concerned about the risks of going out in such weather when he thought that. It was the risk he was taking when he came back, as he knew he would, with or without her husband. He cursed the weakness in him that wouldn't let him stay away from this woman.

When he was all bundled up in his heavy winter gear, Lilli gave him the coal bucket.

Without a word, he walked to the door and took hold of the latchstring. He faltered for a second, then pulled the door open with an impatient jerk and pushed himself outside, shutting the door quickly.

The cold and the whirling snow hit him, bringing him up short for a second. The thickening gray clouds were creating a premature darkness, stealing much of what was left of the afternoon. Webb moved briskly to the side of the shack where the coal was piled and filled the bucket, brushing off the snow that had collected on the black chunks.

Lilli must have been waiting at the door, because she was standing next to it when he returned with the full bucket. He set it down and turned to leave again, but the tense silence needed to be broken. He couldn't just walk out without saying something.

His hand was on the latchstring and he looked at the door, his head tipped down as he spoke. "It's getting dark out there. Keep the lantern turned all the way up so a light shows."

There was a wretched tearing inside Lilli. Involuntarily, she reached for his arm to keep him with her a second longer. "Webb, be careful." The anxious words rushed from her before she could stop them.

The downward angle of his head shifted

slightly in her direction as he looked at the hand on his coat sleeve. She pulled it away as if she had touched something hot.

"Don't you mean 'Mr. Calder'?" The line of his jaw was hard, and his voice had a bitter ring. While she was still groping for a response, Webb was out the door and gone.

The black gelding balked when Webb tried to lead it outside. The horse knew the weather wasn't fit for man or beast to be in even if its rider didn't. In the end, the gelding obeyed with its rider's command, but under protest.

Within minutes after riding out from the yard, the horse and rider were enveloped in the grayness. The snowflakes had turned to pellets, whirling around Webb like white buckshot, stinging and pelting. The wind had picked up, drifting the snow on the ground and reducing the visibility to less than a half a mile. There wasn't much chance of cutting Stefan Reisner's trail. Between the newly fallen snow and the blowing wind, his tracks would have been covered by now. Webb set a zigzagging course toward some broken country south of Kreuger's place and west of here. It was about the only area where there was still some wild game to be found. The advent of the drylanders had driven most of it into rougher country where plows had little success.

The man should be on his way back now, if he hadn't gotten lost. With luck, Webb could intercept him. The black gelding might not like the idea of being ridden double, but that's what Webb intended — if he found Reisner.

The numbing cold took away all perception of time. It seemed he had been riding through this hell's freezer for a lifetime. Webb was losing the feeling in his legs and had to keep pounding them with his hand to retain any sensation. He couldn't feel the cold anymore and knew that was a bad sign. If Reisner hadn't found shelter, the old man was bound to freeze to death.

The rimrock country was around him when Webb suddenly realized the wind had shifted into the northeast, the thing he'd been both expecting and dreading. How long ago it had changed, he didn't know. He halted the gelding to quickly orient himself. He was about equal distance from both the Kreuger place and Lilli. There was a good chance Reisner might have gone to his neighbor's since it was a mile closer. It was possible he had gotten a horse there and ridden back to his place. It would explain why Webb hadn't seen any sign of him.

He was faced with two choices — either head for Kreuger's and confirm Stefan Reisner had come that way, or turn around and ride back to

Lilli. Now that the storm had hit, he could do one or the other — but not both. He had to get to shelter, and those two were the closest places.

Webb didn't think about it twice as he reined the gelding around and headed back in a straight line the way he'd come. The black horse agreed with his decision and moved out smartly for the shed it had so reluctantly left. Webb hunched a shoulder to the wind and tucked his chin into his chest, letting his hat break the force of the blowing cold.

By the time the yellow light could be seen shining out of the shanty window, the horse and rider were blanketed with snow. When the gelding stopped at the shed door. Webb tried to dismount and ended up falling out of the saddle, his muscles too cold to function. He flung an arm over the horse's neck for support until he could get his stiff legs to move.

It was pitch-black inside the shed, but the howling wind couldn't reach them. Webb leaned against the thin wall of the shed and listened to the rustle of straw stirred by the horses and the inquiring whicker from one of the big mares. They were warm sounds. He gathered his energy and lifted a hand to his mouth, tugging off a glove with his teeth. His fingers were too numb to hold on to a match, let alone strike one to light the lantern by the door. Webb shoved the hand inside his jacket and tucked it up under his armpit to warm it.

Once the lantern was lit, he could see the two Belgian mares standing in crude stalls. The black gelding was standing patiently in the small, closed-off feed area, crusty snow covering its shaggy coat until the animal's color was unrecognizable. The beef carcass hung eerily in a shadowed corner.

Before he could seek the warmth of the shanty, Webb had to take care of his horse. The stock saddle seemed three times as heavy when he pulled it off the horse, his cold-stiffened muscles finding it awkward to handle the cumbersome weight of it. When he had the gear stripped from the horse, he grabbed hand-fuls of straw and began rubbing the animal down, wiping off the icy snowcover before the horse's body heat melted it.

When the gelding was bedded down for the night, a part of Webb wanted to lie down and bury himself in the pile of straw in the corner. But there was a stronger urge that drove him out into the storm and across the intervening space to the shanty.

The storm was raging full force now, the Arctic wind blasting the air from his lungs. Although his memory told him the tar-paper shack was only twenty yards from the corral shed, the driving snow hid it from him. There wasn't even the gleam of the yellow lantern light to show him the way. Trusting his instincts, Webb forged ahead in the direction he believed it to be. In the back of his mind he knew men had gotten lost and frozen to death five feet away from their door.

15

The wind howled around the one-room shanty, whistling through the smallest crack to send its piercing chill inside. Lilli stirred up the coals in the stove, trying to convince it to send out more heat to combat the increasing drafts. She walked again to the window, wearing a path into the floor, but it was impossible to see outside. Both Stefan and Webb were out there, and she didn't know which one she was worried about most.

She started back to the stove to stir the bean soup, flavored with salt pork, and make certain the coffee was hot. A blast of wind rattled the flimsy structure, threatening to blow it away. Lilli glanced apprehensively around the room, as if she expected to see some sign of damage from the battering wind. There had been other winter storms, but nothing like this. The wind was so loud she could hardly hear herself think. She knew she'd never hear anyone approaching the house in this storm.

Something fell against the door, startling her. Before she could react, the door popped open and a snowy figure lurched inside and leaned against the door to close it. An angry wind blew its icy, huffing breath into the single room and wrapped its coldness around Lilli. For an instant, the sudden invasion of frigid air held her motionless; then she was running to the snowman in the white-frosted cowboy hat.

"My God, you're frozen solid, Webb," she declared in a murmur and began tearing at the ice-encrusted knot of his wool scarf.

His dark eyebrows and spiked lashes were completely caked with snow. Even his normally sun-browned skin looked colorless. Only the black pupils of his eyes continued to shine with life. When she pulled off his scarf, she removed his hat along with it, scattering chunks of melting snow all over herself and the floor. The buttons of his jacket were frozen in their holes. Lilli had to dig them loose with her fingers before she could get his jacket off. He appeared unable to summon the strength to object to Lilli's removing his outer garments rather than letting him do it.

"Come over by the stove." She grabbed hold of his arm to help him and felt the coldness of it through the layers of a gray wool shirt and long-sleeved underwear. Webb managed a nod of agreement and accepted her support as he stumbled across the room on leaden legs.

When she had his shuddering body next to the stove, Lilli wrapped his hand around a cup of hot coffee, then left him to get the straw broom leaning in the corner. His pants were encased in a mixture of snow and ice.

"Stand still," she ordered and began sweeping at him.

"Your floor is getting all wet," he warned in a voice that cracked.

"Better to have all that snow on my floor than on you," she replied briskly.

Something prompted her to look up from her task. The bluish tinge was gone from his mouth. The corners of it were turned upward to match the crinkling smile lines around his eyes. She felt an unexpected glow light up inside her and hesitantly returned his faint smile before brushing the last of the snow from him.

"We'd better take those boots off," she suggested. "Your feet must feel like ice." She dragged one of the chairs from the table so he could sit on it. "I guess you didn't find Stefan." Her questioning glance didn't quite reach his face.

"I figure he went to Kreuger's." Webb

lowered himself onto the chair seat, the suppleness slowly returning to his muscles. "He's probably waiting out the storm there." At least, he hoped the man was — for Lilli's sake.

She appeared reassured by his suggestion. "He usually goes hunting with Mr. Kreuger. It's likely that he did today, too, even though he didn't mention it." She faced him and reached out a hand. "Give me your foot."

His boot was wet and cold, the leather stiff. It took some tugging before she succeeded in pulling it off. But she didn't stop with removing his boots. She peeled off his wool socks as well. His numbed feet tingled painfully from the shocking exposure to warm air.

Lilli took one look at his frosty white feet and reached for the basin. A kettle of water was warming at the back of the stove. She emptied it into the basin and bent down to immerse his feet in the hot water. Webb was barely able to muffle an outcry at the shooting pain that traveled through his nerves from his nearly frostbitten feet.

"You really should take those wet pants off before you catch cold," she remarked.

Granted, he could feel their dampness through his longjohns, but Webb didn't think the situation called for such drastic measures. "I think I'll keep my pants on," he stated dryly.

"If it's all the same to you." He arched an eyebrow at her, certain she hadn't considered her suggestion all the way through.

The faint blush that rose in her cheeks seemed to confirm it as she avoided his gaze, but her mouth stayed in a determined line. "I am a married woman, Mr. Calder, so I have seen a man in his underwear before."

"It's back to 'Mr. Calder,' is it?" he murmured with a trace of irritation that she had managed to destroy the sense of intimacy that had been growing.

There was no response from her as she turned away, and no further argument about the wisdom of removing his pants. "I have supper hot." She changed the subject entirely. "Would you like something to eat? It's just bean soup —"

"That sounds fine," Webb interrupted her before she could apologize for the plainness of the meal.

"You soak your feet in that hot water while I dish it up." She laid his socks out to dry, steam drifting up from them.

He wouldn't have been a man if he didn't find it pleasing to be waited on by a woman, his every need anticipated. With unhurried movements, she set the table with flatware and a loaf of bread and a knife on a flat board. Two bowls of soup were dished out and placed on the table. Then she walked to the far end of the room where the bed sat and took something out of a trunk. When she came back, she handed him a towel and a pair of dry socks.

"You can wear these," she said.

Webb held them a second, aware they belonged to her husband, then set them on his lap to wipe his feet dry. There was only one chair at the table, so he brought over the one on which he had been sitting. The melting snow from his clothes had left little puddles of water on the floor. His stockinged feet got wet when he crossed to the table, but Webb didn't mention it.

"Smells good." He sniffed appreciatively at the thick soup and accepted the slice of bread Lilli handed him. "Thanks." The soup was too hot to eat right away, so he dipped a corner of the bread into the liquid and ate it. "It tastes as good as it smells."

Her only response was a brief smiling glance; then Lilli was dipping her spoon into the soup and blowing on it to cool it. The silence lengthened. Webb was irritated by it.

"Are you always this quiet at the table?" he questioned, throwing a hard glance across the table at her.

"I'm sorry." She lowered her spoon to the

table, appearing ill at ease. "It's a habit, I'm afraid. Stefan doesn't believe you should talk at the table, not while you're eating."

"I see." He bent his head, struggling with the grimness he felt. Then he shot another glance at her. "Well, if you don't mind, I prefer to talk while I eat. Or do you share your husband's opinion?"

"No, it's just always been the custom in our home." The wind picked up its fury and rattled the tar-papered sides of the shack. Lilli tensed at the noise, feeling it push at her.

"Something wrong?" Webb asked.

"I can't get used to the wind," she admitted and dipped her spoon into the soup again. "It never seems to stop blowing out here."

"It will get to you if you let it," he remarked.

"How do you prevent it?" she asked with an attempt at a smile.

"Think about something else." He shrugged.

"That's easier said than done," she replied. "When it blows like that, I just feel so cooped up in here."

"Cabin fever," Webb diagnosed her ailment with a slow smile.

"What's that?" She looked at him with an interested frown.

"It's a common malady around here," he explained. "It comes from spending too many days inside with the same four walls looking back at you all the time. The symptoms are restlessness, irritability, and melancholy."

"I think I've come down with a bad case of it," Lilli declared. "What's the cure?"

"I don't know of any." Webb smiled sympathetically. "Eventually it just goes away. My mother said it used to help to have company come."

"Yes." She seemed to consider that thought. "It is nice to have someone to talk to."

"Other than your husband, of course." He wanted to bite his tongue for mentioning that.

"Stefan isn't much of a talker." She shrugged and ate her soup.

"I gathered that," Webb murmured dryly.

"He's a quiet, simple man, very strong and gentle." She paused as if thinking about something. "He's changed a little in some ways since we came here."

"Oh? In what way?" His voice attempted to conceal the curiosity her seemingly innocent remark had aroused.

"There was a time when he hated the thought of owing anyone money. But when we sold our crop this year, he didn't pay off the loan we had at the bank. He borrowed more money to buy some additional land," she explained, then quickly defended his action.

"I'm sure it will be a good investment, though." She glanced at his nearly empty bowl. "Would you like some more soup?"

"No, this is plenty," Webb refused and wiped the bowl clean with the crust of bread.

"I'll get you some coffee." She pushed her chair away from the table to fetch it.

The heavy sweater made a lumpy shape of her as Webb studied the shine of red in her hair under the lantern light. The sights and sounds in the room were pleasing to him — the smell of coffee in the cup Lilli brought him, the soft swish of her skirt, and the look in her eyes that she didn't always hide.

"I could get used to having a woman do things for me." Webb smiled as he took the cup from her.

"Most men can." She moved to her own side of the table, poised and showing no sign that she took his remark personally. "First their mothers look after them, then their wives. Men generally don't like to do things for themselves."

His gaze narrowed a fraction as he sensed there was something derogatory in her observation of the male sex. "I suppose some men marry for the convenience of having a wife to take care of them and satisfy their needs."

He suspected it of a few married couples he

331

knew. Their attitudes toward each other were in marked contrast to the special relationship between his parents. Maybe that's why he'd noticed it. Maybe that's why he hadn't been willing to take a wife, because he envied what his father had and didn't want to settle for less. He'd never thought about it much before now.

"I suppose some men do." She suddenly seemed reluctant to share her opinions with him.

Irritation rippled in him at the way she alternated between being natural and open with him and pulling back in aloofness. "And I suppose some women marry for the convenience of having a man to take care of them and satisfy their needs." The hard tone in his voice made it an accusation. He was immediately sorry when he saw her pale slightly.

"If a man and woman are satisfied with what they have, I don't think an outsider's opinion of their arrangement is important," she retorted stiffly.

"Are you satisfied with what you have, Lilli?" he asked quietly.

"That is none of your business, Mr. Calder." The anger that flared in her eyes seemed to mask pain. "I shall ignore your rudeness this time."

His mouth thinned into a silent line. He

wasn't about to apologize for the question, so he drank his coffee instead and let the conversation die.

Outside, the storm prowled around the shack, isolating them on an island of warmth. The two of them were blizzard-bound alone. Webb had known this could happen when he had turned around. There was a part of him that had counted on it. He wasn't responsible for the storm, but he had used it, fully aware that Lilli would never turn him out in it. He didn't feel too damned honorable when he considered it, either. A man liked to think he'd do the decent thing, but his father had warned him there was good and bad in every man. Webb just never thought he'd learn it about himself. Yet he'd known all along there was just one room in this cabin — and just one bed. And it was night.

The clatter of dishes broke the lengthening silence as Lilli began gathering them off the table. Webb got up from his chair and walked to the stove where his outer clothes were drying.

"I'd better put my boots on," he said, feeling the need for words, "before the leather dries stiff and hard."

His own socks were a little damp, but not enough to be uncomfortable. Webb took off her husband's pair and put on his own, then forced his feet into the slant-heeled boots. He heard the slosh of water as Lilli added some from the bucket to the heated water in the dish basin. He reached for his coat and hat and began putting them on.

Out of the corner of her eye, Lilli saw what he was doing and turned to frown at him. "Where are you going?"

"Outside." With the scarf tied over his hat to protect his ears, Webb pulled on his gloves. "I thought I'd get a couple pails of snow and bring them inside so we'll have a supply of water come morning."

Lilli turned back to her dishes, aware of him taking the two empty pails and walking to the door. When the door was opened for the brief moment it took for Webb to step outside, the wind roared louder. Its whipping cold rushed over her face, then was gone. The room felt strangely more empty without Webb.

It was all so different than when Stefan was here. With all his quietness, she almost regarded him as a piece of furniture at times forgetting he was even there. It was impossible to do that with Webb. He filled the room with a kind of vitality that unsettled the quiet tenor of her existence. It was a difference that was rooted in personality rather than the attraction she felt toward him. Webb stimulated, mentally and physically, while Stefan soothed. Lilli closed her eyes against the confusion of emotions as the door opened and Webb returned, stamping at the cold and snow.

"It's bitter out there." He shook off the snow like a great dog and took off his outer clothes to move vigorously toward the stove.

"How long do you think it will last?" The dishes were nearly done, leaving no more tasks to occupy the time.

"The worst of it will pass in about twelve hours. Then it will just be blowing snow and cold." He held his hands over the stove, warming them. "Do you need any help?"

"No, I'm finished." Lilli wiped the last dish and put it on the shelf.

"I'll add some more coals to the fire and get it stoked for the night." As he reached for the coal bucket, Webb was aware of the tension his remark had created. His side glance noticed her wary expression that she didn't fully conceal. "I'll bed down here by the stove, if that's all right."

"I'll get you a quilt." She walked across the room to the trunk and knelt down to open it. The folded square quilt made an awkward bundle as she lifted it out and stood up. A pulse was hammering in her throat when she turned to carry it to Webb. He met her halfway to take it from her.

Lilli surrendered it to him without meeting his gaze, without looking at his strong, chiseled features. She was on guard against the stirrings inside herself; yet, at the same time, she was unsettled by his failure to make any amorous advances toward her as he'd done in past encounters. Lilli was aware of the contradicting feelings that both wanted him to and didn't want him to try something. Tempering her silence was the desire not to be guilty of inviting anything.

When she'd given the quilt to him, she turned and walked to the foot of the bed, listening to the sound of his footsteps going toward the stove. She reached behind her and pulled the heavy sweater over her head. Under the circumstances, Lilli deemed it best to sleep in the blouse and long skirt she was wearing.

So far, Webb felt he was winning the struggle with his low urges as he laid the quilt on the floor in front of the stove. Its width would allow him to sleep on half of it and cover himself with the other. The wide pool of light from the lantern was showing him too much of the other side of the room where Lilli was standing by the lone bed.

"I'll turn the lantern out." He announced his

intention before moving to the center of the room.

Webb started to take her silence for assent, but as he reached up to turn down the wick, he glanced at Lilli to make certain she had no objection. Her back was turned to him and her hands were above her head, pulling the pins from her hair. The dark red mass tumbled down her back. A raw tightness gripped his chest, catching his breath.

"Your hair is beautiful." Somehow he'd known she'd make a stirring picture with her long hair all loose about her shoulders. As she turned with the sound of his voice, Webb moved toward her, drawn by a compulsion stronger than his control. He stopped short of her, still staring and searching for anything that would reveal her thoughts at this moment, but she wasn't letting him see anything.

"Are you happy, Lilli?" He needed to know. Maybe if she could convince him she was, he'd find the decency to walk back to the other side of the room.

"I was —" Lilli cut her answer short, stunned to hear herself speak in the past tense, because it revealed something she hadn't meant Webb to know. She tried to turn away, but his hands were on her shoulders to keep her facing him.

"Does he make you happy?" This time it was

337

a demand, not a question.

"I don't know. I'm so confused anymore that I —" She looked at him and knew it was a mistake. His hair gleamed black and thick, as dark as his eyes gleaming down on her. His features were handsome and rugged. Her gaze lingered on his mouth.

"Don't look at me like that, Lilli, unless you want me to kiss you," he warned thickly, his voice a deep well of emotion.

"Don't you see? That's just it. I do want you to kiss me." The admission tumbled from her in an emotional protest at her own confusion.

But Webb didn't hear the protest within the admission as he gathered her into an embrace that they both had fought against and lost. The long, urgent kiss they shared was drugging in its force. Her arms were around him, pressing him ever more tightly against her, while his fingers combed into the thick tangle of her hair and held its weight against the back of her neck. The blood was pounding through her veins, making her feel light-headed and giddy, weak at the knees and in need of his body to support her.

His roaming hand was alternately caressing and arching her spine to press her more fully to his male form. When his mouth slid off her lips to roll moist kisses over her cheek and temple, she could hear the labored rhythm of his breathing that sounded as disturbed as her own. His moist breath warmed skin that already felt feverishly hot. Passion and desire were new sensations for her, and Lilli wasn't comfortable with them.

"I knew this would happen if you ever came back," she murmured in a choked voice. His hard chin was near the corner of her mouth, the smell of him exciting her senses.

"Haven't you realized yet that you can't keep me away?" Webb asked, resting his forehead against her so their mouths could nearly touch and their breaths mingle. "God knows I've tried, but I can't stay away from you."

The tantalizing nearness of his mouth was more temptation than she could bear. She shifted her arms to curl her hands around his neck and bring his head down while she lifted herself on tiptoe. This small display of aggression sparked his, and the driving pressure of his responding kiss forced her lips apart. When his invading tongue mated with hers, Lilli shuddered at the igniting impact on her senses.

There seemed to be no right or wrong in what was happening. It was all too inevitable. Having Webb kiss her, hold her, and caress her seemed to be the reason she was born. When his lips began exploring the lobe of her ear and the curve of her throat, chills raced over her skin, awakening her already aroused flesh.

While his nibbling and intimate kisses on her neck arched her backward, his fingers made short work of the little buttons on her blouse. Some thin undergarment barred him from her flesh, but it was like a second skin. When his cupping hand closed on a tautly rounded breast, she felt the hardened point of her nipple in his palm.

Lilli moaned silently with a need she couldn't express. All this kissing and touching had not been part of her experience, and certainly she had never been aroused like this before. With Stefan, he had merely expressed a desire to mate, then mounted her with few preliminaries, and even those had been tentative. She was beginning to understand that this hollow ache she felt in her loins was a direct response to the virile hardness of Webb.

"I love you." His mouth rocked over her lips as he murmured his declaration. "God help me, how I love you."

Those were words she'd heard from only one other man in her life, and that was Stefan, her husband. A sense of guilt invaded her, bringing with it the first resistance she'd shown to his embrace. Lilli averted her head from him and brought her hands down to his shoulders.

"Don't say that." She was all tangled again in confusion.

"I love you," he repeated and cupped her face in his hand to turn her toward him. "Not saying it won't change the way I feel."

The gleaming darkness of his eyes seemed to draw her into them. He almost made it seem possible, but it wasn't. Despair began to deaden her senses.

"When this storm blows over, we'll leave here together," he began in a low, urging voice. "We'll go away somewhere and find a place of our own."

"I can't." She slowly shook her head. "I'm married. This is my home."

"Leave him and come away with me," Webb persisted. "You don't love him, not like this."

"No, not like this," Lilli admitted, only half-aware that she was admitting she loved Webb. "But I am his wife."

"Only as long as it takes to get a divorce. Then we'll be married and you'll be my wife," he stated.

"Divorce Stefan?" She looked at him with a sad anger. "On what grounds? That he's kind to me and good? That he trusts me?" The acknowledgment of her betrayal pushed her out of Webb's arms. "I can't leave him. I couldn't hurt Stefan like that."

"What about me?" His features darkened in a frown. "I love you. Do you have any idea of the hell I'm going through? The physical pain of wanting you? The agony of loving a married woman?"

"What about what I'm going through?" she stormed in anger, near tears. "I made a promise before God. At the dance, you claimed your word meant something. I gave my word to Stefan, and that means something to me! And you want me to forget that."

He straightened, pulling back from her, his features hardening into a mask. Lilli faced him, rigid and proud, hurt by his lack of understanding for her position. When Webb pivoted sharply away from her, something splintered inside. It was a full second before she realized he was putting on his hat and coat. By then, he was striding to the door.

"Where are you going?" She blinked her eyes in bewilderment. "You can't leave in this storm."

"I'm going to sleep in the shed with the horses," Webb snapped.

"But —" She never had a chance to finish her protest as he cut in.

"Don't ask me to sleep in here, because if I do, it will be in that bed with you!" he declared thickly. "As crude as it sounds, this thing between my legs doesn't have any conscience and I've only got a scrap left of my own, so allow me this one act of decency."

Then he was out the door, slamming it closed behind him. Lilli trembled, feeling suddenly very cold, but it was an inner cold, not one caused by the icy draft and swirling snow that had managed a brief invasion of the shack.

The black gelding turned its head and whickered a curious inquiry when Webb stalked into the shed. After the lantern was lit, the horse snorted its disapproval for the noise its rider was making. Brisk and grim, Webb kicked more straw into the pile along one wall, then hauled the saddle and blanket over to it to serve as pillow and pad. It was cold in the shed, but he'd slept in colder places. And the cold was what he needed to freeze out his desire.

With his straw bed as comfortable as he could make it, Webb walked to the lantern. The door burst open and he swung around to face it. He went rigid at the sight of Lilli, the shawl slipping off her head.

"What are you doing here?" he growled and immediately didn't want to know. "Get out!"

"I brought you the quilt." She smoothed her hand over the folded bundle in her arms. "I thought you'd need it."

Lowering her gaze, she crossed silently over to his straw bed and knelt down to lay out the quilt. Webb swayed like a man caught between two conflicting forces. Then he finally moved to take over the chore.

"I'll do that." He didn't want Lilli making his bed.

"I'm almost through," she protested, then sat back on her heels to watch him finish it. Her gaze lingered on the harshness of his features, knowing she had caused it. "Webb. I am sorry."

He paused with his hands on his thighs and turned to look at her across his shoulders. His dark eyes were narrowed and hard. "I guess we're both sorry about a lot of things," he concluded grimly.

There were so many things she wanted to say, but it would only make the situation worse. So she said the mundane instead. "Will you be warm enough?"

"I'll never be warm enough, Lilli, not if your body isn't next to mine," he told her.

She choked on a little cry and attempted to rise, but he grabbed her arm and pulled her around to him. "You think you're hurt," Webb mocked bitterly as frustration raged inside him. "You have no idea what it's like to want

344

someone so much that you can't look at anyone else."

"Webb, don't." She didn't struggle in his hold.

"You shouldn't have come out here, Lilli," he groaned, then crushed her hard in his arms, his weight driving her backward into the straw. The rough kiss was a punishment for tempting his control by coming to the shed. Lilli understood. It was a situation where neither and both of them were to blame for the position they now found themselves in. Lilli understood that better than Webb. Men preferred to believe they had control over what happened to them; Lilli knew better.

As suddenly as the angry embrace had begun, Webb was rolling his weight from her and sitting up to hunch over his knees. The hat came off as he raked a hand through his hair and kept his head lowered, breathing raggedly. "Get out of here," he ordered in a hoarse voice.

Aware his control was teetering on a thin edge, Lilli finally acknowledged the subconscious decision that had prompted her to come to the shed. Right or wrong, she wanted him to make her feel alive. There was no more thinking, no more restraint. Webb was here now, and the problems tomorrow might bring were blown away before this primary reasoning.

Not moving from her prone position, half on the quilt and half on the straw, she lifted a hand to touch him. "Webb, I don't want to go," she said. His body went still. "I wanted this to happen. The restlessness — the cabin fever, you said — that isn't what it was. I don't think I've thought about anything else but this moment for a long time. You've been in my mind since we met at the depot, taking up more and more of it until —"

His stillness was broken as he slowly turned, bringing his hand down and prying into her with his gaze, uncertain that she knew what she was saying. With a faint curve of her mouth, she opened her arms to him, inviting him to come to her. He lowered himself onto the straw beside her and curved an arm possessively across her. For a long second, it was enough just to look at her.

Her fingers wandered over the ridged bone of his cheek. "This is all I can give you, Webb." She wouldn't leave Stefan, and she wanted this to be enough, even though she knew it wouldn't be. A time would come when they would both want more, but that time wasn't here.

The straw rustled as Webb moved to warm her lips with his kiss. Her hand curved to the back of his head to increase the pressure and deepen the kiss, guided by the instinct of desire. Webb had already discovered in past encounters that she knew little of the preliminary arts that led to the act of love. He wanted to take it slow and teach them to her, but the need in him was a hot, fierce rod that impatiently demanded satisfaction.

Outside the shed, the blizzard howled and whined, dropping the temperature everywhere except in the corner where the bed of straw was located. There, the friction of two bodies trying to get closer created its own warmth. The black gelding snorted at all the rustling noises coming from the straw pile and turned its head to eye the entwined couple.

Their clothes were an encumbrance that couldn't be removed in this cold, only temporarily shifted out of the way so their hands could seek and invade chosen areas. His mouth grew more hungry for her, eating at her lips and clashing with her tongue. Her breasts strained under his cupping hands, stretching the material that bound them and kept him from touching her warm flesh.

The heat of her body was burning through what restraint he possessed. Little panting moans were coming from her throat as she turned into him with her hips and legs. Webb sensed her uncertainty, her confusion that he hadn't already taken her. It destroyed the rest of his control, sending hot blood coursing wildly through his veins and blocking out all other considerations with his need to have her.

The weighty material of her skirts was an irritating barrier to be lifted to reach her pantalettes. The heat of her skin burned through the cotton undergarment, warming his hand and briefly distracting him. He spread his hand across the rounded cheeks of her bottom, feeling the tautness of them. Then he was shifting her squarely onto the straw, his hand coming around to the front and gliding to her pubic bone. Her astonished gasp of pleasure nearly drove him over the brink. Impatiently he tugged at the undergarment, and her hips arched to help him ease it down.

When he slid into the tight opening, the swelling need inside him nearly exploded on contact. He went rigid, gritting his teeth to check it. She shifted under him, exciting all his senses. His hands dug into her to stop all motion.

"Hold still," Webb ordered thickly, the muscles in his jaw flexing with the tearing effort. "Or it will be over before you've had a chance to begin."

"What?" There was a trace of confusion in her throaty voice.

It gave him the edge of control he needed as his mouth rubbed over her moist lips. "I'll show you what I mean."

While he took possession of her mouth, his hands slid down to her hips and held them still as he moved slowly against them. But the pressure grew, bringing with it the roughness and the wonder of searing desire. She was all motion under him, her tongue pushing into his mouth to make demands from him. Her breath began coming quick and fast and Webb drove into her, letting the thing that rocked them both take over. Sensation kicked through him.

The storm's frigid chill eventually made itself felt, and exposed skin was covered, clothes bundled around them once more. Contentment brought a serenity to her features when Lilli finally looked at him. There was a tightness in his throat, emotion choking him with the need to tell her all she'd given him. The ache in his loins was satisfied, but it was more than that.

"I wondered if it would be like this," she murmured, gazing at him from her pillow of straw. "Now I know."

"Just this isn't enough." His hand cupped her face, his thumb rubbing at her lower lip. "I'll want more of this — and more beyond this."

"You have me. I can't hold back from that anymore." The lightness left her face.

"We'll never be satisfied with that, Lilli. The kind of closeness we're craving isn't satisfied with the breaching of flesh walls," he warned. "I want to eat with you and talk with you and sleep every night with you in my arms. I love you."

Her blue eyes became brilliant with tears. "This is all we've got, Webb. At least we have this much." Her voice was choked. "I can't leave Stefan."

His argument was silenced by the sad but determined line of her mouth. Webb brought his hand away, conscious that she shivered from the loss of contact. "You'd better go back where it's warm." He rolled to his feet and waited for her to stand up, too.

Slowly she arranged the shawl like a hood over her head. "Aren't you coming?" Her eyes clung to him.

"No. That's Stefan's bed inside. Mine's here," he stated, wondering at the peculiar lines men drew. He had taken the man's wife, but he didn't want to sleep in his bed. There was no regret in her eyes, no remorse for her actions. At least he had that.

After she had left, Webb stared at the door for a long time before he finally turned the lantern out and crawled under the quilt. He piled the straw around him, then rested his head on the saddle. There was a flatness in him now. No happy end could come from this, and it would scar her worse than it would him.

He shut his eyes and watched the tormenting images of her in his mind. She had come to him smiling. In some things, women were braver than men.

Sleep was a long time coming, and even then it was in fitful dozes. Along about three o'clock in the morning, he was awakened by the nervous snorting of his horse. He was vaguely conscious that the storm had abated; then he heard the barking exchange of a wolf pack. They'd probably found the entrails from the butchered cow and were feasting on it. When that was gone, their noses would lead them to the shed and the beef carcass hanging in the corner. The man smell would probably keep them from trying to get at it, but just to be on the safe side, Webb reached out from under the quilt and slipped the rifle out of its scabbard to lay it alongside him. The gelding snorted again.

"I hear 'em," he murmured, and the horse seemed to blow out a satisfied breath.

16

A noise awakened Lilli from her fitful slumber. At first she thought it was the wolves again. Then she recognized it as a different sound and tiredly pushed off the bed, pulling the loose shawl more firmly about her shoulders. It sounded like a horse outside. She wiped at the sleep in her eyes and pushed back the hair she hadn't bothered to braid last night.

In a flash it hit her that Webb might be leaving without saying good-bye. She raced to the door and flung it open, then stopped cold when she saw Stefan sliding off the bare back of a draft horse. There was a second horse, carrying Franz Kreuger. She darted a worried look at the shed, wondering if Webb was still there or if he'd heard the riders come in.

"You vere vorried about me," Stefan judged by the hint of concern in her expression. "I am fine. I stayed vith Franz. As soon as the storm ended, I told him I must get back to my Lillian."

"I hoped you were there," she said and stepped back from the door to admit the two men.

"Vere you all right? I vorried about you being alone." A little frown creased his forehead. His vague bewilderment increased when he noticed the wisps of straw clinging to her hair and the straw chaff on the back of her shawl as she crossed to the stove. "Have you been out to take care of the horses this morning already?"

"No, I haven't." Her back was to him as she bent to open the stove grate and stir up the coals. "As a matter of fact, I haven't stoked the fire or put coffee on yet. I've been sleeping. I guess it was the sound of your horses that woke me up."

She had been sleeping in her clothes? And her hair wasn't in its nightly braid. Stefan's frown deepened. Neither of these things was normal for her. She straightened from the stove to pick up the coffee pot and carry it to the water pail, giving him a side view of her.

"And you needn't have worried about me being alone," she said, busying herself with filling the pot with water. "Mr. Calder came by. He went out looking for you before the storm began, but he couldn't find you. He barely made it back here himself."

"Calder vas here?" A bitter anger began to fill him with its birthings in jealousy and fear.

"Yes. He slept in the shed with the horses last night." The information came out with a certain quickness that pulled Stefan's gaze to the particles of straw in her hair. "I haven't seen him this morning, so I don't know whether he's left or not."

"You vere in the shed vith him." His voice rumbled in accusation, surprising a slightly stricken expression to cross her features before she stopped it. For all her outward show of calm, Stefan sensed a tension about her, and his hand tightened its grip on the rifle.

"I took him a quilt," she admitted, lifting her chin a fraction.

"Look at her eyes." Franz Kreuger stood at Stefan's side and leaned slightly toward him when he spoke, as if to share some secret knowledge with him. "They are puffy and red. She has been crying. What do you suppose happened to make her cry?"

The question only increased Stefan's dark suspicions. He was vibrating with the anger that welled within him. "Did he violate you?" He glowered at her, channeling his rage into vengeance to justify its existence.

"No!" she denied, her shocked gaze flying to Franz Kreuger, then back to Stefan.

"Look at how frightened she is." Franz turned the brooding fire glittering in his eyes on Stefan, certainty burning in his expression. "He has threatened her. She is afraid to tell the truth."

"Stefan, don't listen to him," Lilli protested in alarm.

But Stefan looked at the evidence his own eyes had seen and the supporting observations from his wise friend, and drew his own conclusions. Revenge was much nobler than the jealousy of an old man for a younger one. Always a man of few words, Stefan did not speak of his intentions as he turned away to stride toward the door, his rifle in hand.

"Stefan!" Lilli pushed the coffee pot onto the stove and ran after him, but Stefan ignored her cry as he bolted out of the shack and levered a bullet into the rifle chamber.

The black gelding stirred restively, its ears swiveled to the human activity outside, and its animal instinct sensed something was wrong. The horse's movements roused Webb from a deep sleep, his subconscious picking up the primitive warning from the animal. Automatically he reached for the rifle lying alongside him, still not fully awake, and expecting to hear the snuffling and clawing of wolves outside the shed as they had been doing off and on through the predawn hours.

When the door was thrown open, suddenly and violently, instinct took over, bringing Webb to his feet in a crouched, defensive posture. The rifle was aimed low from his hip as he prepared to meet this unknown attack. All in the same instant, Webb recognized the whiskered man charging into the shed as Lilli's husband and started to relax his guard before he saw the murderous look in the man's eyes.

An explosion, red tongues of flame from the rifle in Reisner's grip, and a woman's cry all mingled together as Webb was spun backward by the impact of a bullet fired at close range. It knocked him against the carcass hanging in the corner. He grabbed at it for support, his own rifle lost somewhere in the straw.

The neighing of frightened horses surrounded the second explosion of the rifle. This time the bullet was buried in the frozen beef carcass that Webb had instinctively used as a shield when he'd heard the clicking of the rifle's lever action. He knew he'd been shot, but shock kept him from feeling any more than a burning sensation in his side.

Defenseless against the attack, Webb knew he had to get out of the corner. He could hear Lilli screaming for her husband to stop. When he saw her struggling for the rifle, a shutter clicked in his mind to hold the picture in his memory. He lunged toward the pair as Reisner pushed Lilli out of his way. The rifle was swinging around to bear down on Webb again when he slammed into his assailant and drove him against the shed wall. He grabbed for the rifle to disarm Reisner.

Something cracked against the back of his head, sending an excruciating shaft of pain through his body. Exploding lights blinded him; then all was blackness.

"Webb!" Lilli gasped in horror as he crumpled to the ground, felled by Franz Kreuger's blow. She rushed to his still form, falling to her knees beside him. The left side of his shirt was wet with blood, its stickiness reddening her hand when she touched it. Relief quivered through her when she saw he was still breathing, even though it was frighteningly shallow. "He's alive."

"Stand avay from him," Stefan ordered.

She looked up at him, consumed by fear. "No," she refused in a half-plea, then saw the rifle Stefan was pointing at Webb and reinforced her refusal with defiance. "No, I won't let you kill him."

"Come away from him, woman." Franz Kreuger added his harsh command to Stefan's and moved to enforce it by taking Lilli by the shoulders to pull her away. "This is a man's business. It is no place for a woman."

"No!" She struggled wildly, frightened of what Franz Kreuger might goad Stefan into doing. "You can't kill him in cold blood! For God's sake, listen to me, Stefan!" she stormed through her tears, straining against the iron talons of Kreuger's fingers.

"No one vould convict a man of defending his wife's honor." Stefan flashed her one brief look.

"Oh, Stefan," she sobbed in defeat, forced to condemn herself. "If there is any guilt, I must share in it. He did nothing I didn't want him to do." She saw the shattering effect of her confession and wanted to die for hurting Stefan that way. He stared at her, a broken man. And, most shaming of all, the man whose respect he sought above all others' was there to witness the ultimate humiliation, his wife's faithlessness.

"You have done this to me?" His voice murmured.

"Stefan, please let me explain?" Lilli asked to be given the benefit of a doubt. "I won't leave you. I wouldn't have done that to you."

"You make of me a cuckold and I am to forgive?" he replied in a flat voice. Then he lifted a weary hand and turned his face from her. "Go to the house."

Lilli had stopped fighting Kreuger's restraining hands. At Stefan's last statement, he let her go. But she made no move to leave the shed, her gaze searching Stefan's averted profile.

"What are you going to do with him?" she asked, glancing briefly at Webb's motionless form. "He'll bleed to death if he doesn't get help."

"I don't know." His shoulders lifted in an impatient shrug at her continued concern for this other man. "I vill take him to his family." The decision was difficult for him.

"But there's a doctor in town," Lilli argued weakly.

His head came up with a semblance of his old pride. "I do not vish the whole town to know of vhat transpired here," he informed her coldly. "Go to the house."

There was no need for him to explain that he was not concerned about the town knowing of the shooting, but rather the cause of it. At this point, there was nothing else Lilli could do except obey him. She paused at the shed door and took one last look at the crumpled body on the straw, her eyes clouded with tears.

Not a single word was exchanged between

the two men as the team of horses pulled the wagon through the blowing snow. Metal harness pieces and chains jangled loudly in the cold morning air, wagon runners slicing through the crusty surface of the snow. Stefan Reisner looked neither to the right nor to the left as he drove the wagon-sled into the heart of the Triple C headquarters. In the back of the wagon, the unconscious man was wrapped in a quilt, not having stirred or made a single sound during the journey to the ranch.

There was little activity around the ranch-yard. Those that were out and about stopped and stared at the drylander's wagon that never wavered from its course to The Homestead, the big two-story house rising atop the knoll. Stefan drove the team right up to the front steps of the long porch and stopped.

Showing no haste, he climbed down from the wagon and walked to the rear. Franz Krueger was there to help him lower the tailgate. Stefan reached and dragged the quilt-wrapped body to the edge, where he hefted it onto his shoulder like a sack of grain. With Franz leading the way, he walked up the steps to the front door and pounded on it with his gloved fist.

From the window in his den, Benteen Calder had already noted the wagon's arrival and was on his way to the solid wood door, reaching it before it stopped vibrating from the hard pounding. He pulled it open, a frown gathering on his face at the sight of the bearded homesteader and the boots sticking out of the quilt he carried on his shoulder. There was no friendliness in the man's cold-reddened face as he carried his bundle inside, uninvited.

"It's your son. Vhere you vant me to put him?" The statement was made in a flat voice, as calmly as if he were announcing he had a rug to deliver.

"My son," Benteen repeated in shock, his gaze racing back to the boots, which was all he could see of him. But the drylander was already walking past him to the living room.

Benteen turned to follow, ignoring the second man, who also entered the house. Lorna was just coming out of the kitchen, wiping her hands on her apron.

"Who was —" She never finished her question as she watched the old but massively strong man dump his quilted bundle on the living-room sofa.

The ends of the quilt fell away to reveal Webb's bloodless face. By then, Benteen was already there, raging inside at the thought that he'd lost his only living child. Long ago, he had taken the lifeless body of their youngest son, Arthur, from Lorna's arms. No man should live to see the death of all his children. He heard Lorna's broken cry, but first he had to know. His hand went to Webb's throat, seeking a pulse, while his gaze began to travel his son's length. It went no farther than his blood-soaked left side and the hole in the material.

"He's been shot." Benteen turned on the man who had brought him, hard demand mixing with his rage. "Who did this?"

There was no reaction in the man's expressionless features. "I caught him vith my vife and I shot him," he stated without blinking.

The explanation that preceded the admission negated any justification Benteen had for his avenging anger. The muscles stood out in his neck as he faced the man his son had wronged, bitterly swallowing his rage.

Behind him, Lorna exclaimed in breathless relief, "Benteen, he's alive!"

A pain shot through his left side when he heard the hopeful words. He clutched at his arm, and glared at the drylander. "Get out," he ordered hoarsely.

"If your son lives, tell him I vill kill him if he comes near my vife again," the man vowed in the same emotionless voice as all his previous pronouncements, then turned and walked from the room with the second man following.

As they left through the front door, Nate Moore and two other curious riders came sauntering in. "What did those two want?" he asked before noticing the body on the sofa Benteen and Lorna were crouched beside. "That's Webb!" He abandoned his lazy pose and rushed to the sofa. The bloodied side of the shirt had been ripped open to expose the bullet-ruptured flesh around the hole wound and the coldly caked blood. "He's been shot."

"The bleeding's stopped, but he lost a lot." Benteen shot a look at Nate, as if just realizing he was there. "Ride for the doctor, and just don't kill the horse before you get there."

"Do you want me to round up the boys to be ready to go after the dudes that did it?" Nate looked at his boss expectantly.

"No." It was a grim reply.

A frown flickered across Nate's forehead. "You don't want me to bring the sheriff back, do you?"

"No!" The second denial was more forceful than the first. "Dammit, I said to get the doctor. Now, go!"

The word was rapidly transmitted to every man and woman on the Triple C in the curiously swift way the invisible range telegraph works. Riders were dispatched to every outstation and line camp on the place, spreading the word that it was not only one of their own that had been shot, but the boss's son. Ruth was at The Homestead within minutes of hearing the news. All the others gathered at the bunkhouse or the cookshack, their attention divided between the big house on the knoll where Webb lay unconscious and the direction from which the doctor would arrive.

Since none of them knew the details of the shooting or the identity of the other parties involved, speculation was rampant. But there wasn't a one of them — especially among the older men who had trailed north with Benteen, fought renegades, and battled rustlers to carve out this cattle empire — who didn't believe there would be some sort of retaliatory response against the perpetrators of this deed. Everyone knew that when someone struck out at a Calder, he got hit back twice as hard. So they waited.

When she heard the jingle of the harness and the whispery rush of the runners attached to the wagon, Lilli wanted to run to the door, but she waited inside, sitting with her hands folded in her lap. Her hair was smoothly piled on top of her head, those damning pieces of straw brushed out. She looked composed and ready to make her explanation to Stefan, but it was all on the outside. Inside, she was a seething turmoil of anxiety, guilt, and torn desires. Her concern for Webb almost blocked out everything else.

It was a long, nerve-racking wait Lilli had to endure. The horses had to be unhitched from the wagon and the harnesses removed and stowed away. An eternity passed before she heard the stamp of his feet outside the door. He walked into the shack and began taking off his winter coverings without looking at her once.

"Stefan, I'm sorry about what happened." She couldn't tolerate his condemning silence.

He looked at her once with cold eyes, then walked to the stove. A helpless anger quivered through her at this silent refusal to listen to any explanation from her. It made her all the more determined to give one.

"He brought us some meat. A cow had broken its leg and he had to shoot it. Then he brought it here for us. You must have seen the carcass hanging in the shed," she insisted.

"I threw it out," he finally responded in a voice that was flat of feeling. "I vant nothing from him. Let the volves feast on it."

A whole beef. But Lilli said nothing of the waste, aware that Stefan's action was a pitiful grasp at pride. "When he found out you had gone hunting, he warned me there was a storm coming. That's why he went out to look for you."

"He vishes I had died in the snow." But it sounded as if he were voicing his own wish.

"Stefan," Lilli murmured brokenly. He didn't appear to be listening to her. "He wanted me to go away with him, but I told him no. I —"

"Enough!" he thundered, then just as quickly brought that spate of rage under control. His expression was wooden when he finally looked at her again. "Ve vill speak of this no more."

"Stefan, you have to understand —"

"No more." It was decisive and cold.

But his words seemed to signal an end to something else — the closeness that had been such a vital part of their relationship. He wasn't her longtime friend and companion, but a stranger who didn't want her to heal the hurt she had caused. Lilli wanted to tell him that he could banish the subject but he could never banish the memory from their minds. Somehow she knew it was hopeless. The years had never stretched so wide between them before.

Benteen had a couple of the boys carry Webb upstairs to his old bedroom. The doctor was taken there when he arrived. He was a relatively young man, a year out of medical school back east. Slightly awed by the size of the house, Dr. Simon Bardolph was a little anxious about his own skills, especially while examining his patient under the intimidating presence of Benteen Calder himself. He'd never treated a bullet wound before. It was an exciting first in his western adventure, but he thought it better to keep that information to himself.

"The bullet passed completely through." He was a little disappointed by that discovery. If he'd had to probe for it, it would have made a dandy souvenir. "Doesn't appear to have damaged any vital organs, which is very lucky," he assured the gentleman hovering on the other side of the bed and tried to make professional comments. "It's a miracle he didn't bleed to death, though. The cold must have prevented that." He smiled at the blond-haired woman who helped apply a fresh bandage to the wound. "Barring any infection, it should heal very nicely. Naturally he'll be quite weak from the loss of blood."

"When will he regain consciousness?" Benteen Calder made it a demand for information rather than a simple inquiry.

"That's a nasty bump on his head." Dr. Simon Bardolph considered his answer carefully. "He could regain consciousness in a few minutes or a few hours, possibly two days." And maybe never, but he chose not to broach that possibility now. "That's about all I can do for him. Naturally I'll come by tomorrow."

"Thank you, Doctor." Mrs. Calder came up beside him, the only one in the room who seemed to understand the limits of his healing abilities. "There's hot coffee and homemade apple pie downstairs. I hope you will have some before you leave."

"That's kind of you, ma'am." He folded together his black bag and moved to follow her out of the room.

"You'll stay with Webb, won't you, Ruth?" Mrs. Calder inquired of the blond-haired girl. "Benteen?" She spoke her husband's name in a tone that prodded him into accompanying her.

Impatience made the stern line of his mouth appear even harder. He flashed a dark look at the woman called Ruth. "I want to know the minute he comes to."

"I'll call you," she promised and drew a chair next to the bed to begin her vigil.

But it was the middle of the second night before Webb stirred. Ruth had just come into the bedroom so Lorna could get some sleep. She was at his side with the first sign of movement.

"He has a slight fever." Lorna Calder wrung

out a wet cloth to lay on his forehead and handed it to Ruth.

As she laid it on his forehead, Ruth noticed his lips moving. She bent closer to quiet him, then froze as she heard him murmur something that sounded like *Lilli.* Her gaze jerked to Lorna Calder.

"Is he conscious?" Lorna asked anxiously.

"No. That is —" Ruth faltered. "Do you know anyone named Lilli?"

A stillness came over Lorna's features. "No, I don't know anyone by that name," she denied. Then she gave Ruth a considering look. "I'd rather you didn't mention this to Benteen."

"The man who brought Webb here, was he fairly old — with a gray beard?" Ruth asked, feeling the sharp pain of suspicion and trying to conceal it.

"Yes. Why?" Lorna Calder eyed her closely.

"I just wondered," Ruth murmured and lowered her gaze. Although she had asked how Webb had got shot, Lorna had indicated to her that she didn't know. At first, Ruth had thought that likely, since Webb hadn't regained consciousness. But if it was the same man who had brought him here that Ruth knew to be the husband of that young woman Webb had danced with at the Fourth of July celebration, it seemed very possible the shooting had been over that woman.

At some point this year, she had lost Webb and hadn't even known it.

17

"Benteen, please remember he's very weak," Lorna cautioned her husband before they entered Webb's room.

"I will." But he was impatient with the minor delay caused by her brief comment. Now that Webb had regained consciousness, he wanted to find out the actual circumstances that had surrounded the shooting. After two days of being gnawed by the old man's claim, Benteen couldn't accept it as true. "But there's some things I've got to find out."

As she opened the door, Lorna gave him another warning look that asked him to stay calm and take it slow. Ruth was sitting on the bed, spoon-feeding Webb some broth. Benteen was shaken by the whiteness of his son's face. It made the blackness of his hair and eyes and the stubble on his cheek all the more pronounced. An array of feather pillows supported him in a semireclining position. Benteen felt a stirring of anger again for the man who had laid low his vital, strapping son.

"Ruth, would you leave us alone with Webb for a few minutes?" Lorna requested.

Benteen needed the time to compose himself and bring his emotions under control. He was trembling, and he shoved his hands deep into his pockets so it wouldn't show. While Ruth gathered up her tray to leave, Benteen ranged alongside the bed, searching the pale features of his grown son. He didn't say a word until Ruth had left the room.

"How are you feeling, son?"

"All right." His voice lacked strength. "I guess it's a good thing I've got a hard head." The effort of speaking seemed to send shock waves through his head, increasing the pounding pain that fluctuated between a steady dullness and a stabbing sharpness.

"I want to know about the shooting, Webb," Benteen stated, broaching the issue that had brought him to the room. "I want to know what happened and who did it."

It wasn't a physical pain that closed Webb's eyes. "Forget it."

"Forget it?" The retort came back fast and sharp, loaded with temper.

"Benteen." Lorna issued a quiet warning from her position at the head of the bed.

372

He struggled to lower his voice and it came out rough with the effort. "I'm not going to accept that. Now, you are going to tell me what happened and why?"

"I said forget it," Webb repeated, opening his eyes to challenge his father. But Lorna saw the film of moisture in them and felt her heart twisting for her son. It was a stupid code that men had to do their crying on the inside, and she wished she could cry Webb's tears for him. "This is my business. It has nothing to do with you," Webb insisted.

"Like hell it doesn't!" Benteen towered beside the bed. "You are a Calder, and that makes it my business, too!" His hands came out of his pockets to thrust a finger at Webb. "Nobody shoots my son — nobody shoots one of my riders — that I don't take a personal interest in the reason!"

"It had nothing to do with the ranch." Webb sank tiredly against the pillows; the argument was costing him what little strength he had.

"It doesn't matter if it's personal or business," his father insisted. His mouth was compressed in a tight line as he waited for a response and didn't get it. "The man who brought you here claimed he caught you with his wife." He challenged Webb to deny the information. When the denial didn't come, he was forced to demand, "Is that true?"

A silence ran through the room before the simple, one-word answer was given. "Yes."

"By God, you'd better have more of an explanation than that." His father's voice vibrated. The line of his jaw stood out, muscles harshly clenched. "How could you become involved with a married woman?"

"I love her." His candor touched Lorna, but it didn't sway Benteen at all. "I would have taken her away from him if I could." Webb didn't expect his father to understand, so he wasn't disappointed by his reaction.

"You weren't raised to take what belongs to another man," his father condemned him in hoarse anger.

"Benteen, I think you'd better leave." Lorna came between them, confronting her husband with a determined look he had seen before. "You found out what you wanted to know. The rest can wait until later, when Webb is stronger."

"How can you defend him?" he challenged.

"He's my son, and he's your son," she countered without hesitation. "Right now, he's too weak to lift his head, let alone take on you." She faced him squarely, not giving an inch. "I mean it, Benteen. Leave the room."

"All right," Benteen conceded grimly. "I'll

wait until he's out of that bed."

He turned on his heel and walked briskly from the room. Lorna waited until the door had closed behind him before shifting her attention to Webb.

No matter how much he had been prepared for his father's anger, it still added to his broken despair. His memory of the shooting was laced with an unreality that didn't quite make anything clear, even less reveal how he had survived. He guessed Lilli had somehow kept Reisner from killing him. Lilli. What had happened to her? He damned the wound that had taken his strength.

When he saw the sadness and regret in his mother's expression, he sighed tiredly and aggravated the fiery pain in his side. "Don't apologize for him, Mother," he said. "I expected it."

She combed her fingers through his hair in a loving gesture and smoothed it away from his forehead. "She is the young woman who was injured at the fire," she guessed, and Webb nodded his head, not surprised by his mother's astuteness. "I thought so," she murmured and changed the subject. "We've had all your things brought over from the bunkhouse. You're going to stay here in your old room where we can take care of you." She ran her hand over his scratchy beard and tried to smile. "You need a shave, but first some rest, I think."

"I am tired," he admitted.

His mother started to leave his side, then turned back. "Webb," she began, "I know your father seemed unnecessarily harsh, but remember — his mother ran away with another man when he was a boy. I thought he'd gotten over it, but . . ." She hesitated. "He knows what that did to his father. It's hard for him to accept that his own son would deliberately try to break up a marriage."

No reply was necessary as his mother left the room. Webb stared out the window at the polar-blue color of the sky. It was a detail of his father's past that he'd forgotten. His mother had told him of it, but it was something his father never discussed.

His pain-troubled mind didn't dwell on that thought long. Soon the color of the sky was conjuring up images of Lilli and the incredible blue of her eyes. "If he laid a hand on you because of me, Lilli, I swear I'll kill him," Webb muttered, already drifting into the blackness of exhaustion.

That evening, Barnie Moore came to The Homestead, ostensibly to report on the effects of the storm, but he was tired of the waiting and speculating. He'd known Chase Benteen Calder since they were both wild pups, and his son Nate was Webb's best friend. Others might not dare to question the continuing silence from The Homestead, but Barnie wasn't one of them.

A fire crackled in the den's huge fireplace. The tongues of flames licking over the logs were the objects of Benteen's brooding attention as he sat in a leather-covered chair, a twin to the one Barnie occupied.

"On the whole, the herds have fared pretty well," Barnie said, wrapping up his discourse on the subject. "So far, the winter kill is running light."

"Good," Benteen grunted, but it seemed to be a response given automatically without being aware of what was said.

"How's the boy doin'?" Barnie started out with a safe inquiry.

"He's regained consciousness. You know that." Benteen slid him a short glance, aware the word had gotten around. Barnie confirmed it with a nod. "He's weak as a baby. It'll take him some time to get back on his feet."

"I figured that." Barnie struck a match and carried it to the tailor-made cigarette, cupping the flame to the tip and looking across at

Benteen. "I expect he was strong enough to tell you how he got shot."

With a flash of irritation, Benteen pushed to his feet and approached the fireplace. "It was an accident."

Barnie managed to blow out the smoke he inhaled before he choked on it. "An accident?"

"He was cleaning his rifle and it accidentally discharged," Benteen snapped at Barnie's skeptical response. "It happens all the time."

"And the knot on his head? I suppose he got that when he fell," Barnie doubted, and was even more convinced when he saw the bunching muscles on Benteen's back, signaling a controlled anger.

"Yes, I suppose he did." The clipped agreement accepted Barnie's reasoning.

"Then how do you explain how those farmers got ahold of him?" Barnie challenged quietly.

Benteen whipped around. "How the hell should I know!" he flared. "Maybe he took refuge at their place to wait out the storm." But he knew the explanation had holes in it, because it didn't provide a reason for Webb's not being at the line camp. "As far as you and everyone else is concerned, the shooting was an accident. That's all you need to know."

Without making a reply to that, Barnie rolled

slowly to his feet and walked to the fireplace to toss the burned match into the flames. "Is it all right if Nate comes to see him?" he asked instead.

"He's up to having visitors." Benteen nodded.

"He'll be by, then," Barnie said. "I'm glad to hear Webb's doin' better. You know we all feel like we've had a hand in raising him."

"Yeah." Benteen wondered if that was the problem. Maybe Webb had too many fathers. Or maybe it was his own mother's blood that ran in his son, making him irresponsible and unprincipled. Maybe Webb was a throwback to her. It had taken him a long time to accept his mother for what she was, but he couldn't tolerate those traits in his son. Some hard and painful decision had to be made.

He didn't hear Barnie leave the room.

Bare-chested, Webb stood in front of the wood-framed mirror. His middle was bound in a wide bandage that completely encircled him, while a pair of Levi denim pants hugged the length of his legs and hips. His face was half-covered with shaving lather, two swaths cut through it by the razor in his hand.

His hand trembled when he raised it to make a third wipe at his beard, his arm feeling incredibly heavy. Webb cursed this frightening weakness that still gripped him after more than a week and attempted to force his hand to carry out its task. He felt the sting of pain as the sharp blade nicked his skin. Cursing again, he reached for the towel to blot the blood from the cut. There was a quick knock at the door.

"Come in." He irritably gave permission for the person to enter.

The door opened and Ruth came in with his breakfast tray. "Good morning." She looked at him as she set the tray on the stand next to his bed. "What do you think you're doing?" she asked as he turned back to the mirror and rinsed off the blade in the basin of water.

"Shaving," he answered shortly, eyeing her reflection in the mirror next to his own.

She took away the towel he had pressed against the cut. "It looks to me like you weren't satisfied with the amount of blood you lost and decided to get rid of some more. Sit down." She gently pushed him toward a straight chair. "I'll finish that for you."

With mixed relief, Webb sank into the chair. His legs were rubbery and weren't up to standing for long periods. He'd been nearly to his limit, so part of him didn't mind letting Ruth take over the chore. He tipped his head onto the back edge of the chair and closed his eyes as the razor began making clean, firm strokes across his beard. He opened them to look at Ruth bending over him.

"You're pretty good at this," he remarked.

"I should be with as much practice as I've had on you." It was a simple statement, not meant to be bold or provocative. "Hold still and don't talk, or I'm liable to cut you. I'm not that good."

Webb fell silent, reminded by her remark of all the hours she'd spent with him since he'd been hurt. She'd fed him, washed him, shaved him, and read to him, not talking unless he did and going quietly about her work when he didn't.

When she finished, she handed him the towel to wipe off the last bits of lather. "Come eat your breakfast before it gets cold."

Webb wiped at his face as he stared after her, feeling vaguely puzzled. Getting up and crossing the room to the bed required an effort. He was breaking out in a sweat by the time he reached it, his strength sapped by that minor exertion. Ruth plumped the pillows to give him firmer support, then set the tray on his lap.

"Do you know you have never once asked me about the shooting, Ruth?" Webb realized. Everyone else had wanted a firsthand account, except her.

"Your father said it was an accident." She avoided his gaze. "I don't care how it happened or why. I just want you to get better."

"A woman who doesn't ask questions. You must be a new breed," he suggested dryly and watched her lips part as if she were going to say something, then come together again. "What were you going to say?"

"Nothing." She shook her head, denying there was any question she wanted to ask him. "Eat your breakfast. I'll come back for the tray in a little bit."

"Ruth." Webb called her back when she started to leave. "Thanks for not asking questions."

Her smile was small. As she left, Ruth wondered if it had ever occurred to Webb that she didn't want to know the answers.

It was well into the third week before Webb ventured downstairs. At first it was just for meals, and gradually it worked into longer periods. He didn't see much of his father. When he did, they had little to say to each other. They hadn't been on the best of terms for quite a while, and the relationship had become more strained since the shooting.

During his long recuperation, he'd had many hours to think about Lilli. It was better if he didn't see her again — better for both of them. Since she had made no attempt to contact him, he had to assume her decision to stay with her husband hadn't changed despite the shooting. Webb didn't want to share her. He didn't want an affair, never knowing when he could see her or how. It was better to leave the door closed.

The evening meal had been finished some time ago, but the three of them, Webb and his parents, were lingering at the table over coffee. Webb drained what was in his cup and set it back in its saucer. His father eyed him from his chair at the head of the table.

"Well." The word was issued in a challenging tone. "Are you up to taking me on, Webb? I promised your mother I'd wait until you were stronger before we had our 'discussion.'"

"Benteen —" His mother attempted to protest.

"It's no good, Lorna," he cut in. "Postponing isn't going to change my mind."

"He's right, Mother," Webb agreed. "There's nothing to be gained by putting it off any longer." He glanced at his father. "Shall we go to the den?" He received an affirmative nod, and both stood up at the same time.

"I'm coming too," his mother insisted and pushed her chair away from the table.

"No, you're not, Lorna," his father denied.

"This is one time when there's no room for a peacemaker. There are things that have to be said, and the talk is likely to get rough. I don't want you there. This is something Webb and I have to settle once and for all."

The showdown had been brewing for a long time, Webb realized as he left the dining room, walking stride for stride with his father across the entryway to the den. He didn't know what was coming, but he felt ready for it. Now that Lilli was obviously lost to him, there seemed to be very little in his life that had any meaning. So there was really nothing to lose.

Inside the room, Webb paused and waited for his father to close the doors. When they were shut, he walked to the fire and poked at the glowing logs until a flame shot up. His side was still sore, and he wasn't back to full strength by any means, but he felt able to take on his father.

"Drink?" His father asked, and Webb shook his head in refusal. "Neither do I. It isn't going to help the taste of anything I have to say."

"Then get on with it," Webb stated.

Benteen Calder looked at him and grunted out a laugh. "That's the only thing you've ever said that sounded like it came from a Calder." He shook his head in a kind of hopelessness and walked to his desk. "I guess you know this business with a married woman was the final straw."

"I didn't exactly plan to fall in love with another man's wife," Webb snapped. "But I don't expect you to understand that."

"Do you know what you are?" His father tilted his head to one side, studying him. "You're a saddlebum. You may not drift from ranch to ranch, but you're just like them in all the other ways. You do your drinking and brawling and whoring with the boys. And you'll never amount to a damned thing. You're always taking the easy way, letting someone else do the worrying and give the orders."

"That's your opinion." Webb set the poker back in its rack, feeling the hairs bristling on his neck at the sweeping condemnation.

"Opinion? You've never shown me you're anything else," Benteen shot back. "Do you see that map on the wall? When I was your age, I'd built that, fought for it, and owned it."

"I'm tired of hearing what you did when you were my age!" Webb flared. "What do you expect me to do? Go out and duplicate it just because it was what you did?"

"No! Dammit!" His temper was ignited by the flash of Webb's. "I've been waiting for years for you to start shouldering some of the responsibility around here, but you don't even

385

want to handle a roundup crew! Nothing you have said or done has shown me that you care what happens to this ranch!"

"Is this going to turn into another lecture about the ranch?" Webb demanded. "Because if it is —"

"No." His father paused, breathing hard as his voice grew deadly cold. "This isn't another lecture. Because I realize you aren't going to change."

"I'm glad you finally got it through your thick skull that I don't want anything handed to me," Webb retorted with a trace of sarcasm.

"I got it, all right. And you're not going to get handed a thing, because I wouldn't put the Triple C in the hands of an unprincipled, irresponsible bum like you," he stated. "You're not going to inherit the Triple C when I'm gone. You're not going to get one inch of this land."

Webb stared at his father, trying to take in what he'd just been told. It was as if someone had just ripped out his soul. A strange rage was building inside of him, thundering through his veins like a stampeding herd.

"You can't do that." His voice was tight, hardly sounding like his own.

"The hell I can't."

"Damn you to hell!" Webb was vibrating

with the force of his fury. "This land is as much mine as it is yours! I was born on it! I've worked it and rode every inch of it!"

"Have you, now?" There was a hard, calculating gleam in his father's eyes.

"You know damned well I have!"

"Do you want it?"

"Yes!" He had resisted it for so long that it came as a shock how desperately he wanted this ranch. He belonged to it. It was as much a part of him as his heart. "And, by God, I'm not going to let you take it from me!"

"If you want it, you're going to have to fight to get it," his father challenged. "You're going to have to show me that you've inherited some guts from your mother and me, because I don't think you have what it takes to hold on to a place like this."

"I'm a Calder, aren't I?" Webb retorted. "I'm your son."

"I don't know if you're a Calder." Benteen looked him up and down. "But you'd better be able to fight like one, because you're taking me on. You've got a helluva lot to learn, boy. You might do all right in a stand-up fight. What happens when it's down and dirty?"

The challenge was a figurative one and Webb knew it, but his combative fever was running high. Physical violence would have been a welcome release for his anger. So Webb responded to the taunt with a half-serious invitation.

"Why don't you and me tangle right here? We'd settle that question real quick," he declared.

The prospect seemed to amuse his father in an arrogant kind of way. "Are you sure you don't want to wait until your wound has completely healed and you've got more of your strength back?"

"No. I figure it would put us at an equal advantage, 'cause you're old and slow," Webb countered.

"Fists never win as many fights as brains do. You're thinking with your gut right now, boy. And that isn't the way to get this ranch from me," his father stated. "All you're doing right now is proving to me that you don't deserve it. You talk big, but you haven't shown me anything."

"We'll see about that." Webb agreed that no more could be accomplished with words. He swung away from his father and let his long strides carry him from the room.

Benteen watched him from the center of the room. He stood tall and straight, his big bones fleshed out and his dark hair frosted with gray. The expression of anger and taunting challenge that had been on his strong-lined face gave way to pride, and the gleam in his brown eyes misted over with tears. A second after he heard the sound of a pair of boots climbing the stairs, Lorna came hurrying into the room.

"What happened?" She searched his face, expecting the worst after the angry, shouting voices she'd heard and the way Webb had come charging out of the room. "Webb isn't leaving the ranch?"

"No." He reached out to take her in his arms and gather her against his chest. He rested his chin atop her head and closed his eyes, trembling relief and gratitude all mixing together. "I finally have my son."

"I don't understand." Lorna shifted in his hold and tipped her head back to look at him.

"He's going to fight me to get the ranch." Benteen was smiling. "I called him in here tonight to tell him he wouldn't inherit it."

"Benteen!" She was shocked at the statement, and more than a little angry.

"I had no choice." He defended his decision calmly now that he knew the outcome. "Up till now, he hadn't shown me he gave a damn about it. Deep down, I think I was hoping he would react the way he did, but Webb has disappointed me so many times."

"But what happens now?" Lorna didn't see

how it was going to work.

"Go up to his room, but don't say that I sent you," Benteen told her. "Tell him that a ranch this size has never been successfully run from a bunkhouse. And tell him that if he expects to have any authority, he's going to have to take it — and it isn't just a matter of giving orders. It's taking charge."

18

Once he had cooled down, it hadn't taken Webb long to figure out that he'd played right into his father's hand. But there was a difference. They weren't playing against each other. They were partners.

On the first day of spring roundup, the morning gather of bawling cattle was bunched about a hundred yards away from the chuckwagon where the bulk of the cowboys had collected. Webb was standing a little off to himself, not joining in with the men and trying to be one of them.

The branding fires were hot, the irons lying in them, ready for an afternoon's work. Webb swirled the coffee liquid and dregs in his cup, mixing them together before drinking the black and bitter stuff.

In a curious flash of memory, he recalled another cup of coffee he'd drunk on a stormy night and the auburn-haired woman who had poured it for him. His thoughts turned to Lilli at odd times, coming to him without warning and stabbing him with their futility. She had said no to him. And the very fact that she hadn't attempted to contact him or make any inquiry about him told Webb she hadn't changed her mind. She intended to stay with the man she had married. Even though he had thrown all his energies into the ranch, he still couldn't forget her.

He shook out the last drop of coffee and wandered over to the wagon to toss his cup into the wreckpan, aware the men were waiting for his signal to start the afternoon's work. But he paused there to light a cigarette, not making a move toward the saddled and fresh horses. In addition to Triple C riders, there were reps from other outfits on hand to claim strayed cattle and drive them back to their home ranges.

Nate ambled over to throw his plate and cup into the wreckpan, then paused to stand with Webb. "Sure feels good to be back on the payroll again after bein' flatbusted all winter." He took out his tobacco and papers to roll himself a cigarette. "Well, boss, are you about ready to slap down a few calves?"

"Soon enough." Webb smiled faintly at the term signifying his authority. It didn't grate as he thought it would.

The majority of the riders, especially the older hands, had regarded his step-up with silent approval, even though they were watching to see how he'd do. Webb didn't mind that, either, because it meant he'd be earning their respect — and they were going to expect more from him than they would from one of their own. It was crazy that he hadn't looked at it that way before.

Maybe he'd finally grown up. Maybe it had taken losing some of that hot blood of youth and getting cracked over the head. It was for certain a lot of hard lessons had been learned. He had wanted Lilli and Lilli had wanted him, but that hadn't made it right. Knowing that didn't make it any easier, but at least he was beginning to accept it.

He was doing it again — thinking about Lilli instead of concentrating on the business at hand. His glance ran to Nate, observing the miserly way he licked the tobacco paper together, conserving his spit for the long, dusty afternoon ahead of them. Roundups were brutal on a cowboy. Rain or shine, he worked every day until his muscles were too weary to know the difference, and never got enough sleep. It would be a grueling six weeks or longer.

"Why don't you smoke ready-mades and save yourself all that work, Nate?" Webb asked.

"I don't smoke as much this way — and it's cheaper," he added the decisive factor. He squinted through the swirl of smoke at the cowboy sauntering toward them. Hobie Evans was not one of his favorite people. Nate was of the opinion that Ed Mace could have chosen a better representative for his Snake M brand — but then, he didn't have much time for Ed Mace, either.

"Well, Mr. Big Boss?" Hobie stopped in front of Webb, addressing him a derisive challenge. "Are you figurin' on standin' around all day?"

Before Webb could respond, Nate inserted, "Sure seemed to me like there's a lot of strays mixed in that herd. More'n usual. Most of 'em were carrying a Snake M brand, too. How do you s'pose that happened?"

"We had a lotta trouble with our fences this year," Hobie was quick with an answer. "Add to that the way the snow drifted. It made regular bridges for the cows to walk over the fence. Those honyockers get right testy about cattle gettin' into their fields," he declared with a grinning smirk. "They sent 'em scattering with no courtesy at all about headin' 'em back to where they belong. The boss really needs to string new fence, but money bein' as short as it is, I don't imagine he'll be able to do much about keepin' his cattle in this year."

"You look all tore up about that, Hobie," Nate remarked dryly.

Webb took a last drag on his cigarette, then dropped the butt and crushed it under his heel. "Might as well get started branding and sorting this batch."

He signaled the start of the long afternoon's work by walking to the big, rangy bay horse he used for roping and swinging aboard. By the time he'd turned his horse toward the herd, the rest of the men were either sitting on their horses or stepping a boot into the stirrup.

It was customary for the ranch owner or his foreman to select the first calf to be branded at the roundup, so Webb rode into the herd and shook out a loop. He smoothly roped the nearest bounding calf and dragged it to the fire, where the branding irons of the various represented ranches were heating to an orange-red. The problem of choosing which brand to use was easily solved by applying one of the basic principles of cowboy lore. The calf would be branded the same as its mother, and a cow was quick to inform a cowboy with her wild-eyed bawling when he'd roped her calf.

Webb took one look at the cow watching

anxiously over her roped calf and called out the brand: "Triple C!" Two of the men on the ground wrestled the youngster down and Old Shorty Niles burned the appropriate brand on its flank.

A dozen more calves were branded in the same manner. Two more ropers joined in with Webb to work the herd. The next calf he snared was a hefty-sized youngster that had the look of a late-fall calf. An indistinct brand was already burned on its hip and it looked suspiciously like the Snake M even though its frantic mother carried the Triple C mark. The bellowing calf was thrown to the ground and the two men holding it looked expectantly at Webb, waiting for him to call the brand.

"Triple C." He shouted the order to blot out the other brand, then picked out Hobie Evans from the other reps around the branding fire. "Evans! You'd better tell Mace to teach his stray calves not to suck Triple C cows," he warned. It might have been an accident that the calf had the wrong brand, but then again, it might not. Webb had known he couldn't let the incident pass without a comment. Silence could have signaled to the unscrupulous an open season on unmarked calves.

The Snake M man had a decidedly unpleasant look on his face, but he made no comment to Webb's cutting advice as the air turned acrid with the smell of singed hides.

When Lilli walked into the general store at Stefan's side, she noticed the quick glances and the whispers from the wives of other dry-landers. She didn't blame Stefan for the knowledge in their eyes. The source was undoubtedly Franz Kreuger and his meek wife, who repeated everything her husband told her. Lilli felt like the heroine in that Nathaniel Hawthorne book, *The Scarlet Letter.* She walked a little straighter into their midst, her head held high. She was accustomed to this silent treatment, having endured so much of it from Stefan. Trust, she was learning, was a fragile thing. Once broken, it took a long time to repair, but the restoration was never total. The cracks were always visible, like a mended piece of china.

The advent of spring had brought her some relief, since Stefan had been in the fields from dawn until dusk. The additional acreage he'd purchased in the autumn meant more ground to be plowed and seeded in wheat, which had necessitated the purchase of another team of horses and the expense of a hired hand, the younger son of one of their new neighbors. No longer content with mere prosperity, Stefan saw wealth around the corner. Lilli suspected his sudden obsession with money was partially a result of his need to prove he was a man and overcome the sense of failure she had caused by her brief interlude with Webb Calder.

There were times in these last few months when her relationship with Stefan had seemed hopeless. On those occasions, she had wondered if she should have given in to Webb's entreaty to go away with him. She had too much time alone to think about him. His ghost haunted the shack and sat at the table during the many silent meals. She knew he had recovered simply because no one spoke of him around her. If he had died, they wouldn't have tried to keep the news from her.

Inside the store, she turned to Stefan, behaving neither subdued nor submissive. "I am going to look at material to make into shirts for you. Mr. Ellis mentioned he was expecting a new shipment when we came to town in April. I'm going to see if it has arrived."

With her intentions stated, she left it up to him whether he accompanied her or not. Stefan shadowed her every time they came to town. Lilli suspected that he believed she would arrange some rendezvous with Webb if he didn't. Wrong as it was, she hoped she would see Webb, not necessarily to speak to him, but just to see him.

Bolts of cloth filled the shelves on the far wall, along with needles, threads, and an assortment of buttons. When Lilli crossed the store to dry goods, Stefan didn't follow her. He knew where she was and could easily keep an eye on her. And Lilli was fully aware of it.

As she approached the bolts of shirt material, several women were crowded around the same shelf area, inspecting the selection of cloth. None of them attempted to make room for Lilli, ignoring her with subtle ostracism. Lilli struggled to be patient and wait her turn, but there was a part of her that was simmering. Finally she moved to the button counter, too angry to notice the two women examining the narrow spools of lace.

"I believe I prefer this one, Ruth. What do you think?" The older woman looked to the blond-haired woman for her opinion.

It was strictly female curiosity that prompted Lilli to glance at the pair and see if she would have selected the same lace, and also to find out who could afford to buy such a luxury item. The blonde's response was lost to her as she recognized the older woman with the dark, silvering hair. It was Webb's mother. There was no question about it. Her pulse quickened, and before she could entertain second thoughts,

Lilli approached her.

"Excuse me, Mrs. Calder." There was a slight break in her voice that made it almost a question.

"Yes?" The woman turned to her, the questioning glance giving way to a steady interest.

"How is your son?" Lilli managed to sound casual about the inquiry. "Is he well?"

"Yes, he is. He has fully recovered from his accident." There was slight stress on the last word.

"I'm glad to hear it." She couldn't hold back all of her smile. Her relief was too natural and genuine to be completely controlled.

"Are you Lilli?" his mother asked with a certainty that said she knew the answer. Webb was the only one who had ever used the abbreviated form of her name.

"Yes, I am," Lilli admitted and mentally braced herself against the disapproval she expected to see. There was something proud in the way she held herself, and something a little defensive. "Evidently he mentioned me to you."

"He has." But his mother didn't elaborate.

A feeling of depression began to weigh on her as Lilli realized this conversation had accomplished nothing beyond assuring her that Webb was well. Everything else remained the same.

Somewhat leadenly, she suggested, "I think it would be best if you didn't mention that I asked about him, Mrs. Calder."

"I understand." She nodded.

"Good day." Her glance skipped to both women as she took her leave and moved away.

This chance meeting with the young woman had answered many questions that had been in Lorna Calder's mind. She absently stared after the tall, straight back and the sheen of dark copper hair swept atop her head.

"How strange," Lorna murmured, then realized she'd said it aloud. Consequently the remark required an explanation. "In some ways, she reminds me of your mother, Ruth." Lorna Calder continued to study the woman named Lilli, so young and so proud. "She has the same strong spirit and boldness, the same determination. I think it's those qualities more than her looks that attracted Webb." She glanced at Ruth to see what she thought. Ruth was not adept at masking her feelings. The wounded hurt she saw in Ruth's expression made Lorna immediately regret so thoughtlessly listing the woman's attributes. "How silly of me," Lorna chided herself. "I don't know a thing I'm talking about. She probably isn't like that at all. Now, which lace did you say you preferred?"

Throughout the summer's hot days, Webb found himself more and more involved in the operation of the ranch. While much of the final authority remained with his father, Webb had the responsibility of seeing that the orders were carried out. It was a full-time job, taking his every waking minute, but he needed and welcomed this occupation that demanded all his time and energy.

Late on an August evening, Webb arrived at The Homestead well after the dinner hour. Tired and dusty after a day at one of the outcamps, he waved aside his mother's offer to fix him something to eat and made his own foray into the kitchen, coming back with some cold beef layered between two slices of homemade bread. He took it to the den where his father was finishing up some paperwork and plopped on the leather sofa, stretching out his legs and hooking a spurred heel across his other boot.

"The hay's up in the south branch." Webb took a bite of the bread and meat and chewed at it tiredly.

"It's time to be getting geared up for the fall roundup. I got a list of supplies here the cookie will be needing." Benteen Calder set the piece of paper to the front of his desk for Webb with only a brief glance in his direction.

"I'll send a couple of the boys into town after

it." Webb didn't rouse himself from his comfortable position to fetch the list, letting it lie on the desk for the time being.

"How long has it been since you were in town?" His father leaned back in his chair, studying him with a prodding look.

"A while, I guess." Webb shrugged and bit into the sandwich. Town was a place he had more or less been avoiding — town and the chance of seeing Lilli. He had needed this time to pass.

"It's time you went and found out firsthand what's happening in the area," his father stated in a decisive tone. "You get the supplies."

"It isn't necessary." Webb ignored the trace of command in the reply. "Besides, the boys have put in a hard summer. They deserve a day in town."

"Take them with you." Impatience flickered across his expression as Benteen Calder pushed out of his chair and came around the desk. "I'm making my own guesses about why you don't want to go into town. But I'll bet there are a bunch of drylanders that have come up with a different reason why you've made yourself scarce. Chances are they're going to think you're too scared. They figure they've got a hold on you. Do they?" he challenged.

"No." It was a hard, flat answer.

"Then you'd better prove it to them," Benteen advised. "And take Ruth along with you. She would welcome a trip into town."

"Why?" A dark frown creased his brow.

"Because you're not going to town hunting trouble. With a woman along, they'll see that," he reasoned calmly. "You aren't going to be hunting trouble, are you?"

"I won't back away if it comes to me," Webb replied.

"You wouldn't be a Calder if you did." His father turned and walked back to his desk.

The minute the buggy and its accompanying band of riders left the boundary of the Triple C land to make the ride into town, Webb was confronted by the changes less than one year had brought. Where once there had been pockets of dryland farms, now there were pockets of cattle range. Assorted shacks and shanties sat on both sides of the road at almost regular intervals. Long bands of wheat alternated with strips of plowed and fallow ground. Those stark and barren stretches of exposed earth created a grim picture of the land's unprotected underbelly. Webb acknowledged the sobering fact that the number of new settlers to the area hadn't tapered off. It had tripled or more.

When they rode into the bustling town of

Blue Moon, Webb had the uncomfortable feeling this was just the beginning. Last year there had been a mere shower of drylanders. They were in the middle of a deluge now. Blue Moon's single business street was busting at the seams, threatening to burst into a second. A half-dozen or more automobiles were competing with horse-drawn wagons for everything from open spaces in front of stores to water from the trough.

As they dismounted in front of the hardware store, Webb noticed Franz Kreuger among the knot of men on the raised board sidewalk outside the building. He hadn't noticed the Reisner wagon anywhere on the street, but he felt a leap of anticipation just the same. If his neighbor was in town, it was likely Stefan Reisner was, too — which also meant Lilli. It did no good to remind himself that nothing would be gained from seeing her.

Franz Kreuger had watched them ride up, and his eyes darkened with a brooding resentment. "Do you see how these ranch men never come to town alone?" He addressed the remark to his fellow homesteaders. "They know that our numbers are greater than theirs. So why do we make such small complaints when their cattle get into our fields and damage our crops? We must be more ready to defend what is ours.

My neighbor, Stefan Reisner, stood up to them. Right was on his side and there was nothing they could do about it. We must be prepared to do as he did, or the harassment will continue."

Kreuger made no effort to keep his voice down. Pieces of his remarks drifted to Webb as he helped Ruth out of the buggy, enough for him to get the gist of it. It was becoming apparent that Kreuger was a troublemaker, the instigator of much of the ill will between the factions.

When Webb approached the homesteaders with Ruth on his arm, his gaze was directed at Kreuger. He touched a finger to his hat in a challenging salute. "Hello, Kreuger. Gentlemen." His greeting was curt, but silence might have indicated he was intimidated. There was no response from Kreuger, not even a nod, but Webb hadn't expected one.

Inside the store, he was checking out a new spool of barbed wire the clerk was touting to be the best on the market when he happened to glance out the front window just as the Reisner wagon passed by. Webb had a brief glimpse of Lilli sitting very erectly on the wagon seat; then she was gone from his view. The urge was strong to leave the store and go after her, just for a closer look, but he fought it down. Yet knowing she was in town tested his self-imposed stricture to stay away from her.

After he'd made the necessary purchases at the hardware store, Webb stood on the sidewalk and watched the supplies being loaded in the wagon. Unwillingly he noticed the Reisner wagon parked at the smithy's, but neither Lilli nor her husband was in sight. It was just as well, he told himself.

Ruth came up to him. "It's nearly noon. Why don't we have something to eat at the restaurant?"

Tense and determined not to give in to his nerves, Webb hesitated, then agreed a little gruffly. "It sounds like a good idea." He hailed the slim cowboy sprawled on the buckboard seat with his feet propped on the kickboard. "Nate. See that everything's loaded in the wagon. I'm taking Ruth across the street to the roadhouse."

"Gotcha, Webb." Nate sat up in the seat to take interest in what was being loaded behind him.

With a guiding hand at Ruth's waist, he escorted her across the busy cross traffic of horse-drawn vehicles and skirted the animal droppings to the building on the opposite side of the street. The noise of people, animals, and vehicles was constant.

"I think I liked this town better when there weren't so many people," Ruth murmured.

Webb glanced down at her, just for a moment allowing his thoughts to be distracted. He saw her unease at so many unfamiliar and unfriendly faces. "It would never occur to you to speak to a stranger, would it?" he observed somewhat wryly, because it would have been as unnatural for Ruth as it had been natural for Lilli.

"No," she replied as if any other answer were unthinkable.

As he opened the door to the restaurant for Ruth, he happened to glance up the street. Lilli was just entering the general store with her husband. There was no indication that she'd noticed him. Webb was a step late following Ruth into the restaurant.

They had their pick of several empty tables and Webb chose one off by itself. He was restless with thoughts of Lilli throughout the meal, offering short responses to Ruth's attempts at conversation until she finally became silent.

It was no good, he realized. He was only fooling himself if he believed he could be in the same town as Lilli without somehow managing to see her and speak to her. In the two glimpses he'd had of her, she had appeared aloof and reserved, traits not natural to her. Perhaps he was only imagining that, but —

Ruth was seated on his right. Webb set his fork down and reached over to cover her hand. "Ruth, I have a favor to ask," he declared huskily, caught in the vortex of his own wants.

The intense probe of his dark gaze, as much as the touch of his roughly callused hand, made its impact on Ruth. She felt the swelling lift of her spirits, the acceleration of her pulse. If he only knew, she'd die for him if he asked her.

"Anything." She ignored the tiny little voice that gave away her eagerness to please.

"I'd like you to arrange for me to meet privately with a . . . certain young woman." He had difficulty getting the words out.

Ruth looked at her plate, a shattering pain destroying that fragile bubble of hope. "Lilli," she guessed in a trembling murmur.

Webb became still. He slowly removed his hand and picked up the fork he'd laid down. "Yes," he admitted in a low, flat voice. "How did you know her name?"

"When . . . you were unconscious, I heard you say it." It was a soft reply, filled with hesitance and hurt.

"Do you know who she is?"

"Yes." Ruth lowered her head.

It eliminated the need for an explanation,

which should have made it easier. Yet Webb felt twisted by a knotting tension. "There isn't anyone else I can ask, Ruth," he said. "I've got to talk to her. I've got to find out if she's all right."

"I don't see how I can arrange it." She inwardly railed at the unfairness of his request.

"I saw Lilli going into the general store before we came in here. She's probably still there." As crowded as the store had appeared, it was a good chance. "Ellis never locks the rear door. I can slip into the back room without being seen. All you have to do is make some excuse for her to go back there." He looked at her. "Will you do it?"

"Yes." Ruth made the bitter discovery that she could refuse him nothing, even at the cost of her own heartbreak.

When she entered the store, Ruth wanted to turn around and run out again, but she made herself move forward, her fingers nervously twisting the strings of her reticule. He face was pale and taut as her darting glance skipped over the many customers inside, strangers nearly all of them.

"Is there something I can help you with, Miss Stanton?" The proprietor's voice startled her.

"No," she answered quickly. "I . . . I'm just looking."

"The material you ordered has arrived. I have it in the back room. Would you like me to get it for you?" he asked.

And find Webb back there? Her heart fluttered wildly in panic. "No, please —" She strained to speak in a calmer tone. "I'd like to look around first. I'll collect it later."

"Certainly." He smiled politely. "If you'll excuse me, I have some other customers."

"Of course." Her breathing leveled off to a more normal rate.

She waited until he had moved away before resuming her search of the store. Maybe the woman had left and she would be spared this, Ruth hoped. But it was not to be, she realized as she spied the woman examining some yard goods.

A tiny rebellious seed tried to grow when Ruth made her approach, but it was quickly suppressed by her promise to Webb. She saw the flash of recognition in the dark blue eyes, an awareness that they'd met although not spoken; then her glance was quickly averted.

Ruth was not practiced in the subtleties of deception. If she took too much time to think about what she had to say, she might not say anything at all. "Would you come into the back room with me?" She blurted the request with nervous quickness. The stunned look she received in response made Ruth realize she needed an excuse. "To look at some material I ordered. I have more than I need and I thought —"

"I can't really afford to buy any," her rival replied. "I was only looking at this . . . dreaming, you know."

"Would you come in the back room and look at what I have? It's just right through that curtain."

Puzzled by the blonde woman's obvious agitation and air of urgency, it suddenly occurred to Lilli that the woman might have something to tell her about Webb. It became imperative that she find out.

"All right," Lilli agreed.

As they reached the curtained opening, Ruth started to lift the material aside when the sharp-eyed proprietor saw them. "Is there something I can get you ladies?"

Ruth was guiltily quick with her answer. "No, I was just going to show her the material I ordered. You did say it was back there?"

"Yes, but I'll be more than happy to bring it out to you," he offered.

"You're busy," Ruth insisted nervously. "We're just going to take a quick peek before we finish our shopping."

One of the other clerks called to Ollie Ellis, requiring his assistance, so he didn't persist. "It's on the right-hand side as you enter, the second shelf."

"Thank you," Lilli said and ducked around the curtain to follow the blond-headed woman into the dim storeroom. "What is it you wanted?" she asked, cutting through any motions of looking at material.

The woman didn't answer except to turn slightly and look into the far corner where sunlight filtered through the dirty panes of a high window. Something moved. Lilli unconsciously stiffened, instinct already telling her who was there.

What light reached the corner broke against the ebony-dark surfaces of Webb's eyes and cast strong shadows under his jaw and the exposed hollow at the base of his throat. Tall and wide in the shoulders, he was narrow at the hips from the many hours in a saddle.

As they faced each other across the slanting light rays, Webb saw the pride and strong will that made her different from any other woman he'd known. Her head was thrown back and the dusty sunlight was picking up the subtle luster of her deep-copper hair. She was wearing a plain russet gown that flowed smoothly down the length of her straight, swinging body. He thought she was going to leave.

"Lilli." The use of her name stayed her, although there was no lift, no urgency, in his low voice.

She appeared to change her mind and came slowly toward him. She stopped with her firm chin angled toward him. Her lips lay smoothly together, not smiling. Webb was conscious of the many disturbing things that kept them both silent.

"Why are you here?" she asked in a lowered voice.

"I had to see you. I had to find out for myself whether you were all right, whether he had mistreated you after — afterward."

The strain began to show on her as she listened to the run of his voice and its repressed feelings. Neither was aware of Ruth fading into the background, a silent sentinel keeping watch with her back to them while the low murmur of their voices added a multitude of little wounds.

"Stefan has done nothing to hurt me," Lilli assured him at last. "You shouldn't be here."

"I'm here. There's no good talking about it." His voice was on the ragged edge of anger. "Wrong or not, wise or not, I had to see you — talk to you."

When she looked at his face, she saw the hunger in his eyes, the reckless reason that had prompted him to arrange this clandestine meeting. It broke through the thin barrier that had held him motionless for so long. He gripped the points of her shoulders and pulled her against him, shutting off her faint cry with a kiss. Webb hadn't intended to be rough with her; he had meant to show her through his gentleness how deeply his feelings ran, but the claiming of her lips bred a desire for a wilder union. Lilli responded with her own rush of feelings. With their arms locked around each other, they swayed, pressing and straining, until Lilli finally slid her face to the side and drew away.

A sadness close to despair took the pride from her slim body and pressed her lips tightly together. The very thing that had driven her out of his arms pushed her back to them, curling her head against his chest. Webb held her loosely, shattered by her terrible, quiet crying.

"Lilli, I asked you once to leave him —"

She pulled back and lifted her chin. Webb had an instant to see the unguarded longing in her eyes before her loyalty intervened to take it from him. "I won't," she dully repeated

415

her previous refusal.

"I've got to be able to see you now and then," he insisted roughly. "We can arrange something —"

"No." She shook her head firmly, rejecting his proposal with no hesitation. "I won't meet you like this again."

It angered him that she could show so little feeling. "I'm letting you stay with another man. All I'm asking is to see you." Dryness rustled through his voice. "You can't possibly love me as much as I love you."

"There are only two people in my life who matter," she returned quietly. "You and Stefan. The last time we were together, you were nearly killed and Stefan was broken. I couldn't endure that again." She looked at him with a resigned sadness. "You are young, Webb. You can forget me and find another woman to love. Stefan is an old man."

"You've finally recognized that," he muttered tersely, attacking the only thing he could.

"Good-bye." She was already moving away. Before he could stop her, she was on the other side of the curtain. Webb turned back, his shoulders sagging, and glanced bleakly at Ruth. She lifted a hand toward him, but he brushed it aside as he left through the back door.

19

The locomotive chugged at intervals in the Blue Moon station while it took on more water and its freight was unloaded. A keening north wind blew across the wide plains, dusted with dirty snow. Winter had its cold, blue hand on the sweep of Montana sky. Webb stood on the station platform with his parents, his collar turned up against the wind and his hat pulled low.

"I still don't know how you managed to get him to agree to this trip, Mother." There was a faint twinkle in his eyes as he smiled at the slight figure she made, wrapped in the warmth of a fur, with a jaunty little hat adorning her silver hair.

"Hush, Webb. You don't need to give him any ideas about backing out," she admonished in jest, then sighed and gazed at her husband. "I doubt it was the letter I received from my mother, letting me know my father wasn't well.

417

It's that bull he heard about. It's always cattle."

A low chuckle came from Benteen's throat. "I can't think of another reason to go to Texas," he declared and put a coated arm around her shoulders, glancing at Webb. "You're going to get a taste of what it's like to be in sole control of the ranch while we're gone."

"I think I can manage to hold things together for a month," Webb said dryly.

"Was that box of presents loaded with our baggage?" His mother turned an anxious glance toward the railroad car. "I told Mother I'd be bringing them so we could celebrate a second Christmas together."

"The porter loaded it," Webb assured her.

"Booarrd!" The conductor called out his long announcement to the waiting passengers.

"That's us," his father declared and extended a hand to Webb. "It's all yours, son. Take care of it."

"I will." His hand was clasped in a solid grip, held an instant, then released. Webb bent to kiss his mother's cheek. "Good-bye, Mother."

Her dark eyes were misted with tears. "Take care of yourself." Her gloved fingers fluttered against his cheek.

"Women," his father murmured with a wry shake of his head. "She's talked about going to

Texas for ages. Now she's crying because we're leaving."

"All aboard!" the conductor called again.

Webb walked with them to the passenger car. "Enjoy yourselves and don't worry about anything here," he said as they paused on the car's platform to wave a last time. Then the conductor was signaling the engineer to move out.

As the train pulled away, Webb stood on the platform, his hands shoved deep into the pockets of his coat. The dusty red caboose rocked over the rails, blocking his view of the passenger cars. He turned and walked to the buggy, climbing in to take up the reins and click to the team of matched bays.

The big house seemed unnaturally quiet that evening. Webb had the feeling it, too, was watching to see how he would handle things. He walked into the den and stopped in front of the desk to look at the framed map. He felt the responsibility the land carried, not only its size, but the well-being of all who lived on it, the cowboys and those with families as well as the animals in their care. He moved his shoulders as if testing the fit. It didn't bind him, yet he felt the loneliness of it. The need for Lilli was strong in him.

The needlework lay idly in her lap as Lorna Calder studied her mother dozing in the rocking chair with her mouth open. The withered skin and the shriveled body went with the thinning white hair, but they didn't match the image that had been locked in her mind for so many years. She had known her parents had grown older, yet she hadn't allowed her picture of them to age. She remembered them so differently.

A smile tugged at the corners of her mouth. Who could ever have imagined her mother snoring? But she was the source of the sound that rose and fell with her breathing. Lorna picked up the needlework to resume the tiny stitches where she had left off.

The afternoon quiet was disturbed by the rattle and chug of an automobile coming down the street outside, its noisy din growing louder as it approached. The stillness was shattered by a sudden, explosive backfire that startled her mother out of a sound sleep. She flung up her hands, the rocker taking off on a noisy creak.

"It's all right, Mother." Lorna spoke up quickly. "It's just an automobile."

"Those noisy contraptions." She settled back in her chair and impatiently tugged the shawl around her shoulders. "The streets aren't safe anymore." She sniffed her disapproval. "They're all over the place."

"They certainly are becoming popular," Lorna conceded.

Her mother sat up straighter, her wrinkled lips pinching together. "It sounds like that thing stopped in front of the house. Probably broke down. Go take a look, Lorna." She waved a bony finger to hurry her along.

Lorna set her needlework aside and walked to the window. Her eyes widened in disbelief when she recognized Benteen climbing out of the car. "Good heavens, it's Benteen." She didn't bother to elaborate as she hurried out the door into the Texas-mild February afternoon. "What are you doing in that thing?"

"How do you like it?" A smile split his sun-leathered face.

"Like it? What do you mean?" She took another look at the black vehicle. "Don't tell me you bought this?"

"I did. I've arranged to have it shipped north with that new bull I bought." He brushed at the dust that had collected on the shiny black fender. "It's one of Ford's Model T's. That's genuine leather on the seat. Climb in and I'll take you for a 'spin' — which is the salesman's vernacular for a ride," he explained with a wink.

421

"Are you sure you know how to operate this thing?" Lorna eyed the machine with a degree of skepticism.

"One of the first things I learned was 'giddy-up' and 'whoa' don't work," Benteen teased. "Get in and I'll start it up." He helped her into the passenger seat, then walked around to the front. "To start the motor, you have to crank it. It's like priming a pump." He began turning the crank handle, which produced a grinding noise and a weak sputter.

"Are you sure you know how to start it?" Lorna chided playfully when he stopped to catch his breath.

"It takes some cranking," he assured her and vigorously turned the crank again.

Suddenly, he stopped, bending over to clutch the front edge of the hood. There was a fleeting moment when Lorna thought he was teasing her. Then he sank to his knees and she saw the hand clutched at his chest.

"Benteen, what is it?" She clambered out of the car to rush to his side. He was laboring for breath, his face pale and contorted with pain. "What's wrong?" She tried to get a shoulder under him and help him to his feet.

"My chest . . . the pressure . . ." His rasping voice explained no more than that as more and more of his weight sagged on her.

"Benteen. Oh, my God," Lorna sobbed, unable to support him. She looked to the house. "Momma!"

Both hands were clamped tightly around Benteen's, so Lorna could feel the reassuring beat of his pulse, no matter how weak and faint. The black-coated doctor folded his stethoscope and returned it to his bag. His silent and serious look requested to speak to her privately. Reluctantly, she let go of Benteen's hand and moved to the foot of the bed.

"How is he? Will he be all right?" she asked in a thready whisper so Benteen wouldn't hear. He'd been in and out of consciousness since the attack.

"I will not pretend with you, Mrs. Calder. His condition is extremely serious," the doctor replied soberly. "I consider it a miracle that he is still alive at all."

Lorna breathed in, and it caught in her throat. She was shaking all over and she tried to hold herself rigid. A response was impossible at the moment. Benteen stirred, drawing her teary gaze. She saw the feeble groping of his fingers for her and moved quickly to his side, taking his hand and pressing it to her lips.

"I'm here, darling," she managed shakily.

His eyelids lifted, showing her the weak but determined light burning in his eyes. "Take me home, Lorna." His voice was thin, without strength. "For God's sake, don't let me die in Texas."

"Sssh, darling." The tears rolled down her cheeks at his plea, and her chin quivered. "You aren't going to die." His eyes closed and she knew he had drifted again into unconsciousness. "Doctor" — she lifted her face to him — "could he survive the train ride to Montana?"

"In his condition, it's unlikely, Mrs. Calder," he replied.

"Will he live if he stays here?" she asked.

"I don't know." He shook his head sadly. "As I said, I don't know how he has managed to survive at all."

Lowering her head, she pressed a hand to the middle of her forehead. She could have explained to the doctor that it was really quite simple. Benteen had provided the answer when he asked her not to let him die in Texas, but she didn't think the doctor would understand. When they had crossed the Red River those many years ago, the Texas dirt had been washed from his boots. It was that Montana land he had craved then, and it was what he craved now. She had gone with him then, not knowing what was at the end; she would go

424

with him now, still not knowing what was at the end.

She ran her hand down her face, wiping away the tears. A calmness steadied her. "I should like to hire a nurse to make the journey with us. Would you recommend one, Doctor?" It was an order rather than a request.

"Are you fully aware of what you are doing?" he asked.

"Yes, Doctor." She nodded. "I'm taking my husband home."

Through her husband's connections, Lorna obtained the use of a private railroad car for the journey north. She hired an experienced nurse to travel with them and sent a wire to Webb. Over her parents' protest and the doctor's, she left Texas with Benteen a second time.

The jolting rock of the private car as it followed the sharp bend in the tracks snapped Lorna awake. Guiltily, she realized she had dozed off, and glanced quickly at Benteen, but he appeared to be sleeping. Her tired muscles relaxed a little in the chair, the effects of the endless journey and the sleepless hours telling on her. They must be very near their destination now. She looked out the window, but the view was obscured by the crystal patterns of frost.

"Are we home, Lorna?" His voice sounded remarkably clear.

"We're very close, darling."

The nurse had been resting in the sitting room of the private car. At the sound of voices, she came to the door and looked in. "Mrs. Calder, the porter came with a message a moment ago. He said to tell you that we had crossed the Yellowstone."

"Did you hear that, Benteen?" Lorna turned eagerly to him. The tightness of pain that had been about his face was smoothed away by contentment. A shaft of cold fear plunged into her heart. "Benteen?" She reached for him with both hands as the nurse came hurrying toward the bed. "No!" It was a cry of rage that ended in a wail of raw grief.

The frigid wind blew the light covering of snow into dancing white spirals around the train depot. It was a solemn and silent cluster of cowboys who waited on the platform to meet the train puffing into the station. The shivering doctor was standing amidst the men huddling in their coats against the cold.

The private car was easily distinguishable from the others. Webb started for it the instant the locomotive reversed to a skidding stop on the ice-slick rails. He swung onto the car and pushed open the door, not bothering to knock. A woman in white turned with a start, in the midst of tying on a long wool cape. After a glance at Webb, she looked toward the open door to the car's second room. Webb went striding to it.

After barely a step inside, he halted. His mother was sitting primly in a chair, her hands folded on her lap. She lifted a stark, tearless face to him. Then his gaze shifted to the bed and the sheet-draped form. He half-turned, his head lowering as he reeled from the blow.

A black wreath hung on the front door of The Homestead. Webb climbed the steps and stopped to stare at it, the disbelief still numbing him. He turned and looked out over the ranch buildings and the jagged horizon, then lifted his gaze to the high blue sky. The cold froze the tears from his eyes.

"It's all yours, son. Take care of it."

That had been one of the last things his father had said to him.

It had taken ice picks, not shovels, but they had buried Chase Benteen Calder this morning. And they had buried him under Calder land.

IV

Stands a Calder man,
All alone is he,
Passing to his son
The Calder legacy.

20

At the head of the table, Webb sat easily in the chair with an arm hooked over the back of it. Initially he had been reluctant to occupy the place that had always been his father's, but his mother had quietly assured him that she preferred to see him sitting at the head of the table rather than look at an empty chair.

The china cup had long been empty of coffee, but he stayed, listening to the animated flow of conversation between his mother and Bull Giles. Bull had arrived at the ranch shortly after he had received notification of Benteen Calder's death, and he stayed on, becoming almost a permanent guest. Webb was glad to have him. So much of his time was spent away from The Homestead and his mother was left alone for long periods. It eased his mind to know Bull Giles was on hand to keep her company.

"Webb, this Sunday you must have Bull

teach you how to drive the Model T," his mother declared with a glitter of excitement in her eyes. "He took me for a 'spin' today. We went so fast that it just took my breath away."

When the automobile had arrived, Webb had thought his mother would want him to get rid of it, since it had caused his father's attack. But she didn't attach any blame to the vehicle. The Model T had been his father's last purchase, and she placed more importance on that.

"Did you drive it?" he asked.

"I tried." She laughed. "It bucked worse than a wild horse. I couldn't get those pedals on the floor to work right. 'Clutching,' is that what you call it?" She asked Bull to verify the term, and he nodded. "And you have to grip the wheel with both hands. It jerks your arms so on rough ground trying to hold on to it that I'll probably be sore for a week. But it was so much fun."

"I can tell." Webb smiled at her. "It's so good to hear you laugh."

Her expression became quietly thoughtful as she smoothed a hand over the waistline of her black dress and glanced at her old friend and companion. "I guess Bull has always known how to make a girl feel good, if only for a little while."

"I try, Lorna. I try." Bull Giles was smiling

widely, but a kind of hurt flickered in his eyes. "Is there any coffee left? I believe I'd like one more cup."

"There is." His mother reached for the service to fill his cup. "Webb, how about you?"

"No —" His refusal was interrupted by the sound of the front door opening. Webb lifted his head as the scuffle of boots and clanking spurs approached the dining room.

Ike Willis and Nate Moore walked in, and removed their hats the minute they noticed a woman was present. Ike's face was streaked with the same dust that powdered his clothes. Both men had serious looks etched in their faces.

"What's up?" Webb glanced from one to the other, his eyes narrowing slightly as he waited for one of them to speak.

"We've got a family of squatters over on the east rim," Ike said.

"The east rim?" A frown was forming. "On our land?"

"Yup. They cut the fence and drove their wagon right through," Ike reported, turning his hat in his hand. "There's six of 'em, a man and his wife, two older boys, and a couple of young'uns. I found 'em camped about a mile in where that big hollow is. They'd chopped down a couple of young cottonwoods growing along that dry wash and were riggin' up a tent. I rode in and told them they were on private property and to git, but the man said you had no claim to the land. And his boys had a pair of rifles to back it up. So I hightailed it back here."

"Get four of the boys and have the horses saddled and ready to ride at first light," Webb ordered.

"What are you aimin' to do?" Nate inquired with watching interest.

"I'm going to have a talk with this family, explain a few facts; then we'll escort them back through that break in the fence," he replied. "The man's got his family with him, so he isn't likely to make trouble."

"I reckon not." Nate nodded in agreement. "Guess we'll see you in the morning. Good night, Mrs. Calder, Bull."

When the men had left, Bull Giles tapped his cigar in the glass tray and slid a sideways look at Webb. "I did tell you there would always be someone wanting to take it away from you, either in slices or the whole pie." He reminded Webb of the conversation they'd had on the porch over two years ago.

"You did," he admitted with a recollection turned grim by the present situation. "Now we've got squatters."

"I can't say that I'm surprised," Bull mused. "All the free land worth filing on has been claimed. The latecomers, the poor ones with no money, can't afford to buy land. They probably don't even have the money to go back to wherever they're from, so they plop themselves down on a chunk of land and try to establish squatters' rights. It's worked in the past."

"It won't work here," Webb stated.

"Don't underestimate them," Bull advised. "They are desperate people. All of these drylanders are, for the most part. I'm not talking about the farmers that came here from Iowa, Minnesota, or Kansas. It's the others, the majority that are immigrants."

When Bull paused, Webb remained silent. He couldn't help thinking of Lilli while Bull was speaking about the drylanders.

"They are hungry for land, so hungry that they'll take anything, good or bad, free land or someone else's." Bull released a short laugh of quiet incredulity. "Just the other day I heard they were filing on land in the Missouri Flats of the upper Madison. At that altitude, wheat can't even mature."

"The others, the ones that were here first, they seem to be doing all right," Webb commented, still thinking of Lilli and her husband,

and the wheat harvests they had made.

"They've been growing wheat, lots of it," Bull conceded. "From what I've been able to learn, it's only enough to get them from one year to the next. Every year, they have to borrow money to buy seed. When they sell their wheat, they pay off the bank and have enough left to squeak through the winter. Next year, they always hope it will be better."

"I've heard that some have bought additional land so they can plant more wheat and increase their profits." It was what Lilli's husband had done.

"What some people fail to realize, and others who don't care, is that three hundred and twenty acres in Montana is equal to about thirty acres in Illinois or Iowa. Double that and you've got sixty. You can't make much of a living off sixty acres."

"Then you are saying they'll never get ahead," his mother said with a tiny frown.

"A few might make it, but the majority won't." He shook his head. "Don't forget, the price of wheat has never been this high. As long as there's trouble in Europe and England and France are at war with Germany, it will probably hold. But you've watched the cattle market go up and down over the years. The grain market isn't going to stay at its present level forever. No one seems to be looking that far ahead. Not even the banks. That new bank in Blue Moon, the one old Tom Pettit's son Doyle has half-interest in, they have outstanding loans that are more than double what they have on deposit. The bottom's going to drop out of everything one of these days." He rolled the cigar between his lips, then took it away to study the building ashes. "I'd be careful where I kept my money."

During the months Bull had been staying with them, Webb had discovered he was a wise counsel. Practical experience had given Webb knowledge of cattle, men, and the market, but he was learning some of the finer points of politics and other economic influences from Bull Giles. The Triple C Ranch was nearly as big as some of the eastern states, but it was affected by what happened outside its boundaries.

"By the way, it's official that Bulfert is running for the Senate," Bull informed Webb. "You might want to give some serious thought to supporting his campaign."

"Are you recommending it?" Webb smiled.

There was a responding smile, tinged with wryness. "Just as long as you don't trust him too far."

It was midmorning when the small band of

riders approached the large depression in the rolling plains of the east rim section. They weren't within sight of the squatters' camp, but Webb noticed the puff of dust ahead of them.

"Looks like they had someone watching for us." Nate had observed it, too.

Webb merely nodded. When they came onto the rounded lip of the hollow, he saw the squatters' camp below. A dirty gray tent stood next to a wagon. Wisps of smoke were curling up from a dying campfire in front of the tent where a woman was hurrying two small children inside. A scrawny lad of about fourteen was trotting two horses toward the thin stand of cottonwoods behind the tent. A second boy, not much older, was standing next to the wagon with a man who was obviously his father.

A clod of dirt was kicked up in front of Webb's horse, followed immediately by the crack of a rifle. The chestnut horse shied briefly, tossing back its head. Webb swung his mount at right angles with the camp and halted it as the riders behind him crowded in and stopped.

"That damned fool just shot at us!" Ike exclaimed.

"We're out of range." Webb had already gauged the distance.

Another clod of dirt and grass went flying two feet in front of them, and a pulsebeat later the sound of the shot came. This time he saw the puff of smoke from the rifle. The squatter was using the wagon wheel for a gunrest. Webb's horse rolled an eye and chewed nervously on the bit.

"Do you suppose he knows we're out of range?" Nate inquired. "Could be just warning for us to keep our distance."

"If he didn't know it before, he knows it now." Webb regarded it as unimportant as he reached to loosen the flap of his scabbard and drag out his rifle.

"If he's out of range, we're out of range." Nate eyed the rifle as if Webb should have figured that out.

"Glad you mentioned that." There was a trace of a smile on his mouth as Webb unknotted the kerchief around his throat and tied it to the end of his rifle. "You boys stay here while I see if I can't ride down there and talk some sense to him before someone gets hurt."

Nate reached down for his rifle. "I got the feeling that ole boy ain't too interested in talking. We'll keep you covered just in case."

The kerchief wasn't white, but the message was just the same. Webb reined the chestnut around, the rifle butt resting on his thigh and the muzzle aimed at the sky with the kerchief waving a truce banner. His mount was not too sure of this whole business and moved forward at a mincing walk. Webb kept his gaze fixed sharply on the man and boy as they were joined by the second boy, also carrying a rifle. He was just passing the area where the first two shots had ripped up clods of dirt when he saw the rifles being lifted to their shoulders.

"Don't be damned fools," Webb muttered under his breath and kept kneeing his reluctant horse forward. It might just be they wanted to keep him in their sights in case he tried anything.

A second later he saw the flash and recoil of the squatter's rifle. In nearly the same instant, Webb sank his spurs into the chestnut and spun it to the right. The horse almost jumped out from under him, issuing a snorting squeal at the sting of a bullet grazing its rump. It bounded into a run, angling for the rounded rim. There was a burst of shots from both sides that left the smell of powder smoke in the air.

The short barrage from the riders had sent the squatter and his sons scurrying for cover behind the wagon, hitting no one but coming close enough to scare them. When Webb had safely rejoined them, the shooting stopped.

"I had a notion they weren't going to be reasonable," Nate declared.

"What now?" Ike looked at Webb. "It'd be a bit foolhardly to go on chargin' down there like we were the cavalry. They got the wagon for cover."

"Do you want me to slip over there?" A new rider with the outfit by the name of Virg Haskell indicated the north rim of the hollow. "The camp would be within range from there. I could start slappin' some shots around that wagon, keep them pinned down while the rest of you ride in."

"No." Webb rejected that suggestion. "There's too much risk a stray shot might injure the woman and those two children in the tent. I've got a better idea. Ike —" He turned in his saddle to face the rider as he gave his instructions. "You, Slim, Virgil, and Hank gather up a good-sized bunch of steers. Once you've got them together, we'll stampede them through the camp and follow them in. The rest of us will stay here and keep an eye on things."

After the four cowboys had pulled away from the knoll to begin rounding up some of the steers grazing this section of the range, Webb swung out of his saddle. Nate hooked a knee across his saddlehorn and began rolling a cigarette.

"That squatter is going to figure you're sending for reinforcements." Nate peered down at the camp while he licked at the paper. "He's already acting nervous about where the boys went."

"He just don't know our reinforcements are the four-footed kind," Webb said dryly as he examined the slight flesh wound that had laid a red track across the top of the chestnut's rump. It shifted nervously under his touch. "You'll live, fella," Webb pronounced and absently stroked its neck.

The sun was almost directly overhead before Webb heard the lowing of moving cattle. There were about fifty steers in the bunch the riders had collected and were driving toward the hollow. Climbing into the saddle, Webb swung the chestnut around to join up with the small herd.

"That squatter is really going to be wonderin' what's up now." Nate chuckled as he brought his horse alongside the chestnut.

"He won't be wondering for long."

Slim Trumbo and Ike Willis were riding the swing position at the front of the herd. Webb and the other riders doubled up in the flank and drag posts. When the steers crested the knoll, rifles were fired in the air to start them running. Slim and Ike raced alongside the leaders until they were assured the steers were heading directly for the wagon. Then they fell back with the other riders, using the herd as a protective shield to enter the squatters' camp.

The running cattle avoided the flapping canvas of the tent and split in two groups to flow around the wagon, forcing the man and his sons to scramble under it or be run over by the range-wild steers. Before the last animal had charged past the wagon, the riders were peeling out of their saddles. There was a brief scuffle with the man and his sons before they were disarmed.

"Check the tent and be sure they're all right." Webb directed the order at Slim Trumbo, then confronted the squatter and his skinny, carrot-haired boys. They were a pitiful sight in their ragged clothes and underfed bodies. The man faced him, his eyes glaring with a pride that showed a fine mist of tears. "I don't know who you are, mister, or what you thought you were doing, but somebody could have got hurt." He had to harden himself against the sight of the hollow-cheeked woman and the two big-eyed children emerging from the tent ahead of Slim. "You should have had a care for them, if not yourself."

"I have a care, and that's to put food in their bellies," the squatter retorted, showing no remorse under the circumstances.

"That fence you cut a mile back was the boundary line of the Triple C Ranch. You're on private property, so I'll ask you to pack up your wagon and leave the way you came."

"Our horses, Pa," one of the boys said.

"They took off with the cattle." Nate explained the boy's remark to Webb.

"Virg, catch up their plow ponies and bring them back," Webb instructed.

"This is just a small patch of ground," the squatter argued. "With all the land your boss owns, he ain't gonna miss this little chunk. Why don't you boys just ride away and tell him that you chased us off? He'll never know we're here."

"That's where you're wrong, because I happen to be Webb Calder. And if I let you stay, I'd be opening the floodgates for others like you to come in, and I have no intention of doing that," he stated. "Pack up and move on."

"But we ain't got no place to go," the older of the boys protested.

"That isn't my problem. You should have given that a thought before you came here." Webb refused to be swayed. "If you don't start taking down that tent, I'll have my men dismantle it for you."

The squatter motioned to his sons. With a

great deal of reluctance, they walked over to the tent and began pulling out the stakes. "What about our rifles?"

"I'll leave them with the sheriff in Blue Moon." Webb walked to his horse, taking the reins from Nate. "And the next time you plant yourself on a piece of ground, make sure nobody owns it."

"You tell me where there is such a piece and I'll go there. That railroad man said there was free land here, but I ain't seen none of it," the man declared bitterly and turned to begin loading his wagon with the few possessions he had.

Nate grumbled to Webb under his breath. "The man's a damned fool to bring his family out here. I hate to see little ones suffer like that. All Ike found in that tent for food was some potatoes and flour, and some rabbit bones."

"Catch up a steer and tie it to the back of their wagon," Webb said in a grim tone. "At least they'll have something to eat until they find a place."

By the time Virg Haskell returned with the pair of roman-nosed horses belonging to the squatter, the wagon was loaded. The woman cried when Nate tied the steer to their wagon, but the man didn't say so much as a thank you.

After they had escorted the wagon off Triple C land, Webb sent Ike into town with the family's rifles to report the incident to the sheriff. As soon as the fence was repaired, they turned their horses toward home.

Wet clothes flapped in the hot breeze, draped over the guy wires that kept the shanty from blowing away in a strong wind. Lilli stirred the clothes boiling in the big pot outside the shanty and glanced at Helga Kreuger scrubbing a shirt on the washboard. She wrung it out and tossed it in another bucket, then paused to press a hand against the small of her back. When she arched her back, it emphasized the protruding roundness of her stomach, indicating an advanced pregnancy.

"I'll scrub the clothes for you, Mrs. Kreuger." Lilli volunteered to take over the job, knowing it must be hard on the woman.

"The men are coming in from the fields. We will finish this later." Helga Kreuger shielded her eyes with her hand and turned to look at her young daughter. "Anna, go put the dishes on the table so we can eat."

Using the wooden stick, Lilli began removing the clothes from the hot wash water and depositing them in another large pail. Heat and steam spilled over her, beading her face and neck with perspiration. When she had finished, she mopped at her face with her apron and turned to meet the arriving men.

"Come into the house. Food is on the table," Helga Kreuger greeted them hurriedly.

"Did you fix that stew today?" Stefan asked. "You must give to Lillian the recipe."

Lilli had received barely a glance from her husband, but she was becoming resigned to that. Franz Kreuger came to a sudden stop and frowned darkly in her direction. Her head came up as she thought she was the object of his displeasure until she realized his gaze was directed beyond her. She turned to see a wagon coming up the lane.

"Who is that?" Franz asked, as if expecting someone to answer.

Food was forgotten as they waited for the wagon to reach the shack. Two red-haired boys were walking alongside it. In the wagon seat, there was a man driving the horse team and a woman with a child on her lap and a second on the seat beside her. A wild-eyed steer fought the rope that dragged him after the noisy wagon.

When the straggly-looking caravan was nearly level with them, the man pulled back on the reins, and the wagon rolled to a shuddering halt. The bitterness of disappointment was in

447

the man's face as he bobbed his head to Stefan and Franz.

"Could you spare some water for my horses?" he asked.

"Gustav!" Franz called to his young son. "Fetch the man a bucket of water from the cistern."

"I'm obliged, sir." He stepped down from the wagon and walked to his horses, rubbing their noses. "Would you know a place where a family could camp for the night?"

As Lilli watched, Franz Kreuger stiffened. There was veiled contempt in his look when he swept the dirty, ragtag boys and the poorness of the wagon and team. The man had not shaved and looked equally unkempt. She had suspected Franz Kreuger was guilty of having double standards, looking down on others and hating those who looked down on him.

"You might ask someone down the road," he told the man. "They may know of a place."

"There's no reason why they can't camp in that stand of cottonwoods at the corner of our property, is there, Stefan?" Lillian spoke up. She didn't care whether Franz Kreuger thought a woman should leave such decisions to men or not.

"That sounds right nice, ma'am." The man tipped his hat to her and missed the silencing look Stefan sent her. "We was just run off the last place."

"Where were you?" Franz demanded with a cold look.

"We'd found an empty piece of ground north and west of here. Good ground, it was. There was a place for my wife to put in a garden, and the land would have grown wheat as tall as your belly." His mouth twisted down in another display of bitterness. "Problem was a man named Calder already owned it."

"Calder?" The look that had been on Franz Kreuger's face vanished.

"Yeah, him and his men drove us off. Me and the boys tried to make a fight of it, but I had the wife and the little ones to think about. There wasn't much I could do." The man shook his head. "No man's got a right to own that much land. I told him I just wanted a small place where I could grow food for my family, but he looked at me with those eyes black as the devil's and told me to get out."

Franz Kreuger's attitude changed completely. "Stefan, didn't you say you needed a good, hard-working man to help you with your farm?"

"Yeah." Stefan took his lead from his friend. "I cannot pay much vages, but you vould have a place to stay and a little room for your vife to plant a garden."

"My sons, maybe they could work, too." The man brightened at the idea.

"We know many people," Franz stated. "We will tell them about your sons. Always someone is needing help for a short time. If they are good workers, they will be hired."

"They're good workers, all right," the man said as he took the bucket of water from the tow-headed Kreuger boy and offered it to his horses. "I was countin' on them helpin' me when we got a place of our own, but I guess that's not to be."

"Next year Stefan and I will help you find some good land," Franz promised. "We must all of us stick together, help each other; then we are all stronger."

When the horses had drunk their fill, the man handed the bucket back to the boy and turned to Stefan. "Where is that place your daughter described?" Lilli winced, knowing how sensitive her husband had become to their age difference.

Stefan pulled his slightly stooped frame to its full height, his expression cold and forbidding. "She is my vife."

The man reddened and cast a vaguely stunned glance at Lilli, then quickly dropped it. "Beggin' your pardon," he apologized immediately, mumbling his embarrassment over the mistake.

After Stefan had given directions to their place, he said, "You vait at our house. My vife and I vill be home soon. I vill show the place for you to camp."

The wagon made a tight circle as the family headed down the lane to the road. Lilli was transfixed by the brand on the steer's flank. Her gaze ran to the family who had seen Webb Calder. A wretching envy tore through her, filling every part of her body until she thought she would burst.

"Come. Let us eat before the food grows cold," Helga Kreuger urged them.

Slowly Lilli turned to accompany the others into the small shack, no larger than theirs although it accommodated three times as many people. Nothing showed on her face. She, who had always let her thoughts and feelings run free, now kept them contained and secret. Sometimes she wondered if she weren't becoming more like Stefan every day. It had been so long since either of them had smiled.

After the meal was finished, they set out for home in their wagon. Stefan sat hunched over the reins, swaying with the rocking motion as the wagon jolted over the hard ruts in the road.

Lilli was beside him, sitting stiffly erect and resisting the rough motion. Her sightless gaze was fixed on the distant horizon while Stefan watched the trotting horses.

"Mrs. Kreuger's baby should come before the harvest." Stefan made a rare attempt at conversation. "That is good."

"Yes." Lilli had a cynical moment when she thought how inconvenient the men would find it if Helga Kreuger went into labor when the threshers arrived.

"This is her second baby since they come here," he said, drawing a glance from Lilli as she puzzled over his reason for this subject.

"Yes, it is," she replied.

For the space of several minutes, there was only the clopping of trotting hooves and the creaking of the wagon to fill the silence. Stefan adjusted his grip on the team's reins.

"Vhen ve go to town again, you go to the doctor and find out vhy you have not had any babies," he stated tersely.

"Oh, Stefan." She breathed out his name in irritation and looked anywhere but at him. "It isn't necessary to father a child to prove to the world – or to Franz Kreuger – that you're a man."

An hour ago she had been priding herself on how well she kept her thoughts and feelings to herself, and here they'd just burst through. It didn't matter that what she had said was true. Her careless remark had hurt Stefan. He was angry with her. She was learning a lot about men, and how sensitive they were about this thing called manliness. Her problem was she had never really thought of Stefan as a man such as Webb Calder. Stefan was her friend, her uncle, her father. She hadn't realized there was this other side of him.

"Is it vrong for a man to vant a child?" His voice was thick in its angry demand.

"No, it isn't wrong." Lilli frowned in helpless frustration, ashamed to discover she did not want Stefan's child. "But this is not the time to have one — not now when we are barely able to feed ourselves." She'd said the wrong thing again. But it was true. The additional wheatland had only put them further in debt. They sold more wheat, but more money was spent for plow horses, equipment, hired help, and seed. It seemed they had less and less money, instead of more.

"Stefan, I didn't mean that you haven't done everything you could to provide for us." Lilli attempted to take the sting out of her previous remark. "You have. It's just that things haven't worked out quite the way you thought they would."

"Ve vill have a better harvest this year," he insisted.

"Of course we will." They were empty words, issued for his benefit. But Lilli knew the rains had come late this year. The stand of wheat was not nearly as good as last year's.

"You find out vhy you don't have babies," Stefan repeated his earlier demand.

"I will," she agreed flatly. A silent dread was on her. If the cause turned out to be Stefan's impotence, it would ruin him completely.

Again silence came between them as they traveled toward their home. Lilli had always thought she knew Stefan so well — all her life. But that had been as a child and a young girl. His quietness came from hiding inside himself so others wouldn't know his failures and weaknesses. He was uncertain and indecisive, his actions swayed and colored by those dominant individuals around him. He wanted to be what he saw in other men. It was their attitudes and behavior he adopted, taking their lead in a situation and pretending it was his own. If Franz Kreuger hadn't been with him that morning, Lilli doubted that Stefan would have shot Webb. He was driven to act by his perception of what Franz Kreuger would have done in his place.

Then Lilli became caught up in her own

confusion. Was she finding fault with Stefan, making much out of his weaknesses, to justify the love she felt for another man? There was only one clear certainty in her mind. She did not love Stefan in the way that a woman loves a man. She cared for him deeply the way a person cares for a close family friend. She owed him much for looking after her when her parents died, although she had been the only one left for him, too. And she owed him a wife's loyalty. If there was a persistent voice inside her head that kept asking if she didn't owe herself some happiness, Lilli tried not to hear it.

That evening after Stefan had fallen asleep, Lilli slipped out of bed, taking care not to disturb him, and stole outside into the night. The coolness of a night breeze wrapped its arms around her, stirring the thinness of her long nightgown. She turned her eyes to the west, the longing in them deep and sharp. Webb lived somewhere over there. Why had she been so damned noble and refused to see him? Why had she denied herself a few moments of stolen pleasure in his arms?

He was so close, but so far. She lowered her head, knowing she would never take the step to lessen the distance. She stood there, uncertain whether she was being incredibly strong or merely stupid.

21

Squatters were a problem for all the ranchers, but the size of the Triple C made it the most vulnerable. For the last four years, Webb had been locked in a running battle to keep them off his land. There were a few shooting scrapes, but most of them left without a fuss once their presence was discovered. He'd set up patrols in an effort to ward off squatters before they crossed his fences and keep the occasional rustling of beef by the starving families to a tolerable level.

There were other ranchers that came down hard on the squatters, Ed Mace foremost among them. It might have been more accurate to say Hobie Evans. Stories had circulated that Hobie was quick to use his rifle, and there had been enough woundings to give validity to the stories. Webb knew there were grumblings among his own men that he was being too lenient with the squatters instead of teaching them a lesson to pass on to others of their kind. But he couldn't look at those squatters' wives without thinking of Lilli.

He'd seen her in town a few times and been tempted a thousand times to seek her out these last five years. But she had rejected him twice, turning down the love he wanted to give her. Webb wasn't about to open himself up a third time. A man had some pride.

And a lot of loneliness. Another wreath had blackened the front doors of The Homestead two years ago with his mother's passing. Pneumonia, the doctor had said, but Webb suspected she just didn't have the will to fight the illness. Not even Bull Giles's constant company had filled the void that had been created when his father died. With her death, Bull had packed up and left. He had looked old – old and very tired.

So now Webb was the sole occupant of the big house. He spent no more time in it than he had to, not liking the hollow sound of his footsteps in the empty rooms. With a late-afternoon sun angling on the ranch buildings, Webb crossed from the barn to the new commissary. Prices for supplies at Ellis's store had risen to the point where it had become practical to set up a private store at the ranch, buying food and equipment at cost from

457

suppliers and selling the excess to the men and their families for slightly higher prices, but still less than what Ollie Ellis charged.

The increased prices for goods were about the only effect the war in Europe had on the area. It was all happening far away – on another continent. The news of battles was old by the time it reached Blue Moon, and the names of the places in Germany and France were unknown to most Montanans, except for the immigrant settlers whose roots and families came from those places.

But the grain and beef from the area fed the American army and became their contribution to the war effort, exempting cowboys and farmers alike from the draft. Some boys from the area went off to war, but most of those were sons of immigrants, eager to prove their loyalty to their new country. Life went on as usual for everyone else, the First World War in Germany becoming merely another topic of conversation and speculation.

Halfway to the store, his steps slowed as he observed Ruth coming out of the schoolhouse. Virg Haskell was waiting for her, taking the books and papers she was carrying and falling in step beside her like some schoolboy walking a girl home. It wasn't the first time Webb had noticed the man hanging around Ruth. The sight of them together stirred a vague feeling of dislike. Webb couldn't fault Virg Haskell in the work he did on the ranch; yet he couldn't shake the feeling that there was some kind of weakness in the man's character, even if it hadn't surfaced. Ruth was a fine woman. She deserved someone better than a common drifter like Virg Haskell.

The barns and corrals were just ahead of Nate as his weary horse plodded toward them, blowing out the dust that clogged its nostrils. Slumped in the saddle, sapped of energy by the searing August heat that had turned the range prematurely brown, Nate felt as weary as his mount. Things didn't look good out there. When he noticed Webb crossing his path, he checked his horse's direction and aimed it toward his boss and friend.

Listless as his body was, his eyes retained their keenness. Nate observed the interest Webb was paying to the couple walking away from the schoolhouse, and the displeasure that tightened his mouth. Nate guessed, with a degree of wry cynicism, that it was a case of Webb not wanting her, but he didn't want anybody else getting Ruth, either.

A second later, Webb recognized the horse and rider plodding toward him with heads hanging low and stopped to wait for them. The horse and rider were a matched pair, their dust-covered bodies streaked with muddy sweat.

Nate didn't waste his breath on preliminaries. "You're gonna have to be movin' the cattle to the north range sooner than you figured. They're walkin' off weight trying to find graze."

The announcement made Webb absently look at the dry and cracked ground at his feet. He had hoped the other sections of the range would hold out another month at least. The north range was well watered and had a fairly good stand of grass. It would have been good winter forage, considering the poor hay crop they'd had.

"It's that bad out there, huh?" It wasn't a question, just a protest against the facts.

"June's usually our wet month. Bet we didn't get more'n a half-inch. And the sky's been bone-dry since then," Nate reminded him. "If you think the grass is in bad shape, you oughta see those drylanders' fields. They ain't growin' wheat this year, but they've got a helluva crop of thistles."

Webb took the news without any outward reaction, but another kind of grim frustration registered inside him. In the previous years, the drylanders had struggled from one growing season to the next. A lot of them had given up when they had proved out the term of their claim, and sold their homesteaded land to the next man willing to try his luck — and there never seemed to be a lack of those. The Reisners, Lilli and her husband, hadn't been among the ones to quit the land. That much Webb knew, but he'd heard nothing to indicate their lot was any better than the next man's.

This season there had been near-drought conditions which might be marking the beginning of a dry cycle. Webb glanced skyward at the haze that filtered out the blue to a dusty color. It was hot and dry — so dry that the perspiration evaporated almost as soon as it broke on the skin, or else became caked with the dirt to clog a man's pores.

"We're going to start the fall roundup early this year and sell all the steers of marketable age. I don't want to carry anything extra through the winter and use up what grass we've got," Webb stated. The cattle prices were high right now with the war in Europe, and he intended to sell his cattle while they had weight on them and could bring top price.

The big Belgian mare stood docilely while Lilli dragged the harness off its tall back and set it on the ground. When she moved to its head, the mare lowered it and tried to rub the bridle off, butting against Lilli's chest. It staggered her backward a step before she tiredly recovered her balance and unbuckled the cheek strap. The bridle was loose in her hands as the mare spat out the jangling bit and walked to the water trough.

Gathering up the harness and bridle, Lilli hauled them into the shed and draped them on their hooks. She paused to chip off a piece of salt from the new white block and let it melt in her mouth as she walked outside. She flopped down in the shade of the shed, exhausted by the dry heat.

Her skirt was pulled up around her bent knees, hoping for some air to circulate and cool her skin. Petticoats were too suffocating in this scorching heat and too cumbersome in the fields. Lilli had abandoned them after her first week in the fields doing a man's work because they couldn't afford to hire anyone. The family they had befriended had moved on, and they hadn't found anyone else willing to work for room and board.

She tiredly supported her head with an arm propped up by a knee. She was so tired she could cry, but there didn't seem to be enough moisture to use for tears. There wasn't a part of her body that didn't ache from pulling the weeds out of the wheatfields so they didn't steal what precious moisture the ground contained. Her arms, face, neck, and part of her chest were so brown from the constant exposure to the sun that it was impossible to tell where the freckles ended and the tan began.

She heard the plodding of horse's hooves on the hard-baked ground and the rattle of metal harness pieces. Stefan was coming in from the fields. She straightened and pushed her skirt over her knees when he came into view.

"Is supper ready?" he asked and whoaed the mare.

Anger flashed through her at the way he expected her to work in the fields and have a supper ready when he came in, too. "No." Her voice was a dry rasp. "I just got the mare unharnessed."

"Vell? She is unharnessed now," he prompted irritably.

It was useless to argue that she was tired. Supper still had to be put on the table, and it fell to Lilli to do it. She walked stiffly into the shack and banged things around. It helped to momentarily relieve her frustrations and growing sense of hopelessness that all this work was for nothing. There was only the slimmest chance that they'd have a third of their usual harvest.

With the potato soup heating on the stove, Lilli went to the wash basin and dipped a cloth in the water to press against her hot skin. A small rectangular mirror hung above the basin. She looked at her reflection — the dullness of her hair, her sun-browned skin, and the hollows under her eyes. She was a very old twenty-five.

"There's no reason to think about him anymore," she murmured to herself. "Webb wouldn't want you now."

She turned away from the mirror, unable to look at herself. The wet cloth was laid aside as she walked to the stove to stir the soup. Outside, she heard Stefan at the cistern, pumping water into a bucket. She stepped out the door to call to him.

"Don't forget to water the garden." It had nearly burned out in this heat, but some of the vegetables might be saved.

Stefan was bent over the bucket, sloshing water on his face. He looked so old and broken, without the will to go on, but there was a stubbornness in him, too. It came from that awful fear of failure that drove him. Although he never told Lilli, he was convinced this long, dry weather was God's punishment for his German birth and the war that raged over there. Instead of shouldering it as a cross, it became a chip. When he cupped his hand to take a drink from the bucket, Lilli frowned worriedly.

"The water hasn't been tasting right, Stefan," she warned. "I've been boiling it before we use it for drinking."

But he paid no attention to her and swallowed several handfuls before he straightened. "It is just varm," he insisted and picked up the bucket to take it to the garden.

Everything was warm, Lilli thought. It never cooled off, not even at night. She went back into the house and ladled the soup into bowls. The table and chairs had been moved outside so they could eat where the air was not so stifling. With this endless heat, it became so close in the shanty that Lilli felt suffocated. But it wasn't much better outside unless the wind blew. Even a hot breeze was preferable to none, although it meant dust being blown into the food. Not that it mattered, since her mouth felt gritty all the time.

Confined and restless, Webb laid down the pencil and pushed out of the big leather chair. The damned paperwork was endless. It multiplied into mounds every time he turned his back on it for one day. He crossed the den to the liquor cabinet and poured a glass of whiskey. After a quick, burning swallow, he shuddered and rubbed the back of his neck.

There was a noise, the faint squeak of a floorboard. He looked up and saw Ruth in the doorway. He attempted a smile. "I didn't hear you come in."

"I tried to be quiet so I wouldn't disturb you if you were working." She glanced at the desk. "Are you all finished?"

"Hardly." He tipped his head back to toss down another swallow.

"I came by to invite you to have supper with Dad and me," she explained.

He hesitated, looking at her, then shook his head. "I'd better pass. I'm liable to spend the evening talking instead of taking care of that paperwork."

"You do have to eat," she persisted. "I promise I'll chase you out as soon as you're finished eating."

"Or maybe you could stand over me with a ruler," Webb suggested in a dry reference to her schoolteaching.

"If you've ever been in my classroom, you'd know I don't do that with my pupils." She smiled tentatively. "You used to stop by now and then, but you haven't been by lately."

"I've been too busy." He shrugged aside the length of time that had passed since he'd been in her company. "I'm surprised you noticed. Haskell seems to be a regular caller nowadays."

"Does that bother you?" She hoped it did. She hoped he was jealous. He had noticed Virg Haskell was paying attention to her even though she had tried to discourage him.

"Why should it bother me?" He frowned his surprise at the question. "You're the one he's seeing." Another thought occurred to him. "Is he pestering you? I can tell him to leave you alone, if you want."

"That isn't necessary." Ruth lowered her head, feeling defeated again. "Will you come to supper?" She repeated her invitation, taking one more chance that he'd accept.

His gaze ran over her, as if measuring her against someone else. "No, thanks," he refused.

A little knife twisted in her heart. "You still haven't forgotten her, have you?" She hadn't meant so say it aloud, but now that she had, she wasn't sorry.

His mouth thinned and came down at the corners. "No, I guess I haven't," he agreed in a clipped voice. Neither of them had to say her name. They both knew she had meant Lilli.

"She's married, Webb." It took a great deal of courage for Ruth to say that.

"I am well aware of that." He gave her a cold, impatient look, as if angered that she had reminded him of the fact.

This friction between them was intolerable. Ruth crossed the space separating them with a rush of quick little steps to assure him that she hadn't spoken to hurt him. She stopped when she reached his side, lifting a hand to rest it tentatively on his forearm and claim the attention he'd turned away from her.

"I'm sorry, Webb. I had no right to say that." It was simply that she had lived so long in hope that he would forget Lilli – and that, when he did, he would finally turn to her.

For a long second, Webb looked at the hand on his arm before he lifted his gaze to her face. The muted coloring of her hair and eyes appeared nondescript, yet despite the blandness of her features, he saw something that appealed to a weakness in him. Everything about her was leaning toward him, wanting to please him and wipe out that coldness.

As he set his drink on a side table, Webb wasn't conscious of the silent debate he had with himself. Then he turned to Ruth and heard her quickened breath with a certain detachment. When he took her into his arms, he wasn't seeking the gratification of his male needs. There were women who took care of that for a living.

He wanted to bury himself in the softness of

a caring woman and find a respite from this consuming loneliness. She was yielding in his arms, her body pressing itself to his length. Her lips were pliant to the demands he made of them. All things were as they should be, but it wasn't enough.

The lonely ache became more intense, tinged with a bitterness. Her kiss couldn't fill the emptiness inside him. Webb became disgusted with himself for using her without a care for her feelings. His hands lifted to her shoulders to push her from him. He tightened his grip and forced Ruth away from him. The sight of the little-girl-hurt look in her expression turned him from her, and Webb reached for the drink he had so recently discarded.

"I shouldn't have done that, Ruth," he said grimly and heard her make a little wounded sound. "You have my apology and my word that it won't happen again."

"No, Webb —"

He brutally cut across her protest. "Ask Virg Haskell to supper. He'll appreciate the invitation more than I do."

There was a kind of finality in the silence that followed. It was several more seconds before he heard her slow footsteps carrying her out of the room. He drank the rest of the whiskey in his glass in one burning swallow, but it deadened nothing.

As she dipped the damp cloth into the basin of water, Lilli cast a worried glance at the unconscious man in the bed. His face was unnaturally flushed and his skin was afire to the touch. Stefan mumbled in his native German tongue, fever carrying him to the point of delirium. She wrung out the cloth and pressed its wetness over his face, trying to cool him.

It had begun so innocently yesterday morning with a throbbing in his head, a stomachache, and diarrhea. Stefan had insisted on going out to the fields, overriding Lilli's suggestion that perhaps he should rest. That night, he was so weak Lilli had had to help him into bed. In the night, this raging fever had claimed him.

Her hearing strained to catch sounds outside the shack. She thought she heard something, but it was so faint she wasn't sure whether she had imagined it or not. She turned her head, glancing at the blond-haired woman by the stove, heating some broth so they could force some nourishment into Stefan.

"I think I can hear a buggy. Check and see if it's the doctor, Helga," Lilli urged the pregnant wife of Franz Kreuger.

470

"Of course." Helga Kreuger left the stove and walked to the door to look outside.

Frightened by how rapidly Stefan's condition had deteriorated overnight, Lilli had gone to their neighbor for help that morning. She hadn't wanted to leave Stefan alone for even that short period of time, but she had to send someone for the doctor. Franz had ridden into town to fetch him, and Helga had left her children in the care of her oldest daughter and returned with Lilli to help however she could.

"It is Franz," she confirmed. "The doctor is with him."

"Thank God," Lilli murmured and blinked at the tears to keep them at bay. This fever seemed to be shrinking Stefan right before her eyes, sinking in his cheeks and shriveling his gaunt body.

When the young doctor entered, he didn't waste time with preliminaries and went straight to the bed. His eyes were already making their examination of the stricken man as he opened his black bag. He didn't appear surprised by what he saw; rather, the straight line of his mouth seemed to indicate it was what he had expected.

Lilli was reluctant to leave the bedside, but Helga Kreuger took her by the shoulders and led her to the other side of the single room. She pushed a cup of broth into Lilli's hands.

"You need your strength, too," she insisted.

It was easier to accept it than make the effort to argue. Her hands encircled it as Lilli moved to the window. There were glass panes in it, virtually the only improvement they had made in the shanty. A film of dust coated the glass and blurred her view of the fallow field outside. A swirling wind ran across the dry ground, kicking up dust devils to spin and swoop in wild abandon. The air was so dry it sucked up any moisture it found.

Off to the side, Lillie could hear Franz Kreuger and his wife speaking to each other in low, unintelligible voices. Her mother had been this sick before she died — different symptoms, but there was still the smell of death. It was something Lilli couldn't forget. Until this moment she had been too busy caring for Stefan to let her mind dwell on the possibility he could die. All her attention had been devoted to making him better; now her thoughts were turning to what would happen if he didn't recover.

Her mind flashed to memories of her parents' deaths, the grief and the anguish, the endless number of things that had to be done. If Stefan died, she'd have it all to do again — finding the money to pay for the coffin, arranging for his burial, and going through all his personal belongings. If he died — she'd be free to go to Webb.

The instant the thought leaped into her mind, Lilli was sickened by it. It was a terrible thing to be thinking at a time like this. She despised herself for it and stamped out the seed before it could grow by brutally reminding herself of her face in the mirror and the sobering fact that years had passed without Webb's making a single attempt to see her. He was bound to have forgotten her long ago.

She lifted her gaze to the dust-laden sky. Her lips formed the silent words, "Stefan, forgive me." There was a sound from the corner of the room where her husband lay, and Lilli turned to look at the erect figure tending him. She walked to the foot of the bed and searched the expressionless face of the physician.

"What is it, Doctor?" She asked for an answer that would rid her of these gnawing fears.

He seemed not to want to meet her probing eyes. "Where do you get your drinking water, Mrs. Reisner?" He swung a raking look over her, catching the signs of youth the sun hadn't burned out. "You are his wife?" His patient was considerably older, although he'd learned that was hardly uncommon among some of these immigrant marriages.

Lilli nodded affirmatively to that question and answered the first. "We have a cistern outside."

"Your husband has typhoid fever," he announced grimly. "Which means your water supply has been contaminated. With the lack of rain we've had this year, it's a situation that's going to become more prevalent, I'm afraid. This isn't the first case I've diagnosed."

Typhoid fever. The words numbed her with their ominous portent. Vaguely she was aware of Franz Kreuger intervening and demanding that the doctor give Stefan something to make him better. Most of his reply was lost as she tried to come to grips with the news.

". . . keep bathing him to bring the fever down and make sure he gets plenty of liquid," the doctor instructed. "I have a couple of other calls to make, but I'll stop back here toward evening. We'll see how he's doing then."

Lilli went through the motions of seeing the doctor to the door and thanking him for coming, but she seemed to be existing in a vacuum, devoid of any feelings or sensations. Nothing made any impression on her, not even the abrasive Franz Kreuger.

The Montana weather had been up to its old,

cruel tricks. A big bruise had shown up in the sky and sent the smell of rain over the country. Rain fell in sheeting buckets for forty minutes and no more, but not everywhere, just in one small area where the headquarters of the Triple C Ranch was located. It turned the parched ground into a quagmire, which made it impossible for Webb to use the automobile to drive into town and shorten the trip.

Instead, he saddled an Appaloosa-marked bay to make the long ride. Not three miles from The Homestead, the grass was tinder-dry. The black clouds were already chasing across the sky, leaving as quickly as they had come, tormenting the dry earth with their fragrance of rain.

A dry wind was blasting the weathering buildings of Blue Moon with its burden of dust. There was a fine coating of it on everything. Few people were on the street, walking with their heads down and faces turned away from the wind. With his eyes slitted against the stinging dust, Webb noticed the motley funeral procession slowly making its way to the new cemetery on the grassy knoll just outside of town.

The long, dusty ride had left him with a dry mouth and throat. He turned his horse into the hitching rail in front of Sonny's place and swung down, looping the reins around the post. When he went inside, he found the restaurant by day, bar by night nearly as deserted as the street. He took note of the occupants, recognizing Hobie Evans lounging against the bar. Pushing his hat to the back of his head, Webb sat down at one of the tables.

"Just coffee," he told the dried-out girl who had made a move to come out from behind the bar to take his order. She looked to be from one of the homesteading families, working in town to supplement her family's meager income. With this summer's drought, more of the older children had been forced to seek jobs to help support their family. There had been a deluge of them at the ranch, willing to turn their hand to anything to make a few pennies.

Hobie sauntered over to the table and pulled out a chair, turning it around to straddle it, not waiting for Webb to invite him to sit. He sipped the coffee cup in his hand and eyed Webb with a complacent look. "It's been a long, dry summer," he remarked.

Webb nodded and glanced briefly at the girl when she brought his coffee and set it on the table in front of him. She paused, her features drained of any expression. "Want anything else?"

"What she means is" — Hobie leaned closer

to murmur his explanation so it would go no farther than the table — "for two bits and the price of a shot, she'll make that coffee stronger."

The hypocrisy of the situation wasn't lost on Webb. When the drylanders had come, they had been righteously opposed to the serving of alcoholic beverages in their midst, yet one of their daughters was willing to break the rules for a quarter.

"I'll drink it as it is." He refused the offer to have it laced with whiskey. The girl shrugged indifferently and wandered back to the bar.

"I'll bet for a little more money a fella could buy more than a drink from her." Hobie watched her leave. "If he didn't mind gettin' hung up on those skinny ribs. 'Course, honyockers aren't my cup of tea, but I didn't know but what you might still have a taste for them."

With a man like Hobie Evans, it was better to ignore his coarse and snide remarks. Any comment would wind up encouraging more of the same. Webb drank his coffee, hot and thickly black.

"I noticed a bunch of wagons leading toward the cemetery when I rode into town. Who's getting buried?" He changed the subject.

Hobie shrugged. "Some honyocker. Some

fever bug is laying 'em down right and left. More power to the fever, I say. Maybe we'll finally get rid of some of those bastards. It should've happened a long time ago."

"A fever?" An eyebrow lifted in a silent demand for a more specific answer.

"Yeah. The sawbones was in here earlier, trying to get a bite to eat, but some scrawny drylander dragged him away on a sick call." A kind of grin lifted a corner of Hobie's mouth. "The doc looked worn to a frazzle, said something about their water being contaminated. He's wastin' his time with the likes of them. If a hundred more of 'em died, it wouldn't be too many to suit me."

Webb lost his taste for the coffee and the company. He scraped the chair backward to stand and tossed a coin on the table to pay for the barely touched coffee. "Hobie, when you die, you're going to be all alone. The sad part is — you won't know it."

Leaving the restaurant, he untied the reins and started to mount his horse; then he caught the sound of voices raised in song being carried by the wind, and paused. Snatches of the melody came to him, enough to recognize the mournful hymn "Rock of Ages."

He wondered about the Reisner well, whether its water was contaminated, but it did no good to wonder. There was nothing he could do about it. He had no right to do anything about it. His boot went into the stirrup as he swung onto his horse and reined it away from the hitching rail to head for the depot.

The black shawl covering Lilli's head was whipped by the gritty wind, but she didn't bow her head as shovels of dirt began falling on Stefan's coffin. People filed past her: friends, neighbors, all offering their sympathy. They seemed to expect her silence and the dullness of her eyes.

No one asked what she planned to do, but she had made her decisions. She was putting the farm up for sale. Franz Kreuger was going to harvest what wheat was in the fields on a share basis. After that, she was leaving. There was no more reason to stay, with Stefan gone. She didn't even let herself think about Webb Calder, because that had been too long ago. It was dead, too, like Stefan.

22

When the doctor climbed out of his buggy, Webb noted the changes from an eager young doctor assuming his first practice to this over-worked physician not getting to eat regularly or enough sleep. He was the only doctor for a hundred miles in any direction and the demands on him were constant. It showed in his prematurely grayed hair and eyes reddened from the lack of sleep.

"I'm sorry I had to call you out, Simon." Webb prefaced his greeting with regret and led Dr. Simon Bardolph toward the bunk-house. "I hope you aren't as tired as you look."

"Hell, I'm past the point of being tired." Simon had ceased to be awed by the Calder name. "What happened?"

"Abe Garvey was stomped pretty bad by a rank horse in his roundup string. We brought him back here and did what we could for him, then sent for you," Webb explained as he opened the bunkhouse door. "He appears to be bleeding inside."

"I'll take a look at him." He entered the bunkhouse, his mind already running through the possibilities. A tired smile broke over his weary features when he recognized the blond-haired woman by the injured man's bunk. "Ah, my favorite nurse. How are you, Ruth?"

"Fine." Her glance skipped past him to Webb, then fell quickly away.

"You really should give up schoolteaching and come to work for me, Ruth." Simon began his examination of the patient immediately, talking while he did so. "Lord knows, I could use the help." He sensed her stiffness and the high tension that hovered just below her placid surface. The cause was easy to diagnose. Webb Calder. It had been obvious to Simon when she nursed Webb after that gunshot wound that she was hopelessly in love with him. Evidently the situation hadn't changed. One look at the injured cowboy advised him that he would require her help — and her undivided attention.

"Webb, why don't you clear out and leave us professionals to take care of him?" Simon suggested bluntly while the other half of his mind was practicing his profession on the patient. "And make sure there's plenty of hot

481

coffee. I'm going to need a gallon when I'm through here."

There was a degree of hesitation before Webb conceded his presence wasn't necessary. "I'll be over in the cookshack."

It was better than two hours later when Simon Bardolph entered the cookshack. Webb poured him a cup of coffee and had it sitting on the long table when he sat down. The doctor rubbed his face, as if trying to push out the tiredness.

"I'd say he has better than a good chance of pulling through" was his verdict. "Whoever set that broken leg did a good job."

"Slim and Nate did that before they loaded him in the chuckwagon to bring him back to the ranch," Webb said. "Grizzly has a steak burned for you."

There was a pause, followed by a short, tired laugh. "I can't remember when I ate last," Simon declared.

"That's what I thought." Webb motioned to the bad-tempered cook to serve up the meal. "I heard there's been a fever hitting the drylanders." He was fishing for information about Lilli, whether he was willing to admit it or not.

"Typhoid." When the plate was set before him, Simon picked up his knife and fork and began cutting into the meat with little surgical precision. "It's been keeping me running from one end of the country to the other. I've tried to spread the word that everyone should boil their water before drinking it, but —" He shrugged to indicate the foolish lack of cooperation and simple laziness of some. "It's the very young and the old I'm losing." He chewed on a bite of steak. "I'd forgotten how good food tastes," he said thickly, not waiting until he swallowed.

"We've got plenty of food, so don't be shy about asking for seconds," Webb offered.

"Don't have the time." Simon talked between mouthfuls. "I've got a maternity case waiting."

"Oh?" The sound was a question.

"Your neighbor Franz Kreuger's wife. She went into labor. If this baby follows the pattern of her others, I should arrive just in time to usher it into the world." He sliced off another chunk of the charred meat. "To tell you the truth, I'm surprised Kreuger even sent for me."

"Why's that?"

"He thinks there was more I could have done to save his neighbor." He shook his head. "The man is irrational at times."

"His neighbor. Which one was it?" Webb frowned.

"An old guy . . ." Simon wagged his fork in

the air, searching for the name. "Richter . . . Richner . . . something like that."

"Reisner. Stefan Reisner." Webb supplied the name, surprised at how flat his voice sounded.

"That's it." Simon nodded and stabbed another piece of meat to pop into his mouth, eating with a haste he would have warned his patients against.

"What about his wife?" Everything inside him was still, waiting.

"What about her?" The doctor didn't understand the question. "As far as I know, she's fine, if that's what you mean. But she was young and healthy, too."

"When did this happen?" It had to have been recent, or Webb was sure he would have heard about it.

"Let's see . . . he must have died two, no — three weeks ago," the doctor decided, then sent a curious look at Webb. "Why?"

Three weeks! Everything seemed to break loose inside him. Frustration mixed with anger that Lilli hadn't attempted to let him know. It confused him, raked him with uncertainties. He pushed off the bench that paralleled the long table, unaware that he hadn't answered the doctor's question.

"Webb?" Simon sat up straighter, thoroughly

confused by his behavior.

"I'll see you later, Simon." Webb threw the remark over his shoulder, not slackening his stride as he left the cookhouse and brushing past Ruth as she was coming in.

Simon Bardolph continued to stare at the door long after it had closed, trying to puzzle it out. Ruth noticed his confusion. "Is something wrong?"

His glance flicked to her blankly; then he shook his head and turned back to his food. "I guess Webb just remembered he had to be someplace."

"Why do you say that?" She glanced toward the door, remembering that Webb had been rather brisk, but she had thought it might be left over from their last meeting.

"We were talking. He was asking me questions about Reisner's death —" he began, speaking and mulling the events over in his mind at the same time.

"Reisner." The name came out in a quick breath. "Lilli Reisner?"

"No. Is that the wife's name?" He shrugged that it didn't matter. "It was the old man that died." His gaze narrowed at the way the light seemed to go out of Ruth's eyes. "Would you explain to me what's going on here?"

There was faint movement of her head in

denial. "Nothing." It wasn't her place to tell him. In any case, it was possible he'd know for himself in a short while.

She had waited so patiently, clinging to the last thread of hope. Now it was unraveling. Tears were welling in her eyes. She excused herself quickly and escaped before the doctor saw that she was crying.

The first two weeks after Stefan's death there had been so many details to take care of, so many things to do, that Lilli had barely drawn a restful breath. The third week, it had all caught up with her and she'd practically slept the clock around. Finally her mind and body were cleared of tiredness and indecision. No more dark hollows ringed her eyes. They viewed reality with a steady gleam of determination.

A restless wind tried to lift the skirt of her russet dress, swirling it about her legs. The shawl around her shoulders was the only black garment she owned. She meant no disrespect to Stefan, but buying black material to make mourning dresses seemed a waste of what little money she had. The wind tore at the bank draft in her hand, trying to rip it from her grasp.

"I'm sorry it couldn't be more, Mrs.

Reisner," Doyle Pettit declared, respectfully holding his hat in front of him. "But with the lack of rain this year, the price of land has dropped. I had hoped for your sake that I could have sold your farm for more."

What he neglected to tell her was that he had purchased the land himself. She had insisted on an immediate sale. So Doyle had paid the present, fair-market value of the land, confident he would double his money on it next spring. He certainly hadn't cheated her out of any profits, merely taken advantage of the situation.

"I understand." After the bank loans had been paid and deducted, there wasn't much left. Not as much as she had hoped, certainly. She folded the bank draft into a neat square and slipped it deep into her pocket. "It was kind of you to come all the way out here to bring it to me."

"It was no trouble, I assure you." He used his charming smile on her and looked appropriately concerned. "What will you do now, Mrs. Reisner? It isn't a great deal of money, but naturally you'll want to invest it wisely. I'd be more than happy to advise you on the matter."

"I have already made plans. It should be enough to buy a small restaurant, perhaps in Butte." Cooking was the only skill she possessed, her only means of making a living, and with all the copper mines around Butte, Montana, it sounded like a good place. Besides, it seemed sensible to leave the area and put distance between herself and foolish dreams about Webb Calder.

"Going into business for yourself, now, that's a big step, Mrs. Reisner." Doyle Pettit had the same skeptical look in his eye that everyone else had. Men ran businesses, and women taught school or took care of the sick. "There's a great deal you need to know."

"I have managed our household for a good number of years, Mr. Pettit. I believe I know something about purchasing supplies and paying bills." Lilli was bristling slightly behind the smile she gave him. "But thank you for your concern."

Not by words or action did she encourage him to stay and chat, not even to the extent of inviting him inside the shanty that was no longer hers. The man was too smooth, too well dressed, and the Model T parked a few yards away showed too little dust. There was a vanity, a self-interest, about him that made him seem superficial. As a recent widow, she probably should have been flattered by his attention and interest, but she strongly doubted it was genuine.

Doyle widened his smile and attempted to cover his confusion over this businesslike reception. He had delivered the draft and she seemed to be urging him to leave. It might have been interesting to console her. She certainly looked more attractive than she had the day she came into the bank wanting to sell the farm.

"If there's anything else I can do, Mrs. Reisner, I hope you'll contact me." There was nothing left but to take his leave of her.

"Thank you." She bobbed her head briefly, never saying she would or wouldn't. The sunlight caught the rusty autumn color in her dark hair.

But he didn't hurry about leaving, turning up his collar and pulling on his gloves. "I think we're going to have an early winter. It almost smells like frost in the air." A drumming sound came faintly to him. Doyle turned to look down the lane. A horse and rider were approaching, still too far away to identify. "It looks like someone's coming."

As she stepped away from the windbreak of the shanty, she pulled the shawl more closely around her shoulders. There was a familiarity about the rider that seemed to trip up her pulse and send it skittering unevenly. Everything had been so settled; now her thoughts started going every which way as the rider came close enough for Lilli to be certain it was Webb.

The horse puffed to a stop beside the automobile, pricking its ears at it suspiciously. Webb sat in the saddle for a few seconds, his expressionless glance going from her to Doyle Pettit.

"Webb Calder." Doyle recovered from his surprise to move forward to greet him. "I didn't expect to run into you out here."

Letting the reins trail to ground-tie the horse, Webb shook the hand Doyle extended to him, a measuring look sliding to Lilli.

She was almost glad Doyle Pettit was here. It gave her time to keep her feet firmly on the ground and not be blown away by this rocking of her senses.

"I stopped by to pay my respects to . . . Mrs. Reisner." The hesitation over the formal mode of address was small but noticeable to Lilli. "I can't say that I expected to find you here, either, Doyle."

"I handled the sale of the farm for Mrs. Reisner. The transaction was finalized today, so I brought the draft out to her," he explained.

There was a flicker of surprise in Webb's eyes at the news she had sold the farm before he reasoned out it was sensible. She couldn't have farmed it herself without hiring a man.

He doubted if there was enough money for that, certainly not with this year's poor crop.

"I must say, Webb, you're being very neighborly, coming by like this and all," Doyle said.

Webb didn't try to keep his gaze from straying to Lilli. She looked so damned composed that it rankled him. Her eyes were a dark midnight blue, looking straight at him. Her lips lay together in an easy line. It was as if she were waiting for him to do something or say something.

He removed his hat, feeling awkward and not liking it. "I thought I'd come by and see if there was anything I could do." It wasn't what she wanted to hear and it wasn't what he wanted to say. But with Doyle Pettit here, he was bound by conventions. So he prodded the man into going. "If you were leaving, Doyle, don't let me keep you."

Doyle sent a glance at the young widow, thinking she might want him to stay. There was something in the air that he couldn't quite fathom. Her expression hadn't changed. There continued to be nothing to indicate his presence was wanted.

"I do have some business in town," he lied. "Remember what I said, Mrs. Reisner. If I can be of any help at all, please contact me."

"Thank you again for coming out," she repeated.

Webb caught the reins of his horse and held them while Doyle cranked his automobile and got it running. While his attention was elsewhere, Lilli took the opportunity to study him. The few years hadn't made any differences in his physical appearance except to add lines to the creases near his eyes and mouth. His flatly muscled body was long and male, and the wind ruffed hair that was thick and near black.

The changes were more subtle than that, the kind a woman who loved him would notice. Before when he'd come to her, he'd been a cowboy — unique in many respects, but still a cowboy. Power and authority were resting on his wide shoulders now, and they sat there easily. Lilli sensed that many things were locked inside him, long controlled — perhaps too long controlled. He had come here to see her, but why? She wondered if Webb was even sure. Pride wrapped its invisible shield around her and kept him from observing that just seeing him again disturbed her.

The departing automobile churned up a choking cloud of dust in the barren yard. Lilli lifted an end of the shawl over her nose and mouth to keep the gritty dirt out of her mouth and lungs and closed her eyes to slits against the stinging dust. The wind picked it up and whirled it away before it had a chance to settle back on the ground. Webb's horse swung around him, whickering nervously after the noisy vehicle.

It was a moment or two before Webb let the reins fall and came toward her again, slapping the dust from his hat. His gaze was on her, probing, searching for something – a reaction, a sign, an age-old signal between a man and a woman that was easily recognized and never defined. She stood a few feet in front of the door, watching him, not unfriendly, but not open to him, either. He half-waited for her to suggest they go inside, out of this dust and wind, but she remained silent. There was some kind of barrier between them, and Webb was undecided about how to penetrate it because he didn't understand the cause.

"One of my men was hurt on the roundup. Simon – Dr. Bardolph – came out to fix him up, so I just found out from him this afternoon about Stefan." He wanted to make it clear that he'd have come sooner if he had known. "I was sorry to hear about it." No, dammit! He hadn't been sorry. Why was he mouthing words of polite convention when there were so many other things he wanted to say? "I wish you had let me know." It was the first honest thing he'd said. "It couldn't have been easy for you."

"I managed." Her chin dipped briefly, then came up again. The boldness was there, but so was restraint.

He wasn't handling this right, but he seemed to be on a course that couldn't be altered. "You sold the farm."

"Yes." Her gaze ran around the dried-up buildings rattling in the endless wind, some distant memories stirring in her look. "I've sold everything — the horses and equipment. There wasn't much point in keeping it." Her attention came back to him. "Even if Stefan was alive, as dry as it's been, I don't think we could have made it through to next year."

"What were you planning to do?" Webb unconsciously used the past tense, yet wanting to find out if she had included him at all in her future plans.

She faltered slightly under his steady regard, then held it once again. "After all the debts have been paid, I have enough money left to buy a small restaurant somewhere."

"You were going to leave." His jaw made a harsh line. "Weren't you even going to come and tell me good-bye?" Webb challenged roughly.

The motion of her hand as it brushed aside strands of hair the wind blew across her face seemed to be a means of avoiding his eyes. "Times change. People change." Lilli offered that as an answer. "It isn't reasonable to expect people to have the same feelings after so much time has passed."

Her reply stunned him, hitting him low as he read into it that she had changed. She turned in an unhurried and graceful motion and walked the few steps to the door. There she paused, her body at right angles to him, and looked at him across her shoulders.

"It was good of you to come by," she said.

The shanty door creaked on its hinges as it swung inward. He was burned with a rawness that wouldn't be dismissed as simply as she had just dismissed him. By the time Lilli had stepped inside and turned to close the door, Webb was filling the opening, a hand braced against the door to keep from being shut out.

"Is that all you can say — it was good of me to come?" When he pushed his way inside, she retreated a step, her eyes now intent on him, watching and waiting. "Why do you think I'm here?"

"I couldn't possibly guess." She was too afraid of being wrong. There were too many reasons that might have brought him here.

"Then explain to me what all that 'times changing and people changing' was about,"

Webb demanded. "Say it out plain if you don't want me anymore." Something flickered in her eyes, and some of his confusion lifted. She was waiting for him to state his reason for coming, to declare his intention. He pushed the door shut and caught her shoulders all in the same motion. "I swear, Lilli, you've got a pride that can freeze a man out," he muttered thickly and claimed her mouth in a quick, hungry kiss so there could be no more doubts about what he wanted.

The pressure of her lips unsettled him like none other could. Her hands rested lightly on his chest, not resisting, yet not inviting a closer embrace, either. Webb was puzzled by the way she kissed him and held back at the same time, not allowing herself to be swept away by the passion of her feelings.

"What is it, Lilli?" He lifted his head and spread his hand over the side of her face, tracing the outline of her warm lips with his thumb. Her lashes remained partially lowered.

"I wasn't sure why you were here." She still wasn't. He could hear it in her voice.

His hand moved along her back, feeling the ripple of bones in her spine and the tension. "I'm here because I want you. I still love you. If there's been any change, the feelings have only grown stronger." There was a degree of tightness in the smiling curve of his mouth. "I was beginning to wonder if it was the same for you. Is it?"

She tipped her head back to look at him and see what was in his eyes. There was a quiet expectancy in her expression, a waiting for something else he hadn't said. "Yes," she admitted without any hesitance. She wasn't satisfied with what she saw in his face and pulled slowly out of his arms. Webb frowned when she turned away from him. "Where do we go from here?" she asked.

The pride of her carriage and the steadiness of her voice began to make an impression on him. Slowly Webb began to understand the cause for her proud reticence. She didn't know what role he was asking her to fill — that of a lover, a mistress, or his wife. She was concerned that he thought less of her because she had lain with him and let her feelings be known to him while she was married to another man. She didn't want to be regarded as less worthy of his respect.

Webb came up behind her and put his hands on her shoulders, rubbing them in a caressing way and feeling the tremor of need that ran through her. She swayed backward a little, surrendering to his touch.

"I'd like to take you straight to my bed." The

clean smell of her dark copper hair stirred him. "But I think we'd better see the minister first."

She swung around, her gaze sweeping his face to be certain he meant it. The rigidity went out of her body as he gathered her into his arms. The deep hunger in her kiss raced through him like fire, shaking him. It was a power she had over him that lifted him to some far height and let him glimpse the glory a man and a woman could know.

When they drew apart, neither of them was satisfied, but it was a simple matter that kisses alone wouldn't satisfy their needs and there was a moment of assurance required on both parts before another step was taken. Her long lips were swollen from his possessive kisses and the short stubble on his face had reddened her skin. The light in her blue eyes was especially for him. She ran a finger above his upper lip.

"You're sweating," she murmured, then took his hand and laid it above her breast. "Can you feel my heart pounding?"

"Yes." His own was racing like a steam engine, and his breath was coming just as rapidly. He slid his hand down to cover her breast, so taut and full against his palm. "Lilli." There were a thousand nights of wanting her wrapped up in the groaning whisper of her name.

She came against him, resting her head on his shoulder and possessively curving her arms around him. An exciting contentment was on her, pleased with him and pleased with herself. She studied the throbbing pulse in his throat and the tanned column of his neck.

"Why didn't you come to see me during all that time?" she asked.

Surprise and bewilderment darkened his expression as he tipped his head down, trying to see her face. "You made it clear you were a married woman and didn't want to see me again," he reminded her.

"I know," Lilli murmured.

"Was I suppose to disregard that?" His mouth quirked dryly.

"Sometimes I hoped you would, even though I was relieved that you didn't." She was aware of the contradiction in her answer and smiled at it, because it didn't make it any less true.

"Is that an example of female thinking?" Webb taunted gently. "You ask me to stay away, but you want me to come. You tell me to forget you and find someone else, then hope I don't."

She tilted her head back to look at him, smiling, all gay and confident. "Yes, that's precisely what I meant."

"That kind of logic is not easily followed."

He kissed at her lips, feeling them cling to his.

Then her fingertips were there, exploring the firm line of his mouth and tracing the crease that ran beside it. "I've only been widowed for three weeks. People will talk if we get married so soon."

That struck a raw nerve. "I don't care if propriety dictates a year's mourning period. You've fulfilled whatever obligation you felt you owed Stefan. You'll be my wife — Mrs. Webb Calder — and no one will dare say anything against you. So let them talk. Nothing they might do or say can touch us," he insisted roughly.

She listened to his words, weighing them against her own feelings. There was a part of her that would have preferred not to rush into marriage, not to allow it to be a solution of convenience to settle where she would go, and to take time to be lovers before they settled into a routine of man and wife.

Her hesitation was obvious, and Webb realized her hint to delay their visit to the minister was a way of obtaining something else. It wasn't hard to understand, given the meanness of her past life and given the blandness of her practical marriage to Stefan.

"You'd like if I would woo you and observe all the niceties of courtship, wouldn't you?" he guessed and observed her surprise at his accuracy. "You want me to win your love all over again."

"Is that so wrong?" There was something half-teasing and half-serious in her look.

"It isn't wrong," he assured her with a faint grin. "It's impossible. One week. That's all you're going to have before the wedding, and I'm taking you home with me today. I have no intention of letting you change your mind."

"You like being masterful, don't you?" Lilli mocked, showing him the bold side of her nature again, rushing in where even fools trod softly. "You like the idea of telling me what to do. Well, it just so happens, Mr. Webb Calder, that it's what I want, too."

It was all that needed to be said. The long, drugging kiss affirmed everything else. The thrusting contours of his body were hard against her straining flesh, arousing a desire that had lain dormant for so long. Her emotions no longer had to be repressed; no longer were they withering inside her, but instead were flourishing and blossoming in a way that was basic and timeless. She shuddered at the stimulating nibbles his mouth made on her ear, on the pulsing vein in her neck.

With an effort, he lifted his head and combed his fingers into her hair. "I want you to pack your things." It would have been easy to continue this embrace through to the conclusion they both wanted. But when she finally lay in his arms, Webb wanted it to be under his roof — not here where she had lived with Stefan. "Only bring your clothes and the personal belongings you want to keep. The rest you can sell or give away. I'll be back a little later to get you."

Her hands curved around his neck, bringing his head down for a last kiss. "I'll be waiting."

23

The scale of it was massive, like nothing Lilli had ever seen before. Two stories, with a wide porch running the full length of the front, the house stood on a knoll, overlooking smaller and less elaborate buildings. The slanting rays of a late-afternoon sun bathed it in a warm orange light that colored the glass panes with a welcoming glow. Gray tails of smoke came from two of the stone chimneys dotting the roof, slanted to shed winter snows, and waved against a saffron sky.

Webb was standing by the opened door to help her out of the automobile. She finally tore her gaze away from the house to look at him, vague disbelief still claiming her. "This is your home?" She let him take her hand as she stepped onto the running board, then to the ground.

"No. It's *our* home," he corrected and held onto her hand while he led her up the main steps to the front doors. "It's commonly referred to as The Homestead."

"The Homestead." She laughed shortly at the unassuming name, finding it inappropriate for such a grand-looking place.

Webb stopped, turning her so she could look out at the endless brown sweep of Calder land. "This is the site that my father filed the original homestead claim on that was the beginning of the ranch. When he expanded his holdings, everyone started calling this section of land The Homestead to differentiate it from the new properties. Gradually, it came to mean this house."

Instead of looking at the land, Lilli watched him, catching the pride of ownership in his voice and his eyes — and the hint of humility. Somehow his status of wealth and power hadn't meant much until she had seen these surroundings. They had demanded a thoughtful study of him, but the man she believed she had known was the person standing beside her. The watchfulness was gone from her eyes when he glanced at her.

"Let's go inside so I can show you your new home," Webb stated.

Lilli was eager to see what the house was like inside. He took her on a complete tour of the first-floor rooms that began with the living room and ended with the library-den.

"Are all these books yours?" Lilli went to the shelves, her fingers lightly tracing across the many volumes. Books were such luxuries that she had never known one person could own so many.

"I'm going to read every one of them," she declared, as excited as a child. Webb was discovering that while she might be awed by things, she wasn't intimidated. Once she became accustomed to the size of the house, she'd turn it into a home for both of them, filled with warmth and laughter the way it had been when his parents were alive.

"What's this?" She was behind the desk, looking at the map.

"The ranch." He came around the big desk to point out landmarks to her so she could orient herself and get an idea of where they were in relation to places she knew. When he had finished, Lilli continued to stare at the map drawn on yellowing canvas. "What are you thinking?" Her expression was unreadable.

"Six hundred and forty acres wouldn't take up an inch on this map," she murmured. That was the amount of land she and Stefan had worked.

"The ranch is big," Webb admitted.

"It's indecent," she retorted, but her short

laugh took any sting from the reply. "And your father acquired all this." Lilli turned her gaze to study Webb and try to imagine what his father had been like. "I wish I had met him."

"He was a remarkable man. It took me a while to realize there was only one Benteen Calder." And that his path would be different from his father's, a continuation, but over new ground.

"Most people don't appreciate their parents until it's too late. I was like that." There was understanding in her blue eyes.

When he leaned toward her, she raised her mouth to him and slid her arms around his middle to bring their bodies closer. His hard kiss forced her lips apart and expressed a need for her that was more than just physical. It was a discovery that came late to her. Every ruler needed a mate who would regard him as just a man. He needed her. Her fingers spread over the tapering muscles of his back, her feminine form fitting naturally to his male shape. The smell of him filled her as Lilli knew it would on many nights, warm and musky, scented with the bay rum on his smoothly shaven jaw. The play of his hands on her back and hips caressed and molded, excited and aroused, with their possessing touch. She lost herself in the embrace, blocking out everything but this raw glory she was discovering.

When Ruth noticed the Model T parked in front of The Homestead, she went to the house. Cold water had washed the redness of tears from her eyes, although shadows of pain continued to linger in her pale face. She had guessed Webb had gone to see Lilli, and she had to learn the outcome of his visit. The dreadful waiting was intolerable.

With her habitual quietness, she entered the house and went directly to the den, the only room Webb used with any frequency. Her coat was unbuttoned, but her hands were pushed into the pockets where they could knot into tense fists. Burning logs crackled in the fireplace, she noticed when she first entered the den.

Ruth was three steps into the room before she saw the couple behind the desk, locked in an embrace that was almost sexual. Shock drained the color from her face, dissolving her of all hope. She spun blindly, wanting to escape before they noticed her, and blundered into one of the double doors, knocking it into the wall with a loud bang.

"Ruth!" Webb's startled voice was husky and laced with the heaviness of his breathing.

Her back was to them and she didn't turn

around. The pain inside was more than tears could wash away, so her eyes burned with dryness. "I'm sorry. I didn't mean to intrude." It was a hurried apology, offered as she took a step to leave the room.

"Don't go, Ruth." He called her back, his voice almost normal. Reluctantly she paused, hearing the two sets of footsteps moving out from behind the desk. Her body was braced and rigid as she slowly turned to face the pair. The pride and gentleness, the love flowing through his rugged features, nearly broke Ruth into pieces. "I want you to be the first to know that Lilli and I are getting married."

Ruth wanted to scream at him that she didn't want to be the first, but it simply wasn't in her to be angry with him. The heat of the repressed emotion put red dots in her cheeks.

"Congratulations." Ruth forced out the word and knew she had to say more. "I know it's what you've been wanting for a long time." She sincerely wanted him to be happy, but it still hurt that she wasn't the one.

"You remember Ruth Stanton, don't you, Lilli?" His arm was around the waist of the auburn-haired woman, keeping her close to his side and maintaining a discreet body contact. "Ruth has always been like one of the family."

"Yes, I remember her." Lilli nodded, her lips

curving upward in a warm and apologetic smile. "I hope our behavior a moment ago didn't embarrass you."

"No. I guess I should have knocked," Ruth murmured an uneasy response, unable to cope with such frankness.

"No one knocks at The Homestead." Webb dismissed that idea and looked intimately at Lilli. "We'll simply have to learn to be more circumspect."

"I'd like us to be friends," Lilli stated with an openness that Ruth found difficult to dislike. "May I call you Ruth?"

"Of course," she agreed. But she needed time before she could handle that kind of relationship.

"You came to speak to me about something?" Webb realized he hadn't asked the reason Ruth had come to the house.

She used the excuse she had made ready. "I only came to let you know Abe was doing better."

"I'm glad to hear it. I'll look in on him later," he said.

"If you'll excuse me, I'm sure you'd rather be alone." Ruth's voice nearly broke. Neither raised an objection, saying the normal phrases of parting before she left the room.

A brief silence followed the closing of the

front door. Webb's hand rubbed absently along the curve of Lilli's waist while he looked thoughtfully at the open doors of the den. Lilli couldn't tell what he was thinking.

"Is something wrong?" she asked.

His glance swung around to run warmly over her features, a caressing sensation in his look. "No. The only way things could be better is if you were already my wife." His arm tightened around her, then relaxed to let her go. "I'll bring your things in and show you where you'll be sleeping."

The main bedroom was larger than the one-room shack. A large bed with an elaborately carved headboard was covered with a goose-down quilt. Besides a dresser and a chest of drawers, a pair of chairs and a small sofa covered in rose velvet were grouped to create a sitting area around the fireplace. When Webb set her worn satchel on the floor, Lilli was forcibly reminded of its shabbiness compared to its new surroundings.

"While you get settled, I'm going to check on Abe Garvey," Webb stated. "Through that door, there's a private bath. I stoked the heater earlier, so there's hot water if you want to freshen up before dinner." He noticed the way she was looking around the room, taking in everything. "Do you like it?"

"Who wouldn't?" Lilli countered with a wry smile.

His gaze lingered an instant on that smile, but he refrained from kissing her. "I'll be back," he promised huskily and walked to the door.

Alone in the room, it all seemed unreal to Lilli for a moment. She was reassured by the sound of his footsteps descending the stairs, and the large room claimed her attention again. She moved around it, exploring, opening up drawers that would swallow her meager wardrobe, testing the softness of the mattress and sitting in the chairs. She paused at the window that faced the south, like the front of the house, and watched Webb walking to one of the buildings. When he disappeared inside it, she let the curtain drop and turned back to the room.

Lilli crossed to the inner door Webb had pointed out to her, turned the brass knob, and pushed it inward. Her eyes rounded in dazzled amazement. There was a porcelain sink with brass faucets for running water, hot and cold, and a white porcelain toilet complete with a chain connecting to an overhead flusher. Lilli tested both of them out, laughing in delight. After so many years of carrying water and heating it on the stove, as well as emptying chamber pots, this was the height of luxury.

She ran her hand along the smooth edge of the large white cast-iron bath, supported by clawed feet, and remembered the small tub she had bathed in when there was enough water to spare. It had been so cramped, her knees poking into her chest, but here, she could stretch out almost full length.

Her eyes was caught by the bottles on the marble-topped stand next to the sink. Opening one, she dipped a finger into the creamy lotion and rubbed the dollop into her hand, feeling the silken texture it gave her skin. With her curiosity heightened, she unstoppered a crystal decanter containing fragrant salts. One whiff and Lilli turned to the bath, a totally feminine light shining in her eyes.

Minutes later, the rubber stopper was in the drain hole and the faucets were turned on to fill the porcelain bath with water, water that bubbled with the fragrant salts shaken into it. And Lilli was shedding her clothes to take the first luxurious bath in her life. A toweling cloth hung from a brass ring on the wall, and there was a large sponge on the sink and a bar of scented soap. Lilli could only guess that these feminine toiletries had been the late Mrs. Calder's, Webb's mother. They were a temptation she couldn't resist. Besides, they had obviously been left there to be used by whoever occupied the adjoining room.

When she submerged her naked body in the mounds of scented bubbles and felt the relaxing heat of the water against her skin, she doubted that anything could be so blissful. Stretching out full length, she braced her toes against one end and rested her head on the curved porcelain back. She closed her eyes to savor the sensation and soaked for a long time until the water became tepid.

Uninhibited, Lilli played with the bubbles, scooping some into her hand and blowing them into the air, laughing silently to herself. With her toe, she caught a drip of water dangling from the hot-water faucet, then let her toes play a game of hide and seek in the scented foam. Finally she reached for the sponge and soaped it to wash herself, humming a tuneless melody of contentment and splashing a little.

When Webb didn't find Lilli downstairs upon his return to the house, he climbed the steps to find out what was keeping her. The door to the master suite stood open. He walked in and saw the satchel sitting on the floor where he had left it, but she was nowhere to be seen.

"Lilli?" He started to raise his voice to call

513

her a second time when he heard the faint splashing sounds from the bathroom. An inner pressure directed his feet to the connecting door, aroused by a stronger force than his sense of proper conduct.

The doorknob turned silently. Lilli wasn't alerted to his presence until the motion of the door swinging open caught her eye. She turned, her lips parting to round in a small o. A split second later, she recognized Webb and her brief alarm faded. A vague self-consciousness took its place, since bathing had always been a strictly private activity in her experience. The layer of bubbles concealed her nudity from his gaze. For some reason, she found it difficult to summon a genuine protest at Webb's invasion of her privacy.

"Do you always walk right in when a lady is bathing?" she challenged.

"When you weren't downstairs, I came up to find you." His voice had a husky pitch that sent out its own disturbing message.

"Now you've found me, so get out," Lilli ordered, still in a bantering tone, trying to make light of the situation even though her pulse had begun to accelerate. The deep brown of his eyes had darkened to nearly black with the intensity of his gaze. When he took a step toward her, she did something that she knew

514

would provoke him. It was totally instinctive. "Webb Calder, will you get out of here?" She tossed the wet sponge at him, splattering drops on him and the floor, while a breathless laugh came from her when he ducked to avoid it.

"Now you are coming out of that bath," he growled a mocking threat.

For a few seconds, it was a playful game as Lilli scrunched down in the tub and splashed water at him to fend him off. The instant his hands caught her wet wrists, the laughter left both of their faces. There was a moment when they stared at each other. Then the steady pressure of his grip urged her from the water. She stood up slowly, strangely unembarrassed by her own nudity.

He couldn't know that no man had ever seen her before, not in the light, not even Stefan. They had always undressed in the dark, with their backs turned to each other. When Stefan had wanted satisfaction from her, their night-clothes weren't removed; they were shifted out of the way. She had never questioned the custom of it, or even wondered if others behaved in the same way.

When Webb released her wrists to span his hands around her slippery waist, she reached for his shoulders, holding on to them while he lifted her out of the water. Her wet feet touched the floor inches from his boots, her dripping body brushing against his clothes. A heady silence encircled them as his eyes took in every intimate detail of her. Lilli trembled slightly, unnerved by the wild heat flowing through her veins.

Webb reached for the thick toweling cloth looped through the wall ring and began blotting the moisture and drying bubbles on her skin. He started at the top with her neck and shoulders and slowly worked his way down over her breasts and tightly indrawn stomach, then crouched to dry her hips, thighs, and legs, finishing with her feet. There was a crazy weakness in her limbs when he straightened. Her breathing was no longer deep but very shallow as he wrapped the towel around her shoulders.

Effortlessly, he lifted her into the cradle of his arms. She automatically linked her hands together around his neck. With his face so close to hers, Lilli gazed at his features, so strong and sun-browned, and severely handsome. There was a rightness to everything that she couldn't explain as he carried her into the bedroom.

In the middle of the room, Webb paused and let her feet settle to the floor. She stood within the loose circle of his arms. The towel had slipped, but an instinctive movement of her hand kept it partially covering her front — not out of any sense of modesty, but simply because it was there. Her gaze drifted down to the wet patches on his shirt. There were more on his pants.

"Your clothes are wet," she said huskily.

With calm deliberation, he unbuttoned his shirt and shrugged out of it. There was a tightening low in her stomach as she looked at the rippling muscles of his chest and the dark hairs that nested on it. The sensation increased when he stripped out of his pants. The long white underwear beneath them was molded to the lower half of his body like a second skin. The boots and socks were gone only seconds later.

"You don't need that." His glance flicked to the towel and she lowered her hand, letting it settle onto the floor with his clothes. "Lilli." He groaned her name and lifted her straight up into the air, pressing his mouth against the roundness of a breast.

Raw and curling desires quivered through her as he carried her, letting her slide down him by inches, while his mouth nuzzled a path to her lips. By the time they reached the bed, she was being consumed by a ravishing kiss. He eased her onto the quilt, his body following hers to partially pin her down. The male hard-ness outlined against her thigh was something Lilli understood, but the absence of any demand for him to receive immediate satisfac-tion was new to her.

His mouth rocked over her lips, his tongue darting in with tormenting touches until she turned the aggressor and made it stay to entwine with hers. His hands were roaming at will over her naked flesh, caressing the rise and fall of her breasts, sliding over her stomach and hips, heating her skin wherever they touched.

She was already drowning in the waves of sensations when he started a more intimate exploration. His lips were on her face, hair, and neck, then lower in the valley between her breasts. She sank her teeth into her lip as he rubbed his mouth over a sensitively erect nipple. Her fingers curled into the thickness of his hair and a moan of pleasure came from her throat when he took the nipple into his mouth.

Then he was rolling onto his back and pulling her with him to lie half across him. Her heavy-lidded eyes looked at him in confusion before he sought her lips. She kissed him, hungry for the excitement the contact pro-duced. Some distant part of her mind was conscious that he was stripping off his underwear. Now it will come, the thought registered — but it didn't.

When he shifted their positions again, it was to lie on their sides, facing each other, bodies touching. There were no more barriers between them. It seemed impossible to get close enough to him. Her breasts strained against the flat wall of his chest while her hands ran over the lean muscles in his back to mold him more tightly to her. His erection made no demands for entry despite the arching of her hips.

The aching fury of need was so intense that Lilli felt she could stand it no more. As if sensing it, Webb pressed her backward with his weight and his legs slid between hers. She tasted the perspiration on his skin as she arched to meet the thrust of his hips. His virility filled her throbbing emptiness. Under the driving power of his hips, she was all motion beneath him, giving and demanding, taking and receiving. No previous experience had prepared either of them for the wild passion of their coupling, the mating of souls as well as bodies.

A sweetly wild contentment flowed through every inch of her body as she lay nestled in his arms. Lilli sighed, laughing softly at the wondrously incredible discovery she'd made, and wrapped his arms more tightly around her, the warmth of his hard body the most comfortable blanket she'd ever known. His mouth moved against her hair.

"Are you as happy as I am?" she murmured, so full of pleasure that she was completely drained of all energy.

"Yes." Although it seemed a tame word to describe a satisfaction that went beyond his ken.

"I feel like silk inside." Lilli breathed in deeply and released another contented sigh. It was too unique a feeling for mere words to describe.

The week of courtship he had promised her had taken a much more intimate turn than he had planned. Webb doubted if he could have stayed out of her bed anyway, but he felt he owed her a choice now that he had taken her before marriage.

"Do you want to push the wedding date ahead? Because I'm not going to leave this room tonight," he warned her.

She shifted sideways in his hold to look at him. Mischief danced in her eyes, surprising him. "Not even to eat?" she asked in mock disbelief, unperturbed by the anticipation of their wedding night and changing the subject to boldly show him. "A big man like you?"

"You noticed." The amusement in his eyes

changed the meaning of her remark.

She colored slightly when she caught the more intimate interpretation, but seemed more pleased than embarrassed. "I noticed," she replied. "That's why I thought you'd have to eat to keep up your strength."

"Tonight I could be satisfied feasting on you." He cupped a breast in his hand and bent down to kiss the sleeping nipple. "There are more ways to make love than just one."

"Is that right?" Curiosity flickered in her eyes to contradict her casual reply. "Just the same, we should eat something." She slipped out of his arms and stepped onto the floor.

As she started across the room, she caught a glimpse of her reflection in the full-length standing mirror. She walked over and stood in front of it, looking at her naked body with new eyes and making a critical appraisal. Relatively tall and slim, she was nicely shaped, she discovered, with firm, round breasts, a slender waist, and flaring hips. Her legs were long and slimly muscled − not skinny.

On the bed, Webb was enjoying his all-around view of her. "What are you looking at?" he asked curiously.

"A woman." She turned to face him, a glow in her expression that took his breath away. Webb thought he had been emptied out, but the pressure was coming back. There was a boldness about the way she stood before him, not trying to cover herself; yet it wasn't a brazen posturing to rouse his lust. It was much more natural than that. "I think I just found out how it feels to be a woman," Lilli declared.

"Come here," he said, and she approached the bed, letting him catch her hand and pull her onto the rumpled quilt beside him. Immediately she insinuated herself against him.

"Do you think we'll ever get enough of each other?" she murmured.

"It's going to take a lifetime for that to happen, if it ever does."

Regret rippled through her. "There's so much we could have shared already —"

"Don't look back." He shifted heavily onto her. "We're going to forget what's behind us and only look ahead."

"Yes." Her hand stroked his side, lightly touching the scarred depression left by the bullet hole, and let him think what he suggested was possible.

With the supper dishes finished, Ruth Stanton straightened the oilcloth covering the table and wiped off the crumbs from the meal. There was a knock at the front door of the wood-frame house she shared with her father. Company was the last thing she wanted tonight.

"Papa," she called to her father in the front room. "Somebody's at the door. Will you answer it?" She walked to the cupboards, making noise so it would sound as if she were busy.

When the second, peremptory knock went unanswered, Ruth advanced to the kitchen doorway and saw her father dozing soundly in his easy chair. His hearing wasn't too good anymore. Impatiently she walked over and nudged his shoulder. He stirred, looking around blankly.

"Somebody is at the door, Papa," Ruth repeated.

"What? Oh." He blinked to rid himself of the sleepy daze. "You had better answer it, Ruth."

In a flurry of frustration, she went to the door and tried to compose a look of calm on her strained features as she opened it. Virg Haskell was standing on the porch, turning his hat in his hand. She felt a sinking sensation. She had thought — had hoped — it was one of her father's cronies coming over to chat about old times or play a game of checkers, someone who wouldn't expect to be entertained with talk from her. Tonight of all nights, she didn't want Virg Haskell pressing his attentions on her.

"May I come in?" His smile was wide, expecting to be welcomed as he usually was.

There was no reason to refuse him admittance into her home, but Ruth didn't respond with any enthusiasm as she opened the door wider. "Of course."

"Hello, Virg." Her father started to rise stiffly out of his chair to greet the man he regarded as his daughter's suitor.

"Don't get up, Mr. Stanton." The cowboy moved quickly to shake the older man's hand.

"What brings you here — as if I need to ask?" he asked with a winking look at Ruth. His failing vision didn't notice the stiffness of her features.

"It's a nice night out — a full moon. I thought Ruth might like to go for a little walk." The slim, brown-haired cowboy turned his earnest gaze to her, a light shining brightly in his eyes.

"I can't tonight. I . . . I have papers to grade," she lied, but her father caught her in it.

"You did those before supper," he reminded her.

"Well, I meant . . . I had assignments to prepare for tomorrow." She made a faltering attempt to cover her lie.

"That won't take longer than a jig-tail," her father rebuffed that excuse. "You go out and walk with your young man and do that when you come back."

With no more excuses left to her, Ruth wasn't able to state that she didn't want to go walking with Virg, which meant she was trapped into accepting. She stalled for time. "I'll need a wrap."

She took an unconscionably long time putting on her coat, but Virg Haskell was waiting by the door when she returned. Her father made some inane remark about having a good time as they left the house.

There was one blessing in the situation. Virg always talked so much, mostly about himself, that Ruth was seldom required to say anything. As they wandered along in the moonlight, she let his voice run past her and didn't bother to listen to the words. Her gaze strayed to The Homestead. There was only one light showing, and it was on the second floor. The sight of it slowed her steps to a halt, a knife twisting in her heart.

Suddenly Virg's face was blocking it out and his lips were on her mouth, exerting forceful pressure. For a second, Ruth let herself pretend he was someone else and kissed him back until he became too demanding.

"Ruth," he groaned roughly while his hands moved over her back, trying to rub out her resistance and make her close to him again. "I don't know how much longer I can keep this up. I've asked you so many times to marry me. What do I have to do to make you say yes?"

She looked at him, suddenly seeing the great emptiness of the life ahead for her. A single woman was nothing – the next thing to dead. She couldn't stand the thought of not being wanted. She'd marry a man she didn't love before she'd endure that. It was a kind of unwritten law of survival – a person had to make do with what was at hand.

"Ask me again, Virg," she said. "I have your answer now."

24

The sunlight flashed on her gold ring, intensifying its color and luster. Lilli turned her hand experimentally and watched the play of light on her wedding band, wondering if all newly married women were fascinated by such simple things. In spite of the cold November day, she had refused to wear gloves to keep her hands warm, because they'd hide the ring she wore with such pride.

Her lips lay softly together, curved upward at the corners with a hint of a secret smile, while she supposedly supervised the loading of her purchases in the buggy. The high-necked coat she was wearing was new, a forest-green wool trimmed in a black-dyed woolskin. The dark green color brought out the blue sparkle in her eyes and the sheen of red in her dark hair.

"Will there be anything else, Mrs. Calder?"

That hint of a smile on her lips deepened at

the use of her married name. "That will be all, Mr. Ellis. Thank you." She noticed the way the proprietor of the general store glanced at her mouth and wondered if he were making guesses about the source of the secret satisfaction that lay behind it. Men did things like that, or so Webb had informed her.

"Come back anytime," he stated and moved past her to reenter his store.

Lilli paused a moment on the raised boardwalk and breathed in the crisp, invigorating air. In her present mood, not even the dust could dull the brightness of her world. Webb was to meet her at the restaurant in twenty minutes. It was early yet, but Lilli started in that direction, wondering if Webb would like the dress materials she'd purchased.

"I did not think you would have the nerve to show your face in this town." The cold and contemptuous voice lashed at her.

She faltered a step, then paused to confront Franz Kreuger as he came toward her. "Hello, Mr. Kreuger." She kept her head high. "I understand you have a new son. Congratulations." Dr. Simon Bardolph had passed along the news when he had come by the ranch to check on the progress of Abe Garvey. "Helga is doing well, I trust."

"A brazen hussy like you is not fit to speak

her name." His mouth curled in disdain. "Stefan was not even cold in his grave before you were climbing into another man's bed. You have no respect for the dead."

There was no reason to tolerate his abusive talk. Lilli made to walk past him, but he stepped into her way. She was stiff with anger, and determined not to give him the satisfaction of thinking that anything he said made the slightest impression on her.

"Stefan was a good and faithful man. He deserved more than an adulterous tramp like you," he jeered. "You are what killed him."

"You have been misinformed, Mr. Kreuger," Lilli replied coolly. "It was typhoid fever."

His glance swept her with disgust. "Because of you, he was ashamed to hold his head up among his friends. Now you come to town in your fine clothes and your ladylike airs, but no decent woman will speak to you."

Aware that his voice was growing louder to deliberately attract the attention of his fellow homesteaders and publicly humiliate her, she made a determined effort to end this meeting. "Your opinions have been most interesting, Mr. Kreuger, but you'll have to excuse me. My husband is expecting me." She tried to walk around him, but he wouldn't let her pass.

"You think because you marry a Calder, it

makes you someone important," he accused.

"I think nothing of the sort," she denied on a vibrating note of temper. "Please get out of my way."

"Ah, yes, you are meeting your husband somewhere." His eyes took on an ugly glint. "The sidewalks are for decent, God-fearing people. Walk in the street — in the gutter where your kind of women belong."

His voice rang out through the still air. A cold rage shook her, making every nerve in her body scream with tension. She wanted to hit out at him and slap his vile words down his throat, but she knew it would only please him.

"Perhaps I would find fewer braying jackasses on the street than I have on the sidewalk." Her fury was so focused on him she was blind to everything else around her.

Suddenly there was a large hand on Kreuger's shoulder, spinning him around. Lilli had a short glimpse of the black rage on Webb's face before his cocked arm drove a fist into Kreuger's face and Franz went flying backward, sprawling onto the boardwalk next to her. Then Webb was grabbing her arm and roughly pulling her along with him as he turned to walk away.

He hadn't taken two steps when a body came hurtling at him from behind. The impetus carried both men onto the hard ground of the narrow alleyway between the two buildings. They scuffled in the dirt, rolling and twisting, trying for advantage over the other. Elbows and knees became weapons as Kreuger fought with savage cunning.

A crowd of onlookers jammed around Lilli, forming a ring to watch the fight. As she looked around the chain of faces, there wasn't a friendly one to be found. They were cheering for Kreuger, one of their own, shouting advice and encouragement. He was the underdog, smaller in size than Webb, but his quickness and strength made him an equal.

Kreuger slipped out of Webb's hold and was on his feet while Webb was halfway on his knees. He saw the booted toe coming and managed to block it with his arm, the force of the kick slamming through his shoulder. Then he was catapulting himself upward, no longer underestimating his opponent. He swung a fist at the lowered face and caught Kreuger on the temple with a slanting blow.

It felt good — the fighting, the hitting, the sensation of blood pumping through his veins, cleaning out his system. His punches were reaching Kreuger, hitting his belly and his chest. The wind whistled through his lungs with the force he was throwing into his fists. A jarring set of knuckles rammed into his mouth as Kreuger knocked an arm aside and made an opening. His lip split against his teeth, pouring blood into his mouth. Another quick punch widened the cut and staggered Webb backward. He shook his head, cleaning it of the roaring sound.

He waited for Kreuger to follow up the blow, and he came, springing like a cat for the kill. Webb stepped aside and lifted a knee, driving it forward into Kreuger's vitals. When his arms dropped in pain, Webb slammed a fist into his nose and heard the crunch of bone. A second swing tore out a chunk of flesh on Kreuger's forehead. Then he aimed low and heard the snap of rib bones.

He felt no mercy, aware that Kreuger would gouge out his eyes and kick in his face given the chance. The man's eyes were glassy and shining; his tongue was caught between his teeth. Webb closed his fingers in Kreuger's collar, holding him up when his legs would have collapsed.

"Stop it!" A pair of hands was clawing at him, hitting him, trying to break his hold. "Webb! Stop it! Let him go!"

Lilli's voice finally pierced the violent rage in his mind. His fingers loosened their grip on Kreuger's shirt as Webb staggered backward a step and let the man slide unconscious to the ground. The muscles in his body began to tremble, the blows they'd taken beginning to spread pain. He lifted a hand to his mouth and looked at the crimson wetness, realizing it was his blood. The deep reach of his breathing was labored and rough.

Two overalled men were bending to help the fallen Kreuger. When Webb saw them, his glance went round to the circle of men, seeing the hostility and resentment in their faces when they met his look. He became conscious of Lilli holding tightly to his arm, facing the same looks with a wary defiance.

"Somebody better get a doctor for him." His voice was a rasping sound as he gestured wearily toward Kreuger. Someone peeled away from the circle and went hurrying behind the roadhouse to the doctor's office. Webb turned his hard gaze on the group of men blocking the steps to the roadhouse restaurant. "Make way for my wife." He challenged them to stand in her path as Kreuger had done.

For a moment, no one moved. Then there was a slight shuffling and shifting of position to make an opening for Lilli to pass. Webb freed his arm from her hold and shifted his hand to the back of her waist, guiding her toward the spot. She walked ahead of him, her shoulders squarely braced and her chin level. Tiredness was invading his limbs, but he followed her, meeting the looks of the men on either side.

When they were on the raised boardwalk of the roadhouse porch, he felt the heavy tension lifting from the air. Lilli opened the door to the restaurant, paused a second to be sure Webb was behind her, then walked in. He noticed the angry sparkle in her eyes and wondered at it.

"Sit at that table." She issued the command to Webb, which he obeyed by pulling out a chair at the table she had indicated. Before he had lowered his body onto it, she was giving sharp orders to the waitress to bring a basin of hot water and a cloth so she could clean and doctor his cuts. Webb was amused at the way she had everyone scurrying to do her bidding, intimidating them with her dictatorial attitude, but when he tried to smile, the action pulled at the long cut on his upper lip and started it bleeding again.

When everything had been delivered to the table, she began cleaning his small wounds. The touch of her hands was gentle, but Webb sensed the repressed anger that smoldered in her eyes. He watched her while she dabbed so carefully at his split lip, her concentration focusing on her task. Since Lilli was responsible for stopping the fight, Webb supposed she was upset because it had occurred at all. He attempted to explain the necessity for his violent action.

"If I had let him get by with treating you like that, there would have been no end to it, Lilli." His words were slightly muffled by her continued ministrations to the cut on his mouth. "He brought the fight to me. If I hadn't finished it —"

"I know," she interrupted with a sharp acknowledgment of his reasons, which puzzled him more.

"I thought you were angry because I fought him," he said.

"I am." She rinsed out the cloth with brisk motions. "I wish I could have hit him. I wish I could have beat him up." Her voice was thick with anger. "It's the first time in my life I ever wished I was a man."

His look became thoughtful, but he hid it behind a light remark. "I'm glad you're not."

She paused, a hint of concern lurking in her eyes. "I probably shouldn't have stopped you, Webb. You don't know Franz Kreuger the way I do. He's the one that goaded Stefan into shooting you. If he hadn't been there that morning, it wouldn't have occurred to Stefan to react like that. I'm sure of it."

"That's in the past. We weren't going to look back, remember?" Webb saw the tension in her face before she made a weak attempt at a smile in response.

"I remember," she said, but silently reminded herself that it was not possible.

"Did you finish your shopping?" He changed the subject.

"Yes." It seemed so long ago since she had supervised the loading of her purchases. Lilli tried to summon some of her previous enthusiasm to assure Webb that everything was all right, when she knew it wasn't. "I found some blue material to make into a dress for Ruth's wedding. I hope you'll like it."

His forefinger pressed against the cut on his lip, as if testing the degree of pain it caused, but the frown that creased his forehead didn't come from that. "I hope Ruth knows what she's doing."

Her glance sharpened on him. "You sound as if you don't approve of Virgil Haskell marrying her."

His mouth slanted in a wry line that didn't aggravate the cut. "Does any man approve of his sister's choice for a husband?" Webb countered.

"I suppose not." Lilli understood that Webb regarded Ruth Stanton as being family, so the reference to Ruth as a sister didn't surprise her.

The door to Sonny's place opened and Sheriff Potter crowfooted in. He spied Webb and angled toward his table. Taking his time, he removed his hat and used the seconds to warily take in Webb's battered knuckles and bruised features.

"I got called over to the doc's," he said. "Kreuger's got a busted nose and some broke ribs. He ain't a pretty sight, but he's all right."

Webb let the information settle and made no comment. Whatever was on the sheriff's mind, it would be said without any prompting from Webb. He had no intention of defending his reason for the fight or his winning of it.

"The town's hired me to keep the peace," Potter stated. "I don't like trouble."

"That makes two of us," Webb stated. "But Kreuger seems to have a penchant for it. So don't talk to me about it."

Potter listened to Calder's voice, not caring about the words, but catching the certainty of the tone. The fight was spilt milk as far as he was concerned. The doc was cleaning up one and Calder's bride of a month was wiping up the other. But the badge he wore on his shirt meant he was obliged to make an appearance in the name of law and order. Potter had his own version of his responsibilities. In the long run, it was safer and cheaper to let men settle their own differences. As long as nothing was stolen, and women and children weren't harmed, it wasn't any of his affair. He'd learned that justice had a way of asserting itself. It was a lot easier than trying to figure out for himself who was right and who was wrong.

"I'll be speaking to him," Potter said, meaning Kreuger. He glanced at Calder's bride, fully aware she had been married to Kreuger's best friend, and made his own guesses about the cause of the fight. He nodded to her politely. "G'day to you, ma'am." With a total lack of haste, he put his hat back on and walked to the door.

Ruth's wedding took place shortly after the New Year. The simple ceremony was held at The Homestead, with the ranch families in attendance. Ruth was white and trembling as she made her vows. Her eyes were dry, all the tears shed months ago. Later, when Webb congratulated her, she even managed to smile.

A winter wedding was the perfect excuse for the cowboys to cut loose and celebrate, making Ruth's wedding day and evening anything but quiet. Despite the cold and snow, she and her new husband were shivareed by the rowdy and celebrating ranch hands that came to drag them out of the house they would be sharing with her father and parade them through the wintry night. Lilli and several other of the wives had prepared refreshments for the occasion, so it was well after midnight before the party broke up.

Ruth was certain it had been the longest day of her life. The gold band on her finger still felt strange and cold. She glanced at Virg as he shut the door on the last of his friends, and knew she was cheating him. Her gaze dropped when he looked at her, and she began a busy attempt to straighten up the room.

"The place is a mess," she murmured when he came up and took hold of her hands to stop her.

"You'll have plenty of time to clean it tomorrow," he insisted. "I think we should follow your father's example and call it a night."

She glanced at the door to her father's bedroom where he'd gone more than twenty minutes before. When Virg began to lead her to the door of the second bedroom — their bedroom — she didn't resist. It was a small room, barely large enough for the big feather bed and the mirrored dresser.

When Virg's hold on her hand loosened, Ruth pulled it free and walked to the mirror to take down her hair and fix it in a braid the same way she'd done it a thousand nights before. Only this time she wouldn't be going to bed alone with her dreams about Webb. She would be sharing the bed with her husband. She watched his reflection in the mirror as he loosened the knot of his tie. There wasn't any room for regrets, not anymore.

While she mechanically brushed her pale blond hair, Ruth studied the leanly muscled man removing his suit jacket. He stretched his neck to unfasten the boiled collar of his white shirt and glanced her way. His gaze met the reflection of hers in the mirror, and he paused to study her with a possessive intensity.

"It's a rare feeling to look at you and know you are Mrs. Virgil Haskell." Then he smiled, a little at himself and at the idea. She caught the glint of satisfaction in his eyes. "I'm a married man now, with a wife to think about . . . and someday, a family. It makes a man look at things differently."

"What do you mean?" Since he seemed to expect a response from her, Ruth made one. She had learned it was easier to ask questions than to make statements. It encouraged Virg to talk so she didn't have to do much of it herself.

"Your pa told me he had some money put aside for you. Maybe we should use it to get a small place of our own," he suggested. "It isn't going to be easy to look after you proper on a cowboy's wages."

The idea of leaving the ranch was a possibility Ruth had never considered. And she didn't want to now, either. This was her home; all her friends were here – and Webb. "My father's health isn't that good," she murmured. "I should be nearby so I can look after him. With what I earn teaching –"

"But I don't want you to teach anymore," he interrupted and sat down on the bed to take off his boots. "You're my wife. Your place is in our home, taking care of things and raising our family. I wouldn't be much of a man if I couldn't support a wife." He pulled off one boot and tossed it in the corner, then raised his leg to take off the other. "Any chance of me being more than a cowboy on this ranch is about zero. Calder doesn't make outsiders into foremen. The only ones who get positions like that are men whose fathers worked for his pa."

"I don't think you're being fair to Webb." Ruth couldn't remain silent in the face of that criticism. "If you talked to him about a better position, I'm sure he would consider you."

"No." The other boot joined the one in the corner. Virg Haskell stood up and walked the few steps to the mirror in his stockinged feet, putting his hands on her shoulders. "Maybe if you talked to him, he might listen. But he doesn't think all that much of me."

"That isn't true." Ruth turned around to face him, defending Webb, as she always would. "I've heard him say to others how hard you work and how dependable you are."

"Next week sometime, why don't you mention to him about me becoming one of his foremen . . . kinda feel him out on the idea," Virg said and let his hand trail down the length of her pale braid. "If it looks like a possibility, I'll go talk to him myself. If I can earn a decent wage, there wouldn't be any reason to leave here."

"I'll . . . I'll talk to him," Ruth agreed reluctantly, because she didn't want to leave.

He grinned and kissed her lightly. "Spoken like a proper wife," he said and moved away to unbutton his shirt.

But she knew she wasn't. It made her look at him and say, "I'll be a good wife to you, Virg," she promised, determined to make up for the fact that she didn't love him the way she should.

His shirt was completely unbuttoned and pulled loose from his pants, but he didn't slip it off. He stared at her for a long second before speaking. "You can start by unbuttoning that dress." His voice was husky and the look in his eyes was avid as he watched her fingers comply with his request. "From this night on, you're going to belong to me — and no one else."

Not even Webb Calder. Virg Haskell had known about him all along. Ruth was his wife by default, but Virg was convinced that he'd won just the same. He had wanted her, and she was his. Nothing would ever change that. It was his name she carried, and it would be his children she birthed. If she didn't love him now the way he wanted her to, she would.

When she stepped out of the dress and stood before him in her lace petticoats, Virg Haskell reached out to take what was his by right. This night her body would know his — and every night to come.

The range had been in poor condition going into the winter months, and the winter turned out to be one of the most brutal in thirty years. The chinooks either were late in arriving or didn't come at all. The strong, warm wind was blowing across the plains to usher March toward its conclusion and offering a respite from the killing cold, melting snow and ice. The Triple C was taking advantage of the brief spate of mild weather to check the ranch stock and tally up the losses that would undoubtedly run high.

Separating himself from the band of riders on shaggy-coated horses, Webb rode over to the Stanton house and dismounted. His knock on the door was followed by a muffled permission to enter. He stepped into the house and shut the door behind him. Ruth came out of the kitchen and faltered slightly when she saw him.

"Webb. I didn't know it was you." She pushed at her hair, trying to smooth the stray wisps into place, nervously gesturing at a chair. "Sit down, I'll pour you some coffee."

"No, thanks," he refused, not bothering to take off his hat because he didn't intend to stay more than a couple of minutes. "We're on our way out to check the herds. I stopped by to ask if you would mind looking in on Lilli while I'm gone today. She hasn't been feeling well this week."

"Oh?" Ruth put a hand to her stomach, aware of the life it contained. The recent bouts of morning sickness had left her somewhat weakened and shaky for most of the day. "What's wrong? Do you know?"

Webb shook his head. "She feels all right when she wakes up, but by the afternoon, she can't seem to keep any food down. I've sent a couple of the boys into town to have Simon stop by when he makes his rounds. She insists she'll be all right, but — I won't be back until late today, and I'd feel better if you checked on her later."

"Of course." She wondered why Webb didn't say anything about the expected addition to her family. Surely Virg had told him. He had spread the word quickly enough through the other families at the Triple C headquarters. She remembered how proud Virg had been when she told him, happier than when Webb had given him a foreman's position.

"Thanks, Ruth." A smile briefly creased his face, showing relief. He reached for the door-knob and paused in the act of turning it. "I heard about your news. Congratulations. You'll make a fine mother."

But not to your child, she thought, then buried it deep. "We are very happy about it." Which was true, because a baby would give her something to love, and she had such a store-house of love.

"I'm sure you are." Webb studied her for another close second, not entirely convinced she was happy with her husband. He couldn't lay his finger on what it was about Virg Haskell that he didn't like. Making him foreman was one of the rare times Webb had showed favoritism, solely because of Ruth. He couldn't fault Haskell on the job he'd done so far. Maybe he'd never regarded Haskell as being good enough for Ruth.

He touched his hat to Ruth and walked out of her house. He would always consider it her house, never Haskell's. She was the one whose roots went into the land as deeply as his own. Webb knew he could count on her to look after Lilli while he was gone. The knowledge helped to ease his concern about his wife.

Lilli couldn't recall any time when she'd been so sick. She watched the doctor closely while he made his examination, trying to get some advance warning in case there was something seriously wrong. But his face showed her nothing — so calm and composed, just as it had been when he was treating Stefan.

"I don't understand it, Doctor —" she began, voicing her confusion and apprehension.

"Simon." He corrected her with a faint smile.

"I feel fine when I get up in the morning. Then, shortly after lunch, I get sick to my stomach. I'm so dizzy and weak I can hardly stand." She repeated the symptoms that plagued her. "Is there something you can give me? Some medicine I can take?" She tried to laugh away her fears. "I know Webb is tired of fixing his own supper every night."

"I have a feeling he'd better get used to the

idea." There was almost a twinkle in his eyes when he straightened, his examination evidently concluded.

"What do you mean?" She looked at him uncertainly, afraid to move her head too much in case the dizziness hit her again.

"I strongly suspect that you are going to have a baby," he informed her with a smile that slowly widened across his face.

"But —" She hardly dared to believe it. All those barren years married to Stefan, she had wondered if she would ever have children despite the doctor's assurances of her own fertility. "Are you sure?"

"It's early," he admitted. "But I'm about as sure as I can be. All the signs point to that. The sickness associated with pregnancy doesn't always come in the morning. Some women don't get sick at all."

Tears filled her eyes. She bit down on her lip, trying to contain the happiness that bubbled in her throat. She reached for the doctor's hand and squeezed it tightly, unable to express all the emotions that were tumbling through her.

"Is Webb back yet?" Laughter ran through her eager question. "I can hardly wait to tell him."

"I'll check with Ruth and see." He winked. "I

think she's still downstairs." He stood up, smiling at her, some of his tiredness fading. "If you two women would take some pity on an overworked doctor, you'd have your babies on the same day so I wouldn't have to make two trips all the way out here to deliver them."

"We'll see what we can do about it," Lilli promised with a laugh and hugged the delicious news to her as Simon Bardolph left the room.

As he reached the top of the stairs, he saw Ruth on her way up. "No need to rush," he cautioned her against the way she was hurrying. She stopped abruptly.

"You're needed downstairs, Simon, right away," she murmured anxiously. "Shorty got in a fight in town. He's in bad shape. Slim brought him here."

There was a time when he first came to this empty country to begin his practice that he would have raced down the steps to treat an injured patient, but he'd since learned to ration his energy. It was rarely a life-or-death situation, so he neither took his time nor rushed.

The cowboy had an assortment of injuries including a dislocated shoulder, some busted ribs, and broken fingers, plus a deep cut that required some stitching. Those were the injuries Simon could treat; the multitude of bruises would have to heal on their own. Niles had been worked over thoroughly, and looked worse than the injuries indicated. Simon was taping up his ribs and shoulder when Webb walked in.

At first, Webb didn't even recognize Shorty Niles. Both eyes were blackened and swollen to mere slits, the purpling bruises were spreading across the rest of his facial features. His chest was swathed in bandages. Red blood was sweeping to the surface of the bandage on his forearm. His puffy lips were split in several places and a couple of front teeth were missing. The only clue to the man's identity was the shortness of his stature.

"What happened?" Webb asked the doctor, then glanced at Slim Trumbo, who also bore some marks of battle.

"He isn't as bad as he looks." Simon Bardolph secured the bandage and handed Shorty his shirt. "Although I guarantee you he hurts like hell."

"How did it happen?" Webb repeated his question, addressing it strictly to his two men as Slim helped Shorty ease his shirt on. Both men avoided looking at him.

"They got into a fight in town," Simon volunteered as he repacked his medical bag and closed it up.

"Who with?" The doctor shrugged at Webb's question and Slim shifted uncomfortably under his steady regard, darting glances at Shorty. "They nearly beat your face into a pulp, Shorty."

Shorty Niles said something that sounded like "personal," but with his missing teeth and battered mouth, it was difficult to understand his words. Slim handed the cowboy his hat.

"You were with him, Slim," Webb stated. "You tell me what happened." Again he had the feeling something was being kept from him as the cowboy glanced at his injured buddy.

"You know how Shorty is," he hedged. "Somebody said something to him that he didn't like and he laid into 'em. 'Fore I knew what happened, they were swarmin' all over him."

"Who?"

Slim shrugged nervously. "Just some nesters," he said without naming names.

"Kreuger and his friends?" Webb guessed.

Slim looked down at his boots and glanced at Shorty. There was a faint negative shake of the cowboy's head, warning Slim to keep silent.

"We didn't catch their names," Slim mumbled, and tried to joke his way out of the question. "They didn't exactly take time to introduce themselves."

"Don't lie to me," Webb stated and gave them both a hard, cold look. Suspicions were already forming in his mind. "You might as well admit it was Krueger, and go ahead and tell me what he said."

"He said something Shorty didn't like, that's all," Slim insisted. "I'd better be gettin' Shorty over to the bunkhouse."

"What was it Kreuger said?" Webb demanded. Their secretiveness convinced him it was something he would find personally offensive. They would have openly admitted if it had been against the ranch or cowboys, but they were trying to keep the subject from him. "Was the remark aimed at my wife?"

Slim licked his lips and didn't say anything, but Shorty spoke, as clearly as he could. "Da bastard was tellin' lies."

"Slim. What did Kreuger say?" Webb challenged.

"Just a bunch of crap about you messin' around with her when she was still married and that you got shot by her husband. He was just callin' both of you names. Shorty tried to shut him up and —" He stopped, looking uncomfortable. "Nobody listens to Kreuger. He's just a bag of wind."

"Yeah." It was a hard, dry word that confirmed what Webb had been suspecting. Anger burned slowly in him, gathering heat and gradually expanding to spread through his system.

Simon nodded to the cowboy to escort the injured man out of the room. This time Webb didn't try to stop him, possessing enough details to fill in the rest of the story.

"You wouldn't happen to have any good whiskey in the house, would you, Webb?" the doctor inquired. "I could use a glass — purely medicinal, of course."

"There's some in the den." It was an offhand reply, given without actual thought to the subject. Webb was thinking about Franz Kreuger. His hands were tied. The drylander wouldn't listen to reason, and the fight he'd had with him last fall obviously had made no difference, so it was futile to think he could silence him. Kreuger was going to continue to spread his malicious talk, and there was nothing Webb could do about it except keep it from Lilli if he could. "How's Lilli?" As he asked the question, he was struggling to control his anger and frustration, removing his hat to rake a hand through his hair.

"She's going to be fine."

"What was wrong with her?" An inquiring eyebrow was lifted at the doctor.

"I'll let her tell you." Simon smiled faintly.

"I'll help myself to some of your whiskey while you go upstairs and see her. I know she's been anxious for you to come home."

Simon Bardolph lingered a moment in the living room to watch Webb Calder climb the stairs. There was glimmer of envy in his eyes as he turned to walk to the den.

25

It was dawn. The entire eastern horizon seemed ablaze with the fiery orange light of the rising sun as it began its scorching track across the sky. According to the calendar, spring had come and gone, but the Montana land hadn't known its green colors. The countryside was still wearing its brown mantle of hibernation, slumbering under its dead covering of dry grass in the middle of summer.

With a coffee cup in hand, Webb stood at the dining-room window and watched the sun come up through the dusty pane. The ever-constant dust was a chafing reminder of the drought that gripped the land. It weighted the air, refracting the sun's rays and creating spectacular sunrises and sundowns. It seeped through cracks and left a film of powdery grit on the tops of furniture. Dusting was a futile chore, because an hour later, the grit would be back.

There had been a few times when clouds had darkened the sky and teased the dry air with a hint of moisture. Thunder had rolled in taunting chuckles and sheets of lightning had splintered from the thunderheads. Then the gray clouds had briefly spit at the panting land and raced elsewhere to play their cruel tricks. Streams were dry and the rivers were shrinking.

All through spring and most of the summer, they had been constantly moving cattle. Webb couldn't run the risk of grazing any section of the Triple C range down to bare earth, so they kept shifting the herds from one section to another. In between those times, the men were constantly checking on the range conditions in other areas, determining where the water supply was stable and where it was within reach of available graze.

Everything was paper-dry. The entire ranch, six hundred square miles of it, could go up like a tinderbox. All it would take was one spark. Smoking and campfires of any kind were forbidden. Patrols and fire watches had become part of the ranch routine. Where no natural firebreaks existed in a section, they were created.

Dust storms were becoming common. They came in a dark wall of wind that shut out the sun and prematurely darkened the sky. Dirt rolled into billowing clouds that hugged the ground, whipping along anything that wasn't nailed down.

Webb tipped the coffee cup to his mouth and drained it. A wry slant tilted his mouth as his thoughts turned back to that evening so long ago when Bull Giles had warned him he'd always have to fight to keep the ranch. He had never expected to be involved in a full-scale war with Mother Nature.

He heard the clatter of horses approaching The Homestead, their iron-clad hooves thudding over stone-hard dirt. Turning from the window, he started to walk to the table to leave his cup and begin another day's work. The sight of his sleepy wife entering the dining room stopped him.

Her auburn hair was loose and disheveled, lying about her shoulders in tousled disarray. There was a Madonna-like radiance about her sleep-softened features that reached out to him and gripped his throat with an aching tightness. Damn, but it was true. The pregnancy had made her more beautiful, more desirable. She was tying the sash of her robe, knotting it above the protruding bulge of her stomach.

"Good morning." Leaving the cup on the table, he walked to her and let his arms circle her, gathering her in close. He kissed at her lips, feeling their pliant giving. His hands moved randomly over her shoulders and spine, enjoying the feel of her essentially slim body.

"The boys are outside." Lilli could hear the familiar shuffle of hooves and chomping bits as she fingered the collar of his shirt, tracing its opening. "I thought I'd be able to have a cup of coffee with you before you left."

"You make it hard for a man to leave his house." He resisted the stirrings in his loins and withdrew his arm to take hold of her hands, kissing her white knuckles before letting them go. "You'll take care of yourself?"

"Yes." She smiled at him, amused by his persistent concern. "Ruth is coming over this afternoon so we can finish the quilts for the babies." With Webb gone so much this summer and spring, Lilli had developed a close friendship with the blond-haired Ruth. It had started simply as a sharing of common concerns, since both of them were pregnant for the first time and their husbands were absent a great part of the day. It grew from there.

"I don't like leaving you alone so much." Especially now that she was approaching the end of her term.

"You have enough on your mind. Don't be worrying about me and little Chase Benteen

Calder." She laid a hand on the top of her stomach, absently caressing it. The day she'd found out she was pregnant, Lilli had told Webb she wanted to name their baby after his father if it was a boy.

"That's going to be a funny name for a girl," he teased and tapped the end of her nose with his finger.

She laughed, and the smiled lingered on her face well after the front door had closed behind Webb.

The kerchief was tied up around his nose and mouth to filter out the dust churned up by the cattle. As they reached the chosen section of range, Webb pulled his horse back with the other riders to let the cows scatter and drift. His dark eyes were squinted against the stinging dust, watching the dull red hides of the Hereford cattle encapsulated in a tan haze. The dry, brittle grass under his horse's hooves crackled and rustled like straw.

A pull on the reins stopped the bay horse. It bobbed its head and snorted loudly to rid its nostrils of the clogging dust. A dry, keening wind whispered through the dead stalks of grass that held the soil in place. Webb gripped the point of his kerchief and tugged it down around his neck. He had stopped his mount on a high bench of land that gave him an overview of the surrounding countryside. To the east, he could see the fenceline snaking over the plains to mark the ranch boundary. The other side belonged to drylanders. His range was in pitiful condition, but it was nothing compared to the wheat farmers' land.

The crops in the fields were stunted from lack of moisture, more thistle growing than wheat. But it was the acres that were plowed and left fallow that sickened Webb. The wind was blowing the dry earth away, drifting it into dirt dunes, piling it into mounds, then tearing them down again. All along the fenceline, dirt was deposited in drifts like black snow; in places, it was piled high enough to reach the bottom strand of wire. It was a bleakly ominous sight. If a torrential rain came now, the topsoil would be washed away, and a man didn't have to dig down very far in this country before he ran out of dirt.

Under his breath, Webb muttered a savage assertion. "I'm glad my father's not alive to see this."

His horse shifted restlessly beneath him as another horse swung its rump into it. "Did you say somethin', Webb?" Nate asked, pulling down his kerchief to speak.

The shake of his head was curtly negative.

The saddle leather creaked as Webb half-turned to look at the other riders. Dirt lay in a dark film across their foreheads and cheekbones, but their kerchiefs had left a mark across the lower half of their faces where the dust hadn't been able to settle in thick layers.

Virg Haskell had taken off his hat to mop the sweat from his forehead. He used the hat to point at the sky. "Looks like we got a lonely raincloud headed our way." He continued to watch the dark patch looming closer. "Funny-looking, isn't it?"

It was changing colors. What had started as a dark gray blot now had an obscene green cast to it. A growing dread began to take hold of Webb as he stared at it. When the angle of the sun's light caught it and gave it a silver sheen, there wasn't any more doubt.

"It's a cloud of 'hoppers." Webb tightened his grip on the reins, announcing what some of the other, experienced hands were guessing.

As the living blanket of insects came overhead, the whirring and clacking sound grew louder. Webb's horse moved restively, nervously swiveling its ears. The grasshoppers began dropping onto the ground, falling out of the sky like hailstones. The range-wild cattle were still in a loose bunch when they were suddenly pelted by the falling insects. Their panic was immediate; the lead cow stampeded to the east and the rest followed, lumbering into a run that shook the ground.

Before the riders could spur their horses after the stampeding herd, the onslaught of grasshoppers hit them. There was a confusion of plunging and rearing horses, whinnying their fright at this noisy rainstorm of crawling things. They beat down on his hat as Webb hunched his shoulders and tried to line his horse out to ride away from the deluge. The precious grass was already being blanketed by the insects, chomping noisily and voraciously on every twig and blade in sight.

The boundary fence couldn't hold back the stampeding cattle. Posts snapped and wire popped under the pressure of the panicked beasts. An eternity passed before the riders got control of their mounts. By then, the surrounding land was covered with grasshoppers three inches deep. They struck out after the cattle, their horses wading nervously through the insects and snorting at the slippery footing.

No one spoke. No one said a word. The grasshoppers were everywhere, covering every inch of ground, every blade of grass, and every thistle stalk. The weight of them bent tall plants to the ground. The noise of the chewing jaws and whirring wings was an eerie sound as they set about denuding the earth of all its vegetation. The riders had to constantly brush the clinging insects from their clothes. Their appetites were such that they'd eat anything, and did.

The devastation was widespread and complete. In the seven days that it took to round up their scattered herd, Webb saw firsthand how much the grasshoppers destroyed. Because of the bigness of the Triple C, the damage they suffered was minimal, confined to the east rim section, which was laid bare. But the destructive force of the grasshoppers hit the drylanders hardest — the ones who were already suffering painfully from the drought.

Fields were stripped of their meager stands of wheat. Where there were trees, not a single leaf or young twig was left. Limbs were scattered on the naked ground, broken by the weight of the insects. Gardens that had been nursed along by the women with the rationing of precious water vanished. When all the vegetation had been consumed, the grasshoppers began devouring roof shingles, leather harnesses, clothing, and board fences, indiscriminately satisfying their hunger.

Their numbers were so staggering, they invaded the shacks and ate the food in the cupboards and the curtains at the windows.

Animals stood helplessly as the insects crawled over them, while the children screamed in terror, certain they would be eaten next when one landed on them. The determined dry-landers battled them, trying to save what little they had left. They tied string around their pantlegs so the grasshoppers couldn't crawl up their legs. They shoveled the grasshoppers into piles, poured kerosene on them, and set them on fire. They chopped up lemons and mixed arsenic with the rinds, then scattered them for the hoppers to feed on; but they ate the poisonous mixture and continued on their destructive way.

When Webb and the other cowboys drove the regathered herd of cattle across the path of devastation to their home range, the aftereffect of the insect hordes was as staggering as their first assault. The air reeked with the odor of the grasshoppers. The water in the few flowing streams was brown and tainted with their waste, totally undrinkable. Any drylander whose well hadn't already gone dry would now find the precious water supply impotable.

That night, Webb stripped and soaped himself from head to foot to rid himself of the smell and feel of the 'hoppers. He'd hardly spoken to Lilli at all. It wasn't until they were lying in bed with the lights out and he was holding her in his arms, the warmth of her body flowing into his, that he began to talk about what he'd seen.

There was no emotion in his flat voice, but a tear tunneled down his cheek. He felt that conflict of emotions, despising the drylanders for what they'd done to the land and pitying them for the devastation they had suffered. And there was gratitude mixed in that so much of his land had escaped the plague, and that Lilli was with him, safe from the horror she would have known with her late husband.

"Thank God the worst is over," Lilli murmured when he'd finished.

"I doubt if it is." He stopped staring at the ceiling and turned his head on the pillow to look at her face bathed by the moonlight coming through the window. "What the drought hadn't ruined, the 'hoppers did. There's nothing to hold the dirt anymore. Thousands of acres of dirt will be blown away. But it's more than that." He paused and let a finger trace the faint dusting of freckles across her cheekbone. "Those grasshoppers laid eggs; next spring they'll hatch and they'll have to be fought all over again. First drought, then pestilence. Where will it end?" he murmured with a frown.

She snuggled closer to him. From the

moment he had walked into the house that night, she had known he was deeply troubled and had waited for him to talk. When she tried to imagine what it had been like, she couldn't. Maybe it was better.

"Simon sent a message to us this afternoon." She hadn't mentioned it till now, but it seemed appropriate that she had waited. "The town well has been contaminated, and he asked us if we would send all the water we could spare."

"I'll have the boys fill up all the barrels we've got and take a couple wagonloads in tomorrow morning," he said. He looked at her, and for a second, he almost felt as if he were being sucked into the midnight depths of her blue eyes. A little moan came from him as he brought his face close to hers. "Sometimes, Lilli, I wish I could just crawl inside you and have you all around me. I envy the closeness our son is enjoying. All warm and safe inside you."

Her hand cupped his lean cheek. She felt the dampness of that tear and pressed her lips against his mouth, kissing him fiercely and loving him with a force equally ardent. For a man so powerful, he was amazingly gentle that night.

Water sloshed against the lids of the barrels

as the horse-drawn wagons rattled into town close to noon the next day. The harsh light wasn't kind to the dusty, weather-beaten buildings. Most of them had been thrown up too quickly, responding to the land boom that had so suddenly stretched Blue Moon's capacity. Now it looked exhausted, teetering on its shaky foundations and aging fast. One small business was already boarded up, an Out of Business sign painted across its dusty window front. The deterioration was as inevitable as the boom had been, Webb realized, because it had been built on hope instead of the land's ability to support it.

There weren't many people in town, but all of them seemed to wear a dazed and vacant look, as if they were in the throes of a terrible nightmare that wouldn't end. Dust lay over the town in a haze, reddening the eyes and coating teeth with grit. A half-dozen wagons were parked around the well in front of the blacksmith's, the well that usually supplied water to the drylanders.

The worn and ragged collection of homesteaders blankly watched the two Triple C wagons and their accompanying outriders approaching them. The drought had dried all expression from their features and the grasshoppers had taken the hope out of their eyes. It was purely survival instinct that carried them now.

The arrival of the wagons loaded with barrels of water brought people out of stores. It was as if they smelled it and came out to see the rare commodity. As Webb turned the black gelding into the hitching rail, he noticed the sheriff and Simon Bardolph make their way through the slowly growing crowd to reach him.

"You got my message." A smile of relief broke across the physician's weary features as Webb dismounted.

"This was all we could carry on this trip." They'd run out of barrels. His glance skimmed the dried-out group of homesteaders. "I'm glad you're here. I'll have the boys unload the wagons, and you and the sheriff can decide how to divide it up so everybody gets some."

"The sheriff can do that." Simon volunteered the man for the job. "How bad is it out your way?"

"We escaped the worst of the 'hoppers, but this drought is still burning us up," Webb admitted. "The rivers are running so low you can wade in and pick up all the trout you want."

"How much longer can it last?" The doctor sighed, not expecting an answer.

Webb turned and signaled to his men to

begin unloading the barrels. Sheriff Potter had stepped away and had tiredly lifted his arms to get the drylanders' attention. "There's going to be enough water for everybody, so let's keep this orderly. I want you to form a line —"

A voice from the back of the group broke in and demanded to be heard. "Where did this water come from?"

There was a slight pause before the sheriff resumed his instructions, ignoring the question. "Form a line over here."

"How do we know this is good water?" The voice insisted on an answer. Webb recognized it before Franz Kreuger forced his way to the front of the group.

"Mr. Calder brought it in from his place," the sheriff responded with marked patience.

Kreuger spat at the ground and glared his loathing for the source. "Don't take any of this water," he warned the others around him. "He has probably poisoned it."

Webb shook his head, tipping it downward in exasperation and disgust. Beside him, Simon muttered something under his breath and moved away to stand with the sheriff.

"Kreuger, there is nothing wrong with this water," he snapped.

"Did you give him the poison to put in it?" Kreuger challenged and lifted his hands that

568

had been hanging at his sides. That's when Webb saw he was carrying a rifle.

"Don't be ridiculous —" Simon began angrily.

"I want nothing that comes from Calder or his whore — or the physician who treats them!" There was a madness in Kreuger's eyes as he turned to look at his fellow homesteaders. "Since we came, Calder has wanted to get rid of us. He has tried everything — burning our homes and trampling our wheat with his cattle. The grasshoppers would never have descended on our fields if his cattle hadn't been driven onto our lands by his men. The grasshoppers followed the cattle, landed on their backs to be carried into our fields. He didn't want them destroying his land, so he chased them onto ours."

"That is a damned lie!" Simon bellowed, realizing Kreuger was playing on the superstitious ignorance of the drylanders. They wanted a scapegoat and Kreuger was giving them one.

"Is it?" Kreuger jeered, then addressed the others. "Is it not true that everywhere his cattle were, there were also grasshoppers?" Heads nodded and looks were exchanged even by some of the more skeptical ones. "The insects ate our crops and our food, and ruined our wells. Now Calder brings us water — water that will probably make us sick. He thinks we are so thirsty — so desperate — that we will take water even from the man who has always been our enemy."

Simon swung away, lifting his hands in a wild gesture of disgust. "The man's crazy," he muttered to Webb. "There's no reasoning with him."

Doyle Pettit had seen the gathering of people and wagons around the community well as he left the bank for lunch. He angled over to see what all the commotion was about, and caught the tail end of Kreuger's speech, enough to piece together with the evidence of the Triple C wagons and men.

A smile made a slow curve across his mouth, his eyes gleaming with a way to use this situation to his advantage. Without drawing attention to himself, he circled the crowd and approached Webb from the livery side, using Webb's horse to shield him from the view of the main party of drylanders.

"Webb." He kept his voice low. "Even if any of them wanted it, Kreuger isn't going to let them take any of your water. The man's got a blind spot when it comes to you. You and the boys might as well take your wagons and water and head back for the ranch."

"But what are they going to do for water?"

Webb muttered, agreeing with Doyle Pettit's conclusion and knowing the problem remained.

A boyish grin flashed across Doyle's features, revealing a pride in his own clever thinking. "I said 'head' back to the ranch, but don't 'go' to the ranch. About five miles outside of town, there's a draw. Wait there for me. It'll take me a couple of hours to round up wagons and some drivers. We'll transfer your water onto my wagons and I'll bring it back into town. These drylanders think I'm one of them, so they won't ask twice where I got it." He looked at Webb. "Is it a deal?"

It was a simple and highly workable solution. Webb nodded. "We'll meet you at Simmons' Wash in two hours."

"I'd stay around to chat, but Kreuger might spot me talking to you and decide I've been contaminated." Doyle backed away as unobtrusively as he'd come, silently congratulating himself. It was his ability to size up a situation and turn it to his advantage that was going to enable him to own half the state someday. A man had to think on his feet, and not let any opportunity slip by him.

Potter was still trying to convince the drylanders the water was safe when Webb stepped into his saddle and rode his horse over to the sheriff. "Never mind, Potter," he said. "We're pulling out. If they don't want the water, we'll use it ourselves."

The sheriff's surprised expression objected to his decision, but Webb didn't wait for him to put it into words as he reined his horse toward the wagons and signaled his men to leave. Their confusion and disbelief were understandable, since they didn't know about the planned switch with Doyle Pettit's wagons. He explained it to them when they were outside of town.

It was better than two hours before Doyle met them at the appointed place with his wagons. He had changed from his spiffy eastern suit and tie into range clothes. It was a trick Doyle had learned, changing his attire to suit the people and surroundings, rather like a chameleon.

In town, he was the businessman. When he called on the drylanders at their homesteads, he'd take off his jacket, loosen his tie, and roll up his sleeves. For ranchers like Webb, he kept a set of worn jeans, a work-stained hat, and a sheepskin-lined jacket to remind them he was one of them — Tom Pettit's son.

None of them looked beyond his facade and good-natured demeanor to see the driving ambition and shrewdness in his eyes. It was common knowledge that he owned the bank, the lumberyard, the granary, and a couple of other businesses in town, plus his law practice. Hell, he owned nearly the whole damned town. But Doyle was sure that few were aware that his holdings were so extensive they rivaled the Calder spread. It wasn't the time for them to know, but it amused him to think about it, especially now in his meeting with Webb Calder.

"It's good of you to give these homesteaders your water," he told Webb. "I'd have the boys haul some from the TeePee," he said, referring to the ranch he'd inherited from his father. "But we're just about bone-dry out there."

That wasn't precisely true. The ranch had some water to spare, but there wasn't any point in giving it away as Calder was doing. In time, those drylanders would be buying water, and that's when Doyle planned to dip into his supply. In the meantime, he could take advantage of Webb's largesse and take the credit for being the homesteaders' savior. It was going to be good public relations.

"I've got a couple of good-flowing rivers." Webb hadn't needed to mention that, since Doyle was well aware of the fact. "As long as they keep running, we'll have some water to spare."

"The way Kreuger's got those folks set against you, I think it'd be best if I send my wagons to your place and let them believe it's coming from me," Doyle suggested.

"That's fine." Webb didn't care what form the ruse took as long as those who needed water, got it.

"After we get this load into town, I'll have wagons go to your place and bring more water tomorrow. These barrels aren't going to go very far." The last barrel was rolled onto a TeePee wagon, and Doyle firmly shook Webb's hand. "Give my regards to your wife. You sure never gave me a chance to give you a little competition for her."

As he climbed onto the wagon seat, Doyle knew he hadn't been seriously interested in the widow Webb had married, but it had been the right thing to say to Calder. Marriage was down the road for him, and he was going to choose carefully – maybe pick a rich eastern bride. An alliance, that's what he wanted. A marriage that would better his position.

Before returning to town, he took the precaution of circling the wagons around it and entering from another direction so Kreuger and his drylanders wouldn't suspect he was actually bringing them Calder water. When the drivers stopped the wagons in front of the dry community well, the crowd of homesteaders gathered around them and readily lined up to get their share.

When someone thanked him, Doyle smiled and modestly shrugged it off. "I'm just glad I could help." His arcing glance caught Franz Kreuger watching him. "We all have to stick together in hard times like these." He knew it was a doctrine Kreuger often preached, and he deliberately voiced it now. He saw the faint nod of approval Kreuger unconsciously made and knew he had the ringleader of these dry-landers in his pocket. "If there's anything any of you need, I'll be at the bank."

In the group, there were at least four home-steaders that he knew were in dire straits. They'd be coming to him for a loan, since he already held mortgages on their land. This time he'd have their animals and equipment. Next spring, Doyle Pettit, the landowner, would pay them a tenth of what their home-steads and possessions were worth and they'd get down on their knees and thank him for it. All of them believed he loaned them money to help them, and later bought them out, out of the goodness of his heart, wiping away their debts and giving them just enough money to get them out of the state. As he made his way through the gathering to return to the bank, he

575

saw the gratitude in their faces and nearly laughed out loud.

With a definite pride, he looked at all the businesses that carried his name. They'd brought him a handy bit of cash, the prices on the goods sold marked up two and three times what he'd paid for them. Since the drought came, most of them had been operating at a loss, but Doyle was convinced it was only a temporary setback. There was a side benefit to the town's present poor economic situation. Businesses that had gone into competition with his were now starting to close their doors. It wouldn't be long before he had the whole town sewn up.

Three riders were tying their horses to the hitch rail in front of the bank. Doyle's interest sharpened when he recognized the old and heavyset man approaching the bank entrance. It was Ed Mace from the Snake M Ranch. There was something tired and defeated about the way the aging rancher carried himself. Doyle wondered how much of that was attributable to his sixty-plus years. Doyle couldn't think of any reason Mace would be coming to his bank unless he needed money. That started him thinking. There just might be a way he could get his hands on the Snake M Ranch.

Before the rancher reached the back door,

Doyle Pettit hailed him, chatted with him on the sidewalk for a few minutes, then invited him inside as if he hadn't known it was Mace's destination all along. In the privacy of his office, Doyle kept the talk away from the bank and loans, discussing instead ranching and range conditions. Slowly he worked his way around to the hardships of the drought and the effects it was having on the area ranchers.

"There isn't a cattleman around that hasn't been hurt by this drought — men like you, for instance," Doyle said. "Ever since I went on the first roundup with my daddy, I've looked up to ranchers like you. You're solid people, and your word is good as gold. I want you to know, Ed, if you ever need a loan to help you over a hump, just tell me and you've got it."

"Well . . . it has been a rough year," he admitted, pride making it difficult to state why he'd come. "I have been considerin' arranging to get a small loan."

"You just tell me how much you want and I'll make a draft for you this very minute." He reached into his desk for the loan forms and picked up a pen to begin filling them out. Then he stopped and looked across the desk at the rancher, as if a thought had just occurred to him. "I hate turning down business, but you might be better off raising money another way."

Ed Mace looked skeptical. As far as he was concerned, he had explored every other option to no avail and now found himself backed into a corner, forced to come to the bank with his hat in his hand. Although, he had to admit, so far Doyle Pettit had made it quite painless.

"How?" he asked.

"You've got cattle, and prices have never been higher than they are right now. Why don't you sell off your breeding stock?" Doyle suggested craftily. "Next year, you'll be able to start building up a new herd at probably half the price that you can sell your cows for now."

Doyle failed to mention that next year Ed Mace wouldn't have cattle to use for collateral, which meant he'd have to mortgage his ranch. After that, buying the ranch cheaply would become a simple matter. It would stretch his own finances thin, but the risk was worth it to get possession of the Snake M Ranch.

26

The leaves had fallen from the cottonwoods and willows growing along the banks of the river. The skeletal outlines of trunks and branches stood starkly against the tan haze of an October sky. Webb had thrust his hands deep into the pockets of his jacket as he stared at the muddy riverbed. Behind him the ranch buildings of the Triple C sat on sun-baked ground and The Homestead was silhouetted against the jagged northern horizon. But it was the muddy pools of water in scattered pockets along the riverbed that commanded his attention.

"This river has never run dry before." He turned his head to Nate. "And it's like this the whole length?"

"Worse," he grunted. "At least here you got puddles. Most stretches don't even have mud in the bottom. The river in the north range still has a trickle running through it." He wanted a cigarette bad, but there were too many piles of dry leaves around and too much dead grass. "What do you figure on doin'?" Nate's question didn't get an immediate answer. "I heard Ed Mace sold all his breeding stock so his range wouldn't get overgrazed this winter."

Webb shook his head to refuse that option. "It's taken too long to build our herds and have the kind of quality breeding stock we've got now. I'm not selling." It was an absolute decision. "We'll throw all the herds onto the north range and hope for the best." He turned away from the dried-up river. "Get a message to Doyle that we can't spare any more water for the drylanders. The well at the barns went dry this morning."

Nate said nothing and blew out a wearily grim breath that seemed to ask when the drought would end. By mutual assent, they climbed the bank and started toward the ranch buildings. Abe Garvey was hobbling as fast as he could toward them, puffing at the effort. He stopped and waved to hurry them.

"Hey, Webb! They sent me to fetch you. It's your missus. It's her time!" he called.

Webb broke into a run, excitement and anxiety claiming him at the same moment. "Send someone for the doctor," he ordered hurriedly. Simon had been at the ranch only yesterday to deliver a son to Ruth.

"No need," Abe puffed. "He was here, checking to see how Ruth and her baby were doin'. The doc's up at The Homestead now."

When Webb burst into their bedroom, the pain of the last contraction was just passing. Lilli was breathing deeply and roughly, beads of perspiration collecting on her forehead and above her lips. When she saw the worried look in his rugged and earthy features, she smiled at him, her own unease slipping away.

"You hadn't better be having second thoughts about becoming a father," she warned him as he took her hand and leaned close to the bed. "Because it's too late for that."

"No. No second thoughts." A half-smile came onto his mouth, gentling it. "Are you okay?"

She nodded, and Webb bent down to kiss her.

"None of that." Simon Bardolph interrupted the affectionate exchange and approached the bed. "Unless you plan on delivering this baby, I suggest you go downstairs and have yourself a drink, Webb."

"Later." He didn't take his eyes off Lilli, her dark hair spilling over the pillow her head was resting on, its red sheen subdued.

"Now," the doctor insisted and gestured toward the door. "Out. It's going to be a while, so go pace the floor somewhere else. I don't want you upsetting our little mother."

Webb reluctantly gave in to that argument, kissed her again, and left the room to wait downstairs in the den. He tried to stay calm, but he kept hearing little noises upstairs, sounds of movement and muffled cries. They worked on his nerves like a file. The sun was making a blazing descent below the horizon before he heard the squawl of an infant. He took the steps two at a time and knocked impatiently at the closed door. Simon opened it with a wiggling bundle in his arms.

"Chase Calder, meet your father." He passed the strapping baby boy into the crook of Webb's arm.

"Lilli?"

"She's fine."

And Webb looked at his newborn son for the first time, all red and wrinkled, a wet mass of dark hair on his head, and a perfectly formed fist flailing the air near his mouth. In a kind of daze, Webb walked to the bed. He could feel the tears glistening in his eyes as he looked at Lilli. Her dark hair was clinging damply to the sides of her face. She looked exhausted, yet remarkably happy.

"The poor thing is as ugly as me." Webb smiled.

"And he'll be as handsome as you are, too," she murmured, a little weakly.

Simon came to the bed, smiling at the three of them. "I think your son would like something to eat; then both of them need to rest."

Webb laid the baby in Lilli's arms and left the room reluctantly for the second time.

After adjusting the hood, Lilli tied it under her chin and glanced at Webb watching her so anxiously. Admittedly she was weak and sore, but certainly not the invalid that he considered her to be.

"I'm ready. Shall we go?" She pulled on her gloves, feeling as bundled up as little Chase was in Webb's arms.

"I think you should stay here," he said for the tenth time. "It's too soon for you to be moving around. You should be in bed. It's only been two days since the baby was born."

"Webb, you're making it sound as if I'm embarking on some hazardous journey," she reproached him with a hint of amusement. "I'm not going any farther than Ruth's house. I assure you I'm strong enough to walk that far."

"But there's no need. I can go." The determined glint in her eye warned him that she had no intention of staying behind. Sighing his irritation, Webb put an arm around her waist and guided her to the front door.

As much as he could, he used his body to shield her and their son from the sharp wind blowing from the north. It swept the dry ground in front of them, brushing up dust clouds to sting their eyes and irritate their lungs.

Virg Haskell opened the door when they arrived at the Stanton house. Webb barely gave Lilli time to push back the hood of her cape before sitting her down in a chair. Little Chase whimpered in his arms, completely covered by the small baby quilt. Webb turned back the corner of the quilt and returned the sugar-tit to his son's mouth to quiet him.

"That's a fine-looking son you have," Virg Haskell said and glanced at the man and woman, trying to figure out why they had come.

"How's Ruth?" Lilli asked.

"She and the little bucko are doing fine." He smiled proudly.

From the bedroom, Ruth called out, "Who is it, Virgil?"

"It's" — he half-turned his head to answer — "Miss Lilli and Webb . . . and their son."

There were sounds of movement from the

bedroom. "I'll be right out."

"Can I get you something?" Virgil offered uncertainly. Even though his wife had become very friendly with Lilli Calder, he doubted that this was a social call.

Dissatisfied with the sugar-tit, the baby in Webb's arms began fussing and waving angry fists in the air. "You'd better give him to me." Lilli reached for her son.

Webb gave him into her care before responding to Haskell's inquiry. "No, nothing, thank you. Lilli and I are here to talk to you and your wife on another matter."

The bedroom door opened and Ruth emerged. It was obvious she had made a hurried attempt to make herself look presentable. A ribbon secured her blond hair in a long ponytail at the nape of her neck, and she was wearing a loose-fitting dress. She was stiff and a little unsteady on her feet, holding on to the doorway before coming the rest of the way into the room.

"Lilli, you shouldn't be up. You need to rest and get your strength back," she murmured anxiously.

"That's what I tried to tell her," Webb responded dryly. "But she insisted on coming."

"I've heard that Indian women have their babies and get right up and do their work,"

Lilli said to dispute both of them. "I'm fine, really. Please, sit down, Ruth," she urged. "Webb and I came because we have something to ask of you."

"What is it?" Ruth gingerly sat on a chair close to Lilli's and gazed at the baby boy wrapped in the blanket quilt in Lilli's arms. "He's a beautiful baby." There was a trace of envy in her voice.

"He's a very hungry baby." Mixed in with the love in her expression, there was regret and a hint of guilt. She hesitantly looked at Ruth. "I don't have enough milk for him. Simon fixed some special milk for him, but it didn't agree with him. He said the best solution would be to find another woman willing to wet-nurse. Webb and I thought" — she paused to glance at her husband, standing beside her chair — "we'd ask you."

Ruth didn't need time to consider the request, accepting it immediately. "Of course I'll do it."

"Thank you." Lilli bent her head to hide her trembling chin and blinked back the tears. Chase began crying again. She tenderly kissed his forehead, then handed him to Ruth. "It would probably be best if he stayed here at nights." It was the hardest thing Lilli had ever had to say. "I'll have Webb bring his cradle and

. . . everything." Her voice broke.

"Don't worry, Lilli." Ruth cuddled Webb's son close to her breast and laid a reassuring hand on her friend's arm. "I'll take very good care of him, just as if he were my son." It was the easiest promise in the world for her to make.

Some kind of maternal alarm clock woke Ruth in the middle of the night for the two o'clock feeding. She picked up her noisy and impatient son and carried him into the living room to sit in the rocking chair. His blond hair was downy soft and curly, his blue eyes showing signs of remaining that color. His given name was Timothy Ely Haskell, but her husband had started referring to him as "my bucko" from the first day. It had seemed to fit him, so that Ruth now thought of him as Buck. She adored him in the special way a mother loves her child, smiling as he tugged fiercely on her nipple and pummeled her breast with his little fists.

But, later, when little Chase Benteen Calder suckled at her milk-swollen breast, there were tears in her eyes. This was Webb's son, different in size and coloring and temperament from her own. She had dreamed of this day — of holding his baby to her breast. It had come true, not exactly the way she had wanted it, but she was nursing *his* son.

The stethoscope was captured by a small hand that immediately decided it was meant to be eaten. Simon Bardolph chuckled and pried the Calder baby's fingers loose from the instrument. Innocent brown eyes looked at him boldly.

"By the looks of you, Chase, you've already had enough to eat," he declared.

"He has grown, hasn't he?" Lilli declared proudly as her nearly five-month-old son began jabbering. He was sitting up straight, firmly balanced, chubby but not fat. "He's already trying to crawl, but he usually ends up scooting backward."

"He'll figure it out soon enough; then you'll probably wish he hadn't," Simon murmured dryly and closed the bag. "I haven't seen two healthier babies than this one and little Buck in a long time."

"You will have some coffee and cake, won't you?" she said and picked up the growing youngster, balancing him on her hip. "Webb should be back shortly. He had to go to the train station to pick up the senator. I know he'll want to see you."

"Can't." Simon shrugged into his coat. "I

have to get over to Kreuger's place. Three of his children are sick. Looks like pneumonia." He shook his head, unwillingly comparing the disparities between this household and the pitiful circumstances of the dryland family.

"I'm sorry to hear that." Lilli held Chase just a little tighter. As much as she disliked Franz Kreuger, she still felt sorry for his wife, Helga. "How is . . . his wife?"

His glance skimmed her briefly, trying to decide if she really wanted to know. "I don't think you'd recognize her." He sighed. "I don't think she eats. I wouldn't be surprised if all the food goes to the children and her husband, and she eats whatever is left."

Lilli felt guilty at having so much, guilty because she hadn't given a thought to the families she had lived among with Stefan. There had been a vague awareness that the drought and the grasshoppers had hurt a lot of families, but she hadn't let her mind dwell on it. But the doctor's remark reminded her of winters when she had been hungry, with little in the house to eat.

"Simon, before you go, stop at the commissary and take a supply of food with you," she urged. "If Kreuger asks you where you got it, tell him the church is distributing it. Take food for other needy families in the area, too."

He nodded briefly, a faint smile of under-standing showing on his mouth. She knew most of those people and felt she owed them something, a brother's keeper sort of thing. She began playing with the baby, and Simon let the subject end with her request.

Senator Bulfert was a weekend guest at the ranch, stopping on his way to Helena. On this occasion, he was alone, unaccompanied by his aides. It seemed to change the tenor of the visit. The usually loquacious and loud politi-cian appeared subdued and less talkative.

At the conclusion of dinner, Webb noticed the senator reaching into his vest pocket, bulging with cigars. Aware that Lilli didn't like the smell of cigar smoke, he suggested they adjourn to the den for coffee. Lilli excused herself from joining them to check on the baby.

Webb poured a glass of whiskey for each of them and passed the florid-faced man one. There was a flash of the man's professionally jovial smile as he lifted his glass in a silent toast.

"Better enjoy this while you can," he declared. "Those Temperance ladies are going to get their wish." The senator breathed out a disgusted sound and stared at the whiskey he swirled in the glass. "All those saloons Carry

Nation busted up in Butte. Thought that movement for Prohibition would end when she died. Hell! It turned her into a martyr."

"The Congress isn't really going to outlaw liquor." The proposition was too unrealistic.

"It's all part of this moral fervor that's sweeping the country because of the war," he grunted, then eyed Webb with a twinkling look. "I hope you got some friends in Canada to keep your cabinet stocked for personal use."

"I know a couple people." Webb smiled. "We don't sell as much cattle to the reservations up there as we used to, but we've still got connections."

"Good." He sipped at the whiskey, then gave Webb a cigar and cut off the tip of one for himself. "Giles is dead." The statement came with no advance warning.

The match flame was halfway to his cigar. Webb stopped, taking the cigar from his mouth to stare at the politician. "Bull?" Disbelief ringed his voice. "When?"

"Three months ago, before Christmas. Just found out about it myself." He puffed on the cigar. "Never was the same after he came back. Started drinking heavy and stopped hanging around with the old crowd. That's why it took so long to hear about it, I guess. He'd a made a good politician — a big, lumbering ox, but smart as a whip," he concluded and swallowed another gulp of whiskey, as if in a silent toast to the man.

Webb did the same and watched the flames crackling in the fireplace. Since his mother's death, there had been no word from Bull. Now there wouldn't be any.

"What do you know about this attorney, Doyle Pettit?" With a narrowed look, Bulfert eyed Webb through the smoke of his cigar.

Webb's head came up, some instinct telling him this was the purpose behind the senator's visit. "I've known Doyle all my life. He took over the TeePee Ranch when his father, Tom Pettit, died about ten years back, and he owns a couple businesses in town. Why?" He was scant with his information until he learned the reason for the question.

"I had a look at the property rolls a couple of weeks ago. He's got title to, or claim to, nearly three-quarters of a million acres."

The size of Pettit's holdings surprised Webb, but he didn't show it. He finished lighting his cigar with a new match, shook out the flame, and tossed the dead match into the fireplace. Doyle had amassed a lot of land very quietly — through the bank he owned, obviously, buying up the claims of home-steaders who had given up. He remembered

Doyle's land scheme of buy and sell, buy and sell.

He looked at the map on the wall. Doyle Pettit. That fun-loving always smiling boyhood friend who laughed and rarely fought. He'd always been something of a show-off, buying the first automobile in the area and wearing spiffy clothes, free with his money, buying drinks for his friends and quick to loan a ten-spot to a hard-up man. Doyle had always managed to become the center of attention. Quietly, so quietly, he had obtained control of nearly three-quarters of a million acres — almost the size of the Triple C.

The man had always been something of a peacemaker, never liking arguments or hard feelings. He rode the fence, never taking sides. The ranchers regarded him as Tom Pettit's son, one of them, and the drylanders looked on him as their friend.

The longer Webb looked at the map, the more uneasy he felt. It made no sense to think Doyle's massive land acquisitions were a threat. They'd known each other too many years. They hadn't always been close, but Doyle just wasn't the kind to move against another man. That wasn't his way. Yet Webb was bothered by the discovery of how big Doyle had grown in such a short period of time.

But his comment to the politician revealed he'd known of it. "When this boom started, Pettit began speculating in land," he admitted.

"If this drought keeps up" — a wryness touched the expression on the senator's face — "he's going to find out he owns land in a dozen other states. The wind's blowing away what he's got here."

Webb's mouth twitched in silent and bitter agreement. Inwardly he was thinking, Thank God for the grass that covered Calder land and held the soil together.

The heavy buffalo robe was bunched around his chin, warming the air Simon breathed, his head bobbing in sleep. His black medical bag sat on the floorboards of the buggy near his feet, with the buffalo robe draped over it as well. Even though automobiles were a faster form of transportation, Simon Bardolph preferred his horse and buggy. It might be slower, but there were fewer breakdowns; it could travel cross-country over terrain an auto couldn't traverse; and if Simon fell asleep, as he usually did, he could be sure of the horse staying on the road and not crashing into some ditch.

The ewe-necked gelding stopped in front of the shanty where a small light glowed in the window. It turned its head and whickered quietly at the man sleeping in the buggy. The sound stirred no response. With almost a disgusted snort, the horse laid back its ears and launched a kick at the buggy, jolting its owner awake.

Simon opened his eyes with a frowning reluctance and looked around for a blank minute before recognizing Kreuger's place. He pushed aside the buffalo robe and shivered at the early-evening coldness. A horse blanket was stowed in the rear of the buggy. He shook it out and draped it over the gelding, tossed some grain into a nose bag, and slipped the bit out of its mouth before putting the grain bag on. After the horse was taken care of, he lifted his black satchel out of the buggy and walked to the shanty.

Franz Kreuger opened the door when Simon knocked. The smell of sickness was in the small and drafty shack. Simon supposed he would never get used to the odor. The cloth curtain that usually partitioned off the sleeping quarters had been removed to let the heat from the cookstove reach to the farthest corner where the bunks were stacked.

Simon had called on the family too many times to waste his energy exchanging pleasantries with Franz Kreuger, because the

595

gesture wouldn't be returned. As he shrugged out of his coat, he looked over at the two older children lying in their parents' bed, and his third patient in a lower bunk. A gaunt and hollow-eyed Helga Kreuger was sitting on the edge of the bunk, attempting to spoon broth into the slack mouth of her son.

As he approached the bunk with his bag in hand, the woman was forced to suspend the feeding by a coughing spasm that had a distinct, consumptive sound to it. It sharpened his gaze, sweeping the woman in a cursory examination. She was wasted and had thin, dark circles under her eyes. The hardship in her life had aged her until she looked old enough to be the grandmother of these children. Simon didn't like the sound of that hacking cough. After he had checked the youngsters' conditions, he intended to examine their mother.

He stopped beside her, conscious that Franz Kreuger was hovering close by. "How's Gustav?" He smiled briefly at the wan and anxious face of Helga Kreuger before he turned his attention on the boy. A second later, he heard the rattle in the boy's lungs. Everything inside him froze for a pulsebeat. Violence was alien to his nature, but it gripped him now. He turned savagely on Kreuger. "Damn you, Kreuger," he swore, and curled his fingers into the man's shirt front. "I told you to contact me immediately if they got worse!"

"They are no worse than when you saw them last," Kreuger denied hotly, his dark eyes pinpoints of loathing and distrust.

Helga Kreuger was on her feet, alarm taking away what little color she had. "Gustav is not worse, is he?"

And Simon realized that she was so desperate for her son to get better that she had refused to acknowledge he had gotten worse. Sanity returned to him and he released his hold on Kreuger's shirt to turn back to the child.

"His condition isn't good," he said gruffly, understating the situation.

"He'll get better, though," she murmured and looked at her child anxiously.

"I'll do everything I can." It was the most Simon dared promise. It would be tough pulling a healthy child through, and the Kreuger children were undernourished and weak. Miracles weren't taught in his profession, and he had a feeling that's what it was going to take.

It had happened other times. In the outbreaks of typhoid fever, Simon had seen all but one or two members of the family die, but it was never easy for him to accept, especially when the victims were children. There was always the feeling that there should have been something else he could have done — that for all his knowledge, there was still something he didn't know but should have.

That's what Kreuger thought when all of his children save one were buried within a week. Simon had tried to shut his ears to the man's accusations. Kreuger was convinced that it was because he was poor and couldn't pay the doctor for his services that Simon hadn't done all he could, sure that if his name had been Calder rather than Kreuger the result would have been different.

Tired and frustrated and plagued by the guilt that haunted him every time he lost a patient, Simon leaned on the table in the middle of his cabin's small kitchen. Dirty dishes from two weeks ago sat in the sink, the last time he'd eaten a meal in his own home and office combined. He looked around at the mess.

"I hired a girl to clean the place for me, but her family pulled up stakes last fall. I haven't gotten around to finding someone else." He apologized to Doyle Pettit for the untidy state of his living quarters.

"If you want, I can find someone for you," Doyle volunteered affably and sipped at the bitter black coffee Simon had poured for him. "You really should take a week off and rest. You look terrible."

"Playing doctor, are you?" Simon smiled tiredly.

"What's on your mind, Doc?" Doyle Pettit leaned back in the straight chair, loose and at ease. "I know you didn't ask me to come by just to pass the time of day – not a man as busy as you are. So there must be something bothering you."

"It's Kreuger – or more specifically, Kreuger's wife. She's got tuberculosis, and this climate – the cold and the dust – are just aggravating her condition. He needs to get her out of here if he doesn't want to end up burying her, too." He ran a hand through his hair, rumpling the ends. "I've tried to explain it to him, but he thinks I've got some conspiracy going with Calder to drive him off the land. I can't get through to him. He just won't listen to me. But you – he's more likely to believe it coming from you."

Doyle frowned, concern etched in his features that were usually drawn in such carefree lines. He swirled the coffee in his cup, studying its black color. "I don't know if anything could separate that man from his land. That place is almost an obsession with him. Out of all those that came that first year to stake a homestead claim, he's one of the few left. I don't know what keeps him going."

"Hate." Simon supplied his belief. "A hatred not necessarily of Webb Calder as much as a hatred of what he represents, a big landholder. There are times when I wonder if he didn't choose his place simply because it butted up to Calder's land."

"Could be," Doyle conceded and drank from his cup. "I'll have a talk with him about his wife, but I don't know if I'll have any more success than you did."

Simon hoped he did. Something told him that Kreuger was near the breaking point. Most men would have quit by now. All he had was a hardscrabble farm that was getting blown away. The drought and the dust were working on everyone, fraying nerves and shortening tempers. Add to that the grief Kreuger had to be suffering. Put those things with his intense resentment of Calder, and at some point, the lid was going to blow.

"Have you seen Webb lately? How's that new baby of his doing?" Doyle shifted the subject to a lighter topic.

"I was out to The Homestead about three weeks ago, before all this started. Everyone was fine, including young Chase." The thought of the healthy baby brought a hint of a smile to Simon's face.

"You know what, Doc? You and I should take a trip back east and find ourselves a couple of wives. When I think about Webb having a son, I get downright envious," Doyle declared without looking the slightest bit serious. "I probably should talk to him about making provisions for his son's future. That's something my father never did for me. He left me a ranch and a lot of debts, and that's about all."

"I guess none of us think we're going to die." Simon laughed without humor and lifted the coffee cup to his mouth.

27

Spring came and brought relief from the winter's cold, but not the drought. Everyone said it couldn't last another summer. Banks made loans to the drylanders so they could buy seed and plant their wheat. June was the rainy season. Everyone waited, watching the sky and holding their breath.

The clouds came, scented the air with the sweetness of rain, then vibrated the dry ground with the loudness of their thunder. Suddenly, they split open and rain fell in driving sheets. The jubilance was wiped from Franz Kreuger's face as he stood outside his shack, drenched within minutes, and watched the torrential downpour carry away the top layer of soil and the young shoots of wheat.

The deluge didn't last for more than half an hour, but the dry ground couldn't absorb so much water in such a short period of time. What the wind hadn't eroded, the rainwater did, carving away sides of hills and gouging out gullies where there had been none. The crop was lost again, this time to the rain.

By late afternoon of that same day, the ground already showed signs of being dried out. Only in the low spots did the gumbolike consistency remain for another day.

The road into Blue Moon was crowded with wagons piled high with the meager possessions of drylanders who had packed it up and called it quits. For them, this last setback was the final blow. They had neither the resources nor the willpower to try again. Chickens squawked protests in their wooden cages and rib-thin dogs trotted alongside the slow-moving wagons, following their broken and dispirited masters. A couple of wagons had a milk cow in tow that they hoped to sell and have a little money to make a new start somewhere far away from Montana and the hard luck they'd known.

With each mile they traveled, Lilli grew more silent. There were familiar faces amidst the homeless bands they passed. Each time Webb drove up behind another wagon, she mentally braced herself, wondering whom she would recognize this time. At the approach of their automobile, the wagons pulled off onto the side of the road to let them pass, giving Lilli a short glimpse of the occupants. It was always a relief when they turned out to be strangers.

She stole a glance at Webb and saw the grimness in his hard-bitten features. She doubted that he was silent for the same reason she was. Despite the rain three days ago, dust was hanging over the land like a persistent cloud of doom. Where once there had been neatly plowed fields on either side of the road, the ground was ripped apart by new ravines and gulches. It resembled something in its death throes, twisted and contorted and writhing in agony. She suspected that a small part of him felt pity for the people who had lost all hope, but mostly he was hurt by what they had done to the land.

Chase squirmed in her lap, inactive for too long. He stiffened out his body, wanting to stand up and see something, but Lilli held him tightly.

Blue Moon was equally cheerless when they reached it. More businesses were boarded up. The street was aswarm with drylanders, those that wanted to stick it out and those that were part of the exodus. Some were lined up at the bank, hoping for another loan to buy more seed or to sell their homestead claim for whatever they could get. Others were trying to sell their livestock or furniture so they could buy what they needed. More were trying to barter for needed goods, or persuade the remaining shop-keepers to extend them more credit.

The only available place to park the automobile was at the train station, where a lucky few who possessed the price of a ticket were waiting for the next train. Lilli was slow to open her door, and Webb came around to give her and the baby a hand out.

"I'm sorry I asked you to bring me to town," she said. She hadn't been to town since before Chase was born. She had been looking forward to it, but it was turning out to be depressing. "I keep remembering how you tried to warn us, but nobody listened."

He stiffened at the way she aligned herself with the drylanders. His hand was holding her left one, and he rolled his thumb across her wedding ring. "It happened. There's nothing you can do about it, and nothing I can do." He tucked her hand under his arm and smiled. "Where would you like to go first, Mrs. Calder?"

"Home." Which was the truth, but she immediately changed it, aware that Webb couldn't empathize with her desire to avoid this scene. He hadn't shared the kind of dreams these people had lived on the way she had. "No." She smiled quickly. "We'll go to Ellis's store so I can buy some material to make Chase some clothes. He's growing much too fast and you don't have any more old shirts left."

In front of Sonny Drake's restaurant, Webb almost bumped into Ed Mace. The rancher stopped, his breath reeking of whiskey. His bulk had gone to paunch, and there was a flatness in his eyes.

"Come inside, Webb." Ed grabbed his arm, the grip of his hand lacking strength. If he noticed Lilli and the baby at all, he didn't acknowledge them. "I want to buy you a drink."

"Some other time, Ed," Webb refused calmly.

"Won't be no other time." The man breathed in, and the resulting sound resembled a sniffle. "I had to sell out."

"What are you talking about?" His gaze narrowed on the old man, trying to decide if he was sober enough to know what he was saying.

"I sold the Snake M. That rain we had — well, I'd just bought me a bunch of cows to start buildin' up my herd again. There was a flash flood on my place. More'n half of 'em got caught. They drowned." He looked out to the street with a vacant stare. "It busted me, that's what it did. I'm finished. It's all gone — everything I worked for all my life is wiped

606

out with one rain."

"You sold the ranch?" Webb still couldn't take it in.

"Yeah. Pettit took it off my hands." He paused glumly. "I've said bad things about him, but I think Old Tom would be proud of the way his son stands by his friends." His attention was drawn to the baby in Lilli's arms. The little billed cap tied on his head was askew from his constant twisting to see all that was going on around him. Ed Mace staggered closer, putting out a gnarled and work-worn hand for the baby to investigate. "You've got a fine-lookin' son, Webb. Never had any kids myself. I guess it's a good thing." His tongue was rambling the way a man's does when it's loosened by liquor. "What could I leave him? I lost the ranch — lock, stock, and barrel. Got me enough money to get to Mexico. Maybe I can find me a little place down there where I can run a couple of cows, and have one of them dark-eyed señoritas cook for me."

"You're going to Mexico, then." It was hard for Webb to meet the man's eyes. He felt pity for him, and despite all Ed's talk, he had too much pride to tolerate anyone feeling sorry for him.

"Got me a ticket." Ed Mace nodded, still letting the baby grab at a callused finger. Then

607

his hand dropped and his eyes became watery. "Hell, I never did like tequila, but at least it's legal down there." He rubbed a hand across his mouth. "I'm gonna have another one of Sonny's specials. Take care of that boy, Webb."

There was no repeat of his invitation to buy Webb a drink as the former rancher turned and lurched back inside the roadhouse. All Prohibition had accomplished in Blue Moon was to raise the price of a drink. Sheriff Potter had already shown a willingness to ignore what was in the cups served to some of the customers. It was pretty much business as usual. In this dry country, liquor was more plentiful than water.

There were a lot of things Webb was mulling over in his mind, but he didn't mention any of them to Lilli. It wasn't just drylanders that were cutting their losses and selling out; ranchers were going under, too. There were simply more of the former. He was curious how many properties would end up in Doyle Pettit's name.

There was a small commotion in the wagon-crowded street. One glance and Webb spotted the cause of it. Hobie Evans and the two hardcases he ran with were getting their kicks out of harassing those drylanders who were pulling up stakes.

"You thought you could come here and take what didn't belong to you, didn't ya?" Hobie was tormenting one family piled onto their wagon to leave town. The children were cringing from his jeering face. "You thought you'd come to the Promised Land, but it turned out to be Hell, didn't it? Your crops burned up in the fields; your wells went dry; and your land was blown away. It was the Promised Land, all right, because when the first of you came, I promised to make it Hell for all of you." His laughter was a harsh, mocking sound that seemed to carry above the rattle of wagons and the clopping hooves of horses. "I'm the son of the Devil. Didn't you know that?"

He made a lunge at the children and they shrieked in terror. He laughed again and slapped the flat of his hand across the rump of the spavined-looking draft horse. It jumped in surprise, and the drylander had to saw on the reins to keep his team from bolting into some pedestrians crossing the street in front of them.

"Hey, Hobie!" The breed cowboy had found another subject, now that the other wagon was leaving. "Look over here!"

A homesteader was hawking a mantel clock from the tailgate of his wagon. It was the most valuable possession he owned, a family heirloom that had traveled across oceans only to be sold on a dusty street so he could buy food for another journey.

"What you got there, mister?" Hobie sauntered over to the wagon. The man protectively clutched the clock in his arms, warily eyeing the three men converging on him. His wife anxiously tugged at his sleeve, trying to persuade him to climb into the wagon with her. "Ain't ya going to let me see it?" Hobie challenged with a sneer. "If a man's interested in buyin' something, he's got a right to look at it first."

"I'll sell it for ten dollars." The desperate man reluctantly offered the clock to Hobie for his inspection. "It's worth ten times that."

"Hell, this thing's old. Do you see how old this is?" He showed it to his friends. "I bet it can't even keep time."

When he shook it, Lilli's hand tightened on Webb's arm. He didn't even look at her as he slipped out of her hold. "You stay here, out of the way." He vaulted over the porch railing to the ground and started to make his way along the crowded street to the wagon in front of Ellis's store.

"It don't look worth ten dollars to me." Hobie Evans made as if to give it back to the man, but just before the drylander's outstretched hands reached it, Hobie let go. The clock's chimes dinged as it fell to the hard ground. The woman cried out at the sickening sound of splintering wood. "It sure as hell ain't worth ten dollars now." Hobie laughed as the man bent to carefully pick up his broken clock. Lilli's shoulders sagged. It was too late; the damage was done; and Webb wasn't even halfway there yet. "It's no good, mister," Hobie sneered. "Just like you're no good. We don't want your kind around here. We never wanted you. This land's gonna be cursed until all of you leave. So git!"

A bottle was thrown at the wagon. Lilli heard it crash against the side and break. Pieces of glass struck the horses. One of them reared and Webb grabbed at the bridle, hauling the animal down. No one seemed to notice him except the two little girls huddled together on the wagon seat. All the attention was focused at the rear of the wagon, where the drylander was setting the clock on the tailgate, trying to keep the broken parts together.

"Did you hear me?" Hobie challenged. "Nobody wants your trash. So climb in your wagon and git! And take your junk with you!"

It was all too much for the drylander. The one thing he had of value to sell was now broken. He turned on Hobie Evans, trembling and near tears. Without warning, he hurled himself at the cowboy. Hobie easily side-stepped the blind charge, clasped his hands together in a single fist, and brought it down on the man's back, driving him to the ground.

"Damned fool tried to attack me," he declared with a laugh, as if he'd just swatted down a pesky mosquito.

Webb had the horses settled down and had taken a stride toward the rear of the wagon when an explosion shocked everyone on the street into stillness. Hobie was lifted up on tiptoes, his mouth opened in stunned disbelief as his hands clawed at his arched back. His legs began to fold under him, but he managed a half-pivot to look for the unknown assailant who had shot him. Lilli covered her mouth with her hand when she saw the small red hole in the middle of his back.

Thirty feet away, Franz Kreuger stood poised with his rifle to his shoulder, a faint white trail of smoke curling from the barrel. As Hobie crumpled into a heap on the dusty ground, his two comrades back-pedaled, slinking away before the rifle was turned on them. But Kreuger kept it reined on the dead man.

His eyes had the look of a crazed man, pushed over the brink by too many battles with opponents he couldn't beat — the drought that had ruined his farm and the disease that had taken his children and made an invalid of his wife. Hobie Evans finally represented something he could destroy. His life could be taken as the drought had taken the life from his land and the disease had claimed the last breath of his children.

Everyone recognized his demented look and no one took a step toward the dead man or the man with the rifle, afraid that he might become indiscriminate about his next target. Webb knew something had to be done and fought the coldness in the pit of his stomach. When he started to move toward Kreuger, a hand clamped itself on his shoulder to stop him. His head jerked to the side as Doyle Pettit moved silently up on his left.

"You'd better stay out of it, Webb," he murmured and eyed Kreuger with a steady coolness. "He'd just as soon shoot you as look at you."

From the other side of the street, Sheriff Potter was threading his way through the crowd with a double-barreled shotgun in hand. Doyle Pettit left Webb and angled over to join up with the law officer.

With a brassiness that Webb couldn't help but admire, Doyle walked jauntily to Kreuger with a bright-eyed, innocent look fixed on his handsome face. His hands were thrust in his pants pockets, casually pushing his jacket open to subtly prove he was unarmed. Hobie had been unarmed, too. Kreuger's side glance at Doyle was full of suspicion, but Doyle stood there, looking at the crumpled body in the dirt.

"He was a mean one, wasn't he?" he said in a light, dispassionate voice.

"He deserved to die," Kreuger declared. "No one should take pleasure from other people's suffering. He should have been killed long ago. I have said over and over that we must all stick together and help each other out. But we are letting people like him drive us from our lands. It is time we stopped them."

Doyle appeared to give a lot of thought to the embittered declaration the man made. "You know, Kreuger, I think you're right." He nodded. "We've got to stick together in this. You and me and the sheriff should sit down and come up with a plan. That Hobie Evans has given the sheriff nothing but trouble from the beginning. Isn't that right, Sheriff?" The question invited Potter to come forward.

The sheriff kept the shotgun pointed at the ground, not making any threatening motions toward Kreuger. The weapon was easily explained away by Doyle, since Potter had only heard the gunshot and had not known what kind of trouble to expect or from whom.

Within minutes, the two were guiding Kreuger up the street toward the sheriff's office. Doyle Pettit kept Kreuger talking and listened attentively to everything he had to say.

Two cowboys came forward to carry Evans's body over to the smithy's shop, who also did double duty as a coffinmaker. Lilli was white and trembling when Webb returned to her side. He immediately guided her away from the milling throng into the roadhouse and found a quiet table in the corner. With the excitement of the shooting, it was several minutes before he managed to have the waitress bring coffee to their table.

Lilli held Chase's arms down to keep him from grabbing the cup of hot coffee while she took a sip of it. It seemed to steady her nerves.

"Are you okay?" Webb asked, and she nodded.

"I think I've always known Kreuger was capable of killing someone in cold blood," she murmured. "But seeing it —" She shuddered expressively, not needing to finish the sentence.

"It's over now." His hand closed over hers.

"Is it?" She looked up at him, her blue eyes wide with doubt. "Or is it just the beginning?" Webb didn't answer, stunned by the quiet conviction in her voice. "I've heard all the stories about long dry spells that have driven people berserk. Kreuger has always advocated violence. He's shown he's willing to commit it. What's to stop him now?"

"The sheriff has him in custody, Lil. You don't have to worry about him anymore," he insisted.

"I wished I believed that," she murmured, because the knowledge didn't reassure her.

The door to the roadhouse opened and Simon Bardolph walked in. He was halfway to an empty table when he spotted Webb and Lilli sitting in the corner. He changed course to join them.

"You saw it?" he asked as he pulled out a chair to sit down. There wasn't any need to refer directly to the shooting. It was the only topic being discussed in town. Webb nodded. Simon leaned both elbows on the table and wiped at his face, smoothing the shaggy hair behind his ears. "I've just been over to look at the body so I can write up the death certificate. I knew Kreuger would snap sometime. Too many things have been piling up on him."

"Has Kreuger sold out? Is he leaving?" Webb asked.

"The only way he'll leave that place is feet first." The physician shook his head and sighed tiredly.

Chase was trying to put his fingers in Lilli's mouth. She absently took hold of them and pushed his hand down. "What about Helga?" she asked, suddenly concerned about Kreuger's wife. "Did she come to town with him?"

"I doubt it. Just about any kind of exertion starts her coughing. I'm sure she stayed at their place with her daughter," Simon guessed and motioned to the waitress that he wanted coffee, too.

"Someone has to tell her what happened," she said, feeling pity for the woman and wondering what would happen to her.

There was a heavy sigh from the doctor. "I'll drive out there. She'll probably need me." He didn't look forward to it, but he was the logical person under the circumstances.

Voices were raised outside the roadhouse, cheering remarks filtering inside. When the door was opened, a half-dozen people spilled into the restaurant area, fighting for the chance to shake Doyle Pettit's hand and congratulate him on the way he had so quietly handled Kreuger. His gaze swept the room, stopping at Webb's table. It took him a few seconds to disengage from the group and approach their table.

"I'm glad to see you, Simon." He pulled out a chair next to the doctor's and sat down. "I was looking for you, and somebody said they'd seen you come in here."

"What is it? Are you having problems with Kreuger?" Simon asked, rousing himself to sit up straighter.

"Not exactly. Right now he's locked up in my office. We took him there rather than alarming him by taking him to the sheriff's," Doyle explained. "I've closed the bank for the day so we can figure out what to do with him."

"He's at the bank?" Simon frowned.

"He isn't going to cause any trouble for a while." Doyle dismissed the concern that came into their expressions. "I slipped some laudanum into his coffee. He's sleeping on my couch. He'll be out for a couple of hours or more."

"Then what's the trouble?" Simon didn't understand, unless Doyle and the sheriff wanted him to keep Kreuger sedated.

"Kreuger's been under a lot of stress. He cracked today." His glance darted around the table stopping to study a point in the middle. "I guess we can all be glad that nobody else was hurt but Evans. I can't say I blame him for killing Hobie. There have been times when I wanted to strangle the man myself. If Kreuger is locked up until the trial, I think he'll go completely over the wall. I'd like you to help me convince the sheriff to release Kreuger in my custody. I can control him. I can take him and his family out to my ranch where they can get plenty of food and rest."

"Are you saying you think he was justified in killing an unarmed man because that person was Hobie Evans?" Simon stared at him faintly angry.

"That isn't for me to decide. That's a jury's job. I'm not saying he should go free," Doyle insisted. "But, because of his condition, I don't think he should be jailed until the trial. After all that man's been through, he deserves some compassion. Desperate men sometimes do desperate things." He paused and studied the doctor with an earnest look. "Will you speak to the sheriff for me?"

"Are you really prepared to be responsible for him?" Simon murmured.

"I can handle him. Besides, I'll have men watching him all the time. It isn't just Kreuger I'm thinking about. It's his wife and what all this will do to her," Doyle argued persuasively.

"I hope you aren't making a mistake." Simon breathed in, still skeptical, but willing to go along with the suggestion.

"Good." His mouth curved in satisfaction as he leaned back. "The sheriff's over in my office, keeping an eye on Kreuger just in case he wakes up. We'll go over and talk to him."

"Let me go back to my place first and write up a death certificate." The waitress came with his coffee. He pushed it toward Doyle. "You drink it. I'll be back in a few minutes."

As the doctor left them, Lilli silently hoped he wouldn't be able to convince the sheriff to go along with Doyle's plan. She didn't like the sound of it, even though she didn't understand the cause of her misgivings.

But when two of the most respected members of the community put the proposition to Potter, he succumbed to their assurances. Kreuger was still unconscious when they bundled him into the doctor's buggy and drove out to his farm to get his wife and daughter.

Doyle studied the sky, a haze of dust without a cloud in sight. The shooting this morning had been a stroke of luck as far as he was concerned. Whether Kreuger knew it or not, Doyle owed him a debt. There had been a run on the bank, draining his cash to a dangerously low level. The shooting in the street had given him the perfect excuse to shut the doors before the money ran out and people started to panic. Because of his handling of Kreuger, the town regarded him as some kind of hero. They'd accept any excuse he gave why the bank wouldn't be open tomorrow. Then it would be the weekend. By Monday, he should be able to raise the cash to cover the deficit.

Buying the Snake M had put him in a bind, but it was going to be worth it. If he had guessed Mace would sell so soon, he could have made provisions to have the ready cash instead of dipping into the bank's supply. It didn't matter now, though. Everything was going to work out.

"You look like the cat that got the cream." Simon observed the faintly smug smile on Doyle's face.

"Do I?" The smile became more pronounced. "I guess it just feels good to help other people." He turned to look at the doctor. "You know what they say: Cast your bread upon the waters . . ." The biblical quotation didn't require completion.

A horn tooted behind the buggy and Simon pulled on the reins to angle the gelding onto the hard shoulder and let the automobile pass. Webb was behind the wheel. He lifted a hand as they went by.

They hadn't stayed in town to do any shopping as Lilli had intended. She'd lost her desire for the outing. When she recognized Simon's buggy and guessed at its destination of the

Kreuger place, all her uncertainties came flooding back.

"I'd feel much better if I knew Kreuger was in jail." She had to speak loudly to make herself heard above the noise of the motor.

"He'll stand trial. You can be sure of it," Webb replied.

But she wasn't.

28

Lightning flashed along the horizon, but Lilli wasn't fooled by it. It was heat lightning, not the forerunner of rain. The night wind lifting the curtains at the window was warm and dry, but it lessened the stifling temperature of the upstairs bedroom, even if everything would be covered with dust in the morning.

She tunneled a hand under the mass of auburn hair and lifted its weight from her neck as she turned to glance toward the crib where Chase was sleeping. His little nightshirt clung to him, damp with the perspiration on his chubby neck, but he slept soundly, indifferent to the heat.

The warm wind curled around the exposed skin of her neck, cooling it a degree. Lilli had blamed the summer heat for the restlessness that had pushed her out of bed, but the endless heat wasn't responsible for the thoughts that kept turning around in her head.

Tomorrow was the day of Franz Kreuger's trial. Three weeks had passed since the shooting, yet she was still apprehensive. No one had mourned Hobie Evans's passing. Lilli hadn't liked him any more than the next person, but Kreuger had murdered him — shot him in the back. If he got away with that, there would be no stopping him. He would consider himself above the law, justified to avenge any real or imagined wrong. Sooner or later his target for vengeance would be Webb. He had despised him for too long and the hatred ran too deep.

She had attempted to confide her fears to Webb, but he didn't truly understand. Kreuger would stand trial and be punished for his crime, Webb had insisted, but despite his assurances she didn't have much faith in the law, and told him so. It had been one of their typical spirited disagreements. They had argued angrily over it, which now troubled Lilli as much as anything.

With the thought of him uppermost in her mind, her gaze swung to the bed, intermittently illuminated by the flashes of heat lightning through the window where she stood. Even in sleep, his rugged features held their strength, his solid lips lying together in a firm line. Most of the covers were kicked off him. She studied his asymmetrical and thoroughly masculine body, relaxed now. Emotion swelled in her, a deep, abiding love that knew no end.

Silently, she slipped off the cotton nightgown and glided into bed. At the touch of her, Webb automatically gathered her into the crook of his arm, but she leaned onto his chest, her hair falling over her shoulder to brush his cheek. When her lips probed at the stillness of his mouth, he stirred, wakening slowly. As the hunger in her kiss made itself known, he combed his fingers into her hair to press her head down and deepen the kiss.

When he rolled her over onto the mattress, there was a moment when the contact between their lips was broken. "Make love to me, Webb," Lilli murmured in that space.

Slowly and passionately, they made the union last a long time. Neither seemed able to get enough of the other. Even when it was over and they drifted to sleep in each other's arms, there was a sense that it hadn't been enough — that there would never be enough loving.

Dawn came with its fiery range of reds and oranges to herald the rise of a blazing yellow sun. Webb stopped the Model T in front of the Stanton house and let the engine idle. His glance shunted to his wife and son in the passenger seat. He reached out a hand to affectionately rumple the unruly mass of dark hair on his son's head, but it was Lilli who claimed his attention.

"Are you sure you want to go to the trial?" he asked.

"Yes." It was a determined answer that warned him she wouldn't be budged no matter how strongly he felt she shouldn't attend.

With Chase in her arms, she stepped out of the car and climbed the porch steps to the door. Ruth had heard them drive up and opened the door before Lilli knocked. Chase recognized her and became excited, reaching out his hands to be held by her and laughing. Ruth was a second mother to him, so he never raised much of a fuss when Lilli left him with her.

"He's already had his breakfast," Lilli said as she let Ruth take him from her. Little Buck came crawling to the door, and Chase immediately began wiggling in Ruth's arms to be put down so he could play with her son. "I'm not sure when we'll be back. It will depend on how long the trial lasts."

"Please don't worry about Chase while you're gone." Ruth set him on the floor. "I'll take good care of him."

Lilli watched her son crawling across the floor, so completely at home. When she lifted her gaze to Ruth, there was a vague tightness in her throat. "I know I don't have to worry about him when he's with you, Ruth. You love him as much as I do, I think." Impulsively, she reached out and squeezed the woman's hand, then turned quickly to walk back to the car. They had a long drive ahead of them to the county seat.

Before they entered the courtroom, Doyle Pettit drew the handcuffed Kreuger aside, out of earshot but under the eye of Sheriff Potter. He could see the dark suspicion and mistrust for the trial proceedings in Kreuger's face and needed to allay them before the man stopped listening to him.

"A lot depends on you doing exactly as I say," Doyle murmured. Hopefully, Kreuger would never know how much depended on it. "You're going to have to plead guilty and throw yourself at the mercy of the court."

"I won't go to prison." There was a threatening gleam in his eyes.

"If you do what I say, you won't." His palms were sweating. He wasn't sure if he could convince Kreuger. And he had to, because there was too much to lose. "Have I ever misled you about anything? I'm trying to help you, Kreuger." The man said nothing and showed signs of listening, however sullenly. "The twelve men on the jury are all drylanders, so they know what you've been through. They'll be sympathetic. Don't worry about the judge, either. There isn't any way Calder has gotten to him, so you don't need to be thinking that. He's my man." Thanks to an overdue loan the judge had with his bank, but Doyle didn't mention that. "Now we've got a few minutes. Do you want to run through it again?"

"I am not an ignorant man." Kreuger straightened, reading an implied insult into the question. "You have already told me several times what it is I should do."

"All right." Doyle didn't go into it again, although he would have felt more confident if they had. Kreuger was so damned unpredictable. He was taking a big chance risking so much on this man, but if he could pull it off, all his own problems were going to be behind him. People were beginning to wonder why the bank wasn't open every day. When he ran out of excuses, it was all going to collapse unless this scheme succeeded.

People were packed in the courtroom like steers in a cattle car. Lilli and Webb found seats in the second row behind the prosecutor's table. When they saw Simon Bardolph searching for a place to sit, there was such a gabble of voices that it was useless to call to the physician. Webb stood up and motioned to him that there was a small space next to them. Lilli squeezed closer to Webb so Simon would have room to sit.

"I didn't know you were coming." Simon shouldered his way into the space and kept his elbows tucked in close to his sides.

"Lilli insisted on coming." Disapproval was in Webb's voice, but he carried the subject no further.

"They're calling me to testify as to the cause of death." His mouth twisted wryly. "It's going to be a five-word answer. A bullet in the back."

A hush came over the courtroom as the lawyers arguing the case entered, followed by the defendant. Both Doyle Pettit, who was the attorney for the defense, and Franz Kreuger remained standing by their chairs. Their action stirred a murmur of confusion that ran through the courtroom crowd.

"Good God, what's she doing here?" Simon uttered angrily under his breath, and Lilli noticed the tubercular-wasted woman being led to the front, a man on each side, half-carrying her to an empty chair behind the defense table.

"She shouldn't be out of bed."

"Doyle obviously plans to play on their sympathy." Dryness rustled through Webb's voice as a grim watchfulness came over him. It was a clever move. Its brilliance was made even more apparent when the jury filed in and Webb saw it consisted of wheat farmers. He had the uneasy feeling he had underestimated Doyle Pettit for a second time, although he couldn't see what Doyle hoped to gain by getting Kreuger off. Surely he stood a better chance of getting Kreuger's land if the man were convicted.

Once Helga Kreuger was seated, Doyle Pettit sat down and motioned to his client to take the chair next to him. Kreuger did so slowly, his look turning malevolent when he saw Webb Calder in the second row.

"Calder is here," he told Pettit.

"Don't think about him now," Doyle ordered, barely moving his lips as he issued the low warning. "And wipe that look off your face. If the jury sees it, you'll wind up with your neck in a noose."

"That's what he's hoping will happen to me." Kreuger turned to face the judge's bench.

"Then we'll just have to fool him, won't we?" Doyle looked at Kreuger and smiled with his eyes. There was a moment when he thought his appeal wasn't going to work; then Kreuger's expression changed to one of blankness. Doyle mentally reminded himself that Kreuger might be a simple matter to maneuver.

The judge entered and everyone stood as he pounded the gavel and called the room to order. The trial began.

With the entering of the guilty plea, Doyle Pettit then sought to prove that the act was committed under extenuating circumstances. Within minutes, Webb realized that it was Hobie Evans who was on trial, not Franz Kreuger. A dozen witnesses testified to the physical harassment and abuse they had suffered at the hands of the murder victim. When Evans was painted blacker than the devil, Pettit eloquently set about detailing all the hardships and losses Kreuger had endured — the killing drought, the crop wiped out by a plague of grasshoppers, the deaths of his children, and the debilitating illness of his wife. He compared his trials with those that beset Job in the Bible, trials he had borne in silence until he'd seen a neighbor suffering at the hands of a cruel, villainous blackguard. Then it had become too much for him. In summation, Pettit pleaded with the jury to show mercy for this man and his pitifully ill wife who needed him.

Webb listened to it all. Beside him, Lilli was transmitting her tension to him, strain whitening her complexion. When the jury filed out of the courtroom to arrive at a verdict, he took her hand and threaded his fingers between hers.

She couldn't find any comfort in the gesture, although she held tightly on to his hand. No one left the courtroom, as if they all suspected the jury of twelve good and true men wouldn't deliberate long over the verdict. In less than twenty minutes, they filed back in and took their seats.

When the judge read the verdict that found Kreuger guilty of a lesser charge and suspended the sentence, Lilli came to her feet. "No!" She angrily protested the decision that set Kreuger free. "No, you can't do it!" Her hands were knotted into fists, clenched rigidly at her side.

Then Webb was standing and taking hold of her arms to restrain her. "It's no good, Lilli." His voice was low and rough. "You can't change it." His grip forced her to turn away as he guided her down the row to the aisle so they could exit the courtroom. She didn't resist him, but her body remained stiff, everything held tightly in check.

Other people were already milling, some pausing to watch the touching scene as the handcuffs were taken off Kreuger's wrists and he was reunited with his wife. Simon separated himself from the Calders and made his way through the crowd to Helga Kreuger, concerned that the trial had been too much for her.

Tears were streaming down her sallow cheeks as she lay in her husband's embrace. She was too weak to cry or cough, making feeble attempts at each that just drained more of her strength.

Simon turned his scowling and angry countenance on Doyle Pettit. "Get her out of here," he demanded. "She needs complete quiet and bedrest – and plenty of it."

"I have a room for her at the boarding house up the street." Doyle showed little concern as he signaled to the two men who had brought Helga Kreuger to the courtroom to take her back.

Franz protested, "I will take her home."

"She's in no condition to travel," Simon Bardolph snapped. "Can't you see she's sick? She needs rest, and I don't just mean an hour or two. I'm talking days and weeks."

The terrible sound of her cough convinced Franz when the doctor's warning failed.

Grudgingly, he assisted one of the men to help his wife to her feet and supported her while they made their way through the thinning crowd.

"How could you put her through an ordeal like this?" Simon looked narrowly at the man he had believed to be a compassionate individual.

"I had no choice."

"No, I suppose she was a necessary tool in obtaining Kreuger's release," he said firmly. "So you used her and won. I hope you know what you're doing by setting a man like that free."

"I didn't set him free. The judge did that," Doyle reminded him smoothly. "As a doctor, it's your duty to do all you can to save a patient. And it's my duty to defend my client to the best of my ability. The right and wrong of something is for the judge and jury to decide. I can't do that any more than you can play God."

It was an unarguable comparison, but Simon still didn't like it. It was written in the sternness of his expression as he pivoted away from Pettit, his opinion of the man rapidly dropping.

Outside the courthouse, Webb paused with Lilli on the sidewalk. She hadn't said a word, but he'd seen the I-told-you-so look in her eyes the one time she had glanced at him. It had been her fear all along that Kreuger would somehow be set free, and he hadn't believed it was possible. He had killed a man, shot him in the back in front of a score of witnesses, and he was walking out of the courtroom a free man. Webb watched Kreuger carrying his frail wife the last few yards to the waiting buggy.

"Webb, I want to go home. Now." Lilli was seized by the urge and couldn't shake it. It was an unreasoning kind of fear that she couldn't explain. But it was suddenly imperative that they go back to the ranch this afternoon.

He took his watch from his vest pocket and looked at the time. "It's late. We'd never make it before nightfall, and I'm not going to try to travel over those roads in the dark."

"Please. I have this feeling we should go." She looked at him earnestly, silently imploring him to listen to her. "I want to see Chase, and make sure he's all right."

Webb hesitated. For an instant, Lilli thought she had won him over; then he shook his head. "No. We'll spend the night here as we planned and get an early start in the morning. Ruth's taking good care of our son."

"Yes." She admitted that, but with more than a trace of agitation.

He put his arm around her waist and fitted her close to his side. "This business with Kreuger has spooked you." He smiled warmly at her. There was pride in his eyes for this slim, strong woman who carried his name. She was beautiful and spirited, with a will to match his. Even now, she was pushing away the fear that shadowed her eyes.

"Maybe so," she conceded.

"Do you suppose I can persuade a certain married woman to have dinner with me tonight?" he murmured, his voice growing husky.

"You can try," she replied on a faint note of challenge.

The afternoon sun was leaning toward the west, slanting its rays through the boarding-house window. Franz Kreuger pulled the blind so the light wouldn't disturb his wife. She had closed her eyes only minutes ago, finally drifting into a much-needed sleep. He slipped quietly out of the room, and down the stairs to the parlor.

"How is she?" Doyle Pettit looked up briefly, then finished pouring liquid from his pocket flask into a glass.

"She finally went to sleep. She will be better." Franz Kreuger refused to believe anything else. He moved to the window, an impatience claiming his actions; his gaze was restless and hard. "We should be going home. We have been away from our place too long. So much work has been left undone for so long."

"It looks as if it's going to be some time before your wife is in any condition to travel." Doyle took a drink of the bootlegged whiskey.

"I'll have to leave her here until she is better." Franz was confident his wife would understand. She had never disagreed with any of his decisions, and she would see the sense of this one. "I have decided to go this afternoon."

"Calder won't be leaving until in the morning, so it's probably a good idea that you leave today." Doyle nodded his agreement. "I'll arrange for Mrs. Rogers to look after your wife until she's better."

Kreuger faced him, suspicion lurking in his narrowed eyes. "You have done much for me, and I can't pay you."

"But you will." Doyle smiled away that concern. "I pride myself on being a good judge of character, Kreuger. You are the sort that always pays your debts. This drought won't last forever. And as long as you have your land, you'll be harvesting wheat one day. That means business for my grain elevator, my bank, and my hardware store. By helping you,

I stand to gain a lot, too." Much more than Kreuger ever suspected. Doyle was confident that everything was going to work out as he had planned it. He lifted his glass in a silent drink to it.

When Kreuger saw the many ways Pettit stood to profit from helping him, it eased his mind. The day would come when he would pay him back. He accepted charity from no man. Pettit indicated he respected him for that, which pleased Kreuger. He'd rather die than grovel at the feet of any man, so he didn't offer his thanks for the help Pettit had given him. The man would be paid, so gratitude wasn't necessary.

"I will leave now," Kreuger announced. "Please tell my wife that I will come to fetch her in three weeks."

"Of course." Doyle inclined his head. Not until after Kreuger had left the boarding house did a smile spread across his face and a different light began to shine in his eyes. "Hurry home, Kreuger," he murmured and chuckled softly. "Hurry home."

Early the next morning, the Model T was on the road, making the return journey to the ranch. Webb and Lilli passed families of drylanders, a common sight now. Some were on foot, others in dilapidated trucks, and still more in wagons. But the dust didn't seem as bad. And the wind generated by the fast-traveling automobile made the hot temperature bearable. There were stretches of land blackened by range fires, and more acres mounded into dirt dunes, dotted with thistles that were fodder for milk cows. They drove by hardscrabble farms with chickens scratching futilely in the dirt and bone-thin pigs wallowing in the dust.

It was a relief when they reached the unmarked gate to the Triple C Ranch. Here the rolling country was covered with brown grass, dried out and burnt up, but it was a covering that held the rangeland intact.

"We're almost home." Webb took his eyes off the lane long enough to glance at Lilli.

The blowing wind had freed strands of dark hair for the sun to set on fire. Her wide mouth was lifted in a faint smile at the prospect of journey's end. "I wish we could go faster."

Ahead, there was a straight stretch of fairly smooth road. Webb pushed down on the foot pedal to increase their speed, blurring the landscape in his side vision. They were nearly halfway across the stretch when, all at the same moment, there was an explosion and the steering wheel was suddenly wrenched to the right, nearly ripped from his hands.

A blowout. Webb fought to regain control, but the automobile careened violently to the right, bounced wildly into a ditch, and came to an abrupt stop as it gouged into an embankment. It was a full second before Webb realized they were no longer moving. The instant he turned, he saw Lilli slumped against the door.

A wild fear clawed through him as he reached for her, calling her name. Her body was limp when he gathered it into his arms. Already an ugly bruise was coloring her right temple. His fingers found the pulse in her neck, but it wasn't very strong. His own heart was thudding loudly in his chest, the blood pumping with powerful thrusts. As carefully as possible, he laid her down on the seat and reached behind him to open the door.

There was a whanging thud of a bullet ricocheting off the metal frame, and Webb threw himself across Lilli. It hadn't been a blowout. Somebody had shot out the tire. Another searching shot plowed into the upholstery of the seat only a few inches above his head. He reached over to open the small compartment in the dash and take out the revolver that was always kept there. It was mostly for snakes, which were prevalent in this part of the country. It wasn't uncommon to encounter one while changing a tire. Whoever was shooting had a rifle, but at least Webb, too, was armed.

Aware that he had to draw the fire away from the car, where Lilli might get hit, Webb waited until the third shot broke the windshield. He kicked the door open and rolled outside, counting on surprise. He hit the ground and kept moving. Two shots were snapped off in rapid succession, kicking up the dirt behind him as his unseen assailant tried to bring his moving target into his sights. Erosion had exposed an outcropping of coal just ahead of him. Webb lunged for the shelter it offered, grabbed a corner of it, and swung behind it. Another bullet fragmented the coal edge under his hand, coal splinters peppering his hand as he yanked it back and flattened himself against the ledge rock.

He was breathing hard; perspiration was breaking out on his forehead and upper lip. All the shots had come from the same rifle. There was only one person out there. Judging from the direction of the shots, the man had to be in that stand of dead pines on the hill across the way. Webb checked the revolver. There were only five bullets, the hammer resting on an empty chamber. He turned it and wished he'd grabbed some shells.

There was a chance a Triple C rider was in

the vicinity and had heard the shots. But with Lilli hurt and unconscious, Webb couldn't risk waiting for help to come.

So far, his attacker was unaware he was armed, which gave Webb a slim advantage. With only five bullets, he couldn't trade shots with the man, which left him with the only other option – to stalk his attacker. There was little covering around him. The ambush site had been well chosen. The hill and the stand of trees gave a commanding field of fire. Webb would have to rely on the folds of the land to conceal his stalk, but first he had to verify the location of his prey.

He made a move as if he intended to bolt for the protection of the Model T and let the rifle fire drive him behind the outcropping of coal again. This time he watched for the stabs of red in the pines. They came through the branches of the lowest tree on the slope, brown and brittle needles hiding the shooter behind their screen.

There hadn't been a sound from the Model T, nothing to indicate Lilli had regained consciousness. His lips were dry with fear and he moistened them. He couldn't risk thinking about her, not now when all his concentration had to be on this stalk.

As quietly as he could, Webb bellied down

on the ground and left his hat by the coal ledge. Then he started out, crawling like a snake through the grass and using every available dip and crease in the land. It was all so open around him. Any minute he expected to hear a bullet whistling near his head. But it was the openness that was his protection. It lulled his attacker into believing there was no way he could be approached in this deceptively flat-looking land.

It seemed to take forever to crawl around to the side slope of the hill. His nose and throat were constantly tickled by the dust and the smell of dried grass. A persistent wind partially covered the rustling sounds he made. Webb paused, his shirt drenched with sweat, and tried to gauge how close he was to the trees. He flexed his fingers, tightening his grip on the long-barreled pistol.

The low, suspicious whicker of a horse came from his right, snapping Webb's gaze in that direction. A tall, gaunt draft horse stood ground-tied on the back of the hill, eyeing the dark object in the grass with puzzled alarm. There was second of shock as Webb recognized the animal as one of Kreuger's plow horses. Kreuger! He was the attacker!

Webb cursed himself for not listening to Lilli's warnings about the man. But even if he had, there was nothing he could have done about it. The law had tried Kreuger and turned him loose — to kill again.

The horse snorted. There was no more time to wonder about how things might have been different — or how close he was to Kreuger. Kreuger would have heard the horse and become suspicious about what was alarming it. He had to make his play now.

Pushing to his feet, he squared his body in the direction he expected to find Kreuger and cocked the hammer of his gun. Kreuger was backing away from a tree, half-turned to look up the hill instead of to the side where Webb stood.

"Throw down the rifle, Kreuger!" Webb had the gun leveled on him, his finger resting against the trigger.

Not even a split second passed between the sound of his voice and the whirling move of the drylander. He didn't take time to bring the rifle to his shoulder, snapping off the shot as he came around. The bullet tugged at the sleeve of Webb's shirt. In pure reflex, he squeezed the trigger and felt the revolver buck in his hand.

The impact of the shot hit Kreuger full in the chest. He staggered a step, but came on. This time he raised the rifle and took aim. Webb fired again, stepping to his left as the

644

rifle barrel jumped with a stab of flame. He heard the whoosh of the bullet go by him. Kreuger's left arm was hanging limp at his side, a crimson stain spreading down his sleeve. Still he tried to balance and aim the rifle with his good arm. Webb gritted his teeth and fired again, realizing the man wasn't going to stop until he was dead.

The rifle was torn from his hand as Kreuger was spun around and knocked to the ground. Webb started forward, keeping the gun on the man as he would an animal of prey that was downed but not dead. With almost super-human effort, Kreuger was trying to drag himself to the rifle. Webb reached it first and picked it up. Kreuger twisted his head to look up at him. The hatred in his eyes hadn't dimmed.

"Dammit, Kreuger. Why?" Webb growled, hearing the gurgle of blood in the man's lungs.

"You burned my place." Blood was coming from his mouth, running red over his lip. "You sent your men to burn my place. Pettit warned me you might try, so . . ." His voice grew fainter, becoming unintelligible as the light in his eyes dimmed.

"Pettit?" A dark frown rimmed his hard features. Crouching on his heels, Webb grabbed the shoulder of Kreuger's shirt. "What the hell do you mean – Pettit warned you?" But he was looking into sightless eyes.

Kreuger was dead and the cracked and thirsty ground was already drinking in the wetness of his blood. Webb let go of the shirt, the lifeless body slumping. His stomach felt queasy till he thought of Lilli. Then he was hurrying down the hill, spurred by his fear for her.

She was lying on the seat as he had left her, no sign of having stirred. Her pulse was weaker, her breath barely stirring against his hand. He had to clench his teeth together to hold back the sobs.

"Lilli. For God's sake, don't die. I need you." His voice was a hoarse plea that vibrated above a whisper.

Reluctantly he moved away from her to inspect the damage to the auto. The right front fender was wedged against the embankment, making it impossible to change the flat tire. He tried to start the motor to reverse it onto open ground, but it wouldn't turn over. As Webb started to raise the hood to locate the problem, hooves drummed the ground, signaling the approach of riders. He walked quickly to open the car door and gathered Lilli into the cradle of his arms.

When Ike Willis and Nate Moore rode into

view, he was standing in the middle of the road, waiting for them. They reined their horses into a plunging halt.

"We heard shooting. What happened?" Nate asked, swinging out of the saddle, a worried eye darting to the limp woman in Webb's arms.

"Kreuger. His body's up there." Webb jerked his head in the direction of the hill. "I'm going to take your horse, Nate. Ike, you ride for the doctor. It's her head. She hit it —" He choked up, unable to finish the sentence. Nate held the reins to his horse while Webb climbed into the saddle with Lilli in his arms.

Nate was left standing in the road as the two riders took off in opposite directions. He was good at reading signs, so it didn't take him long to figure out what had happened.

Simon had been standing helplessly beside the bed, watching life slip from Lilli's body with each passing minute. There was nothing he could do except to monitor her vital signs of pulse and respiration. Webb was huddled on a chair pulled close to the bed, his big hands gripping her hand in a silent effort to will his strength into her body. There was a haunting bleakness in his dark eyes and a ghastly pallor about his sun-browned features.

Leaning over her, Simon searched again for a

pulse with his stethoscope and found none. She had left them so quickly he couldn't even say when the exact moment had come. There were tears in his eyes when he looked at Webb.

"I've lost her," he said. "I'm sorry."

Simon braced himself for the disbelief, the denial, he expected from Webb, but it didn't come. The dark head was bent. The pair of hands were wrapped so tightly around hers that the knuckles showed white. The silence was harder for Simon to endure than an outpouring of grief and protest.

When Webb spoke, his voice was unnaturally low and gruff. "Let me be alone with her."

As Simon left the room, his chin was quivering and his eyes were so blurred with tears he could barely see the door. He closed it and leaned against it, breathing in shakily. From inside the room, there came the scrape of a chair leg moving.

Webb sat on the edge of the bed, tears streaming down his face. He gathered Lilli into his arms and buried his face in her dark copper hair. Great, racking sobs tore through his body. He held her like that until there was no more warmth in her body.

29

No expression showed on his face, all the grief locked behind his stony features, as Webb stood beside the open grave, his feet slightly apart and his nearly one-year-old son in his arms. The minister droned out his prayer for the living to the mourners. With the exception of Simon Bardolph, they were all Triple C riders and their families.

A swirling wind kicked up dirt from the freshly dug earth mounded beside the grave and swept it over the mourners. Little Chase rubbed a fist at his nose, making a face of dislike at the stinging dust that pelted him, but Webb was mindless of it.

With the close of the prayer, Webb stepped forward and shifted his son to the crook of one arm. A shovel was planted upright in the earth mound. He gripped its handle and scooped up the loose dirt with a push of his foot, tossing it into the grave. The larger chunks made a hollow noise as they landed on the wooden coffin below. Webb dipped the shovel into the dirt a second time and shifted his hold on the handle to raise it, offering it to his son. The small hand eagerly closed on the dirt to grab up a fistful. Then Chase gave his father a bright-eyed look, thinking they were playing some game.

"Throw it down, son." It was a flat request, accompanied by a nod of his head toward the grave.

With a wild fling of his arm, Chase released the dirt in the general direction of the grave and clapped his hands together. He reached for more dirt, wanting to do it again, but Webb emptied it into the grave. He then turned and passed the shovel to Nate Moore, standing with his parents. He stepped back, a lonely figure in his black broadcloth suit, too impassive and too silent. And the youngster in his arms only made the picture more poignant.

A darkness was filling the sky to the west when the last mourner added his shovelful of dirt to the grave. Anxious glances were cast in its direction. No one mistook the looming cloud for a billowing thunderhead. They had seen similar formations too many times not to know it was a wind-driven wall of dust, commonly referred to as a black-roller.

Before the group of mourners splintered to go to their individual homes, Webb approached Ruth Haskell and her husband. Chase immediately reached out his arms to the woman who was his second mother, and Webb handed him to her.

"Take care of him for me, Ruth," he said and walked away.

Like the others, Nate had observed Webb's action and was vaguely puzzled by it. His interest sharpened when he realized Webb was heading for the barns instead of The Homestead. He followed him out of concern and curiosity. Nate finally caught up with him inside the barn, where he found Webb saddling a dingy-colored buckskin.

"Where're you goin'?" Nate wandered over and combed the horse's mane with his fingers, eyeing Webb in a side look.

"Town." He snugged up the cinch and wrapped it around and through the ring.

"What for?"

"I got some questions to ask Pettit."

"Can't it wait?" It was already growing dark outside. "There's a dust storm fixin' to blow in."

"Nope, it can't wait." Webb took up the reins and stepped a booted toe into the stirrup.

"Then I'll come along with you," Nate

volunteered, wanting to find out why it was so all-fired important for Webb to talk to Doyle Pettit.

"Thanks, but I don't need company." He walked the horse past Nate and out the opened barn door into the ranchyard.

The black and billowing dustcloud was casting a long, dark shadow across the land, shutting out the sun's rays and turning the day into a false dusk. He rode most of the way to Blue Moon ahead of the storm, but it caught up with him five miles from town. The storm enclosed the horse and rider in a blowing shroud of dust. Its accompanying wind whipped the horse's scrubby tail between its legs as the buckskin lowered its head, pinching its nostrils together to shut out the clogging dirt particles, and plodded blindly down the road. Webb turned his collar up and tied a kerchief around his nose and mouth, hunching his shoulders against the sandblasting wind.

The buildings were all shuttered and boarded when Webb rode into town. Some of them were permanently closed and some were just battened down against the storm. The street was littered with blowing papers, rolling cans and bottles, and tumbleweeds. Shingles were torn off roofs to become flying missiles.

There was a Closed sign on the bank. Webb

turned his horse down the alley that ran alongside it, the near building breaking the fury of the wind. A light showed in a rear window of the bank. Webb dismounted by the back door and took a gun and holster out of his saddlebag, strapping it around his hip. The buckskin sidled closer to the building, taking advantage of its shelter from the storm.

When Webb tried the back door to the bank, the knob turned freely under his hand. He pushed it open and stepped inside. pulling down his kerchief and breathing in dusty-smelling air.

The source of light in the darkened building came from Doyle Pettit's private office. The door was ajar and Webb walked to it, nudging it open. The howling wind thrashing around outside had covered any sound Webb had made. Yet when Doyle Pettit looked up from his chair behind the desk, he didn't look surprised to see him.

A whiskey bottle was sitting in front of him, more than half empty, and a glass was in his hand. The stubble of a beard growth was on his cheeks, and his shirt looked as if it had been slept in. He stared at Webb through liquor-reddened eyes. His mouth flashed briefly with a smile that belonged to the Doyle Pettit Webb had known all his life, and intensified the contrast between that man and the broken, desperate person now sitting behind the desk.

"Hello, Webb." Even his voice was peculiarly flat, as if Doyle had stopped caring about living. "I knew you'd show up sooner or later. I'm glad I don't have to wait anymore."

"You know my wife is dead." He stepped into the room, but didn't take a chair, even though there was one empty in front of the desk.

"Yes, I know." Doyle couldn't hold his level stare and looked down, reaching for the whiskey bottle to refill his glass. "I don't expect you to believe me, but I am truly sorry about that."

"Before Kreuger died, he said you had warned him that I might burn his place." Within the statement, there was a demand for an explanation.

"It wasn't exactly that way." Doyle lifted the bottle in Webb's direction, silently offering him a drink, but Webb shook his head in mute refusal. Doyle's hand was trembling as he raised the glass to his mouth and took a quick drink. "He believed you would do something like that, and I encouraged him to keep thinking it."

"So you burned it, knowing he would blame me," Webb guessed.

"I paid a couple of drifters to do it, but I ordered them to stay until the fire was out to make sure it didn't start a range fire," Doyle said, as if that precaution in some way made up for the other.

"You knew Kreuger would come after me. You knew he'd try to kill me. That's what you wanted him to do. Why, Doyle? Why?" Webb demanded coldly.

The chair creaked noisily under his weight as Pettit leaned back and looked at the ceiling. "I'm finished. I've lost everything." He dragged his gaze down to look dully at Webb. "The bank, the lumberyard, all my land — even Dad's ranch. I've lost it all. I could see it coming and I was desperate to stop it. I always wanted to be big, Webb." His eyes came alive with the zeal of ambition. "I wanted to have it all — money, land, power, and everything that goes with it. I was almost there, Webb, but I needed to lay my hands on a lot of cash or some assets I could borrow against."

"You were after the Triple C." The wind was rattling the glass panes in the window, its incessant howl always in the background, but Webb's attention never strayed from the man behind the desk.

"You've got to believe me, Webb, if there'd been any other choice I would have made it. I wouldn't have taken the ranch." He tried to explain. "With you out of the way" — Doyle avoided the word "dead" — "it would have been a simple matter to have myself appointed as administrator of your son's estate. I would have kept it for your son. If I could have just gotten a loan on the Triple C, it would have carried me through this. I'd have paid it back."

"So you sicced Kreuger on me to get me out of the picture." The line of his jaw was inflexible. He had no sympathy for Doyle, not when Lilli was lying in her grave because of him.

"You don't know the hell I went through that day after the trial." His head sagged and bobbed to the side as Doyle lifted the whiskey glass again. "I kept wondering whether you were alive — and wondering whether I could live with myself if you were dead. It's almost a relief to see you standing there. I know you don't believe that, but it's true."

Rage spilled through Webb as he knocked the glass from Doyle's hand with an angry sweep of his arm. "I could kill you for what you've done." The bitter words sifted through his teeth in a low growl.

Doyle absently wiped at the whiskey splattered on his shirt. A sad smile was on his face when he looked up at Webb, towering over the desk. "It would be an act of mercy if you did.

I'm ruined. These last couple of days, I've thought a lot about suicide, but I haven't got the guts. I guess that's why I've been sitting here waiting for you to come."

When he'd strapped on the gun, it had been with killing in mind. Now Webb stepped back from the desk and smoothly pulled the gun from its holster. Doyle was sitting back in the chair, his wrinkled white shirt making an easy target. Webb flipped the gun, gripping it by the barrel, and laid it on the desk blotter.

"You've always persuaded someone else to do your dirty work. If it wasn't Kreuger, it was those drifters you hired to burn his place." His low voice was riddled with contempt. "If you want to die, you're going to have to pull the trigger. I'm not going to make that easy for you, too."

He swung away from the desk, his shoulders and back rigid as he walked to the door. "Webb, no!" He heard the sob in Doyle's voice, and kept going. "Don't leave me! Come back!"

He was in the hallway, reaching for the knob to the back doorway. He hesitated only a second, then yanked the door open and plunged into the false darkness of the dust-storm. It swirled about him, obscuring the buckskin pressed against the building, its head hanging low. Webb picked up its trailing reins and began leading it out of the alley. The howling wind was punctuated by a popping sound. It could have been anything — the snap of a shingle tearing loose from a roof, or the crack of a bottle breaking against a foundation.

Crossing the street, Webb led the horse down the alley and ended up behind Sonny's place by the house where Simon had his practice. He put the buckskin in the shed in back of the cabin and let himself into the cabin. Simon hadn't returned, probably holing up somewhere until the storm blew over. Webb poured himself a drink and stretched out in a chair, letting grief take over his expression and empty his features. At some point he fell asleep.

It was the silence that wakened him. The blasting storm had rolled on. As he stood up, he arched stiff and cramped muscles. His first thought was to get back to the ranch so Lilli wouldn't worry about him; then he remembered she wouldn't be at The Homestead. A heaviness dragged at him as he went out to the shed and saddled his buckskin.

When he led it outside, he saw the sheriff coming and paused. "Pettit's dead," the sheriff announced, his glance running over Webb's face to judge his reaction. Nothing showed. A gun was tucked in the waistband of his pants. The sheriff took it out and showed it to Webb. "Is this yours?"

"Yes." Webb took it and slipped it into his empty holster. Turning, he stepped into the saddle and adjusted the reins.

"Pettit left a note. Don't you want to know what was in it?" the sheriff asked. "There was a message for you. He wanted you to forgive him."

Webb made no comment as he nudged his horse forward. Maybe Lilli could forgive him, but Webb couldn't. There were tears at the back of his eyes for the woman he'd lost. It was a grief he'd have in him for a long, lonely time. He pointed the buckskin toward the ranch and gave the horse its head.

EPILOGUE

From the front porch of The Homestead, Webb watched the early-morning sunlight glisten on the river's surface as it curled through the sprawling valley and around the ranch buildings. The cottonwoods were budding green and the vast grassland beyond was showing its spring colors. Overhead, the sky was a sharp blue, finally washed free of dust a few years ago when the rains came to signal the end of the killing drought.

He pulled his gaze from the upthrust of range to glance at Nate Moore. His stance was loosely hiplocked while he rolled a miserly cigarette, taking care not to lose a scrap of tobacco. There was something comforting about watching this cowboy building a smoke: a carrying-on of the old ways to keep a tradition going.

Three saddled horses were tied near the bottom of the porch steps, patiently waiting for their riders. The roundup crew and its accompanying remuda and chuckwagon had left an hour earlier when the sun broke over the eastern horizon.

"When we was in town for the doc's funeral, I heard the old Beasley place north of here was bought by some sailor, home from the war, name of O'Rourke." Nate passed on the information as he scraped a match against his pants and carried the flame to his cigarette.

"I met him." Webb nodded. "He came and introduced himself to me. His tongue was a little too glib for my liking."

Some of his pleasure in the morning went out of him as his mind turned to thoughts of Simon Bardolph. He'd been a good friend. Maybe that's what made his death seem so senseless. Some drunken cowboy had decided to find out how fast his truck would go and slammed into the back of Simon's buggy, killing him instantly.

"Yeah, I guess O'Rourke talks like his cows are only going to have heifers." Nate grinned. "It's a poor piece of land he's got — a lot of rough country and not much water."

O'Rourke hadn't been here during the prolonged drought. And it was something that those who stayed and weathered it out didn't talk about. But of the nearly eighty thousand homesteaders who had come to till the dryland, over sixty thousand had abandoned their farms and moved out. It had turned into a massive exodus, leaving deserted farms and towns in their wake and more than two hundred failed banks.

So much had changed in such a short time. Anyone going into Blue Moon would find it hard to believe it had once been a boom town, a thriving community bursting at its seams. Most of the buildings had been burned when a transient had started a fire in a vacant store so he could keep warm.

The roadhouse was still standing, owned by a man named Jake. It had turned into a Montana version of a speakeasy, catering to the hard-drinking cowboy crowd that once again populated the region. Another building had been converted into a gasoline station, grocery store, and post office. The hardware store across the street had started carrying a dry-goods section when Ellis's emporium had gone up in smoke along with the livery. The railroad had abandoned its tracks into Blue Moon. It was just another wide spot in the road again.

All traces of what had been were wiped out. But the land still bore the mark, and it would never be the same again. Except where there was a source of water to irrigate, it had reverted to livestock range, domain of the cattleman. But the native grass never came back to the areas where the plow had turned the sod — that rich, high-protein grass that put hard weight on cattle. New, tough grasses were sown on the millions of eroded acres, but it wasn't the same. The difference was starkly apparent when contrasted with the preserved range of the Triple C where the grassy plains survived.

The front door burst open and a young boy with a mop of dark hair and bold brown eyes came hurtling onto the porch. Webb turned, catching the boy and sweeping him into his arms to ride high. Chase was five years old, going on six, and eager for each new experience. When he looked at his son, Webb caught glimpses of Lilli in the boy's boldness and determination, even though Chase didn't have her coloring. It tightened his throat and stung his eyes — and deepened the love he had for the boy.

"I told Buck I was gonna rope a calf. I can, can't I?" he demanded eagerly.

Webb had made it a point to take his son with him whenever it was possible. This would be his first roundup, but certainly not his last.

"As much as you've been practicing, I don't see why you can't." Webb smiled, then became conscious of someone standing in the back-ground.

He glanced over his shoulder. Ruth was waiting near the door holding a bedroll and a saddlebag stuffed with the boy's extra clothes. Her own son was standing beside her, not quite as big-boned as Chase. Buck's mouth was pushed in a pouting line as he stared enviously at his young friend.

"Better go get your things from Ruth so we can start out." He set the boy down and watched him run over to take his gear.

It was almost more than Chase could carry, but Webb didn't offer to help. The boy had to learn to do for himself, and he might as well find that out while he was young.

Nate clumped down the steps and waited beside the placid sorrel horse that Chase rode. It was a full-grown horse, not pony-sized, and trained to work cattle. Its gentle disposition had made it a suitable mount for a child, negating the need for a broken-down nag that couldn't be kicked out of a trot.

Chase managed to half-carry and half-drag his saddlebag and bedroll down the steps where Nate took them and secured the gear behind the child-sized saddle, specially tooled by a Triple C craftsman. Chase had figured out how to mount his horse without help, hauling himself up by the stirrup. When he was in the saddle, his legs were barely long enough to grip the horse's side. He took the reins Nate passed him and looked at his father.

"You comin', Dad?" he called.

"I'll be there in a minute," Webb assured him and turned to Ruth. "If anything comes up, you can send one of the boys to fetch me."

"Take care," she murmured, and watched him move away to join his son.

"Why can't I go?" Buck complained. "Chase gets to go."

"Yes, but his father is taking him," she reasoned quietly.

Buck looked longingly after his departing friend. "I wish he was my father."

The words tugged at her heart, but she said nothing. Webb was a widower now, but she was still married to Virg. She had made peace with her heart and learned to be content to take care of Webb's home and his son. It was all she could have, and it was better not to want more.

As they rode out of the ranchyard, Nate trailed behind the father and son. It was a custom of the range not to ride ahead of the boss. When Webb set the pace at a walk, Nate followed suit.

As they passed the barns with their big wooden beams and the vast range spread out before them, Webb slid a glance at the small boy perched atop the big horse. "All this is going to be yours someday, Chase."

It was a fact he was determined to instill in the boy. After Lilli died, it had been easier to let Chase stay at the Stanton house where Ruth could care for him. But that only lasted four short months until Webb realized it was a mistake. Chase was a Calder; he belonged at The Homestead. He had to learn that he'd never be anything else; more would always be expected from him. Webb didn't want Chase making the mistake he had made. He'd always be Chase Calder, and never an ordinary cowboy.

"It's a lot of land, Chase, but it's gotta be this big to fit under a sky like this." There was pride in his words, pride in the legacy that would come to his son.

When the stock market crashed and the Great Depression of the thirties came with its collapse of financial institutions, Montanans had already lived through the like nearly a decade earlier. When the lower Plains states suffered through the drought years that turned the land into a dust bowl, Montanans could have told the farmers what it was like. Rains spared their land from suffering through it a second time.

When the land is abused, nature has a way of striking back. Land will eventually go back to what nature had intended, but the cost is high. The land is what it is, no matter what man does or thinks he can do. Benteen Calder knew it, and Webb learned it.

Hopes die and man moves on, but the land stays.

THORNDIKE PRESS HOPES you have enjoyed this Large Print book. All our Large Print titles are designed for the easiest reading, and all our books are made to last. Other Thorndike Press Large Print books are available at your library, through selected bookstores, or directly from the publisher. For more information about our current and upcoming Large Print titles, please send your name and address to:

THORNDIKE PRESS
ONE MILE ROAD
P.O. Box 157
THORNDIKE, MAINE 04986

There is no obligation, of course.

F.